THE LAST FAOII

Tahani Nelson

For my husband, who is willing to stand next to me no matter the battlefield.

Stupid morning bells. Stupid, stupid morning bells. Kaiya cast a baleful glance at the grand, iron banes of her existence as she slogged toward the chapel. The bells ignored her and continued sounding with an unnecessary clarity in the otherwise silent dawn. Next to her, Mollie pulled impatiently at Kaiya's elbow.

"Come on, Kai. I'm not going to get stuck mucking stables again just because you can't get up like a regular Faoii for chapel."

Kaiya wrinkled her nose and yanked her arm away, making a face at her redheaded shield sister.

"It's not that it's hard. It's unnecessary," she mumbled as she trudged up the hill. "The Goddess doesn't ask for our worship through words or songs. She cares about our love of justice and strength. Our faith in honor and virtue. She cares about the strength that comes from being *us*. We don't have to worry about pleasing *Her*." She huffed and added under her breath, "Why would it matter to the Eternal One whether I got up at dawn or two hours later?"

Mollie must have heard anyway, because suddenly the redhead stopped and spun toward Kaiya in a single graceful movement that spoke heavily of her Faoii training. Her eyes were dark with irritation. "Don't presume to know more than the Cleroii, Kaiya. You know it's our strength of discipline that makes the Goddess proud of us."

"Yeah, yeah, yeah," Kaiya growled. "And the songs help focus the Cleroii. Save it, Mollie. I've heard it a thousand times." She scrunched up her face and mockingly droned out one of the daily mantras in a poor imitation of Cleroii-Belle's voice.

"'Kaiya-Faoii, you must be *disciplined*. Kaiya-Faoii, you must *sing*. Kaiya-Faoii, I see that piece of bread you keep sneaking bites of.' Bleh. It's all bull, Mollie. None of it makes us better Faoii."

Mollie opened her mouth to reply, but Kaiya continued before she could. "We're fighters, Mollie. We're not Cleroii or Preoii. 'Our blades will sing with the voice of every throat that has cried out against injustice and dance with the steps of every innocent child.'"

"'And we will lead the choir, and the voices of our swords will deafen the ears of our enemies.'" Mollie finished the Oath with a resigned sigh, pulling away from Kaiya enough to fist her hands in front of her, one over the other as though grasping an invisible hilt. Kaiya smiled.

"Exactly. I'll make a good Faoii out of you yet." She slapped Mollie on the shoulder and began the trek once more.

"We'll see which one of us gets our Faoii rank placed before our name first, Kaiya. I'll ascend to Faoii-Mollie while you're still mucking stables for being impetuous. The Goddess respects discipline."

"You wish," Kaiya shot back. "The Goddess loves me for following my instincts." She grinned, and Mollie sighed.

"Seriously, though, Kai—did you really sneak bread into the chapel?"

"That's not the only thing I sneak in," Kaiya whispered gleefully, motioning to her boot. Mollie glanced downward, gasping at the iron hilt she saw there. She stuttered to a stop, green eyes wide in disbelief.

"Kaiya! You can't just—"

"Ready at all times, Faoii."

"In mind and spirit! You can't bring weapons into chapel!"

"Really? So I don't have to go?" Glee colored Kaiya's eyes, and Mollie glared. "I am Faoii, after all. 'Wherever I am, there will a weapon against injustice always be.'"

"That's why you have hand-to-hand training! You can *be* a weapon without *carrying* one! If one of the ascended found out—"

"'All things are sacred, and all souls worthwhile. But my blade shall be held above all, for it protects all, and shall be a part of me, for I am Faoii.'"

"Stop quoting the Oath at me!" Mollie fumed, stamping her foot.

"'And my tongue will never forget the words of truth, for when I speak, then will the Goddess hear, and I am only Faoii in Her presence.'"

"Ugh. You're impossible."

"And you're about to make us late." Kaiya motioned to the path, vacant save for a few stragglers. Mollie's eyes widened with shock and betrayal. Kaiya would have felt bad if it wasn't so damned funny. She grinned as she crossed her arms and settled her weight on one hip, raising an eyebrow at her flabbergasted shield sister.

"You . . . you tricked me."

"Yep. The Sight didn't see that one, did it?"

"I saw deceit, but I thought it was about the knife…"

"Maybe it was." Kaiya laughed and kissed Mollie's forehead. "Come on, Moll. We can still make it." Mollie nodded and took off at a trot. Kaiya matched her, then increased the pace.

Flying across the monastery grounds, they arrived at chapel just as the last bell sounded.

The chapel of Illindria, great Goddess of the Faoii, was large and open, its marble walls curving gracefully upward toward a peaked roof. Sunlight fell through the large, glassless windows, trickling through tree branches that bowed into the open chamber. The scent of lavender drifted in from outside, and Kaiya noted that the tapestries normally used to keep out drafts had been pulled away from the dewy morning air. She glanced around as they passed the first window, idly breaking off a sprig of sweet-smelling vielen and twisting the purple leaves between her fingers. At least she and Mollie weren't the last ones to arrive to chapel (something she silently thanked mighty Illindria for as they stopped to kneel before Her statue), and none of the Cleroii seemed ready to strike at the girls with their hated staves. Maybe today wouldn't be so bad after all. Weaving the vielen into a lock of hair that rarely stayed in place, Kaiya guided Mollie to one of the well-worn benches.

Once Kaiya and Mollie were seated, all Faoii eyes were naturally drawn to the marble figure that stood at the chapel's head, wreathed in the light from the eastern windows. Illindria's gentle gaze was inviting. Beautiful. In Her right hand was a glistening fantoii. In Her left, a sprig of healing chinol. Kaiya smiled. *That* was the Goddess—a creature of duality. A deity of life and death. War and healing. Perfect.

Someone was talking, but Kaiya ignored them, ensconced in her own thoughts. It was probably the same drivel as every other day anyway. Besides, the Goddess would definitely prefer it if Kaiya used this time to better understand the nature of Her being, rather than listen to an old Preoii prattle on. She was sure of it.

Duality. She is a creature of duality. Of course She was. A person has two eyes, two ears, two hands. A person, like a coin, has two halves, or like the sky, two shades. Light and dark. Good and evil. A scale must have two platforms in order to balance. What equilibrium could there be found in three? Or one?

She also probably likes to sleep in. Kaiya smiled as she stared up at the Goddess and Her eternal beauty. The graceful sculpture seemed to understand, looking down upon Kaiya with a serene smile, the plaited braid hanging over one shoulder from beneath Her ivy-covered helm.

Movement at the base of the Goddess's unclad feet caught Kaiya's eye, and she came back to attention just as Preoii-Aleena spread her arms, her sermon evidently finished. Immediately, the girls in the pews in front of Aleena fisted their hands, one over another, and bowed their heads. Kaiya did likewise, and they spoke as one.

"I am Faoii. I am the harbinger of justice and truth. I am the strength of the weak and the voice of the silent. My blade is my arm, and as such is the arm of all people. Wherever I am, there will a weapon against injustice always be. And with this weapon, I will protect the weak and purge all evil in the land. I will be ready to perform my duty for the weak at all times. And through this, I shall remember that all things are sacred and all souls worthwhile. But my blade will be held above all, for it protects all, and shall be a part of me. For I am Faoii. My tongue will never forget the words of truth, for when I speak, then will the Goddess hear, and I am only Faoii in Her presence. We are the Weavers of the Tapestry. We see the threads through all the world and guide them with the Goddess's eye. Above all, we are Faoii."

The chorus of women's voices grew. "Our blades will sing with the voice of every throat that has cried out against injustice and dance with the steps of every innocent child. We will lead the choir, and the voices of our swords will deafen the ears of our enemies. For we are Faoii."

Kaiya grinned. As much as she complained about early morning chapel, she could not hate this part of it. The power in the room swelled, and the staves of the Cleroii glowed in the presence of the Oath. The Oath was strong and sacred. Beautiful and powerful. Perfect.

The warriors around Kaiya smiled as well, and even calm-eyed Mollie had irises that glinted like steel. "We are Faoii!" The cry was unstoppable, irrepressible, and swelled out of each girl with an indescribable force. Released, the power gushed from the room, causing the chandeliers to sway and the trees outside the glassless windows to dance in an unnatural breeze. Flushed and limp, the girls relaxed, grinning at each other with shining eyes. Preoii-Aleena beamed and nodded from her dais.

The Cleroii and few young Preoii rose and began their first song. The power that built here would not be as explosive as the Oath, but it was soothing, and Kaiya leaned back, letting it wash over her. These songs were magics of healing rather than war, the craft of the Cleroii rather than the Faoii, but she enjoyed listening anyway. And besides, this was always the best time to mess with

Cleroii-Belle.

"What do you think Cleroii-Belle would do if I sharpened that dagger in Chapel?" Kaiya whispered to Mollie. "Do you think she'd cause a huge scene here or just wait until afterward? Could she even hold it in that long?"

"You wouldn't!" Kaiya could hear the fear in Mollie's voice and laughed as she dug around in her boots. "Blessed Blade, Kai. *Please.*" But Kaiya was already running her whetstone over the dagger's edge. The faint *skkksh* barely rose above the Cleroii song.

Somehow, Cleroii-Belle heard it. Because *of course* she did.

Kaiya could almost sense the older Cleroii hustling down the aisle, grey eyes intent on the back of Kaiya's black braid. Kaiya did her best not to smile and waited to see what would happen, the "my blade will be held above all" section of the Oath ready on her tongue. A dozen nearby faces turned toward the odd noise of Kaiya's whetstone, intrigued. Cleroii-Belle arrived at the end of their aisle.

"We're in for it now," Mollie sighed. "I've never seen her so angry." Kaiya wondered whether she was actually hearing a smile under Mollie's morose tones. It was possible; few of the students around her were successfully hiding their amusement. Kaiya controlled her urge to grin and instead looked up at the Cleroii with wide, innocent eyes. A dozen Faoii held their breath to see what would happen next.

Their curiosity would never be sated.

As the aging Cleroii opened her mouth to speak, the doors to the chapel crashed open and Faoii-Leigh rushed in, her bronze breastplate splattered with crimson. Chunks of flesh slid down across its markings. Her dark eyes sparked with anger, disgust, and . . . *fear? Could that actually be* fear *in her eyes?*

If it was, the woman's voice belied it with an order that rang out like steel on stone. "The monastery is under attack! Faoii, on your feet!"

Kaiya had never seen a Faoii breastplate marred by blood before. But here Faoii-Leigh stood, her braid disheveled and her armor soaked in crimson. Red droplets flicked from her fantoii as she barked for silence.

The Cleroii, mouths gaping, stopped their song. Its power drifted in the breeze like shredded ribbons before disintegrating. A heartbeat passed before a roar of leather, metal, and shifting bodies sounded through the room as dozens of fighters shot to their feet, standing back-to-back with piercing eyes. Kaiya pressed her shoulder blades against Mollie's, who straightened in response. All eyes turned to Faoii-Leigh, whose voice rang out with venom and battle lust.

"We show no fear, Faoii! We do not lose, and we do not fail! We are Faoii! We have trained to be the hand of justice! We are prepared for this enemy!" Faoii-Leigh's voice sounded like clashing swords and broken chainmail as she struck her fantoii hilt against her shield with each new phrase.

"Faoii-Leigh," Preoii-Aleena began, pulling her own blade from behind the grand statue, "where is Faoii-Caril?" Faoii-Leigh did not quite look at the Preoii when she replied.

"She has fallen." Kaiya was near enough to see the tears in Faoii-Leigh's eyes. "They appeared so suddenly. There was no time . . ." Faoii-Leigh's voice trembled for a moment before she steeled herself. "May the Goddess grant her better battles."

A murmur ran through the room. Though young, Faoii-Caril was ascended—accomplished enough to have her rank placed before her name. If she had fallen, would the young, unascended maidens gathered here be able to stand against her enemy?

"Is there time to gather weapons, Faoii-Leigh?" a young voice rang out. Faoii-Leigh opened her mouth to speak but was drowned out by Cleroii screams. She turned and raised her shield just quickly enough to block the blow of one of the burly invaders who swarmed through the open doorway. No one had seen them approaching through the glassless windows.

Faoii-Leigh and the others who jumped to her defense tried to hold their own, but it didn't take long before they were overpowered by the swell of invading bodies and shoved across the marble floor. Faoii-Leigh took the brunt of the blow with her shield, and Kaiya thought she saw the hardened warrior rise again, but couldn't be sure with the swelling horde between them. Above the din, Preoii-Aleena's voice called out, "Faoii! Form ranks!"

The remaining students squared their shoulders and stared down the rows of armored men, who were already forming their own ranks at the front of the room. There they stood, posed for battle but eerily silent. Kaiya's gaze roamed over the motionless lines of soldiers. *Who are they? What are they waiting for?*

Each invader wore a horned helm adorned with a scowling, demonic faceplate. A few of the youngest girls shrank back from the blood-soaked blades they wielded, but Kaiya only bristled. Behind her, Mollie gasped.

"Kai. Third row in. Is that a Faoii?" Kaiya peered at the sea of metal bodies. A hundred masked faces stared impassively back. Her eyes narrowed at the smaller warrior that Mollie had indicated before she shook her head.

"No. A child soldier," she finally said through gritted teeth. And then: "Goddess grant you a good battle, sister."

"I will be at your back until the end." As meek and quiet as Mollie often was, there was no doubt that she was Faoii. Her voice betrayed no fear, and her shoulders were squared. Even without a weapon, she was far from weak. Kaiya pulled her lips back in a tight grimace and glanced around. Dozens of other girls stood tense and ready, posed to strike at Preoii-Aleena's command. A bristling tension vibrated through the room.

Tensed to spring, Kaiya trained her eyes on one of the masked invaders but stopped short. Someone else had entered. Tall and lean, with skin as dark as hers and pale eyes, this new man did not match his soldiers. Intricate tattoos covered his bare crown and torso, and his booted feet pounded against the marble floor, wordlessly barking for silence. Even the rustle of his robed waist was apparent in the sudden, deathly quiet. A moment passed before several girls around Kaiya broke free of his trance and sprang.

Their battle cries were barely past their teeth when the invader waved his bloodstained blade, knocking them back with a crackling force. They landed heavily and remained still.

Kaiya grimaced as one girl skidded back to land at the base of an adjacent pew. She could not even bend over to close the lifeless eyes.

What magic is this? What could kill Faoii so readily? No one was trained in magic outside the monastery. Only Faoii were worthy of Illindria's greatest gift.

She stared, more angry than horrified, as the tattooed man passed his immobile army and walked purposefully toward Preoii-Aleena.

"You are not welcome here, Croeli-Thinir." Those that had been preparing to attack stopped uncertainly. The Croeli were gone, exiled generations before and decimated by their own brutality. Even mentioning the banished order was considered taboo amongst the Faoii.

The smiling invader did not reply. Preoii-Aleena moved toward him, her sword raised, but he only lifted a fist toward the open-domed roof and tore it back down with a violent wrench of his tattooed arm. Lightning struck the Goddess statue's ivy helm with a resounding *boom*.

The Faoii watched, horrified, as a single crack jagged its way down mighty Illindria's head and body. It jolted with sporadic movements before finally stopping at Her unshod feet.

Time froze as the Eternal One stood serenely, smiling at all Her children . . . before shattering into a million pieces of powdery dust.

The explosion caught Preoii-Aleena full-force, flinging her across the room and into a far wall. Kaiya lost sight of her as the army of burly men suddenly moved, swarming out into the pews, hewing down those who met them in the early morning light.

Kaiya, Mollie, and a hundred other Faoii screamed their

defiance at the coming horde.

Chaos exploded in the chapel. Every woman, be she Faoii, Cleroii, or Preoii, launched herself into the battle. Battle cries and healing songs clashed against each other in the air as the women rushed against the invaders. Kaiya and Mollie joined the swarm, flowing between men and women alike. Even without needing to speak, they knew their goal.

Kaiya had already dropped her whetstone. She dodged beneath a man's wide swing, then straightened and rammed the blade of her dagger into the soft flesh beneath his jaw. The screams of the dying echoed in her ears as she lunged past another sword. Bracing down, Kaiya pushed an opponent's shield upward and, with Mollie's help, forced it forward into his mouth. Blood and teeth splattered the floor.

Another took the fallen man's place, and Mollie slid forward to break his kneecap with her booted heel. Kaiya finished him off with a head butt that drove his nose into his brain. The stench of blood and death surrounded them, but Kaiya only squared her shoulders, intent on finding a man she couldn't yet see over the crowd.

The swarm got denser as Kaiya and Mollie neared their adversary, but they saw Faoii-Leigh hacking her way toward the sorcerer. Awed at her strength even without a shield mate, the girls pressed harder. The number of bodies behind them was insignificant compared to the mound that surrounded the stoic mage and his crackling blade.

Dozens of lifeless eyes stared at Kaiya as she danced her way around another man. This one moved too slowly, and as he lunged, she brought her knife down on his arm, piercing it before jumping up and using her entire body weight to snap the bone.

She tore the brutish sword—*criukli*, she vaguely remembered from one of the classes she thought she'd slept through—from the man's limp hand and sliced at him again. His gauntleted fist clattered to the floor.

Undeterred, Kaiya spun, her arm outstretched, aiming for the weak armor encasing his neck, but was stopped by a violent kick to her abdomen. She stumbled, trying to focus around suddenly empty lungs and teary eyes. This new opponent had already brought his foot back down to better stabilize the man that Kaiya had injured, and his eyes only momentarily flicked to the bloody stump cradled to his comrade's chest. Then he refocused his gaze on Kaiya, and the fury there was palpable. Using his shield arm to support his wounded comrade, the new warrior swung a jagged criukli over his ally's shoulder, aiming for Kaiya's head.

Kaiya ducked. Without a shield to protect her, it was her only choice. But too late did she remember to shove Mollie out of the way. She tried to bring her sword back up to block the blow, but it had already passed her.

Behind her, Mollie's skull split open under the sword's weight. She dropped limply, her final battle cry unspoken.

Kaiya could only stare as Mollie sank to the ground, her green eyes open and unseeing. All training, all anger, all fear was forgotten. Something landed heavily against her chest, but she barely felt it, did not try to catch herself as she fell. Instead, she simply lay where she was and stared at her best friend—her lifelong companion, her first love, eyes wide above the growing pool of her own blood. This was not a reality Kaiya could accept or understand. This wasn't right. Her vision swam as a furious rage pulled at her brows.

It felt like ages passed before Kaiya realized she was on her feet again.

"I am Faoii." The words rang out of her mouth as her sword launched at the nearest horned helm. She didn't even know if it was Mollie's destroyer or if he had turned to attack a different Faoii. It didn't matter. She blamed them *all*. "I am the harbinger of justice and truth." Blood sprayed. "I am the strength of the weak and the voice of the silent." Mollie's eyes stared at her, her mouth white and partially open. "My blade is my arm, and as such is the arm of all people." Another Faoii fell to her right, brought low by a Croeli blade. "Wherever I am, there will a weapon against injustice always be." She cut down a struggling man that lay broken to her left. "And with this weapon, I will protect the weak and purge all evil in the land."

Through the fray, Kaiya caught the glint of the ivy helm of an ascended Faoii somewhere toward the end of the hall. She quickened her onslaught. "I will be ready to perform my duty for the weak at all times." She heard a hint of a healing song rise above the noise in the room, but it was cut short. "And through this, I shall remember that all things are sacred and all souls worthwhile." She held her blade still just long enough to allow a young Cleroii to pass under it before slashing down at the Croeli in pursuit. "But my blade will be held above all, for it protects all, and shall be a part of me." The flash of an ivy helm again, closer now. "For I am Faoii. My tongue will never forget the words of truth, for when I speak, then will the Goddess hear." She passed a piece of Illindria's broken statue. "And I am only Faoii in Her presence."

She continued forward, screaming now, unaware of what she hit or whether she herself was injured. "I am the Weaver of the Tapestry. I see the threads through all the world and guide them with the Goddess's eye." Blood oozed from a dozen superficial wounds, but she felt none of them. "Above all, I am Faoii, and my blade will sing with the voice of every throat that has cried out against injustice and dance with the steps of every innocent child!"

She could see the sorcerer now, above the heads of fighting armies. Could see the ivy helm of Faoii-Leigh, too. "I will lead the choir, and the voice of my sword will deafen the ears of my enemies." Her voice rose to a fervor she wouldn't have believed possible. *"For I am Faoii!"*

She was there now, swinging her sword at the head of the tattooed destroyer. The glistening ivy helm that had served as her beacon moved just barely as Faoii-Leigh struggled to push herself back up, one arm clutched to her bleeding side. But the seasoned Faoii was not dead yet, and her eyes flashed as she straightened. With a painful heave, she brought her bronze shield up just long enough to block the sorcerer's blade, still crackling with magic, as he swung it toward the screaming Kaiya.

Kaiya's blade, slick and gleaming crimson, collided with the tattooed head. But no blood sprayed. There was no crack of bone or splattering of brains. Instead, the sword rang out with the sound of a grand bell. It echoed through eternity.

As the chime faded, it seemed to Kaiya that the entire room was deathly silent except for the soft laughter of this unnamed fiend. She blinked. The chapel was gone. The girls, the sunlight, the Goddess. All gone. She was alone, and the biting air of a winter that hadn't come yet clung to her body with icy fingers, pulling at all parts of her except for a spot of warmth that swelled outward from her belly. She looked down and blinked again. Surely that knife covered with blood was not coming out of *her* stomach. Surely that red ooze was not *her* life covering the floor. Her vision dimmed and tilted. Surely that laugh was not still ringing in her ears . . . Surely . . .

3

The laughter continued for a long time, sometimes mixing with the deep tone a bell. Kaiya listened. Cheers floated toward her from far away. A man's voice. *This is the last temple. Our unjust exile has finally ended, my brothers.* More cheers faded into the distance. Kaiya drifted between emptiness and nothingness while the laughter and voices slowly washed away, only to be replaced by . . . *by what?* She strained her ears. Singing?

Yes. Singing. It was dim . . . so dim. But striking and enchanting. A beautiful, comforting song. So far away. So familiar.

Kaiya was sure she should be sharpening a blade, but she couldn't find it. Why did she want to do that, again? It seemed so important at the time.

Oh, well. It'll show up eventually.

She drifted. Slowly, peacefully. It would be easy to just . . . float away. That would be nice, right?

That sound again. What was that?

Faoii, can you hear me? Can you open your eyes?

Maybe she should answer before floating away. That would be the nice thing to do. Mollie said she should be nicer. Kaiya tried to blink her eyes open. Tried to respond.

Can you hear me?

Kaiya tried to move.

Her groan was louder than the song's quiet whispers. Silence prevailed for a moment.

"Who's there?" The call was tired and weak, but Kaiya heard it. Again she tried to respond. Why couldn't she open her eyes? They were coated with something . . . sticky. And thick. Honey? Sap? Slowly . . . oh, so slowly . . . she peeled her lids apart.

Blood. There was blood everywhere. Surely even oceans were not as wet as this. And bodies. Women, men, Faoii, Cleroii. Everyone. The bodies were not laid out or peaceful in their passing, but were left how they fell: broken and wide-eyed. Kaiya felt bile rise in her throat.

Something heavy was on top of her. Struggling, Kaiya managed to lift it away, and the obstruction fell to the side with a clang. *Faoii-Leigh's shield.* The warrior lay next to her, pale and still, her blood staining the scattered pieces of Illindria's statue. Kaiya reached over to close the unblinking eyes, her arm shaking.

"Better battles, Faoii," she whispered.

"Who is there? That clatter...who are you?" the voice continued, and Kaiya at last rose. Awkwardly, like a newborn foal, she stood on shaky calves.

"I'm here." Kaiya spoke uncertainly, afraid of who would be looking for her in a battlefield like this. But the voice did not seem frightening.

"Come in front of me. I cannot see you. I can only sense you... Faoii. Yes, I am sure of it. You are Faoii. Come closer, child. I cannot sing anymore." Kaiya turned around slowly, looking for the whispers' source.

She found it, but nothing could have prepared her for what she saw. The chandeliers in the center of the room had been broken and torn from the ceiling. From their dangling skeletons, long, thorny vines with broad, flat leaves snaked their way around Preoii-Aleena's wrists and torso, and she hung limply in midair.

The vines clung to the Preoii's head in a bloody diadem and twisted through her eye sockets. Kaiya felt the bile rise in her throat again but fought it back down. Trembling, she dragged her feet forward.

It seemed like she crossed miles before reaching her destination. "Preoii . . ." Her whisper seemed deafening in the silence, and Kaiya hit her knees. Slowly, she lifted quivering hands to touch the Preoii's thorny feet. "Preoii-Aleena, I'm so sorry."

"You must not touch me, child. I fear that this plant may be bred from ton—" The Preoii stopped herself and started again, her voice quiet. "Something evil from long ago. I am afraid, little one, that you must leave me like this."

"Preoii-Aleena, I can't. I—"

"Shhh, Kaiya-Faoii. It is pretty little Kaiya, is it not? Of course. I'd recognize that undisciplined aura anywhere." Despite everything, the Preoii smiled, chuckling under her breath. "Of course it would be. Pretty little Kaiya. So much older now than when you came to us. We never thought we would get your thick, stubborn curls into a braid—" She was wracked with a rattling cough.

"Kaiya-Faoii, I am sorry I could save only you. My songs once could have healed twice as many as those that have fallen here, but these vile thorns have torn through the magic of this place. It is not a very fitting end, I'm afraid. Our fallen sisters deserve to be laid to rest where there is still magic. Where people will sense for centuries to come that this is where Faoii lived and died. But the Croeli have desecrated even our legacy."

The vines tugged on the skin of Preoii-Aleena's forehead, and she clenched her teeth shut with a snap. The muscles in her arms tensed against the pain, and for the first time Kaiya realized how strong the Preoii really was. Beneath the soft ivory skin and auburn hair, Aleena was still Faoii. And her voice was filled with vengeance, drawing power from her hatred for the Croeli foe, when she said, "May the Goddess strike down the Croeli with Her eternal blade. She has seen the ending of this tale. When the Everlasting Tapestry frays, Croeli-Thinir will be at its center—if She does not destroy him first."

The vines slithered forward as the power around her grew, and Preoii-Aleena sagged beneath them, the last of her strength sapped by the dark magic of their source. When she spoke again, her voice was barely a whisper.

"Kaiya-Faoii, you are the last of our Order. You are not just Faoii as you were, but you are now all Faoii. Every throat that ever sang in these walls, every breath and cry and laugh, is part of your blade now. You carry all of the Order with you." Preoii-Aleena stopped as another cough tore through her. Blood splattered the floor at Kaiya's feet. "You must not be afraid, Faoii, for as long as one blade still sings, there will be justice. Tell the world what has happened here. Tell them to fear the Croeli's destructive horned god. You are strong, little Faoii. I, and the Goddess, have faith in you." Tears mixed with the blood of Preoii-Aleena's ruined eyes as she gasped for breath. "Arise, Kaiya-Faoii . . . as Faoii-Kaiya."

Kaiya rose. There was no cheer or sense of honor as she had always expected would come with her ascension. There was only a cold whistle as a breeze passed through the dying chamber and a soft *shuck* sound as the vines continued to snake their way over Preoii-Aleena's skin.

"To the armory, Faoii. You must prepare for your crusade. I cannot go with you to help you find the blade that is meant to be your arm, but I have faith you will find it. Go. And know that you are all of us."

Kaiya stuttered for a moment before dropping her eyes. "Preoii-Aleena, I couldn't even hurt him. My sword just rang off his skin. I can't do this. I can't—" Kaiya saw the faintest hint of a smile on Preoii-Aleena's face.

"Of course you can, Kaiya. You're so much stronger than you know." Her words softened as her head dropped forward. "Your mother would have been so proud . . ." The last whisper was barely louder than the whistle of the wind in the halls, but Kaiya's head snapped up, regardless, desperate to hear more. But there was no more sound. Just the soft *shuck, shuck, shuck* of the vines. She stood there, stunned into silence. Dust and plaster sprinkled down from the rafters as the creepers continued their slow slither in the darkness.

Kaiya did not know how long she stood there. Hours? Years? Time held no meaning for her. An eternity might have passed when, body shaking and knees weak, Kaiya turned toward the door. She lifted her eyes toward the ceiling as a single ray of sunlight struggled its way through the crumbling dome. For the first time, her eyes flooded with tears as she realized the enormity of Preoii-Aleena's words.

"I am Faoii."

4

The stars were hidden by smoke when Kaiya finally urged the solitary gelding she'd found in the stables down the rocky cliffs leading away from the Monastery of the Eternal Blade. A smallish, grey beast, it had not surprised her that the large Croeli with their heavy armor had left him and the weakest mares behind. Not that it really mattered now. *Not that any of it really mattered anymore.* Her face was dark with soot and ash, but no new streaks of salty tears had washed away the grime.

Though never heavily guarded, the armory had always been forbidden to the unascended, and Kaiya had never been inside it before today. She had not been surprised to find that the room had been raided, though little was missing. The swords there were too light and the armor too small for the Croeli to value.

She wrapped a gloved hand around her sword hilt. While perfectly capable of wielding a classic blade or even the jagged criukli if necessary, Faoii were trained from childhood to use the smaller, quicker fantoii. Years of practice had honed her skills, each hour aimed at the goal of eventually receiving her own weapon. The hilt in her hand was her greatest accomplishment; the mark of a true Faoii.

Kaiya spit to the side. *Yeah, right. Some accomplishment.*

There had been no ceremony, no sense of honor. No one alive knew that Kaiya had at last been granted ascension—that she was Faoii-Kaiya instead of Kaiya-Faoii. So no one went with her to find the breastplate, ivy helm, and fantoii that were the symbols of her rank. Kaiya had just dug through combat gear, tossing aside broken remnants before selecting a shield and an ivy helm at random from the discarded mess. Even the breastplate she'd found was too big for her. She sighed, disgusted with herself. She felt like a vulture picking through carrion.

The fantoii had taken longer to find. She must have swung a dozen blades, hoping to hear the one that would sing with the voices of all she had promised to uphold, but each one only whistled in the tomblike hall. She'd thrown several down in frustration. Didn't the stories always talk of a connection between fantoii and Faoii? Wasn't there supposed to be a cry or song with each swing of the blade? Faoii-Leigh's sword had *screamed* in battle. It had cried out with the voices of a hundred souls and had reassured the unascended that they had the Goddess on their side, that they would always prevail on the side of good. That assurance had often lifted Kaiya's heart during the more frustrating moments of monastery life. It had been beautiful.

Kaiya had looked for the blade that would respond to her touch with such a chorus but had only been able to find one that... hummed? She wasn't sure. It wasn't *right*, but Kaiya knew there was something different about the fantoii she finally chose. That was enough. It *had* to be enough.

But the unease in her gut never faded. She knew this blade hadn't been made for her, and she doubted that it would be any more effective against Thinir than her last sword had been. Her arm still ached from where the pilfered criukli had bounced off his tattooed skull, ringing with the force. She felt so useless.

"Sisters," Kaiya prayed, "if someone else was meant to wield this fantoii, I'm sorry. I didn't mean to steal your glory. Or your blade. But please help me to guide it in your absence, Faoii. And Illindria grant you a thousand glorious battles once I give it back."

She smiled for a moment as she remembered that she would see her sisters again someday on Illindria's infinite battlefield; she would dine with them again in Her great hall. But a sudden chill in the air brought her back to the present, and the comfort faded. She blinked tears out of her eyes and cast one more glance at the sky. "Don't forget about me, sisters. I'll come when I can." The wind caught Kaiya's whisper and pulled it upward to mix with the wisps of smoke above her head. She waited, hoping for some sign that her fallen loved ones or the Goddess had heard.

No answer came.

It did not take Kaiya long to reach Resting Oak, the ever-growing town that sat at the base of the monastery's cliffs. As Resting Oak's main protectors, the Faoii never had trouble getting supplies here or finding a friendly face with whom to trade stories. She shivered at the familiar streets. The Crow's Caw Tavern had always been a favorite haunt on summer evenings, and the town's familiarity stirred up bittersweet memories as Kaiya rode through the dusty gates.

It was early morning now. People would start waking soon, and Kaiya needed to find someone who would listen to her story, who would heed the warning of Preoii-Aleena and the Faoii. The tavern seemed a good place to start, but Kaiya didn't think she could stand to see it. Mollie used to always buy the first round of drinks when they came this way.

Instead, Kaiya turned her mount toward the city square. Lord Boyer, ruler of Resting Oak, lived in a manor there. He'd know what to do.

Destination in mind, Kaiya rode through the eerily silent streets purposefully. All was quiet and dark, save for the distant glow on the horizon behind her. A tickling worry tugged at her.

Strange. The Croeli didn't come here afterward. Goddess knows it would be easy to take now.

But the worry was something more than that. The air was different here than it should be. When she'd made her way down from the monastery, she had assumed it was simply the smoke from the burning monastery mixed with the scents of death and blood. But something was . . . off.

Is someone cooking rotting meat? No. It's more of a feeling than a smell. Something's wrong. Maybe someone... Kaiya's thoughts broke off suddenly as she realized what was different. *Broken Blade. It can't be...*

The signs of the Goddess, the emblems and handicrafts that normally decorated windows and doorways, were gone. But Kaiya was surely mistaken. The simple inverted triangle with its clockwise spiral inside was such a simple way to invite Illindria into your home. It was... bizarre that anyone would fail to hang one. But there were none. Anywhere. The protective embrace that usually filled Resting Oak was gone, leaving the streets empty and chilled. Kaiya shivered.

"Goddess, what could have—" Kaiya was cut off by a man's voice booming from around the corner. A small, meek tone responded but was overwhelmed by the first man's thundering reply.

Kaiya turned onto a nearby street and heard the words more clearly. "I won't!" The meek voice forced a bit of strength into the outburst. "You can burn the chapels and tear down the symbols, but the Goddess remains! The Faoii will hunt you down!"

"The Faoii?" A man's dark laughter grated on Kaiya's eardrums. "The Faoii are gone! Look! See that glow on the horizon? It's too early to be sunlight, isn't it?" He snorted with glee. "Now, what do you suppose could be up there?" Silence answered him, and he laughed harder. "Go on! Go see! I'm sure you'd like the gifts Croeli-Thinir left you."

"You're lying." The smaller voice did not sound so sure, but it strengthened and continued, "The Faoii are undefeatable, and there are no Croeli left."

At last Kaiya found the alleyway that was the commotion's source. She dismounted and entered it silently, warily drawing her fantoii. A hulking brute in hardened leather armor stood with his back to Kaiya, his attention focused on the only other people in the alleyway. A middle-aged woman stood facing him defiantly as she clutched a Goddess symbol with white knuckles. A slightly older man had one arm wrapped protectively around her shoulders. The battered old sword in his other hand was shaking.

The beastly man stepped closer, looming over the pair, and

Kaiya's eyes narrowed. She doubted the couple saw him reach for the dagger at the small of his back.

"Your divine hag and her Faoii have no place here. She will follow her pathetic worshippers to the hell we sent them all to." A laugh rolled out of him like smoke billowing from a funeral pyre as the couple stared back in dismay.

Kaiya's blood boiled, but she didn't speak. She released no bold, hate-filled battle cry to summon war magic. She did not even melt into the shadows that steeped the street in gloom. She simply sprinted, determined and spiteful, toward the Croeli, blade unsheathed. He didn't have a chance to react—she swung her blade, and his laughter faded into a soft gurgle.

Kaiya sheathed her fantoii as the man's shaved head rolled toward her feet. She stopped it with a booted heel and looked down at the lifeless eyes. "Only one of us ended up in this hell, you bastard," she whispered before stepping over the gore and stalking back to the now-gaping townsfolk.

Kaiya stopped before reaching them, suddenly at a loss for what to say.

"I . . . uh . . . sorry," she finally stammered, looking down at the body at their feet. "It's been . . ." She didn't know how to finish. She had been planning to say *a long day*, but it sounded like a sorry excuse, even to her. Preoii-Aleena had said that executions, however just, were not supposed to be a spectacle.

Ashamed of her thoughtlessness, Kaiya stared down at the headless body as crimson blood pooled around the fleshy neck. The silence and the bloody puddle slowly filled the space between her and the people of Resting Oak.

Ages passed before the woman finally released a shaky, nervous whisper. "We thank you, Faoii. I am Astrid. This is my husband, Ray." The couple bowed their heads and raised their hands to form an inverted triangle at chest level—the common citizens' sign for Illindria. These two, at least, recognized her for what she was.

Kaiya fisted her hands in front of her and lowered her chin a bit as she spoke. "I am Faoii-Kaiya of the Monastery of the Eternal Blade. I'm sorry I scared you."

"Better to be frightened and alive than whatever this man was planning to do to us," Ray replied before glancing around uneasily. "There isn't much time, Faoii. The others will look for him. We have to get rid of the body."

Kaiya frowned. "I thought Illindria's word was still law here," she said as the couple broke formation and began dragging the headless corpse across the cobblestones. "The Faoii are Her enforcers. Our actions are above reproach."

"Normally you would be right, Faoii," Ray whispered fiercely, "but these men do not follow the Goddess or Her laws." Astrid mentioned a refuse pile, and he nodded before ushering her through a gate that led to another alley and helping her to drag the body after them. Kaiya picked the head up by its greying beard and followed. Ray continued between grunts as he lugged the heavy body forward, "An army appeared at our gates before daylight yesterday. Literally *appeared*, Faoii. Out of nowhere. A few of the warriors stayed here when the others disappeared again. They've destroyed all signs of the Goddess and have been jailing everyone that speaks against them. They're already in control of everything here."

"We aren't fighters," Astrid said. "We sent word to the monastery for aid, but no one came." She paused for a second, staring fearfully into Kaiya's eyes. "They took our blood, Faoii.

All of us." She rolled up one of her sleeves to reveal a shallow cut on her forearm. Kaiya frowned.

"Did they say why?"

"No. But we did hear a man in the market say that someone named Thinir—Croeli-Thinir—was collecting blood from conquered towns all across the country. For a spell."

Kaiya tried not to let the worry show on her face. "No one practices blood magic anymore. Not even Croeli. Don't worry." She hoped that she at least *sounded* sure, but as she pictured the sorcerer that had destroyed her home, she was less than certain.

"The bastards——" Ray grunted as he pulled the body over a broken stretch of road. "The bastards claimed that the troops that disappeared were off to destroy the monastery, but that's impossible. No one can defeat the Faoii." He stopped for a moment in order to meet Kaiya's gaze. Licking his lips nervously, he lowered his voice as though hoping Kaiya wouldn't hear. "They didn't take the monastery, did they, Faoii?"

Kaiya's face was grim as she forced herself to respond. "They did."

A squeak escaped Astrid's lips, and she faltered. On reflex, Kaiya moved to assist with the body, tucking the beard attached to the severed head into her belt. She could almost hear Preoii-Aleena's guidance: *Don't show weakness. They need you to be strong.*

Be strong. Kaiya could do that. She was Faoii, after all.

Her body obviously didn't hear her brain's determination, though, because as she leaned over the Croeli torso, Kaiya's head spun in a sudden, dizzy exhaustion. She shook it away with effort and heaved the body forward.

The couple said nothing as they helped her drag the man down another alley that ended with a rubbish heap. After adequately hiding it beneath the refuse, they straightened again, grimly looking over their completed task.

"No one will find him here?" Kaiya asked.

"Eventually, sure," the aging man replied. "But people bring their pigs here when feed prices get too high. Hopefully, if they do find him, he'll be too far gone to recognize."

"And the blood trail?"

"It is beginning to rain, Faoii." Kaiya looked up, surprised to have missed something so obvious. "We should head back," he added softly.

Nodding, Kaiya spun on her heel to return the way they'd come. The movement was too quick, however, and the alleyway tilted. She sagged against a clammy wall, willing her eyes to clear. By the time they did, she realized with an uncomfortable jolt that the couple was supporting her.

"Are you all right, Faoii?" Kaiya was ashamed that anyone would have to ask her that.

"I'm . . ." she took a deep, steadying breath. "I'm fine. I need to speak to Lord Boyer." Kaiya was confused by the sound of her own voice. Were her words always so thick and slurred? Carefully, she pulled herself free of the couple's supporting hands and straightened. "Lord Boyer," she repeated, her words clearer.

"I'm afraid that won't be possible, dear." Kaiya bristled at the endearing term and turned to face the woman who'd dare say such a thing, but she paused when the world spun again. It righted itself more quickly this time, and she found herself looking into the worried eyes of a woman who, in another life, could have been her mother. Kaiya softened her gaze.

"Why not? Isn't he at his manor?"

"His head is in the courtyard, Faoii," Ray answered quietly. "We don't know what they did with the body. Either way, I don't think he's the man you need to see."

It took a moment for Kaiya to comprehend what he was saying, and her knees sagged as realization struck her.

Lord Boyer was dead, and the Goddess had been pushed out of Resting Oak. There were no allies for her here. Or at least no one with the ability to fight back against the Croeli. She needed warriors. She needed Faoii, not scared citizens that could barely lift a sword. When Preoii-Aleena had said she was the last, Kaiya had not truly understood the magnitude of that statement. Where else could she go? Who else could she turn to?

For the first time, Kaiya realized that she was completely and utterly alone.

The sudden weakness in the Faoii's stance did not go unnoticed, and the hovering woman was there immediately.

"Ray, let's get her home. We can't leave her out here."

"Come, Faoii," Ray replied. "It is not safe here."

Kaiya strengthened her knees, pulling her arm from Astrid's shoulders. She let go and Kaiya walked, though sluggishly, on her own two legs. "My horse."

"We're almost back to the street where you left him. I'll stable him for you once you're safe."

The walk to the couple's house could not have been a long one, but to Kaiya it seemed like ages as every step caused her entire body to scream in pain. At one point, they'd tried to convince her to mount her gelding, but the task had seemed too arduous at the time. As she walked, she tried to focus on a specific hurt and enter a simple healing trance, but she could not focus on anything other than the constant sound of her sisters' screams echoing in her mind. If her eyes closed, she was back in the chapel watching

Mollie's head split open. A thousand images and sounds from throughout the day—*Goddess, it hadn't even been a full day, had it?*—came flooding forward. Kaiya wanted to scream, to cry, but only forced herself to keep walking with her face rigid but expressionless and her steps sluggish but straight.

The rest of the journey seemed to happen in pieces. At one point, she was walking next to her gelding, her hand tangled in its grey mane as it plodded steadily beside her. Then she was walking next to Astrid and a heavy rain had begun to fall, plastering black ringlets to her breastplate from beneath the ivy helm. Later she was in a soft, warm room, and someone was pulling off her boots as she fumbled with her armor. Then there was no one, and it was quiet. Kaiya lay in the silence, her eyes staring, unfocused, at a thatched ceiling.

She did not know how long she lay there, still hearing the screams of her sisters, but when she at last plummeted into a hard and dreamless sleep, she found herself thinking of the abhorrent name that both Preoii-Aleena and Astrid had given her.

Croeli-Thinir.

"There are nine horses left at the monastery," Kaiya explained to Ray as Astrid dressed the wounds on the Faoii's battered back. "They're corralled in the pasture beneath the cliffs. There aren't any stallions left; the Croeli took them and our largest mares. My mount was the only gelding left, and I need him. But the rest should be worth something." She tried to give the couple a reassuring smile. "They're yours if you want them. Maybe you can make a life where the Goddess is still welcome."

"The Goddess is always welcome in our home, Faoii," said Ray.

"I know. That's why I'm offering them to you."

Ray bowed his head. "We accept your gifts with gratitude, Faoii, and are humbled that we could share our table with you. Your presence brings hope that the Croeli may yet fall."

Kaiya looked at her fantoii resting against the table leg. "As long as one Faoii still wields a sword, her blade will sing with the voice of every throat that has cried out against injustice and dance with the steps of every innocent child. She will lead the choir, and the voices of her sword will deafen the ears of her enemies." The Oath was cold and heavy on her tongue. Ray nodded grimly.

"I hope that your choir does not grow any larger, Faoii. But I wish you luck in your journey."

"And you in yours." Kaiya winced as Astrid wrapped her torso, but remained silent.

"You have four broken ribs, Faoii," the woman said softly. "And the wound in your stomach concerns me. There may be damage beneath the skin." Kaiya looked down at the purple bruise blossoming on her belly. It was dark and tender to the touch, but she couldn't repress her smile.

"You should have seen it when it was a stab wound." Astrid and Ray gaped as Kaiya pulled on her worn tunic and leather jerkin. Then she donned her bronze breastplate and took Astrid's shoulders in her hands. "May Illindria bless you always, and may you never forget Her truths."

"Thank you, Faoii."

Kaiya gave Ray her blessing as well. He thanked her softly and turned toward the door.

"I'll retrieve your gelding."

"Where will you go?" Astrid asked quietly after her husband had gone. Kaiya thought for a moment.

"To the capital," she finally decided. "The Faoii don't have a lot of political strength behind the king's walls, but we're still respected as diplomats. If I'm quick, I can warn the capital before Thinir sets his eyes on it." Kaiya did not stoop to call the sorcerer by his title. "With the king's help, I can rally against these... beasts."

"It seems a good plan. Goddess guide your footfalls, Faoii."

"And yours as well."

Ray arrived with Kaiya's horse. She thanked him and mounted silently. The beast perked its ears forward and pranced uneasily in the Goddessless street.

"How much do I owe you for the stable?"

"Nothing, Faoii. The proprietor asks only for your blessing as you pass, if you would be willing to give it to a man who has removed the Goddess's symbol from his windows."

Kaiya frowned. "He wasn't the one who tarnished Illindria's name here. I can't blame him for choosing obedience over death."

Astrid smiled sadly. "Nor can I, but I wish he'd come with us now that we have an idea of what to do. We can take the horses you have offered and make our living far from here. In the country, we can hang our symbols and feel Her protection again. But Leonard . . . he won't leave his stable and his smithy. His wife is buried in our graveyard, and he's still hoping his children will come back some day. Resting Oak is his home."

"I understand." Kaiya smiled warmly at the poor couple. "Don't worry. I'll ask the Eternal One to watch over your friend."

As Kaiya spoke, it dawned on her that she was Cleroii now too— worthy of singing Illindria's songs of praise and glory. But more importantly, she was Preoii. She could truly bless people and not worry about insulting Illindria with a tongue unworthy of Her voice. As the last of her Order, Faoii-Kaiya took on all of its roles.

The thought was frightening, but she didn't let them see.

The streets of Resting Oak were quiet. Rain pattered softly, dampening the smell of ash. Most of the villagers ducked their heads as Kaiya passed, peeking out from beneath their brows in shock or shame. Kaiya read all the signs. The eyes that used to show awe or reverence were now chagrined as they appraised the Faoii. Many knew what she was, but none dared to even hail her. Kaiya tried to bury the feeling of betrayal as she moved forward. Mostly, she felt pity. It was like she was riding through a graveyard; the people around her only shades. Did they feel the chill in the air or see each other as they passed? Could they remember what laughter was, though it had only been two days since this gloom had fallen? Rather than being offended, Kaiya ached for these people. But she could not defeat the Croeli by herself, and any mention of the Goddess would only bring a gruesome death by the hands of the Resting Oak's new overlords. If she stopped to right the evils here, Kaiya knew she'd never reach the king or stop Thinir.

With straight shoulders but a heavy heart, Kaiya rode through a town that was letting itself die and, worse, was preparing to bow to those wielding the blade.

The smith was not hard to find, though Kaiya had never sought him out in her travels here—the Faoii crafted their own blades and armor. She heard the steady *clank, clank, clank,* of a hammer on anvil long before she saw the open shop, little more than a roof on raised support beams. She slowed her gelding as they approached.

A huge man with arms bulging from tattered sleeves stood behind the anvil, his hammer releasing a remorseful, continuous toll. His braided beard was greying, but his arm still rippled with the force of each mallet strike. Kaiya gave a cursory glance to the aging smith, prepared to whisper a blessing as she went on her way, but she found herself frozen under the piercing gaze of Leonard's too-bright eyes. An overwhelming flood of sorrow and regret rippled out from him, washing over her even from across the street.

Stunned, the Faoii gripped her reins and watched flashes of a life that was not hers dance sporadically over the damp cobblestones. A wife who had loved the Goddess and crafted delicate tapestries in Her honor. Two children who had sat on the crates in the back of the shop and watched the hammer fall rhythmically before growing up and moving on. A grave with an iron Goddess symbol at its head, crafted by the smith himself. A rainy night and bloody hands tearing the marker from the ground. A broken edge. A tortured cry.

Kaiya saw all these pictures in a span of seconds but didn't have to ask in order to know that the Croeli had demanded the tombstone of Leonard's wife destroyed. Even now the smith hammered the Goddess's symbol into an indiscernible mass of iron on the very forge that had crafted it in the beginning. Astrid hadn't been wrong when she'd said that the Croeli had forbidden any sign of the Goddess's existence. They didn't even hold grave markers sacred. And yet Illindria's presence still remained.

Kaiya concentrated, searching for the magical domelike sense that an Illindrian symbol creates. Her ears picked up a steady dripping that did not come from the rain, and her heart sensed a glow from a fire that no longer burned. Kaiya's eyes narrowed in on the smith's bulging arm and saw blood drip steadily from it.

Beneath the tattered sleeve, the Goddess's symbol could be seen, and in another flash of memories that were not hers, she watched Leonard carve it into his own flesh with the rusted edges of his wife's broken gravestone. Blood still dripped from the unhealed gashes. His gaze still froze her to the spot.

Kaiya realized now why Leonard had asked for a blessing. It was not to make this life better or to feel the Goddess's embrace during times of darkness. Leonard knew the Croeli would never overlook his self-inflicted brand. He was not looking for a sweet song of summer blessings from a Cleroii on her way out of town.

The smith had asked for a dirge.

As though reading Kaiya's thoughts, Leonard gave an almost imperceptible nod and lowered his gaze back to the anvil. Kaiya closed her eyes and turned away as she felt a song gather in her throat. She sang quietly, trying to ignore the sound of a dozen sabatons as they rounded a corner behind her, steering toward the smithy. She turned down a side street and out of sight, resisting the urge to sing louder as the *clank, clank, clank* stopped abruptly and a crash of iron on stone thundered down the street. She tried to ignore the sound of someone screaming in agony.

But it was no use. With all her heart, Kaiya wished that the song of memories and loved ones could be louder than the sound of pain and loss that rose behind her. Then, when the screaming was cut short, she wished with all her heart that the world wasn't so silent.

6

If there had been anyone on the streets of Resting Oak when the commotion at the smithy started, they weren't there now, but the town still felt full of accusing eyes. *Will he join your choir, Faoii? Even after you abandoned him?* Kaiya shuddered as she tried to push past the loathing in her gut. Even with Mollie at her back, she wouldn't have been able to take down so many Croeli. She'd had no choice. The smith had chosen his fate, and she had done all she could for him.

So why did she feel like she'd betrayed all Faoii with her lack of action?

You were too afraid. You shouldn't be here. Illindria should have chosen someone else.

The accusations echoed in her head incessantly as Kaiya turned onto a street leading out of Resting Oak. Up ahead, a lone Croeli leaned against the city's outer wall. He did not look up as Kaiya dismounted, only waved lazily for her to continue on her way.

Kaiya kept her head down and her gelding between them as she headed through the opening in the outer wall. The Croeli was apparently unbothered by it and didn't even raise his eyes as she passed. Kaiya stopped, suddenly infuriated by his insolence and her own previous inaction. Were the Croeli really so sure of their hold on Resting Oak that this beast could just wave her by, even in her armor and helm? Could they be so *arrogant?*

Or worse—could they be right?

They couldn't be. They had to know that there were other monasteries in the world, that the Monastery of the Eternal Blade would be avenged. There's no way they could have gotten to all eight of them, right? No. Preoii-Aleena would have known whether the other monasteries had been attacked. Even if there wasn't much communication among the monasteries… she'd know. Right?

In truth, though, none of the Faoii monasteries had seen a true threat in centuries—only small skirmishes, and those were hardly reason to call another monastery for aid. Each faction was self-sufficient. In control. They'd never *needed* to talk to the others. Did Faoii messengers even exist?

We became too sure. We were unprepared. The watchers at the gate, the patrols and lookouts—all these things seemed so insignificant and ineffective now. *We should have been ready for an attack like this. We were overconfident.*

Only a part of Kaiya truly believed this, though, as she thought of how fiercely the chapel fight had raged, despite a group of unarmed girls facing trained assailants. She thought about the bodies she had passed in those halls; so many had been Croeli.

Her sisters had done more than should have been possible. They were not weak. They had never been weak. She felt ashamed for thinking otherwise.

"Hey there, sugar," someone drawled, pulling Kaiya from her thoughts. "You plannin' on goin', or you waitin' for me to make an offer? I got a few coins on me." Kaiya bristled. She wasn't even sure how long she'd been lost in thought, and only *now* did this so-called "guard" take notice of her? And, worse, she was still hiding her face from the other side of her gelding. Why was she avoiding a fight here? She couldn't have fought the soldiers that rounded on the smithy, but this was a solitary Croeli. One who dared mistake her for a common harlot. She'd started fights outside the chapel for less than that.

We had no messengers. We had no fear. These men will not be as lucky.

Kaiya's hands clenched, and her heart raced as she stepped around her horse.

"I am Faoii. Not 'sugar.'" The guard's eyes widened in surprise, but then he laughed.

"Funny, lass. No one could escape Thinir and his soldiers. None of the previous Faoii did, and none from up that mountain coulda, either. So my guess is ya found out the Faoii bitches were gone, and ya decided to strap on some armor that's too big for ya and call yourself a warrior now that them whores ain't able to say otherwise. Heh. Yer a little stern-lookin' to make much money around these parts, though those pretty eyes o' yers sure are somethin'. Never saw eyes like that on a dark girl. But if you wanna go make men's fantasies come true since the Faoii are just stories now, ya might make yerself enough to buy yer own brothel." His chuckle smelled of smoke and ale. "That little outfit o' yers ain't perfect, but it's close enough to make some men go hard just lookin' at you." He grinned. "Wanna try yer first attempt at Faoii-playin'? I seen them whores when they were still alive, even played with a few when they couldn't fight back anymore. I can help ya make yer name." He reached out toward Kaiya, who sidestepped swiftly. His eyes narrowed, but realization came too slowly.

Kaiya's fantoii sprouted from his outstretched palm. The man gaped, but before he could utter a sound, her elbow was wedged against his throat, pinning him to the wall even as his eyes bugged.

"Listen, Croeli," Kaiya hissed, bringing a knee up against his groin. "I'm not going to kill you even though I should. Blades, I should turn you into a eunuch after what you've done to my sisters." She paused. "Maybe I should anyway. Even a eunuch can be a messenger boy." The stench of sweat and ale mixed suddenly with urine, and the knee of Kaiya's breeches became warm and wet. The man blanched.

"Here's your message, filth. Go to your superiors. Go to your brothers. Go to the other murderers and rapists. Tell them that the Faoii are still alive and that they sing with the chorus of a thousand vengeful voices. My sword swings with the strength of every dead sister, and the voices will not quiet until each of you lies unburied in your own stench. I will find each one of you and cut you down. And in the end, Croeli-Thinir will stand at the base of your piled bodies, sick and weary. And I will be there to end him. You tell him that he cannot escape the choir."

She brought her knee up with a sudden jerk, and the man crumpled forward, his neck pressing into her elbow. He gasped audibly, trying to suck air into his lungs, but Kaiya only pressed harder, her teeth clenched in anger and disgust as she thought about this *scum* pleasuring himself at her sisters' expense. She thought about Leonard's resigned eyes as he pounded away at his wife's burial marker and of Preoii-Aleena's tortured body hanging from the chapel.

His eyes streaming, the Croeli frantically tried to pry Kaiya's arm off his throat, but she yielded nothing. His eyes bulged and his lips turned blue as his throat swelled under the pressure of her elbow. Finally, his purple tongue fell from between his lips, and Kaiya relaxed her forearm. Fantoii flashing, she released the man and pulled at his tongue. Her blade sliced through it cleanly.

The Croeli crumpled, trying to grab both his crotch and his mouth at the same time, blood and urine spreading across the cobblestones. Kaiya flicked the swollen tongue at him as he writhed. "You will live, Croeli, and you still have most of your parts. I have been merciful. In return, you will spread my message, even without your forked tongue. Go." Kaiya watched as the man crawled away from her, weeping. Then she mounted and guided her gelding out of the gate.

The capital was waiting.

Croeli-Thinir chuckled darkly as he peered into the chalice's inky water. The Faoii, Kaiya, had fought him bravely in her chapel. But she was young. Inexperienced. Weak. She was filled with hatred and anger now, but that would fade. Soon, she would return to the Faoii's more natural temperament. They had all grown soft around the eyes, quick to smile and slow to anger.

She had no concept of what her land needed, what the people needed. She was Faoii, there was no denying that, but the Faoii had grown indulgent in their unopposed reign. She might have had the steel to tear down her enemies, but that willingness to fight was never forefront in her mind. She, like the others, had grown accustomed to ease.

He sneered into the chalice, spitting into the dark water. The image faded, and his own reflection glowered back at him. How could it be that he knew so much more about this child than she knew herself? Had her precious Preoii kept so much from her?

Even after all that he had accomplished, it had not surprised Thinir that this would be the Faoii to stand against him when all others fell. After all, he knew of her, knew the traits that she herself did not realize she possessed. It was only fitting that she should continue through the maze that he had steadily built over the last decade. She was the most fitting piece in the puzzle.

He was sure that her parents would agree, and that made him smile.

Thinir ordered the refurbished slave in front of him to remove the goblet as he drummed his fingers on his blade.

The Faoii Order was sick, festering. Its injuries were covered and decorated with silken finery, but the wounds below oozed with decay. The people "protected"—"ruled" would be a better term—by the Faoii Order smiled as they stabbed each other in dark, fetid alleyways, far from the influence of the "all-encompassing" light of the monasteries. In the Faoii's quest to protect the citizens of the heartland, the women had forgotten justice. They hid in their chapels and offered prayers or songs that did nothing to feed their people. Meanwhile, in the villages, the sickness showed itself.

In a land that had grown accustomed to having more than its share, the people had acquired a taste for wealth. The Faoii had the power to make sure that it was doled out evenly so no one starved while another thrived. But they did not. Instead, they sang, they prayed, and they *failed*.

He could fix that. His people were starving, but all starved equally. When the Faoii lands were in his control, there would be balance. All people would have enough to eat. All would have enough land to live in comfort. He clenched his fist until his palm bled, thinking of the acres of unsown pastures around the Faoii holds.

By the rich Goddess's broken blade, those lands would belong to his people.

Thinir chuckled again as he pulled an elaborately carved ebony box from beneath his seat. Defeating the final monastery had gone better than he had expected. Puzzle pieces he had not foreseen had settled into place with only the smallest push. Setting the box on his knees, he lifted the lid slowly. A simple bronze dagger rested on a velvet pillow, the blade still coated with rust-colored blood.

He had been correct in his assumption that Aleena would heal Kaiya-Faoii before the others. The Preoii's prolonged death had served him far better than a simple beheading would have. It had been a stroke of luck—*no, not luck; it was in her blood, after all*—that the pretty little Kaiya had reached him in her fury. That he had been able to plant his blade in her belly so readily.

And then the soft-eyed Aleena had healed her and sent her on her way.

It was perfect.

"Go, little Faoii," he whispered, watching his pale eyes reflect in the bronze of the dagger. "Go. I will wait."

Kaiya sighed as she passed a rickety barn and another too-lean cow. She'd always assumed the people protected by the Faoii were happy and content, like those in Resting Oak, but the farther from the monastery she traveled, the more desolate her surroundings became. Many houses along her route had been abandoned or burned; many pastures lay fallow and barren. Had it always been this way, and she and the other Faoii had not noticed? Or was this the aftermath of the Croeli rampage they'd failed to protect the people from? She wasn't sure which answer would upset her more.

A young girl carrying two buckets came around the corner of the barn and stopped when she saw Kaiya riding up the path. Kaiya nodded at her, but the girl did not move, did not even put down her load. Kaiya frowned and continued forward. She'd never met a person who did not bow their head, make the sign for the

Goddess with their hands, or at least offer a smile at her passing. But things had changed. Now, only three weeks after the fall of her monastery, the people only stared in awe or fear, and no one tried to hide their disbelief. Those that she tried to speak to ducked their heads and scurried away or made anti-curse signs in her direction. Somehow, even in so short a time, word had spread. The Faoii were dead, and the Croeli would not tolerate anyone who dared suggest otherwise. Kaiya was either an impostor or a ghost. Neither was welcome at most tables.

Three weeks. How could so much change so quickly? While Kaiya's life had crashed and been rebuilt in an awkward, slanting shanty of partially forgotten ceremonies that didn't mean anything in this new world, the rest of the world had simply . . . lived. There was no outcry, no rage. Most of the Croeli-occupied towns bore some sense of emptiness and sorrow, but even that was repressed and quickly forgotten as the townsfolk went on with their lives.

It hadn't taken her long to start living like the fugitive she'd suddenly become. For the first time in her life, Kaiya had to hide that she was Faoii. She hid her breastplate and ivy helm beneath her cloak and begged for food along her route. When she could, she probed people in taverns for news of the Faoii downfall. More than once she heard a quiet whisper of "same whip, different tyrant," but had to hide her fury at the words. How could anyone consider the Faoii and the Croeli similar?

Days passed. The sun still rose and fell as it always had. Birds still sang and cocks still crowed, but to Kaiya it all sounded muted and dull. The rolling hills that spread before the capital lost their splendor in the dark world she had wrapped around herself like a frosted, comfortless cloak. Even her horse had caught the air and plodded on with gloomy determination over the final rise of their journey.

In the valley below, Clearwall sprawled on its glittering dais. Even in the early morning, the city had begun to come alive as a thousand firefly-like torches dotted the valley with splatters of golden light that shone like jewels. Nestled in the rocky cliffs overlooking the Twilight River, Clearwall's mighty castle cast its unwavering gaze over the town. The palace's white marble walls glistened in a glowing array of orange and gold.

"Kai, look at the sunrise. Have you ever seen so many colors in one place before? Isn't it gorgeous?"

A laugh and a light smack on a red head. "Where were you raised, Mollie? Underground? You've never seen a sunrise before?"

A thoughtful quiet before an equally thoughtful reply. "No. I've seen many sunrises. But I've never seen this sunrise. And it is the most beautiful because it's alive right now. It is more than just memory and thought. It... is."

A casual shrug. "If you say so. It looks like any other sunrise to me."

Kaiya sighed and brought her hanging head to sit solidly atop squared shoulders, fixing a stern gaze into place. Her horse perked its head up too, and with a feigned air of the invincibility and pride that Kaiya no longer felt, they made their way to the city gates.

I wish I'd listened to you more, Mollie. I wish a lot of things.

Kaiya fretted with the idea of keeping herself hidden in Clearwall, but she'd only been here for an hour and she was already hopelessly lost. There wasn't enough time to waste in the maze that was the outer city, and if anyone would still welcome a Faoii, it would be King Lucius Clearwall III and his subjects. Clearwall had always respected the Order, which is why she'd come here for help. She would be safe here. For the first time in weeks, Kaiya lowered her cowl.

The city did not follow any sort of grid or pattern. The streets were curved and twisted, sometimes wide enough that six horses could walk abreast without the riders brushing thighs, and sometimes so narrow that Kaiya's boots scuffed against the long-worn walls that loomed around her. She had heard whispers that the streets of the outer city had been designed this way in order to dissuade invading armies, but she had no way to verify that. Still, there must have been some method to the insanity that was Clearwall's outer city, because men and women shuffled through the streets, scurrying to their destinations without looking up.

Kaiya refrained from biting her lip, a childish sign of worry that she'd convinced Preoii-Aleena she'd grown out of. Faoii do not show such weakness. But she could not completely banish her uncertainty. Like everyone else she had passed since leaving Ray and Astrid's home, these people did not even try to acknowledge her presence. There was no sign of Croeli influence, but still she went unhailed. How was it possible? Could word of her monastery's massacre have reached this far already? Why hadn't Lucius done anything in retaliation?

Kai tried to take a steadying breath against the uncertainty but wrinkled her nose at the inhale. The air was odd here. Not with the disconcerting strangeness that she had experienced in Resting Oak, but something subtler. Everything in Clearwall was too chaotic, too fast-paced. The curved, jagged streets broke up the magic that would usually form around such an emotional and bustling city, so there was an unnerving lack of power in the air. Normally you could feel the Eternal Weave more clearly as more people who were tied to it gathered in one spot. But despite the throngs of people, there was nothing. *Have these people grown up surrounded by this . . . void?*

Kaiya was pulled from her thoughts as an armored man turned onto the street she was navigating. He walked purposefully toward her, and Kaiya brought her gelding to a stop, the reigns held loosely in one hand. The stranger's sabatons rang on the cobblestones, and the sound echoed for a moment even after he had stopped in front of Kaiya.

"Madam Warrior, King Lucius Clearwall III requests your presence." Kaiya raised an eyebrow and looked down at the soldier. Her own face stared back from his shiny helm, awkward and oblong in its reflection. It surprised and pleased her that the king was already on the lookout for Faoii, even this soon after the monastery's fall. Maybe there was hope for help here after all.

"All right," she replied, nodding to the soldier, "but I will need to stable my horse."

"We will take care of it. Follow me." Without waiting for a reply, the soldier turned on his heel and started forward. Kaiya had her horse follow, watching in surprised awe as people parted before them without raising their eyes. They'd barely moved through the throng when another armored guard stepped from the crowd to join the first. A little further and a third man, young and without a helmet, joined the march. Kaiya frowned.

"I didn't expect an armed escort. Am I being arrested?" The words came out more sullen than intended.

"Only criminals are arrested. If we have no reason to imprison you, we will not." Kaiya frowned. It was not a no.

"I'm sure, Fa—" the young soldier began before clamping his mouth shut at a sharp glare from his superior. He cleared his throat and tried again. "I am sure, *Lady*, that our honorable king will treat you as expected." Kaiya peered down at the newest escort through her ivy helm, careful not to turn her head or draw attention from the other guards that now made her more uneasy than relieved. The man was light for a soldier, his hair tied back away from his face. But he held himself with the strength of someone who knew his sword. Kaiya studied his face.

"You're hiding something." Her whisper was low and carried softly, and she spoke out of the corner of her mouth so that the other guards could not see or hear. "I don't read *deceit* in your face so much as . . . implication." For a moment, the Sight showed fear and a hint of regret in his features, and his steel-grey eyes darted to the other two soldiers who accompanied them. He relaxed when they showed no sign of having heard and gave one jerky nod.

"You know that I am Faoii." Kaiya felt the air strengthen at the word. The man might have felt it too, because he stiffened marginally. "Will anyone else recognize me as I am?" The soldier squared his shoulders and didn't respond. Confusion colored his eyes. She tried again. "Will anyone else affirm the Faoii Order?"

The head jerked once to the left, then to the right. *No.* Kaiya pondered for a moment. "Can I trust the king?" The guard's shoulder flicked. The tiniest of shrugs.

Kaiya refrained from biting her lip before continuing. "Soldier, do you still honor the Faoii and Illindria, the Great Goddess?"

The nod was immediate and sharp. The movement caught the attention of the guard on Kaiya's right, and he turned to study the young soldier as they marched on. The boy used his shoulder to scratch his right ear, and the other man lost interest. Kaiya repressed a grin.

"You're quick," she finally whispered after a few minutes. "What's your name?"

Another minute passed, and Kaiya thought that the soldier wasn't going to respond, but suddenly there was an obnoxious clatter that caused several people nearby to jump in surprise.

The other two guards swung around and Kaiya stopped her gelding, watching the soldier try to gather his fallen sword belt and coin purse while still gripping his shield with one hand. Small gold coins rolled through the street, and people flocked to retrieve them.

"Harkins! Damn it, boy, didn't anyone ever teach you how to dress yourself?" The original guard roared with indignation, his cheeks purple with rage. Harkins said nothing as he buckled his belt on again before falling into step next to the gelding. They continued in a silence that was only occasionally interrupted by the senior guard's angry mumbles.

The road continued along its twisted route, and Kaiya realized with dismay that she had been so focused on talking to Harkins without the others knowing that she hadn't been paying attention to where they were going. They were nearing the end of the valley now, and the walls of the inner city rose ahead of them, built directly into the cliffs that supported the ever-regal Clearwall Keep.

It was both glorious and imposing. Kaiya studied the high turrets and alabaster walls, awed by the stained glass and stone gargoyles. This was different than her monastery. Faoii buildings were designed to incorporate the natural world in their construction. Archways and pillars curved like tree branches, and decorations were green with living things. The great keep she was approaching now was not one of the Goddess's organic-inspired structures, yet it was no less impressive.

They arrived, and Kaiya dismounted, handing her reigns to an expectant guard that led the gelding away without a word. Harkins held open the great metal door as his superior led Kaiya inside with a pompous air of authority. Kaiya matched his pace, her booted heels ringing on a mosaic floor.

The palace was as grand on the inside as it was on the outside, and Kaiya almost faltered in her step. Rich tapestries hung from white stone walls, coats of arms etched in gold thread gleaming from the woven fabric. Lighted chandeliers with real glass encasings hung above them, casting blue and purple shadows on the floor tiles before the grand alabaster staircase that dominated the entranceway.

Kaiya stared for a moment at all the glittering sights the palace had to offer before stopping and narrowing her eyes. Silently, she scrutinized one of the stained-glass windows next to the door.

"This isn't defensible at all," she muttered, stroking one dark hand against the polished wooden table beneath the window. Hadn't her history lessons praised Clearwall for its stalwart defenses? They never said anything about floor-to-ceiling windows of easily-shattered glass.

Kaiya turned away from the window, suddenly unsure. Would Clearwall be safe from the Croeli threat? She could sense the old fortress—the keep that had been built of rock and desperation and had repelled swarms of enemies over its lifetime—still lay somewhere beneath the glistening white walls and reflective tiles. But this was not the fort that had housed generations of noblemen and saved countless peasants during grand wars. This building was a boy wearing his father's finery.

They'll do the same to the monastery, too, someday. They'll rebuild what you burnt down. But they won't know how. The Faoii will just be painted pictures in storybooks when you're gone.

Suddenly angry, Kaiya turned to the stairs with an impatient stride. She couldn't let that happen. She needed to see the king. She needed to stop the Croeli. She needed to give the world a reason to remember her Order.

She needed the Faoii to endure.

The stairs brought Kaiya and her guards to a soft-carpeted hallway that ended at a broad wooden door. The older guard removed Kaiya's sword belt with a practiced ease while Harkins held the door ajar. He stood completely straight as Kaiya passed, and she took the opportunity to study his expression.

There was fear there.

"Who have you brought to me, General?"

The booming voice almost made Kaiya jump, and she turned away from the frightened Harkins in order to face the king.

King Lucius Clearwall III had once been a strong and comely man. He still had a strong chin and imposing features, but his black beard was streaked with grey and his dark eyes peered from behind deepening crow's feet. His shoulders were still broad and straight, but his middle had thickened and his arms had softened during the years that he had wielded a quill rather than a sword. Kaiya knew the man had once been a fierce and stalwart hero, part of the family of nobles that had been guarding Clearwall for more than twelve generations. It was because of his lineage that the city had gone from being a handful of homesteads to the sprawling jewel that was now the nation's capital. King Lucius looked down his nose at Kaiya as he waited for the soldier's reply.

"Your majesty." The guard bowed. "I have brought a woman dressed similarly to the recent traitors to the crown, milord. As instructed, we have kept a lookout for any suspicious figures in the city." He pushed Kaiya forward, apparently trying to make her stumble. She did not, but instead took a sturdy step toward the throne. She looked up at the king on his raised dais, framed by the high vaulted ceilings and story-tall windows of the throne room...and froze.

For a moment, Kaiya stood awkwardly, not sure of what to do. Faoii bowed to no one. She had never been taught the correct way for a Faoii to address a king.

Finally, Kaiya fisted her hands in front of her and bowed her head. Her words came smoother than she expected.

"Your Majesty, I am Faoii-Kaiya of the Monastery of the Eternal Blade. I'm sorry that you see me as a potential traitor. I was not aware that your people and mine were at odds." The king looked her up and down carefully.

"Eternal Blade? The Illindrian monastery to the north? To look at you, I would have expected you to say you were from the south. Most of our northern brethren are of fair complexion." He stroked his greying beard thoughtfully. "You have traveled quite far, young lady. I trust all is well with your kind?" Kaiya was put off by his failure to use her title but said nothing.

"No, sir." *See? I don't have to use titles either.* "Our temple was attacked, and I am the only survivor. The nearby town of Resting Oak has been taken over by vicious men, and the Goddess has been pushed out of the cities between here and the northern sea. Even the people here in the—" she stopped, recognizing something in King Lucius's eyes. His face remained completely still, a look of rapt attention, surprise, and slight concern on his features, but it was...false. Behind his eyes and in the curve of his lips there was...deception, pride, and a sly joy. Mollie had always been better at using the Sight than Kaiya was, but Kai knew enough.

The king was false-facing.

Kaiya didn't know what to do. She had come here looking for an ally against the Croeli and had only found another ruin. No wonder she had felt no hint of the Goddess's presence here. It had nothing to do with the twists and turns of the city breaking up the flow of magic. Illindria had been forced out of this city by the Croeli long ago. And now Kaiya had fallen into their trap.

Kaiya shivered as ghostly replays of Lucius declaring fealty to Thinir suddenly superimposed themselves upon the throne room, unseen by everyone except her. Images of his grisly deeds and orders to execute other Faoii who'd come to the capital made her stomach churn. She barely heard him beneath the white-hot ringing in her ears.

"Continue your story, girl. I am listening."

"You mean that you find it entertaining." Kaiya kept her hands from shaking in rage as she spoke through clenched teeth. "You already know what I'm going to say. It's a story you've heard a dozen times, and yet you haven't gotten tired of it. Have you, Croeli?" A piercing, heart-wrenching rage made her insides scream and her fingers clench. She could not keep her eyes from filling with tears as she continued in icy tones. "You've known. And you did nothing to stop it."

The king's face had lost its smile, but Kaiya saw it there, lurking in his features. He straightened in his high-backed throne, and his voice rang through the court.

"You dare accuse the king of such things! Get her out of my sight! She is a traitor like the rest of them!"

Kaiya could not repress her rage. She leapt at the monster king, knowing as she did that it was futile. Her hands hooked like claws, and she sailed through the air with a grace that would not have been possible in a heavier breastplate. Her battle cry was sharp and piercing, and she thought for just a moment that she saw fear in the king's eyes. But it was quickly replaced with humor.

Kaiya heard the click before she felt anything. She had no time to react before a crossbow bolt sprouted just above her hip, buried in the exposed leather below her breastplate. Her momentum carried her to the king, but he was already up, grabbing her by her outstretched wrists. Time slowed as Kaiya stared into the familiar pale eyes of Croeli-Thinir. They were colored with glee.

Kaiya wanted to tear those eyes out of the stolen skull they had settled in. But there was no time. The false king swung her quickly, and, as a farmer throws a bag of grain onto a loft, Kaiya flew across the hall with unnatural force. She thought she heard laughter and a bell as she landed heavily on her uninjured hip.

"Croeli-Thinir!" she screamed, trying to scramble back to her feet as men in plate armor surrounded her with glinting long spears. She tried to push past but was beaten down. "You have to let me go! The king is taken!" But her cries went unheeded and were then cut short as a booted foot pounded into her stomach, doubling her over.

The bell and laughter were sounding again, but there were words there too. "Take her to the dungeon. I will deal with her personally." There was a pause before the voice continued, "Oh, and do be careful. She is the last, after all." Kaiya could only glare and pull against her captors as the laughter took control again.

Croeli-Thinir growled as he clutched his head in pain and anger. How dare Lucius defy him? He was completing the work of gods, and some insignificant, *mortal* king felt he held enough power to disobey orders? Now pretty little Kaiya not only knew that the monarchy was not her ally, but was to be thrown into a cell, and for what? So that a single man could satisfy his most base desires and flaunt his power over the last of the women that had refused his reign? Imbecile!

But... this could work. Kaiya was resourceful. She could adapt. She wasn't even aware of how strong her bloodline was. And there were other resources in those cells. Ones that Thinir could still use to his advantage, even if not in the way he had originally intended. Kaiya was alone and frightened. Surely, she would take whatever help she could, regardless of the source.

This could still work. Even if Kaiya could not escape the prison, even if she did not use his gifts to her... he could still succeed with his original plan. Most of the country was his already. Those few that still opposed him would come of their own accord.

Until then, he would continue the horned god's work. His control must be complete.

And there was a sad little king that needed to be punished.

Kaiya said nothing as her hands were bound and she was lifted forcefully to her feet. She kept her head down and tried to think through the humiliation of having fallen into a trap like this.

There were not very many twists and turns through the long hallways, and some part of Kaiya knew she should be paying attention to their route. But the Faoii could only focus on her hatred and listen to the sound of booted feet as spear tips prodded her breastplate at random. Even with her head down and her eyes misted in a red haze, Kaiya refused to let the spears affect her stride. She never faltered in her step, never stumbled or fell out of sequence with her captors. Until suddenly, the ground wasn't there anymore.

Kaiya tumbled down the stairs she had not noticed in front of her, trying to catch herself with arms that had been bound behind her back. She fell six or seven steps before she could catch herself in a crouch, using her legs to steady herself and stop the disconcerting spill. The men above her laughed and jeered, their comments reverberating against the stone walls. Stubbornly, Kaiya straightened her legs and rebalanced herself, turning with a determined stride until she was facing downward.

This time, Kaiya started the descent more carefully, angry at herself. She should have realized where she was. The air was chilled here and smelled of mildew. It was obvious that this passage led underground, and she should have been able to sense it before reaching the first step. Disgusted, she finished the descent with a grace that quickly quieted the men behind her. The last few stone steps rang out under her booted heel.

The men were not gentle as they stripped her of her breastplate and leathers, tearing through her armor and casually discarding knives and tools as they found them. There was a sharp pain as someone ripped off her jerkin, and Kaiya looked down to where the crossbow bolt had struck her. She was pleased that the leather had stopped all but the very tip of the shaft, and the wound was minor. It was only after both sets of armor had been stripped that the men paused, looking over the plain cloth tunic that Kaiya wore underneath everything else. It was well worn and threadbare, and the dust-colored cloth contrasted with her dark flesh. Kaiya squared her shoulders and eyed the men, waiting. The sound of dripping water echoed through the cavern.

Without warning, one of the guards behind Kaiya suddenly lunged forward, wrapping his arms around her torso. She convulsed as she felt him poke against her lower back, throwing the back of her head forcefully into his wide smile. The soldier roared with pain, and Kaiya felt something warm and sticky splatter the back of her head. She straightened again as the other men looked between her and the wounded man. She stared back.

Come at me, then.

Kaiya felt the dam break moments before they moved. She tried to prepare for it, but without her arms, she was only able to kick two others down before the rest were on top of her, and without balance she was only able to bite at their fingers, ears, or arms as they pushed her down to the floor. She felt the hard stone against her back and smelled moldy hay, but ignored it as she continued to fend off her attackers, determined to fight with everything she had.

When someone pulled up her tunic and forcefully tried to spread her thighs, Kaiya could not hold back her battle cry as she brutally rammed her knee upward. There was a choked shout followed by the sound of someone vomiting. Kaiya smiled as she lashed out again.

Kaiya wasn't sure how many cries of pain she had elicited before a sharp metal point pricked her neck. She froze, eyeing the iron spear in silence. At its end, a man stared down a bloodied nose to glare at her with dark eyes.

"Now, you just lie still, Faoii-witch," he growled, pressing the blade against her jugular. "The king wants you alive, and alive you'll be. But I will cut out your eyes and break both your legs first if that's what it takes. Now, you just lie there for a minute until we can grab our wounded. Then you get your disease-laden body into that cell. Do you understand?" Kaiya glared and resisted trying to swallow against the pressure on her throat. Instead, she narrowed her eyes, straightened as much as she was able, and gave a single nod, ignoring the spear and the resulting bead of blood as it pricked her. The guard stared at her, and she read distrust and uncertainty in his features. After a moment, however, he seemed satisfied and pulled back his spear. She heard scrambling and a few pained groans as the other men made their way back to the stairwell.

Kaiya didn't move until the bloodied man finally motioned her toward an open cell a few strides away. She scowled up at him and pulled at her bound wrists, which were quickly going numb under the weight of her back. It took the man a second to understand, and when he finally realized what was wrong, he let out a cackling laugh.

"Not so big now, are you, witch?" He lowered the spear and reached forward to pull Kaiya up by the tunic. Kaiya couldn't keep the smirk out of her eyes as she curled her legs under her and pushed herself up forcefully by the strength of her calves, ramming her skull into the guard's already-broken nose. He stumbled back, screaming in agony. Kaiya straightened as best she could and used what little maneuverability she had in her hands to pull down the back of her tunic. Then, with slow, measured steps, she walked to the open cell. The guard glared at her from the other side of the room, holding his face with one hand and his spear in the other. Kaiya lifted her chin.

"You may close the door now, soldier." Her voice was stern with the full authority and power of the Faoii. Slowly, the soldier crept toward the cell, then swung it shut with unnecessary force and slammed the bolt into place with a resounding clang. Still eyeing Kaiya, he backed away before turning and rushing up the stairs.

For a long time the only sounds were dripping water and the ghostly whistle of air drifting through the prison. Kaiya fidgeted with the ropes at her wrists but could not break them despite her struggles. With a frustrated exhale, she gave up, stamping her foot in irritation. The force of it bruised her bare heel.

The gloom of the prison was dingy and grey, and the barred window in Kaiya's door only offered her a glimpse of the cell directly across from hers and a ray of pale, flickering firelight. There was no evidence that any guards remained in the catacombs. They'd probably all escaped to the sanctuary at the top of the stairs.

Kaiya stood silently, listening to the quiet *plop-plop* of dripping water somewhere nearby. But there was . . . something else, too. She perked her ears and lifted her head again, trying to glimpse more of the underground chamber.

"Who's there?" she called out. She heard a soft exhale, then silence again.

"Who's there?" Kaiya's voice was more forceful this time.

No reply.

"Answer me!" Kaiya kicked the iron door in front of her, using her heel rather than her toes, and the action gave a resounding thump that accented her command. The bruise that had already formed there protested under this continued abuse, and she hissed in pain. Something shifted in the shadows of the cell across the pathway.

"There is no need to shout, Faoii. I can hear you." A man materialized out of the darkness. Tall and thin, with sharp, angular features, he held her gaze with pale blue eyes through his own barred door. Kaiya straightened, clenching her teeth.

The man's dark features were familiar to her, and she hated them with everything she was.

"You... you Croeli bastard! I'll kill you!" She gnashed her teeth and pulled even tighter at her bonds, angry that the man she was seeing was not quite the man she wanted to be screaming at. Though not exact, he looked so much like Thinir. He *had* to be a relative of some sort. And in her mind, that made him just as responsible as his kin. "You look like *him*! You son of a bitch! You're one of them!" It was a long moment before the other prisoner responded.

"You're speaking of Thinir, aren't you? Be careful what you say. I don't look any more like him than you do, Faoii." The reply was soft and even. Kaiya's blood seethed.

"How *dare* you?" she screamed. The figure slipped back into the shadows. "How *dare you?*"

"Look to your own reflection, Faoii. You hate me because of my dark skin and light eyes, even when you are as dark as I am and have eyes like drops of pale jade?"

Kaiya felt that she could almost break the ropes with just her rage. Who could dare compare her to the beastly Croeli so casually? She was about to scream her fury at the pretentious prisoner, but he continued, "The contrast is not a common trait, so I do not begrudge your assumption that I know of whom you speak. But don't be so quick to throw rocks in a mirrored hallway."

Kaiya seethed. "I am Faoii. I'm not one of those murdering beasts! But you—!" There was a soft grunt as the other man presumably lowered himself to the ground of his cell. "You look just like that sorcerer. You're one of *them.*" The sigh echoed again.

"You know nothing of me, Faoii. Judge me as you wish; it is of no matter now. Though"—He paused, and Kaiya had to strain her ears to hear his soft finish— "though, it does sadden me to see you here."

Kaiya wanted to scream her frustration and hurt at the man, but she could not. Instead she only sank wearily to the floor, the adrenaline of her encounter with the guards and the fury of being so close to an adversary but unable to reach him sapping her strength. She shivered on the stone floor and twisted at the ropes that bound her hands behind her back. The man was right; it was rare to have pale eyes and dark skin. Had she ever met another person with those features? No. In all her life, she had never realized her own strangeness. Why hadn't it occurred to her as soon as she had seen the Croeli sorcerer? It would have occurred to anyone.

Had it occurred to Mollie?

Mollie's wide, unblinking eyes stared into Kaiya's memory, and she could not help but try and use her Sight on the face floating there. Did she read betrayal? Was that last look of terror actually directed at her more than at the Croeli or death?

Did she die thinking I was somehow associated with those monsters? Why else would I duck out of the way so she could fall?

Kaiya didn't realize she was crying until the sound of her own racking sobs pulled her from her stupor.

"Stop it, Faoii," the other prisoner was saying. "You are stronger than this." Kaiya wondered how long he had been speaking to her. But his voice was gentle, and as much as she hated it, she felt comforted. She wiped her eyes against her shoulders and leaned back on her heels.

"How do *you* know how strong I am?" She tried not to sniffle or let her voice shake. She failed. There was a gentle chuckle from across the corridor.

"I know so much about you, Kaiya-Faoii. If only you knew…"

It surprised Kaiya that she was more upset about the improper title than that a strange Croeli knew her name. Still, she could not help but bristle.

"I am Faoii-Kaiya of the Monastery of the Eternal Blade. I have earned my title." Her voice still trembled, but Kaiya realized that she was still somehow proud enough of her place in the world that she could demand respect, and that strengthened her. The soft chuckle sounded again.

"Apologies, Faoii-Kaiya. I did not know of your ascension. That must have happened after last I saw you."

"What? Were you there? With them at the end?"

The stranger was quiet for a long time before he spoke. "No. I was a . . . scout. I was sent to watch your monastery's movements several years ago, and I . . ." His voice softened. Was that regret she heard? "I am always thorough." Kaiya wasn't sure whether he was even still speaking to her, his voice was so low. "I am not proud of it now, but I gathered as much information as I could and sent it to my superiors. That is why they knew of your weaknesses." He paused, and Kaiya wanted to scream out in renewed rage and hatred, but something in his voice stopped her. There was shame in his words. Shame, regret, and pity.

The prisoner released a breath as he moved restlessly. "I tried to save your people, Kai—Faoii-Kaiya. But I could not. I tried to warn the king, but Thinir had already claimed the heart of the nation as his own. Even I did not know that his influence had spread so far. My betrayal was dealt with accordingly." Kaiya could almost see him gesturing around the prison. "But I did try." As he finished, the silence became absolute again. Kaiya frowned.

"Stand up, Croeli, and tell me all of that again. I want to see you say it."

"You mean you want to test your Sight on me."

"Yes." Kaiya did not bother trying to lie. The chuckle was softer this time.

"Well, at least you're honest about it. It will be too dark in here to do you much good, though, Faoii."

"I don't care. I want to see you say that you did not intentionally kill my people." Kaiya used her legs to push herself into a standing position and stared out through the bars on her door. After a few moments, the Croeli appeared in his window. He moved his face as much into the light as he could before speaking.

"I tried to save your people, Faoii-Kaiya. I was not able to, and I regret my actions that led to their fall." Kaiya watched his face carefully. She saw no indication that he was trying to falsify his features, but she did catch something else. "It was never my intention to hurt you."

"You're not lying. Or if you are, you're better at false-facing than I am at using the Sight." He turned to move away from the door again, but she stopped him. "No. I know you're hiding something. There's something you want to say. There's a longing in your eyes. And fear." The man said nothing, only held her gaze. Kaiya narrowed her eyes. "Keeping secrets won't get me to trust you, Croeli."

"I don't need you to trust me."

"But you *want* me to. I can read it all over your face. Ugh! Did they even try to teach you how to false-face in that barbaric land of yours?" The man grimaced, his face somewhere between a wince and a snarl. Despite herself, Kaiya regretted the words.

"You're better at the Sight than you let on. You have not yet been wrong."

"So what are you hiding? Tell me." The demand in her statement burned the air between them. "*Tell me!*"

"You would not believe me if I did. Look at me. Tell me yourself what you see."

"I see eagerness . . . frustration . . . apprehension . . ."

"No!" The Croeli's pale eyes narrowed as he stared at Kaiya from across the corridor that separated them. His voice rose in pitch as he spoke. "Don't look at the emotions in the face! Look at the face itself! Look at the bridge of the nose, the angle of the ears, the apex of the eyes! What do you *see*, Kaiya?" Kaiya tensed at the casual use of her name, but stared hard, searching his features. Her gaze roamed his face, his ears, his nose, his eyes . . .

And she saw it.

Broken blade. No . . .

The shock came almost like a mortal blow, and Kaiya stumbled backward, landing heavily on the floor. She stared at the base of the door that separated her from something she did not quite want to admit out loud.

"You . . . you look like me. You're . . . my cousin? My uncle?" The words sounded foreign as they passed her lips.

"No, Kai—" He caught himself and tried again. The words were low, but clear, and each new phrase hung in the air between the cells. "You don't know me, but I've known you since you were born. I watched our mother drop you off at that monastery before bringing me to the Croeli grove north of here, near the Blackfeather Wilds. I have always known you."

The Croeli's voice was low, almost a whisper. "I went to your monastery every chance I could, and I watched you grow. I wanted to know the sister I was never allowed to see. I was supposed to hate your kind, and a part of me did. A part of me loathes everything you are and everything you stand for, but I still watched. I watched you learn to walk and sing. I watched you learn to fight and dance. I watched you become a goddess in your own right—a warrior goddess and a strong woman that knew nothing of the plight of my people. I watched you become an embodiment of all the things the Croeli despise.

"When our father sent me to watch your temple, I knew my people would try to breach the gap that your kind had forced between us. I had hoped that future negotiations would allow me to speak to you as a brother and an ally rather than as an enemy. I never knew that one of my superiors had meant to destroy a people that, despite our differences, were truly beautiful. The Faoii were majestic. I realize that now. I thought that all of my people were in agreement—that they were planning to strengthen both races by offering an alliance. Had I known . . ." he drifted off, but Kaiya could not get her mouth to make any sounds that could serve as a proper response. "I am sorry, Kaiya. I always wanted to be nearby so that I could protect you. I did not realize I would need to protect you from me."

Kaiya tried to scream that she didn't need his protection. She didn't need a brother. She tried to tell him to stop saying her name, because *by the eternal blade, he did not deserve to speak to her at all.*

Instead, the words came out differently. They were strained, barely louder than a murmur.

"What should I call you?"

"My name is Croeli-Tendaji."

Tendaji.

She had a brother named Tendaji.

There was silence for a long time, and Kaiya knew he was waiting for a response. She could not come up with any. After several minutes, she heard a weak groan as he lowered himself to the ground once more. She realized now why it had taken him so long to bring his face to the window in the door. Her heart clenched involuntarily.

"You are injured," she said. It was a statement rather than a question.

"Yes." It was an equally simple statement, and Kaiya was surprised at his honest response. She felt that she would have tried to hide weakness from a stranger. An enemy.

But a brother?

Kaiya leaned her head against the wall and looked at the ceiling. The blackness of the cell hurt her eyes.

"And that makes Thinir . . . what?"

"Our uncle. A traitor. An enemy."

Kaiya shut her eyes. She didn't want to hear any more. Not while she was trapped here, in a cell next to a man she didn't want to know, imprisoned by the hands of everything she despised. She couldn't sit here listening to stories that changed everything while all that she'd ever loved lay forgotten and desecrated somewhere beyond these barred walls. She let the darkness and the quiet envelop her.

Eventually the solitude of her own mind became too much to bear, and Kaiya licked her lips. "How long have you been down here?" she finally asked the darkness. There was a rustle of cloth, and Kaiya could almost visualize the shrug that accompanied it.

"I have lost count. It was spring when I arrived in Clearwall. It could not have been more than a few days later that I woke up in here." Kaiya pinched her brow. It was almost autumn now. He had been left to rot here for months. He could have died from the cold and damp. As though reading her thoughts, Tendaji coughed dryly from his cell, but the hiss that followed was one of pain rather than illness.

"How bad is it?" Kaiya whispered. She did not want to admit to herself that she cared about the response, but she waited in nervous anticipation for the reply.

"It…" A pause. "It is not good, Faoii." Kaiya frowned, thinking hard.

"If I can get us out of here, would you be able to walk until we got somewhere safe?" That slight chuckle again. Kaiya wasn't sure whether she was beginning to like it or hate it.

"If you can manage that, I can manage to hold my own."

"Good."

It couldn't have been much past midnight when Kaiya heard a single pair of boots make their way down the stairwell. She wasn't sure, but it seemed like the newcomer was trying to move stealthily. She listened to see how Tendaji would react, but heard nothing. Warily, she stood and waited for what would come.

"Faoii?" The whisper was louder than necessary, and sounded awkward in the silence. Kaiya raised an eyebrow.

"Harkins?" She moved to the door and looked through the window there. Harkins stood uneasily in the torchlight, peering through the darkness. He straightened when he saw her.

"You can call me Emery, ma'am. I tried to come earlier, but I could only get this night shift. They don't like young soldiers watching the prisoners."

"Don't apologize, Emery. I was not expecting any aid at all." She peered at the young man. His steel-grey eyes were wide with nervousness and fear. No, not just fear. Absolute terror. She sighed through the bars. "Emery, are you sure about this? You can go back upstairs, and no one would ever know. You don't have to commit treason." He gave her a slight grin, and some of the fear faded away.

"In my opinion, Faoii, the real treason is following that... thing." Emery undid the bolt as silently as he could, but the rusted metal rang through the room. They both froze and listened for sounds on the stairs. After a moment, Emery eased the door open.

"You knew about Lucius's usurpation?"

"I knew that the man who was giving me orders was not the man I'd sworn fealty to. And after I watched him kill the Faoii that came before you . . ." He shook his head. "I would have been gone by now if I didn't have a feeling there was still something I could do." Emery cut the rope that bound Kaiya's wrists, and she rubbed her hands together, trying to bring the circulation back. She smiled at him as she did.

"That was the Goddess speaking to you. I'm sure you've made Her proud."

"Thank you, ma'am, but I think we should go." He fumbled with his sword belt and removed it hastily. "I brought your fao . . . fan . . . I brought your sword, Faoii." He handed her the belt with a too-large scabbard attached, but Kaiya recognized the fantoii's hilt. She buckled it over her worn tunic as Emery moved toward the stairs. "Follow me. I've loaded up a wagon with your armor. We should be able to make it there before anyone realizes that no one is on guard."

"Wait." Kaiya moved to Tendaji's cell. Emery pulled at her wrist.

"Don't, Faoii. Do you know who's in there? He's one of *them*." Emery's hiss was shrill and desperate, but Kaiya didn't pause.

"I know who he is, Emery. He's coming with us." Emery eyed the door warily but said nothing. Tendaji's bolt loosened with less of a screech than hers had, and Kaiya swung the door ajar.

Tendaji was almost a head taller than Kaiya, and she'd been one of the tallest girls in the monastery, despite her young age. He was thinner than she had expected, but as she looked at his high, jutting cheekbones and gaunt features, she wondered if that was from malnourishment. His ragged tunic hung limply on his atrophied frame. The stained and bloodied side of the tattered cloth also hinted at a man who had suffered for too long at the hands of a captor who showed no mercy. Despite herself, Kaiya pitied the Croeli. Even the nomadic Danhaid Tribes to the south took care of their prisoners.

Tendaji's pale blue eyes were piercing and steady, but he stooped more than was comforting and kept an arm carefully wrapped around his middle. Even so, when Tendaji moved, he flowed more than walked, and his steps were light and silent. Kaiya was impressed. She could move in shadows with the grace and prowling instinct of a cat if she wanted to, but this Croeli seemed capable of becoming the shadow itself. A world of difference from the horned demons that had attacked her home.

Tendaji glided into the central part of the prison before inclining his head thoughtfully to Emery. "I thank you for this release. I hope I may prove to you that I am not the traitor you think I am." Emery did not reply but looked to Kaiya. She drew her fantoii a short way from its borrowed sheath.

"We'd better get moving. Croeli, will you be all right?" Tendaji nodded once, straightening his shoulders without so much as a grimace. Kaiya nodded to Emery. "Lead on, soldier."

Emery was no thief, but he did a decent job of sneaking as he led the two prisoners from the dungeon. His movements were quick and sometimes awkward, but not bad for an untrained youth. Kaiya and Tendaji followed him like panthers stalking their prey, watching in all directions for trouble. They were lucky. With Emery's guidance, they turned down several empty halls, and (with the exception of one heart-pounding minute of crouching behind a low-set table as an unexpected servant passed) they reached a dark, barren room without incident.

"Where are we?" Kaiya whispered after Emery closed the worn wooden door.

"In an overstock pantry, ma'am," Emery whispered back, pulling an unlit torch from the wall. "It's not being used right now, but it'll be filled by the end of the season." He lit the torch carefully and crept to a trapdoor at the far end of the room. Kaiya and Tendaji followed close behind and peered down into the blackness. "I'm afraid it's going to be cold. It would have looked suspicious if I'd grabbed cloaks." Kaiya glanced at Tendaji, who was hunched over the trap door, still clutching his side. The tremors in his arms and legs were more pronounced, but Kaiya couldn't tell whether they were from fever, exhaustion, or pain. Maybe it was a mixture of all three. She frowned.

"But *why* the pantry, Emery?"

"It's the taxes pantry, ma'am. It leads to the tax collector's office. That's where I left the cart." He frowned. "I know it's not fitting for a Faoii, but I didn't know another route . . ."

Kaiya smiled. "It's perfect, Emery. Thank you." He blushed a bit as he descended the steps. Kaiya followed, and Tendaji came last, reaching up to close the trapdoor behind him.

As he reached upward, Tendaji's tunic shifted, and Kaiya saw the true extent of his injuries for the first time. Blood caked his tunic, and shiny crimson flowed from a wound that must have been aggravated in their escape. With a sickening twinge, she eyed the bulge of a rib that had not been allowed to heal properly and a back covered with the crisscross markings of a whip. She couldn't imagine the pain a rib like that would cause Tendaji every time he shifted, and for the first time in her life, she wished that she had trained to be Cleroii instead of Faoii.

Tendaji stumbled a bit on the last step, but Kaiya refrained from assisting him. It seemed wrong to damage the man's pride when he had apparently made it this far on will alone. She did, however, hum the slightest hint of a tune under her breath, gathering pale ribbons of strength and encouragement to her estranged ally. She might not know how to heal someone, but she did know how to use war magic to bolster soldiers.

Tendaji straightened again, eyeing her with a look that was neither gratitude nor repulsion. Kaiya did not try to read his features but turned to follow Emery, who had started down the hall.

The air was chilled by the enclosed stone and earth, and Kaiya shivered in her tunic. There was no sound besides that of Emery's footsteps ringing off the walls, but she kept her hand on her fantoii hilt anyway. She did not expect an easy escape from the king's prison, no matter who assisted. Next to her, Tendaji was rigid and tense, his arms held in a state of readiness. Even Emery had pulled out a long dagger and held it before him while he used the torch to illuminate darkened corners and shifting shadows.

They'd been in the tunnel for several minutes before Kaiya caught a glimpse of the stepladder at its end. She relaxed as they approached. Soon they would be out of the capital city and in a safe place. There, she could think about what she was going to do about . . . well, about everything. Her home's destruction, the king's usurpation, her brother . . . She shook her head and pressed forward. They still had to make it through the twisted, broken streets at the center of a twisted, broken empire.

Emery motioned for the other two to remain at the bottom of the ladder as he climbed up first. Kaiya waited apprehensively as he disappeared into the darkness above.

It felt like hours passed before the soldier's head appeared in the opening again. He set a finger to his lips and motioned them upward with his other hand before moving away from the trapdoor. Kaiya climbed up deftly, and Tendaji oozed after her.

The tax collector's office was large and lavishly furnished. Plush couches and deep purple curtains contrasted with golden accents and silver candelabras. Kaiya heard Tendaji growl under his breath as he looked around. She glowered too and thought about the bony cow she had passed on her way to Clearwall. It wasn't fair that so much wealth would be shared with only a few.

Scowling, she reached out for a heavy silver candlestick, testing its weight in one hand. She made a few bashing movements in the air and, satisfied, tossed it underhand to the currently weaponless Tendaji. He caught it easily.

Emery crept over to the window and drew himself up to it. Too quickly, he dropped back down, and Kaiya shook her head at him. Quick movements were more likely to catch someone's attention. He would have done better to stay in the window and remain still than to jerk hastily out of the way. She released her breath slowly and dropped into a crouch, eyes facing the door. If someone had seen him, she wanted it to end quickly and with as little noise as possible.

She silently drew her fantoii from its sheath. Next to her, Tendaji dropped too, his stance matching hers despite the bulge on his ribcage that she could just see out of her peripheral vision. With a glance, she shifted her weight away from him. Tendaji mirrored the movement, and in a moment they were crouched back-to-back. The stance of shield mates.

There was a heavy knock on the front door. Kaiya's heart sank. They'd been spotted. She tensed and centered herself on the balls of her feet. Emery sighed and reached out to unlatch the bolt with one hand. The door swung open forcefully, knocking the young soldier back as two armed warriors in studded leather armor pushed their way through. Their cloaks had King Lucius's seal on them.

"What are you doing in here, Soldier?" one of the guards growled. "All off-duty militia are supposed—" He stopped suddenly, staring at Kaiya and Tendaji.

"Why, you traitorous—!" The guard stepped back half a step and opened his mouth to yell, but Emery rammed the hilt of his dagger into his throat, choking his airways. The older man sputtered and fell to his knees.

The second guard was quick to act. His sword came loose with a forceful tug, and he swung it up toward Emery's chest. Emery barely hopped out of the way in time, his eyes still focused on the downed man that was already trying to regain his feet. Without pause, the standing sentinel brought his sword up again, preparing to swing down from the shoulder.

Kaiya didn't give him the chance to strike.

Biting back her battle cry, the Faoii rushed forward in a crouch, her fantoii at her side. Just as she reached the soldier, she spun on her toes, using the momentum to carry her body and outstretched sword arm in a half circle that sliced across the man's chest. A bright red streak appeared, starting just below the exposed armpit.

Normally a fantoii is not strong enough to cut through studded leather when the blow is just from the shoulder, but Faoii are trained to use momentum and pressure points to give their weapons extra potency. With the combined momentum of her sprint and entire body spin, the thin blade sliced through the man's skin under his arm and then continued for more than half of his chest piece. As the fantoii caught in the leather, she yanked it out, her continuous momentum carrying her just under 180 degrees around. Here Kaiya crouched, her back to the man and her blade at her side, his blood dripping from it onto the painted rug.

Then it hit her.

It had felt so *right* to have a shield mate again that Kaiya had not thought about whether Tendaji was capable or even willing to defend her. The maneuver she had just performed left a Faoii exposed and vulnerable to her opponent, as it would take precious seconds to readjust her stance so that she could roll forward and out of the way. It was the shield mate's job to finish the weakened adversary off before his sword could fall. Even as she rebalanced and centered herself onto the balls of her feet, Kaiya was painfully aware that at her back there was a wounded man with his sword raised high. And she'd just entrusted her life to a Croeli.

Before she could even finish the thought, the metal sword rang out as it hit something solid. Kaiya tumbled forward and away from the armed guard. There was a sickly *sluck* sound, then a grunt and a heavy thud. Out of the corner of her eye, Kaiya saw a sword fall limply to the floor as she gathered her feet back under her. Another thump came a second later as Kaiya rose with one swift motion. She glanced down. A bloody candlestick lay next to her foot. Emery had jammed his knife into the other man's throat, and the dying guard gurgled a weak call for aid. Kaiya wondered whether dead soldiers would heed the call, because there were no living to hear.

"Blades. I wish they hadn't been here." Her voice was quiet as she used her fantoii to cut the remaining man's femoral artery. He passed quickly.

"Do you regret having killed them?" Tendaji asked quietly, his crystalline eyes intense.

"No. We needed to kill them to escape. But I wouldn't have gone out of my way to hunt them down. They were only doing their jobs."

"If we had not killed them, they would have only continued to aid the false king, and in doing so further hurt your people." Tendaji shook his head at her as he bent to retrieve one of the fallen swords. "Why are Faoii always ready to decide who lives and dies without seeing the consequences? Sometimes, the enemy must be taken down or people suffer." He sighed at Kaiya's infuriated glare as she rifled the soldiers' pockets.

"I cannot hate a man for a crime they have not yet committed," she whispered as she straightened and lugged one of the bodies onto her shoulder. Emery opened the hatch for her, and she tossed the corpse into the pantry below.

"If you know a man is going to kill his wife and you do nothing, you are as heartless as he, Faoii." Tendaji's voice softened as he helped her roll the other body. Kaiya tried not to notice the *crunch* she heard as he bent at the waist. "I know it sounds heartless, but the Croeli... we used to swear an Oath before Thinir came into power. We knew our duty and we did not shy away from it." He nearly smiled as she spoke, his words tinted with a nearly forgotten power. "We were the harbingers of justice and truth. We were the strength of the weak and the voice of the silent. Our blades were our arms, and as such were the arms of all people. Wherever we were, so would a weapon against injustice always be. We were ready to perform our duty for the weak at all times." Kaiya froze, half bent at the waist with one arm on the trap door. She broke out into a cold sweat as she pushed the body down.

Tendaji turned to her and his eyes were stern. "If someone is alive now and they will be murdered later, the injustice is still part of the Unbroken Tapestry's glorious weave. If a good man is going to eventually burn down a schoolhouse, then the evil must be purged as soon as possible. We were taught to be ready at *all* times, Faoii. Even before a fateful event occurs." Kaiya couldn't move.

She had never heard the Oath from a man's lips before.

When Tendaji said *we*, she knew he meant the other Croeli, but did he realize that he could be talking about her just as easily? Her stomach rolled.

"We need to go," she finally whispered, willing her voice to break the chill that shrouded her. Tendaji nodded and turned toward the door.

Emery was thorough. As promised, all of Kaiya's possessions had been loaded into a caravan-worthy wagon just outside the tax collector's plush abode. He ushered the fugitives out with a jerk of his head and held up the edge of a weatherworn tarp. Kaiya ducked under it, folding a knee underneath her on the warped wood of the wagon's bottom. Crouching thus, she kept a wary lookout as Tendaji mounted and leaned his back against the wagon's side. His complexion was decidedly greyer than it had been in the castle's cellar, and Kaiya felt a pang of worry. She looked away from his bulging rib and bleeding back and locked eyes with Emery. There was fear there, but he tightened his jaw and gave a quick, furtive nod. Then the tarp was secured and darkness prevailed.

The ride was not as unpleasant as it could have been, though with every jarring bump Kaiya could not help but glance to the silhouette across from her. Sometimes a pained gasp would tear from Tendaji's lips, but mostly there was only silence.

Kaiya must have dozed off, because a sudden, harsh whisper woke her.

"Faoii-Kaiya." She mumbled a reply and began drifting off again, comforted by the steady rocking of the carriage. "Kai!" The whisper was fiercer now, and Kaiya forced the sleep from her eyes and looked to where Tendaji's silhouette could just be seen. His posture was rigid and tense. "We are going toward the docks rather than the city gates. Where is your friend taking us?" Kaiya blinked twice, pulling her brows together.

"He . . . he never said." Her eyes narrowed dangerously, fully awake now. "But I can find out."

With careful movements, Kaiya crept toward the front of the wagon. The tarp was secure, but with a flick of her wrist the fantoii slit its side. She poked her head through.

"Harkins!" The hiss was louder than she'd intended, and the young soldier nearly leapt out of his seat. He quickly transferred the reins to one hand and twisted around to face her. Kaiya made an effort to soften her voice. "Where are we going?"

"Where...? Why, to the other Faoii, ma'am." He spoke as though the answer was obvious. Kaiya stared at him as though he'd just sprouted feathers. Her head swam as she tried to process this new information. "Are you all right, Faoii?"

Finally, Kaiya's tongue felt like it could work again, and she managed a stuttered reply. "The other... There's another...?" She pulled her head back through the tarp and stumbled her way back to where Tendaji sat. She felt his eyes upon her but could only sink down next to him, her stupor not yet faded. Finally, in a bliss she was not sure she'd ever feel again, she sighed.

"There's another Faoii. I'm not alone."

Tendaji chuckled. "Alone? No. I suppose you wouldn't be, would you?"

10

There was no question that the leader of the docks was Faoii. Kaiya could feel her presence even before she was in sight. There was an aura that surrounded her hidden barracks, a clamminess in the air that could not be explained away by the putrid sewers beneath the docks. But it was not the hush of terror or tyranny, nor was the clamminess chilled with evil intent. Instead, it was like a machine, so well-oiled that the idea of stepping out of one's station was unthinkable. And thus Kaiya, Tendaji, and Emery were led through a maze of statuesque soldiers and twisting sewers—completely silent except for the sound of dripping water and their booted feet.

Faoii-Eili was a large, brusque woman. Her mouth was set in a perpetual scowl, which could only be partially credited to the mass of deep scars that covered the left side of her face. A milk-white eye gazed unnervingly through the web of scar tissue, and the remaining azure eye softened for only a fraction of a second when she saw Kaiya.

"Hail, Sister." Kaiya was surprised at being recognized despite her attire. A dust-colored tunic and bare legs hardly represented the Faoii. However, she diligently fisted her hands and bowed her head.

"May Illindria guide your battles, Faoii-Eili."

The unscarred side of Eili's mouth twitched. "My soldiers told ya my name, did they? Stupid. Don't know nothin' about custom." There was humor and fondness that echoed in her voice despite the rough tone, but Faoii-Eili spat to one side for good measure as she guided Kaiya to a dry platform furnished with a rough-hewn table and chairs. "What's yer name, girl?"

"I am Faoii-Kaiya of the Monastery of the Eternal Blade." Kaiya glanced around. The sewer system was old, and it looked like they were in a section that was no longer used regularly. While the clearing they were in was only sparsely furnished, Kaiya could smell wood smoke and roasting meat somewhere nearby. Quiet whispers and laughter echoed down the tunnel. Despite herself, Kaiya could not help but feel awed by this hardened Faoii, who had created a sanctuary for a rebellion in the very heart of the Croeli empire.

"Faoii-Kaiya? Yer ascended, then? Youngin' ain't ya? But no matter. What brings an ascended to this rotten city?"

"I . . ." Kaiya wasn't sure what to say. "I came for help." The words sounded small and weak. Faoii-Eili let out a barking laugh.

"So ya came here? To a broken king on a tarnished throne? Poor girl. What could ya possibly have expected to find here?" There was no sympathy in Eili's voice as she gazed at Kaiya with a sort of matronly disdain. Kaiya took a deep breath and met the woman's stare.

"I didn't know about the king, and when the rest of my monastery—" Kaiya stopped short as Faoii-Eili's eyes suddenly sharpened and focused on something behind Kaiya's right shoulder. Adamant hatred darkened her features, and the table shook as she stood with a violent jerk. With roughly the same amount of ceremony a rhino shows when it charges, Faoii-Eili shoved Kai to one side and drew her fantoii.

Immediately aware of the battle spells woven into the air, Kaiya spun around just in time to see Tendaji limp his way into view. Her eyes widened and darted to Faoii-Eili's hand. The fantoii glinted in the torchlight.

"You've been followed!" Faoii-Eili's scream rang through the darkened tunnels, and Kaiya barely had time to register the blonde warrior's swift attack. Always at the ready, Tendaji had dropped into an unsteady crouch as the scarred Faoii sprinted for him.

Kaiya cursed herself as she sprang forward. She had only been in the sewers for a few minutes and had already shredded what little bit of trust she could expect from the only other Faoii in existence. She should have known better than to let a Croeli follow her before she'd had a chance to explain. Her anger at herself and her fear for the coming fight spurred Kaiya forward, and with a passionate cry, she leapt outward, colliding with the armored woman's back. Her unclad shoulder immediately protested the collision with Eili's bronze breastplate.

Both women stumbled, and Kaiya used her momentum to tumble forward, spinning as she landed. She crouched defensively in front of Tendaji as Faoii-Eili regained her feet. There was no repressing the rippling growl that leaked between her lips, and Kaiya was surprised at herself. Would she really be willing to raise her blade against another Faoii sister in order to save a Croeli?

Always ready to decide who lives and dies. Wasn't that what Tendaji had said? She would have chuckled if the situation wasn't so dire.

"Stop!" Kaiya's hiss was more feline than she had intended, but she willed all the power she could muster into it. It cut through the air and rang against the walls. Faoii-Eili just barely faltered in her tracks. Seeing her opportunity, Kaiya lashed out with her left hand, the movement blurring. Viperlike, her dark fingers wrapped tightly around Faoii-Eili's pale wrist and *squeezed.* Eili's fantoii clattered to the floor.

Without breaking eye contact, Kaiya used her calves to push herself upward. Rising slowly, she met the older woman's toxic gaze.

"He is with me. And he is wounded. You cannot hurt him." Faoii-Eili's piercing stare only darkened, dripping venom, but Kaiya forced herself to meet it. Finally, the veteran warrior yanked her wrist from Kaiya's grip as though her fingers were simply paper. Kaiya's hand hung in the air awkwardly for a moment before she slowly let it drop. The two women stood in silence for a long time, eyeing each other with distrust and unspoken curses.

"You ain't lyin'." There was a hint of surprise in Faoii-Eili's ragged tone. "You actually believe this Croeli bastard's an ally." She looked down at her wrist. Kaiya was ashamed to see bruises already forming on the pale skin. "And you've been well-trained. If yer a traitor, yer a skilled one." With a seemingly effortless flick of her arm but with the full magical force of an ascended Faoii, Faoii-Eili's open palm slammed against Kaiya's face with a resounding smack. Kaiya rolled her head with the strike, but she still felt her cheekbone crack under the blow. Slowly, she brought her face around to look Faoii-Eili in the eyes again.

"I'm no traitor." She paused, but Faoii-Eili only continued to stare. "I'm no traitor, but I do owe this man my life. He's no threat to us." Eili's entire body tensed.

"Us?" Eili spat. "*Us?* You've been in my territory for less than five minutes and have brought the Faoii's oldest enemy with you. What in Illindria's graces could possibly make you believe there's an *us*, girl?" Kaiya could have cut the tension between them with her fantoii.

"Because we are the last of the Faoii. If we don't work together, there will be no more to follow after us. Ever." Kaiya held the woman's gaze, aware of the anger, the distrust, and the faintest hint of fear in Faoii-Eili's eye.

It seemed like an eternity before the battle-hardened woman finally broke the silence that stretched out between them.

"What's happened?"

"Let me tend to my comrade and I will tell you everything."

Eili narrowed her eyes dangerously before glancing back at Tendaji. He approached cautiously. With an impatient wave of her hand, Faoii-Eili bent over to pick up her fantoii and intentionally turned her back on the Croeli visitor. "Sing yer song then, girl. I won't stop ya." Kaiya faltered. Her uncertainty and confusion must have been clear, because Faoii-Eili released another barking laugh. "All yer training next to Cleroii and Preoii, and you never learned a single healin' song? You daft, girl? What? Daydreamin' during chapel?" With an impatient jerk of her chin, Faoii-Eili motioned Tendaji to a ledge nearby. He slinked toward it, keeping his eyes toward the Faoii and his back to the sewer wall. Finally, he sat gingerly, eyeing her as a hawk eyes a mouse, or possibly the other way around. Her gaze matched his perfectly.

Without preamble, Faoii-Eili spread her fingers as though she was standing in front of a fire on a snowy night. Her song welled forward like ice cracking against a shore.

The song was nothing like what Kaiya had heard in chapel. The words did not flow; they were not beautiful or even comforting. Instead they were clipped and short, and the spell shot through the air like icy arrows. Kaiya remembered the Cleroii songs. They had drifted through the air like silken ribbons. In contrast, this spell made her wince.

Tendaji's head snapped backward as the spell struck him, and Kaiya started forward, but an angry glance from Eili stopped her. Stomach churning, she watched in silence as Tendaji's mishealed rib snapped back into its regular place.

Faoii-Kaiya was not sure how long the healing lasted, but try as she might, she could not look away from it. The reopened scars on his back restitched themselves in jerky movements, stretching and pulling as necessary. When the song finally ended with a clipped note, she was trembling as much as Tendaji, but he made no protest. Grimacing around clenched teeth, his pale blue eyes met the icy stare of Faoii-Eili's remaining iris.

Finally, he whispered, "Thank you."

One did not need to be trained in the Sight to see the surprise that registered on Eili's face. She hid it almost immediately, however, and glowered at the panting man. "Stand up, Croeli."

Even Kaiya was caught off guard by the demand, but Tendaji only exhaled slowly and rose, one arm still wrapped around his aching side. Eili's stare stretched into eternity.

"Who are you?" The question was cold, biting. Tendaji squared his shoulders.

"I am the outcast Croeli-Tendaji-Tendir."

"Croeli-Tendaji? Yer ascended, then?"

"Yes. Though it is likely that the title no longer applies."

"What's the Tendir on the end of yer name?"

"The name of my superior officer. Our people attach the name to our rank."

Eili thought about this new bit of information for a moment, then continued, "You are dark-skinned. Are the others in your tribe of the same complexion?"

"No. Just me and one other."

"Why were you cast out?"

Tendaji considered a moment before answering. "I learned about the plans my tribe had for the Faoii and for my own people. I could not condone the coming slaughter, so I buried my criukli into my superior's chest and deserted." There was no hint of regret or remorse in Tendaji's response, but there was no pride either. He could have been explaining what he'd eaten for breakfast. Despite herself, Kaiya shuddered. This was the Croeli she had always heard of in the stories.

Faoii-Eili seemed unfazed. "Detail your dealings with the Thinir Tribe."

The interrogation continued for a long time. Tendaji spoke of his superiors, first of his true commander, then of the one he had killed, and finally of his uncle. He spoke of rarely being with the tribe itself, often scouting in far corners of the country; about how things slowly and subtly changed between every visit, until finally the place he returned to was not a home at all. He spoke of his desertion and his attempts to gather other deserters to his cause against Thinir, and of the outrage he faced. He spoke of hatred and battles that he had experienced, both firsthand and from the lips of those he had considered brothers. Of his audience with

King Lucius. Of his conversation with Kaiya in the cell below the keep.

Faoii-Eili asked question after question, digging into every aspect of Croeli culture and any plans Tendaji might have been aware of. Kaiya watched in silent disapproval as her superior questioned the weakened man without pause. His answers came continuously, his voice unfaltering. Kaiya watched Tendaji carefully, but she never saw any sign of him false-facing.

Emery, who had entered shortly after the interrogation began and who was only briefly glanced at by Eili before being casually ignored, stood by Kaiya in an uncomfortable silence.

Eventually, as the interrogation dragged on, Kaiya's insides filled with stone. She straightened her shoulders and narrowed her eyes, indignant that a Faoii could treat another human being, Croeli or not—*brother or not*—with so little humanity. Tendaji had long since proven his intentions, and the questions that dug into his private affairs held no use for the Faoii other than a sick determination to make him fully realize his current helplessness. Kaiya strode to Faoii-Eili, determined to stop this torture, but was forcibly halted by a sudden and violent change in the sewer's surroundings. With a swiftness that made her head spin, a new and ghostly scene superimposed itself on the area, and new people swam before her eyes.

Kneeling at Tendaji's feet was an emaciated, naked man with grey and tattered wings, hands set firmly on the grime-covered ground. Across from him, an angel of orange and yellow fire cascading from her ivy helm continued the never-ceasing tirade of questions. The answers flowed continuously from the broken man's mouth, and Kaiya's heart tore as she studied his bent and shaking shoulders. In her mind's eye, she reached out for her ailing brother, only partially aware that the image she saw was not real.

Or, she imagined a familiar voice whispering, *is it the only true thing you've ever seen at all, Faoii-Kaiya?* As she did, the grey man's head jerked up.

From the sunken sockets of that crippled, dingy apparition, the piercing amber eyes of a wolf returned Kaiya's stare, so full of strength and surety that she could only choke back a surprised gasp. Under that gaze, Kaiya felt a storm building in her, around her, and through her, filling her heart and mind and the sewers that surrounded them all—so passionate and powerful had the air become. Awestruck by this… *Vision? Hallucination? Dream?* … Kaiya tottered to a stop.

Eventually, the figures faded, and though the amber eyes did not dissipate for a long moment, Kaiya was at last able to redirect her attention to the real-world interrogation between Eili and Tendaji. Slowly, as though underwater, their words floated toward her.

"How old were you when your mother abandoned you to the Croeli?"

"Nine years, eight months, and six days."

"How did they respond?" Several more minutes went by before Faoii-Eili finally paused in her questions. Kaiya followed her gaze into Tendaji's steady eyes.

Wolf eyes? No. Pale blue. Like frosted ivory.

Finally, Faoii-Eili asked the question that she had evidently been building up to: "You have not lied to me. At all. Why?"

Shaken from her slightly disoriented reverie, Kaiya looked to her brother for an answer. The simple, too-little asked question of *why* was one of the most important. What motive did he truly have to help them? Were blood ties enough to banish an entire lifetime of separation?

The answer came in the same unemotional tone as the others had: "If you do not trust me, you will never trust her." A long, slender finger pointed directly at Kaiya. "She has vouched for me. And you need her." Faoii-Eili looked like she was going to say something but changed her mind. Tendaji continued, "She's right, Faoii-Eili. If the last of the Faoii do not work together, then there is no hope for this world and its Goddess. The husks of the people may not die, but their hearts will decay until they become as my people have." He paused, and Kaiya sensed the slightest hint of a shudder.

"Thinir and his army have almost succeeded in destroying Illindria's hold. You must have sensed it by now—the chill in the air. The void that wasn't there before. You have to stop him." Tendaji sighed, and for the first time, his voice seemed unsteady.

"The rot and corruption that is my fellow Croeli sickens me. They follow their orders—no matter how dark or twisted— without question or understanding. Their eyes lose the light that makes them human, and they travel the world like empty husks. When I dream at night, a woman's voice tells me to add my strength to your Order. To my sister's Order. So I will. Illindria demands it."

Faoii-Eili's eyes grew wide with an uncontrolled bloodlust. "Blasphemy!" The older warrior shrieked as she stepped forward. "Blasphemy!"

Kaiya stopped her with a gentle hand. "Listen." A song had formed in the air like needlework through a handkerchief. It was not a sound so much as an invisible beam of sunlight as diaphanous as a string of silk from a spider's web. But it was everywhere, filling the Faoii and the sewer.

Moments passed, and Kaiya released a breath she had not been aware she was holding. With it, a flood of uncertainty and doubt left her, and she was filled only with the Goddess's embrace. As the song continued, rising and drifting through Kaiya as a wave breaks over a sandy beach, joyful tears and laughter poured from her. She lifted her arms in longing and ecstasy, her fingers brushing the stained cobwebs of the sewer's walls. But the sewer was gone; she saw only Illindria's fields and earth while a warm sun and gentle breeze pulled at her braid.

When Kaiya opened her mortal eyes again, Eili was crying, her already-broken face cracking with sudden emotion.

"The Goddess's presence is not known in this city," Faoii-Eili whispered to no one in particular. "With all the prayers I offer, with all the Oaths I swear, I thought I still knew what Her embrace felt like. Has it been so long…?" The older woman's knees shook, and she hit the floor with a dazed expression. Kaiya resisted the urge to help her stand. Eili was true Faoii again, in tune with the Goddess for the first time in many years.

She would have to remember how to stand on her own.

"All right, girl."** It hadn't taken long for Kaiya to figure out that Faoii-Eili moved her spoon when speaking, which usually resulted in her flicking stew carelessly across the table. Kaiya maneuvered away from the projectiles as she pleated her curly black hair into its familiar braid. She had been in the sewers for three days, and Faoii-Eili's resolve for action was catching. They only needed a plan. "We can't be the only Faoii left. Too many girls were given orders outside the monasteries to have all been caught. We just have to find 'em." Moving her stew bowl to one side, the blonde warrior unrolled a map onto the table, pinning it down with a stone at each corner. "Most of the girls that came to the capital were imprisoned or killed immediately. There were a few I got to before Lucius, but even then, there was nothing I could do except keep them comfortable until they passed." She wiped a hand over her face. "Goddess, if I'm not a Preoii yet, I should be. Too many dirges for too many young."

Kaiya bowed her head for the fallen, picturing those that had straggled their way to the capital from distant monasteries, broken and bloodied from a war they had not been prepared for. The images swam before her eyes, memories that were not her own.

She watched young girls supporting each other as they dragged themselves to the city gates, their eyes full of hope and pride that they had made it this far. Some had barely made it into the outer city before they were escorted away by armored guards; others were received by hooded vagabonds who had brought them here, where they'd lain in burning agony and delirium before finally passing into Illindria's embrace.

Tendaji, sitting across from Kaiya, furrowed his brow. "The fevers you describe…Some of the Croeli have might have recently begun coating their blades with criukli poison. It has no antidote and incapacitates its victims quickly." He studied one of the daggers as though there was writing on it that only he could see. "Odd. It was not widespread when I left. And Thinir would never have condoned its use…" He drifted off, contemplating.

"Leave it to the Croeli to create something so horrible." While still not friendly with Tendaji, Eili had adopted a cool, dispassionate tone when speaking with him. "I tried to find out what afflicted those poor maidens, but I had no luck. They always spoke of bells before they passed. I didn't know a poison could do that."

Tendaji's eyes darkened. "The poison doesn't cause the bells. Thinir does. They're somehow connected with the magic that his war god has provided. They're the signal that lets him dig into your mind and play with your head. If you hear them, they start to color Thinir's words, and you *want* to follow him. Everything he says starts to make sense." Tendaji's voice was low. "Your people are not the only ones who have spoken of this."

Kaiya thought of the bells and the laughter she'd heard in the monastery, and then of Preoii-Aleena's calming voice that had quieted the other sounds. She shuddered. Thinir had been in her head. Somehow, his power had had hold of her. And yet she had lived when no others could say the same.

"Why poison 'em, then? If he wants to get in their heads, he must want 'em alive."

"Some of the Croeli who fought the enslavement believed that criukli poison could drown Thinir's whispers out—"

"Superstitious nonsense," Eili cut him off. "People used to believe that tonicloran poison could turn you into a god or some such, too."

"Maybe. But superstitions always start from somewhere."

"Listen to you, knowin' nothin' and everythin'. Don't know why I ever let one of your kind sit at my table anyway."

"How many Faoii eventually reached the city?" Kaiya cut in, hoping to avoid another argument. Eili's voice softened as she redirected her attention to the young Faoii.

"I know of twelve for certain. Six pairs that at least had each other in their final days. That is somethin' to be grateful for, if nothin' else." A silence loomed over the table. "No one should die alone." Kaiya refrained from biting her lip.

"Faoii-Eili," she finally whispered, "may I ask…?" Kaiya dropped off, not sure how to finish.

"What happened to my shield sister?" Eili's good eye twinkled and got a faraway look. "King Lucius—or Thinir, if your story is true—had our old barrack burnt down. The coward attacked in the middle of the night. A beam fell across our bed. I dug at it until my fingers bled, but the flames only rose higher. Elsa . . ."

She trailed off, bringing a hand to her scarred cheek. The silence reigned again. "Goddess grant her better battles."

Suddenly, Kaiya feared that Eili would ask about Mollie. Kaiya had not fought nearly so hard to save her shield sister, the person she loved more than anyone on earth. *Did I even close her eyes?* Kaiya frowned, ashamed. She could not remember. Mercifully, Eili did not ask.

"That was four years ago. I shoulda known then that there were darker powers at play than an agin' king. The Croeli have been in power longer than I dared fear." Suddenly the woman slammed a fist down onto the table, causing everyone except for the ever-stoic Tendaji to jump. "Damn our Order for being so independent! We shoulda kept better contact with the other factions. We coulda known when the winds changed!" Kaiya said nothing. Agreeing now would not help anything.

"How long has it been since you've seen another Faoii besides me?" Kaiya finally asked. Eili rolled her shoulders, bringing her emotions back under control.

"Eight months. Those last two girls were slightly more coherent than the others had been, and their story was similar ta yers. There was no warning, no time to prepare. One mornin' the Croeli were suddenly at their gates. The attack was quick and brutal, and they had been left for dead. These men were particularly cruel. One of them stabbed them both with his poisoned blade even after they'd been struck down by ordinary steel.

"The fever had already taken most of their minds by the time they reached me, but they spoke of horned monsters that fought like Faoii and of bells that had been burned away by fire. I suppose that their stories weren't so incredible after all. I didn't think an army could just appear outta the blue like that." Kaiya turned to Tendaji, suddenly curious.

"How do you—" She stopped herself and tried again. "How do the Croeli appear so suddenly? From the monastery, we could see for miles. But they just . . . showed up."

Tendaji sat silently for a moment. "I do not know." Eili narrowed her eyes but said nothing. Kaiya read no dishonesty in his features. "I was never part of the infantry. My shield mate and I—" He faltered and moved on hastily. "I . . . we . . . were scouts. Infiltrators." Kaiya raised her eyebrows. She had never seen Tendaji flustered before. "We were trained to move in shadows, but we always had to remain on *this side*." He stressed the words, but elaborated when he was greeted only with blank stares.

"Whatever magic the infantry uses—Blinking, they call it—it gets its strength from numbers. The more people that use it, the more potent it is. It allows Thinir's men to move across great distances in a short time, but they come back . . . different."

"Different how?"

"There is less light behind their eyes. They start following any orders they are given without argument. And they speak of the bells. It's unnatural, and I am sure that it is what gives Thinir his power."

Kaiya frowned. "If it makes people more obedient, why didn't Thinir make you travel that way too?" Tendaji chuckled dryly.

"It's unlikely that he expected to be betrayed by blood. And there was too much chance of missing important information if we used magic rather than skill. We needed to keep our heads clear. Our minds sharp." He looked up, his gaze intense. After a moment, it softened. "I wish I could tell you more."

Kaiya thought for a long moment. Something about Tendaji's

story caught at the back of her mind.

"How long have you been here, Faoii-Eili?" she asked, trying to pin down the tickling feeling that nagged at her.

Eili shrugged. "Nearly five years. I never noticed any change in the king, if that's what yer wonderin'. Originally, Elsa and I had only stopped 'cuz we noticed Illindria's absence here and thought we could do some good." Her face got a faraway look again, and she sighed. "It was Elsa's idea. She was always softhearted."

Eili shook her head angrily before continuing. "I shoulda recognized immediately that our actions did no good. We were threatened often enough by the king and his men that I shoulda noticed somethin' was wrong. I just thought it was 'cuz we refused to wear his bloody dresses and our girls beat his soldiers at the field games that first year. Sure, he called us a cult, but no one seemed to mind us. Then he barricaded our doors and set the place on fire. The few of us that survived were picked off in the followin' weeks. Girls couldn't even go ta market without disappearin' off the street. And the streets are so twisted, no one ever noticed when or where it happened. I never got an answer about any of my missin' girls."

The twisted streets. That was it. Kaiya brought her head up sharply. "Have you ever seen Lucius's army mobilize?"

"What in Tapestry are ya—no. No, I haven't." Eili narrowed her eyes, suddenly perplexed. "Whatcha thinkin', girl?"

"What about you, Emery? Has the army ever left the inner city?" Kaiya tried not to look too excited as she pressed the question. Emery thought for a long moment.

"Not as far as I know, ma'am. But there really hasn't been a need."

"What about with the nomadic tribes to the south? The

Danhaid? That war was only five years ago. Didn't the king send soldiers to fight them?"

"I'm sure, ma'am. But I don't remember it. I was just a stable-hand then."

Eili caught on and rose to question one of the guards in her underground rebellion. He admitted that he had worked as a soldier but had never been asked to leave the city during the Danhaid Wars.

"I never saw them mobilize. One day I just happened to notice there were fewer soldiers around than there had been the day before. I didn't think it too strange at the time. We were at war, after all."

"You 'didn't think it too strange' that you never saw an entire army move in or out of town?" Eili growled. The guard frowned but didn't respond.

"They must have used the horned god's magic," Tendaji said, furrowing his brow. "An army that size moving that far? They must all be completely loyal to Thinir's will, now. Which means your King Lucius has been out of power for at least five years."

"And that the Croeli have had at least that long to gather and mobilize the attacks that brought down the Faoii." Eili's glare was fierce as she spoke. Kaiya shook her head, still confused.

"But why expend men to fight the nomads? The Danhaid Wars must have cost Thinir at least something, and he couldn't have gained much. They still don't follow Clearwall's laws. They don't pay taxes or farm crops. If the Croeli were planning to go against the Faoii, why sacrifice men in battles that they had nothing to gain from and then leave the Danhaid unconquered?"

"Maybe to test their power before fightin' true warriors?" Faoii-Eili shrugged. "Does it matter now? The Croeli are in control, and what's left of the Danhaid don't give a spit about us or the Goddess. They ain't no concern of ours." She caught Kai's gaze with a hungry eye.

"Come on, girl. We got Faoii ta find."

12

Kaiya pulled uncomfortably at the neckline of her dress. Her flowing sleeve snagged on the unnecessarily slimming corset, and she cursed under her breath, trying to disentangle the ruinous parts of her ensemble. A passing dock worker glanced at her uncertainly before hurrying past. Kaiya took a deep breath and tried to center herself. Her ridiculous heels clicked on the pavement as she moved—*Elegantly? I'm supposed to move elegantly in this death trap?*—forward.

The street was dark, the moon all but invisible in the misty air, crowded out by the looming buildings. Cailivale was smaller than Clearwall, but not by much, and Kaiya shivered again at the seemingly magicless streets that stretched out for miles all around her. Despite being almost two months south of the capital, the air was colder here. It was nearly the middle of autumn, and Kaiya was sure that the first snowfall would come soon.

Cailivale was not quite like Clearwall in its emptiness. There was no gaping void where Illindria had been torn away. Instead, it was more like the Goddess's presence was... covered. Kaiya could almost sense it there, hiding beneath the fog that pulled at her delicate heels.

Kaiya felt more than saw the shadow that detached itself from one of the overhead eaves and oozed toward her like water through cracks in a stone wall. Clenching her teeth in what could possibly pass as some sort of smile while yanking at one of her sleeves, Kaiya growled at her brother. "What?"

"You fidget too much."

"Do you want to wear this blasted dress?" Kaiya hissed as she tried in vain to pull down the immodest front hem of her skirt. She guessed that she might have been capable of walking well enough if the entire thing had been cut to this short length, but some apparently sadistic seamstress had gathered a long train at the small of her back, and it dragged across the cobblestones behind her, catching at her heels. She released a frustrated sigh. Tendaji chuckled under his breath.

"Ah, pretty little Kai. Do you think Mother would be proud to see you now?" He motioned to her low-cut neckline and high-cut hem. His eyes twinkled with silent laughter in the moonlight. With tremendous willpower, Kaiya resisted the urge to punch him. In this outfit, she'd probably do more damage to herself, anyway.

She and Tendaji had been traveling together for two months now, and she had grown fond of her brother's many indelicate remarks. They lightened the increasingly desperate situation somehow. But she still frowned for good measure.

"You are making it exceedingly hard to stay in character, Croeli bastard."

Tendaji shrugged casually. "Nothing I do could possibly make you look any more out of character, anyway." He paused, considering. "Faoii witch." This time Kaiya did elbow him, but he slid out of the way. "It doesn't matter. The Faoii know you are here. They are coming."

"How do you know they are Faoii and not regular whores?"

"If Faoii-Eili is to be believed, most are one and the same in this area." He glanced over just as Kaiya hid her smile. He frowned. "Please, Kaiya, don't insult me. Do you think any mere street woman could move as a Faoii does? Can any untrained girl stalk the shadows like a panther? How do you spot a Croeli in a fight?"

"I just look for anyone that looks like scum. Then I'm pretty sure."

"Well, then by that logic, I looked for whoever seemed the most pretentious. They were not difficult to find." Kaiya rolled her eyes, but Tendaji continued, "I assure you, these women are Faoii. There are others, too, though they are inelegant in their strength, too sure of themselves to have seen battle. Acolytes, perhaps?" Kaiya shook her head.

"Unascended, maybe. There are no acolytes in the Faoii Order." Tendaji shrugged easily.

"As you say. Just do not be surprised if they are overly eager to jump into battle. I did try to warn you." He shifted away from her and melted into the shadows again. Kaiya lifted her eyes to the unseen moon above in a silent prayer before continuing her promenade through the dirty streets of Cailivale.

It was not long before she heard someone turn onto the cobbled road behind her, the steps clear and intentional. Someone wanted her to hear the approach. Kaiya walked on with deliberate steadiness.

"You there. Stop." The words were issued by a soft, airy voice, but there was no doubt that it was a command. The sentence was laced with all the power of the Faoii. Kaiya squared her shoulders before turning around.

The girl before Kaiya was young. Her deep black hair was braided in an elegant design—much too ornate to be considered proper for a Faoii, but normal for a Cleroii. She had a slight build and doe-like eyes, but she held herself with a strength that seemed unnatural in her petite body. The girl stopped a few paces away from Kaiya, arms crossed in front of her. Kaiya looked right through the seemingly casual stance and watched the young Cleroii settle her weight on the balls of her feet, ready to spring at a moment's notice.

"Hail, Sister." Kaiya's voice drifted over the cobblestones like smoke over a campfire as she fisted her hands one over the other. The fawn girl froze in place, eyes obviously wider than they should be, even without using the Sight. A long moment passed in silence. Then two. Then three. Kaiya grew irritated at the lack of response. Wasn't she still an ascended Faoii? Didn't she at least deserve the honor of a reply?

Finally, Kaiya took a forceful step toward the young maiden, feeling the air charge around her as she drew herself up to her full height. The girl was almost dwarfish in Kaiya's presence, but she did not shy away. She did, however, raise her arms in a defensive motion as Kaiya advanced. There was no fear in her eyes, and Kaiya flashed a wolfish smile at the sight of another warrior. The girl's movements were so *fluid*, so *perfect*.

"Why are you trying to hide yourself?" she asked, softening

her eyes. "Look at you. You are true Faoii. One of the few that remain." She hushed the girl quickly as she tried to speak. "No. Don't lie. You may be Cleroii rather than Faoii, but you are of the Order, and I greet you as a sister." Kaiya paused, sensing something in the air. "As do I greet you others, too." The fawnlike girl gave her a strange look, and Kaiya smiled. "You have two companions who are closing in on us. One is coming from the market stall behind me, and the other is in the window to my left." The faintest gasp came from the cracked pane.

"Well. You *are* well trained." The voice was young and smug, though it was obvious the speaker was trying to sound forceful. Kaiya sighed at the sound of the voice. *So young. They— we?—are all so young.* Kaiya turned toward this new voice and tried not to stumble in her heels. The smile she gave was genuine.

"I am probably no better than you, Faoii." Kaiya fisted her hands once more. "Hail, Sister."

This new girl immediately fisted her olive-toned hands in the customary fashion. Long strands of silky, ebony hair fell across her face as she bowed her head. "May the Goddess guide your battles, Faoii." She raised her head and stood with one hand on a leather-clad hip. Her breastplate had been switched out for a subtler leather jerkin, and, unlike Kaiya and the fawnlike Cleroii, she wore dusty, flexible breeches and sturdy boots rather than the obscenely short skirt and feminine heels. Her silky black braid was bound with iron rings. It reached the small of her back, and a glittering fantoii rested easily on one hip. She gave Kaiya a reproving look.

"You look ridiculous." Kaiya looked down at her awkward gown.

"It's . . . hard to openly search for Faoii these days. It's not like I could simply ask around until I found you. So I gave you a reason to seek me out instead." She shrugged one bare, dark shoulder. The leather-clad girl's almond eyes sparkled in wry amusement.

"Well, it worked. Who are you?"

Kaiya smiled and fisted her hands again. "I am Faoii-Kaiya of the Monastery of the Eternal Blade."

"Kaiya. Pretty. I'm Faoii-Lyn of the Unbroken Weave. This is Kim-Cleroii, and the one hiding behind the windowpane is Mei-Faoii. And before you ask, yes, Mei and I are biological siblings, not just sisters of the Order." A smallish girl with the same silky hair and almond eyes stepped out of the house she had been using for cover. A weather-worn crossbow hung lazily from one hand. Its bolt had not been removed. "Welcome to Cailivale, the last Faoii bastion."

Kaiya looked to Mei and Kim. Both wore the deep-cut dresses that whispered of… purchasable affection. And neither looked older than ten or twelve.

Faoii-Lyn followed her gaze, apparently using the Sight to read her thoughts at a glance. "Do not judge us, Faoii. We do what we must in order to put food on the table. We know how to defend ourselves, and the other girls in this town do, too, and there's no shame in that." Kaiya opened her mouth to speak, but Faoii-Lyn stopped her. "And besides, men's tongues grow loose when their blood rushes from one head and into the other. I'm willing to bet my fantoii that I have at least some information that you want, all of which was given willingly and received readily."

Kaiya spread her hands, surprised at the younger woman's pride and strength. "I misjudged, Faoii. I apologize." Faoii-Lyn's gaze immediately softened, and she grinned as she slapped Kaiya lightly on one shoulder.

"No harm done. We'll discuss it when we get to the enclave. Your awkward soldier friend is already waiting for you there." Kaiya cocked her head to one side.

"You already picked up Emery?"

"Yeah. He was almost as out of place as you. We stopped him and found Faoii armor in the wagon, so I locked him up in the enclave. He's not hurt or anything. We knew pretty quick that he didn't kill anyone to get that armor. And he said 'ma'am' so many times I thought I'd go crazy, so we left him there and went looking for the Faoii he claimed was his companion." She shrugged and gestured around her. "And here we are."

"And here you are." Kaiya tried to imagine the nervous but kind-hearted Emery being accused of murdering a Faoii by a bunch of dangerous and beautiful women. Poor Emery.

"What about my other companion?" she finally ventured. Lyn noticeably froze, her entire body straightening. The look on her face was not one of amusement.

"What other companion?"

Kaiya sighed in muted relief. She wasn't sure what she'd do if the women of Cailivale had already discovered Tendaji. She took a step closer to Lyn with her hands raised. No more repetitions of what had happened in the sewers.

"I need you to hear me out, Faoii. Please. I'm here with someone else, and I'm not surprised that he's eluded you. He's greatly skilled, and all but the most perceptive Faoii would pass him by without a second glance. That's valuable in times like these."

"If he has to hide from us, then we can't trust him." Kim-Cleroii seemed nervous as she spoke. Kaiya tried to make her voice as soothing as possible.

"I know. But that's my fault rather than his. Please, sisters. I need you to trust me. I swear on the Tapestry that we're not a danger to you." Lyn eyed Kaiya closely, measuring her words. After a moment, she gave the other girls a nod. Kim pulled a long dagger from her sleeve and tucked it into her belt where Kaiya could easily see it. With an aptitude belying her small hands and young age, Mei unloaded her crossbow.

"Fine. Lead us to him." Kaiya gave a soft sigh and made sure her hands were nowhere near her fantoii as she spoke.

"He's already here." The girls all tensed as they looked around warily. Then, slowly, one of the shadows in the rafters of a nearby building disjointed from those around it and dropped silently onto the cobblestones. Tendaji glided into the street, tucking a throwing knife into his leather belt pouch. He stopped several strides away, eyeing the pack of Faoii with wary amusement. The street had all the commotion of a cemetery.

Mei's trembling voice finally broke the silence. "Lyn, it's one of *them*." Lyn gave her little sister a sharp glance before turning back to Kai.

"You travel with troubling companions, Faoii." Faoii-Lyn's voice was hard and cold as she crossed her arms. Kaiya noted that the stance brought her right hand closer to the fantoii hilt.

"Then you know what he is?" Kaiya's question was simple and held no implications.

"Of course. No one burns a monastery full of Croeli to the ground without knowing the enemy first."

"And yet there is no fear in your eyes. His presence does not bother you?"

"Don't be stupid. Of course it bothers me. But I do *not* fear him. You've given up your advantage by bringing him into the light. We'll watch him. Carefully." Lyn took a quick step toward Kaiya and looked up into her eyes with a deathly stare. "Just be aware of this, Faoii-Kaiya: if you betray us, I will kill you. And I'll do it slowly." The amount of power that Faoii-Lyn was able to put into that simple statement was enough to charge the air and make the hair on the back of Kaiya's neck stand on end. Kaiya nodded.

"I know. But if it ever comes to that, I don't think I would try to stop you." Lyn held Kaiya's gaze for a moment longer, then turned away.

"Okay then. If that's settled, let's get going. Time to show you the Faoii enclave of Cailivale."

13

The enclave was really two adjacent warehouses that had been connected over time. Its many exits made it easy for the women inside to avoid the scrupulous gazes of what authoritative figures Cailivale had to offer, but for the most part, the enclave was Cailivale's most open secret. Commonly viewed as an elaborate brothel, the women of Cailivale had their own brewery, barracks, and chapel hidden amidst the training dummies and weapon stands that filled the massive warehouse situated behind the "entertainment" plaza. Women of all ages and all manners of dress sauntered through the building as Kaiya received the grand tour. Some looked like common street women, shameless and proud as they stretched their long, bare legs with each step. Others were dressed in the more modest and battle-ready leather jerkins that matched Faoii-Lyn's. None wore the bronze breastplate and ivy-covered helm that came with ascension, and except for Faoii-Lyn's glittering weapon, no fantoii were present.

"Only Kim, Mei, and I actually grew up in the monastery," Lyn said as she led Kaiya and Tendaji through the twisted "rooms" created by hanging rugs and beaded curtains. "The rest are girls we found on our way here. They were all either too weak and afraid to stand up for themselves or too proud and headstrong to be anything other than dangerous. Until we came along. We gave them a home and we taught them how to fight the Croeli." She lowered her voice. "None of them are true Faoii, but they don't know that. And they *need* this." She gave Kai a hard look, daring her to shred the fantasy they'd built around themselves. Kaiya thought about her own "ascension" and everything she'd learned since the beginning of her journey and smiled sadly.

"I think we all do."

Lyn grinned as they continued. Most of the women bowed their heads or gave long-legged curtsies to Faoii-Lyn as she passed, and she sauntered through them proudly, leading Kaiya to a changing screen set up near an iron tub toward the back of the building. There was no question that Faoii-Lyn was in charge as she called over a nearby harlot.

"Bring me the armor that the scared boy had with him. Oh, and let him out, too. He's harmless." The woman moved to obey, and Lyn turned back to Kaiya. "I'd ask you what happened to the Eternal Blade Monastery, but I'm pretty sure I already know. Croeli appeared on your doorstep out of nowhere, broke their way inside, and slaughtered everyone they came across? Maybe holed up for a while to rest and heal before moving on?"

"Yes." Kaiya was slightly hurt by how glibly Faoii-Lyn was able to discuss the situation, though she'd had more time to cope with it. "But they didn't stay in the monastery. They were gone before I woke up." Briefly, Kaiya described the fall of her monastery.

"Huh. I wonder why they didn't stay. If they were right and you really were the last, you'd think they'd rest up before continuing. Especially since it sounds like they lost more soldiers in your fight than mine. They must have had something more important on the horizon." Lyn paused, thinking. "I don't know what it was, though. My scouts say they've seen the Croeli army mobilizing in different places, but they never attack anything. They're just…waiting. Whatever they're up to, they've had more than enough time to plan it."

"How long ago did your monastery fall?" Kaiya asked just as the woman returned with her breastplate and leathers. Kaiya let out a sigh of relief as she stepped behind the changing screen and clawed her way out of the form-fitting dress, only too happy to leave it in an undignified heap on the floor. She stepped out again to receive Lyn's answer as she belted on her fantoii.

"Two years ago." Faoii-Lyn picked up the dress and corset and called another young girl over to her. "Take this to Emilia. She doesn't have to give back the gold that the stranger paid her for it." Kaiya almost blushed, but she refrained. She had bought the dress three days ago in a different town. Faoii-Lyn must have read the embarrassment on her face, because her eyes twinkled.

"Yeah. They're pretty much all my girls. At least within riding distance. It's one of the reasons I knew to look for you. Don't know why you picked orange. It looks good on you, but green would have matched your eyes." Her dark eyes twinkled as she helped Kaiya tighten the leather straps on her breastplate. When she'd finished, her petite fingers glided over the bronze detailing and, for a moment, her eyes drifted away.

It was several seconds before Lyn spoke again. "I probably could have gotten to your monastery before they did. I probably could have warned you. But honestly, it didn't even occur to me. We went to the king first, to the capital city. But something didn't smell right in the air, so we kept moving. I just assumed that your monastery had already fallen, being so close. So I came here, started over from scratch. I don't know. Maybe I was afraid of how the Order would judge me, but I never even thought of searching for other Faoii."

"We wouldn't have believed you, anyway. Even if we had, what could we have done? We might have mobilized and sought to face the Croeli head-on, but they move so quickly . . . they would have eluded us until they were ready or ambushed us on unfavorable ground. And if we'd planned on the defensive . . . there were two years between attacks. We would have grown complacent again. In the end, the result would have been the same." The words were bitter in Kaiya's mouth, but they still rang true.

"Maybe that's what the Croeli were counting on. Or maybe they were afraid of your monastery and had to gather more forces before... Hell, I don't know. Does it even matter now?" Lyn paused, biting her lip. Her eyes traced the bronze breastplate again. "I... I never thought I'd see another woman worthy of wearing the ivy helm and breastplate. I..." She straightened her shoulders and met Kaiya's eyes. "I'm honored. Really. It will be nice for the girls to have a true ascended to look up to." Her almond eyes glanced over to Kim and Mei, who were going through the simple steps of a battle dance on one side of the room. Their quiet song drifted through the throng of women that trickled their way into the warehouse.

"You were not offered ascension before...?" Kaiya trailed off, not sure how to finish. Lyn shook her head.

"No. I hadn't yet earned my title when our monastery was

attacked. I gave it to myself when I realized I was the last girl older than thirteen to survive the Croeli occupation. Someone needed to lead those few who were left." She glanced over to the younger girls again. "Please don't tell them that I am not truly ascended. I know that I should not hold pride in a lie, but . . . I told them that it was okay." Kaiya gave the other girl a warm smile.

"Your secret's safe with me." She followed Lyn's gaze. The two young girls had changed out of their short dresses and into the soft leathers of the unascended. They moved in complete unison, their voices and bodies in perfect harmony as they guided their blades through the air in front of them.

"Aren't their blades a little large for their age?" Kaiya asked. The swords were twice the length of the girls' arms.

"They are young, though growing quickly. They completed their sword ceremonies with a broader blade than that." Lyn caught Kaiya's glance. "Where we're from, girls start with the largest blade and work their way up to the smallest." She pulled a disk from one of the pouches at her waist. The dark metal glinted in the torchlight, its razor edges bright. With an almost lazy gesture, Lyn held it between her index and middle fingers. Then, with a flick of her wrist, it was buried in one of the wooden support beams halfway across the room. Kaiya murmured her approval.

"A frightening skill. Useful, I suppose, if your opponent is unaware of you."

Lyn grinned. "Exactly. Why risk danger to yourself or your sisters when the threat can be eliminated without a struggle?"

"Maybe. But it seems . . . wrong. The Goddess praises courage and defense as well as the attack itself. There's no opposition if you strike from the shadows. No . . . duality. And it denies your

opponent the ability to please Illindria with her own strength."
Kaiya pulled her eyebrows together at the thought. Didn't
everyone deserve the chance to at least fight for their own glory?

"You talk like the opponent is Faoii. When would you ever
fight a Faoii in true battle?"

Kaiya was startled when she realized that Lyn was right. Her
"battles" had always been against other Faoii, so they'd always
been for show. A chance for fame and recognition rather than life
or death. Here, in the real world, *glory* didn't seem like much more
than word.

She thought about the brute that had bullied Astrid and Ray in
Resting Oak. She had not given him a chance to prove himself to
the Goddess. Did she regret those actions now?

Mollie's broken body flashed in her mind. A cold bitterness
flooded Kaiya.

"No. You're right. Sometimes it's better if they never have a
chance." Kaiya went to the support beam that housed the metal
disk. She yanked it out with one gloved hand and stood there,
turning it over in her fingers. Her reflection stared back at her
from the darkened mirror. The steel in her eyes was terrifying.

After a moment, Kaiya returned to where Lyn was leaning
casually against the wall, still watching the young dancers. She
took back the disk without taking her eyes from the girls, a slight
smile coloring her features. Kaiya turned to watch the graceful
circles, enthralled.

"They move like shield sisters."

"That's because they are. Isn't it obvious?"

"But Mei is Faoii and Kim is Cleroii."

"You don't know much about our home, do you? The
Monastery of the Unbroken Weave." Kaiya did not deny her

ignorance. She knew next to nothing about any of the monasteries besides her own.

"Well, pretend the Faoii were contacted by a sultan to the south that needed his harem protected but was afraid to have male guards. What would your monastery do?" Kaiya thought for a long moment as she watched the young girls dance.

"That's not uncommon. I guess we'd send two to four Faoii. They would be trained in how to properly address the sultan and follow his orders, and in return he would have to agree that they were not a part of his harem. It wouldn't be hard. Two sentries at each door. An easy but honorable position for an ascended."

"See?" Lyn replied. "That's where we're different. While you would have two Faoii at the door, dressed in their breastplates and fantoii, our monastery would have Faoii dressed as harem girls themselves. In the harem, part of the harem, protecting the women from within and gaining all the secrets the royalty of that land had to offer." She gave Kaiya a wink. "That's what made the Unbroken Weave unique. We are warriors, like you, but our policy was never blades first and a fight to the death. We kill our enemies before the fight even begins. Masters of subterfuge and poisons. Infiltrators. Sweet smiles and sharp blades. And we were never paired with another girl of the same class. A Faoii keeps her Cleroii sister alive with her sword, and the Cleroii keeps the Faoii alive with her song. Sometimes, depending on a situation, the roles must be reversed, so we all had to learn both parts. We *need* our sisters."

Kaiya thought about Mollie and felt her eyes mist, but she batted the tears away quickly. She had always needed Mollie, too.

"The same can be said for all Faoii, Lyn. We all need our shield sister as much as we need our fantoii or breastplate." Lyn shook her head.

"Not like this. Look at them. Focus on the spell around them. Do you sense it?" Kaiya looked, and for a moment she *did* see it. There was a bond, a silver cord that wrapped itself around the girls. It stretched between them, like a scarf in a dervish dance, constantly twirling as they spun their swords. "Some of the Preoii think that it makes us weaker. Neither girl is as strong as a regular Faoii, and neither can sing a song with as much power as a regular Cleroii, but there's something about the bond between a Faoii's will and a Cleroii's spell. It's strong. There's a physical need to protect your sister, an aching when she is absent. But… it's also that much more painful when it's severed." Lyn brought a hand up over her chest and visibly shivered.

Kaiya put a gentle hand on her shoulder. "I am sorry for your loss."

Lyn shook the tears from her eyes and straightened. Her shrug was not as casual as she probably hoped. "You deserve to hear the story, Faoii. I haven't had a superior to report to since we left. There's… so much I could have done differently." Kaiya gave a soft smile.

"Look at what you've accomplished, Lyn. I am sure that there was little you could change and less still that you could have improved upon."

"No, I know that. It's just…" She rolled her shoulders and systematically began popping the knuckles on her fists. Kaiya wondered whether it was a nervous gesture. "Please, Faoii-Kaiya. If you would listen, I would… Well, I… It's just that… Goddess's girdle, Kaiya, I *need* to tell someone." Lyn's voice was harsh as she finally finished, though the whisper was too quiet for anyone else to hear. With another angry sigh, she brought her smoldering eyes up to meet Kaiya's. The uncertainty there was almost tangible.

For a broken moment, Kaiya thought that Lyn's strong façade would crumble in view of her gathered followers—something that could hurt the piecemeal army nearly as much as an outside attack would. Kaiya caught Lyn's gaze and nodded.

"Not here, Faoii. Is there somewhere we can go?"

With a look that could have been relief as easily as anxiety, Lyn straightened her shoulders and led Kaiya to a partially-enclosed section of the building. A pile of mismatched pillows was heaped in one corner, making the area look haphazard and ungainly while warm rugs and rich tapestries struggled to give it an air of authority and luxury instead. A curtain of dull peacock feathers that, ten years before, could have graced a sultan's bedroom, hung awkwardly on the wall behind the "throne." Keeping up her appearances with an intimidating skillfulness, Lyn sank into the cushions and motioned for the women nearby to clear a safe distance. Only after all the other women had moved off to do other things and Kaiya was settled on one of the pillows with her fantoii laid across her lap did Lyn's cold eyes finally begin to soften again. It took several minutes for her to gather the courage to tell her tale.

14

It was dusk at the Monastery of the Unbroken Weave. A soft orange light filtered in through the high windows, giving everything a rosy color. I might have considered it pleasant if it wasn't for the horrible stench of lye.

Blades, I hated laundry day. It would have been completely intolerable if not for Jade. Somehow, even in her silence, Jade always made things better.

I pondered the question that my Cleroii sister had asked a few minutes before. It had been a long-standing tradition that laundry day be passed with hypothetical questions of "who's the better fighter?" and her most recent test had put me up against a lithe barbarian with a machete. Jade was an amazing warrior— more than capable of holding her own. I knew that if my response wasn't perfect, she would know. And even without her saying anything, I would know, too.

Jade had the maddening quality of being able to say anything with just her eyes. She was too kind to outright say that she was disappointed in you, but you always *knew* anyway. Part of me wished that she would at least try false-facing sometimes, instead of just . . . staring. But Jade never lied. Everything was on the table for her. So I thought about her question and made sure to answer correctly.

"From that distance?" I chewed the inside of my cheek as I scrubbed harder. "Hmm . . . Maybe the jugular. Is he behind me or in front of me?"

Jade wrinkled her nose but spoke in her soft, lyrical voice, "Behind."

"Hmm . . . Elbow to the sternum, then." I paused in my task, keeping my face emotionless. I was not some untrained urchin; I knew that answer was a good one. But I waited anyway, afraid of the Preoii-worthy gleam in Jade's eyes when I looked up.

Jade only nodded, smiling brightly as she straightened the thin, coarse sheet held out between us. I grinned.

"All right, Cleroii. My turn." I handed my side of the sheet to Jade and moved to the small stove holding the iron. She followed, her graceful steps barely making a sound. "There are three of them. Average height, but about thirty pounds on the heavy side. Two behind you and one ahead. You have six strides of maneuverability. Plot it."

Jade considered the situation for several minutes, pleating the sheets as I ironed them. I did not bother to repeat the question as the minutes lengthened. Jade always thought every word out before she spoke, never wasting a sound.

"I would—"

I still don't know how Jade would have answered. She was cut off by a shattering crash that echoed through the monastery. We both froze. A single, high-pitched battle cry trilled its way through the halls, rising for a moment before being cut off suddenly. Its echo ghosted through the corridors before drifting into nothingness.

What can I say? We were Faoii. We acted instantly. The iron fell from my hand onto the newly-cleaned linen, forgotten. It took four running steps for me to reach the counter at the other end of the room, and I launched off it and into the crawl space above with a practiced ease. Jade followed after, using the wall as her springboard as she soared into the hideaway that had once been our playhouse. I crouched there, rigid and tense, as Jade jerked the access board back into place. Below us, the thundering crash of booted men rang up from the main floor.

"That came from the great hall." I tried to keep my voice calm as I motioned toward the front of the monastery with one hand. Jade simply nodded and hummed a soft tune, her crystalline, all-knowing eyes staring at me from beneath heavy lashes. Courage and lucidity filled me, and my jittery limbs stilled. With a steadying breath, I pulled one of the edged disks from my belt as the thundering footsteps grew louder, closer. The disk was about the same length as my palm and weighted for throwing. Clean and sharp. I nodded once before easing my way toward the path that led to the entrance. Almost immediately, Jade grasped my wrist in protest and motioned for me to wait.

I wrenched my arm free, irritated and tense. My whisper was harsher than intended. "We can't stay here, Jade. We have to find out what happened to—" I ground to a halt when Jade's eyes met mine, and my stomach filled with dread. "Goddess's girdle. Mei and Kim. All of the urchins are training with Mimi and Kiki."

Jade nodded silently. Frustrated, I flicked my eyes back and forth between Jade and the pathway that would lead to the front door. To the fight. The little ones (fondly referred to as "the urchins" by the rest of the Faoii) trained in the west wing—on the opposite side of the grounds. My limbs tingled as I was pulled between the two destinations.

With a hiss, I turned to the west, pulling Jade behind me as we scrambled down the pathway.

The entire monastery was laced with hidden passageways and secret rooms. The rat tunnels in the ceiling crisscrossed a dozen times between the laundry room and the west wing. More than once we passed other sets of women trying to repel the unexpected attack on our home. No one in the rafters spoke as dozens of Faoii and Cleroii wove through the ceiling passages, setting traps in their wake.

It wasn't until we reached the dining hall that we caught sight of Faoii-Ming and Cleroii-Sung. Our superiors were busy directing younger girls with sharp, authoritative whispers. No one questioned their orders or made any move to slow the pace. It was imperative that we all achieve as much as possible before the invaders discovered the rat holes and passageways that offered us sanctuary. In the bustle of activity, we were barely granted the few seconds it took to ask about the urchins' whereabouts.

"We haven't seen the young ones." Faoii-Ming had to raise her voice in order to be heard over the screaming coming from the dining hall below. She hardly looked at us as she knotted and reknotted a net coiled at her feet. Cleroii-Sung chimed a bit of wounding magic into the knots while Jade and I helped her to set the trap over one of the archways leading into the hall below. "I don't know whether these horned bastards got to them or not, but I doubt it. Mimiko-Faoii and Keiko-Cleroii finished their sword ceremony last week, and your little sister is set to finish hers in a month. They can handle themselves, no matter how young they are." I wasn't trying to false-face, so she must have seen the worry in my eyes when she looked up. Faoii-Ming just smiled and laid a rough hand on my shoulder. "Don't worry, Lyn-Faoii. We'll all be there to see her dance." She glanced through the wooden slats in the floor before finishing the preparations on the trap. "None of the invaders seem to have made it out of the eastern wing yet. We've done a pretty good job holding them off. You go find the urchins. We'll keep these Croeli bastards back." With a nod, Jade and I wove our way through the crooked paths toward the western wing.

"Did Faoii-Ming say Croeli?" Jade whispered to me as we crawled. I only shook my head, unsure of how to answer.

We tried to ignore the screams behind us. Goddess, how we tried. The fact that most were masculine was not as comforting as I wish it was. Every pained Faoii cry was like a sliver in my heart, but I knew I couldn't stop. My little sister was still ahead, and I had to find her.

But the west wing was abandoned.

Jade and I dropped silently into the training room. All those years of learning subterfuge rather than brute force were finally being put to use, and I didn't even notice enough to care. Instead, all I saw was the empty room where my sister should be. Two of the wooden practice swords that the girls were offered to train with before their sword ceremony lay in the middle of the floor while two pairs of shoes lay at the edge of the mat. My heart climbed into my throat at the stillness of the air.

There was no sign of passing. No footprints, no sounds. The trapdoors to the ceiling were untouched, and neither of us had seen any hint of the children while in the rafters. As quietly as possible but with quickening footsteps, we searched the hidden crevices and hidey-holes that dotted the wing, trying not to let the pounding of our heartbeats give us away. But every step was like a new stone in my gut. There was no sign that any of the hidden passageways or doors had been disturbed. The alcoves were empty, the whisper-holes silent. My legs moved woodenly, but I tried to remain hopeful with each failed search. The urchins were intelligent. Surely, they were still okay.

Finally, on hands and knees, I pressed the heel of my palm into a smooth section of masonry at the base of one wall that I vaguely remembered from years before. A tiny section of stone clicked open, and I nudged it aside. There was just a hint of a gasp in the silence from within. The faintest scent of soap.

"Mei? Kim? It's Lyn. Are you there?" Nothing. With a sigh, I turned to Jade. She shrugged easily, and I'm almost positive I saw a smile on her face.

"You always taught them that silence was the key to survival." I tried to ignore that maddening glint in my shield sister's eyes.

"Yeah. Yeah, I know." I rolled my shoulders and ducked my head into the hole. There was only blackness. Muttering, I squirmed my way into the tight passage that stretched forward through the dark.

I had often made my way through this particular crevice as a child, now that I thought about it, but that didn't make it easier. My too-wide hips and shoulders caught against the stone. *Smart girls. No man would be able to make it through here.*

Finally, I pulled myself through to the other side. The darkness of the hidden alcove was almost absolute, so I felt more than saw the practice sword above the opening. I ducked away just as it fell.

"Goddess's grace, girls! It's *me!*" I wriggled in the darkness until a small, moonlike face with doe eyes peered down to look me in the face. I did my best not to sound angry. "Kim-Faoii, it's me!" Kim's face disappeared for a moment before reappearing with an embarrassed smile.

"Come through, Lyn-Faoii." She paused. "Sorry. Mimi said she saw a Faoii fighting with the Croeli. We needed to make sure it was you." I squirmed my way out of the burrow and crouched in a room full of small children, surprised at what I found once my eyes adjusted.

The urchins' professionalism in the face of danger was one of the most amazing things I've ever seen. There was no fear in that dingy, cluttered space. Only a grim determination. A sense of duty. As soon as the young Faoii were sure that I was not a threat, they turned away. Kim rekindled a fire that had apparently been kicked out rapidly not long before, while Mimi and Kiki stirred a putrid liquid in the frying pan that sat above it. The other girls pulled at planks in the floorboards and walls, using their small, quickly-purpling fists at close range to break the boards into serviceable, if jagged, weapons.

"We can't get a cauldron in here, Lyn," Mei whispered as I pulled Jade through the hole and blocked it up again with one of the loose boards. "So we're doing what we can with what we could grab." She shrugged and turned back to Mimi and Kiki at their task. Jade and I followed, curious.

"You're boiling oil!" I'd almost clapped my hands in glee at the girls' resourcefulness. They were Faoii, even then, and I don't think I've ever been more proud.

"We were able to get to the pantry twice before we heard boots in the corridor. We only have enough oil for one more run, and then we'll have to try to get to the pantry again."

Mei jabbed at empty air with her improvised spear, and my eyes brimmed with tears. I just kept thinking over and over, *Illindria bless them. They aren't even afraid. They are true Faoii.* And they were. There was no doubt that those girls were warriors. "We need to meet up with the others for orders," Mei whispered as she thrust her spear up into the ceiling, then prepared to leap after it. I leaned down to give her a boost up, but Mei pulled herself into the hole without assistance. She peeked back over the lip of the frame. "Will you come with us?"

Jade and I didn't even hesitate. "We're right behind you."

The children knew the passageways that wormed through the monastery better than anyone alive. They were smaller and lighter than the rest of us, and were able to use ancient tunnels that Jade and I had walked by a million times and never noticed. The urchins practically danced above the Croeli's heads with complete autonomy. Even I, who was known in the monastery to be more cat than human, was impressed. The little brats were like shades in the night.

Days passed in an ever-more terrifying war against the Croeli invaders. I don't know why we didn't send anyone out for help. The urchins probably could have snuck out unnoticed in those first days before we truly utilized them. But I guess we all thought that if we couldn't do it, no one could. Faoii arrogance at its finest, right?

It was Faoii-Ming that first used the little ones to their full advantage. I often thought to myself that maybe we shouldn't use such young girls as scouts or trap setters, but damn it if Faoii-Ming's tactics didn't work. Between the urchins scampering through the hidden tunnels like mice through sewers and us older Faoii using guerilla tactics in the shadows of the darkened halls, we were more than capable of holding our own. Everything was perpetually slick with blood and gore.

Two full weeks passed in this manner with surprising success. Under Faoii-Ming's careful planning, the Faoii thrived. Attacks were varied and scattered, catching the Croeli by surprise again and again. Sometimes Faoii-Ming would have us wait hours or even days between attacks, leaving the Croeli to worry or wear themselves out while the Faoii forces sought refuge and rest in the hidden alcoves and rooms behind stone walls.

We protected each other by spreading out, clumping in small groups throughout the grounds. Faoii-Ming and Cleroii-Sung always remained in a centralized point near the dining hall, sending messengers to give orders to the scattered girls. Their constant need for scouts forced the urchins to relocate to a smaller alcove behind the fireplace on the dining hall's eastern wall. It was not as secure as the other alcove had been, but it made travel quicker and orders more efficient. For a while we held the advantage again, and we were so sure that we would be able to finish it. We were going to take our home back.

Despite our best attempts, however, sometimes the attacks did not go as planned. There always seemed to be Croeli in the dining hall, leaving only one exit from the fireplace alcove. And as the Croeli began to discover the hidden passageways, fewer routes remained safe. But we still didn't give up. We never tried to flee. I don't think we even considered that an option. What kind of Faoii army sacrifices its own monastery? But, looking back, maybe that would have been best.

The situation kept getting worse. Guerilla fighters would drop down onto a Croeli and not make it up again. Young girls would go to scout for Croeli placements and never return. Messengers would disappear on their way to give orders, causing chaos when assignments weren't received. Those that did make it back from skirmishes moaned in the fevered states, and even Cleroii-Sung could not dull the pain of that new poison they've started using, criukli. These girls were offered a silent death, not only for their own comfort but for the safety of those of us that still had to live in silence behind the walls. The dead began to fill the alcoves that were no longer serviceable for safe passage.

The girls who made it back in order to beg for death were the lucky ones. Sometimes, we would hear our missing sisters' muffled screams and the Croeli's vulgar laughter through the floorboards where we hid. But we could do nothing except close our eyes and pray while our sisters were brutally ravished by armored swine. Any rescue attempts only delivered more Faoii into the Croeli's clutches. The bastards had been well-trained, and our only advantage came from our ability to hide. But the undiscovered avenues and rooms began to dwindle. More and more women were forced into close combat against the devastating criukli. More and more women fell before their blades.

The rest of us stuck to our guerilla tactics as best we could and prayed to the Goddess that those who were caught died quickly.

Things became significantly more difficult during the third week, and by that time we didn't know any more safe routes out of the monastery. Most of the trapdoors had been recognized by the Croeli and were constantly monitored or trapped. Their magic was darker than what the Cleroii were used to, and many girls died in lingering agony while the rest of us tried in vain to heal their wounds. Trips to the pantry became first more dangerous, then virtually impossible as the Croeli set out guards and increasingly dark spells. Our rations began to dwindle.

Faoii-Ming and Cleroii-Sung did what they could to provide more rations for those that remained. Several times they were able to make their way to the pantry and kill those that guarded the ice boxes and preserved goods. But they were never able to get enough. Our stomachs remained hollow and our hearts heavy.

And in the end, the Croeli proved too much for even our strongest warriors.

15

It was cold the night Jade and I waited on the eaves below the dining hall's square window. Scaling the wall that led to this section of roof had been nerve-wracking; we'd all expected an arrow in the back the entire climb. The interior routes to the pantry had been sealed off, and this dangerous entrance was our last chance to gather enough food to continue the siege. So I crouched next to Jade, the rope in my hands loose and giving. Somewhere below, Faoii-Ming and Cleroii-Sung were scavenging what they could, but it had already taken them longer than expected, and a tight knot had formed in my gut.

As though reading my mind, the rope suddenly grew taught. That was the signal that Sung and Ming were ready to be pulled back up with what they had gathered. Hand over hand, Jade and I pulled our superiors back to the window, desperate to return to the safety of the alcoves.

Faoii-Ming and Cleroii-Sung never appeared.

Instead, my stomach lurched as two Faoii maidens, tied in a bundle to the rope's end, their bodies broken and torn, appeared above the sill. Four dark eyes stared lifelessly in terrified, silent agony. Their bruised, blue skin was transparent in the moonlight, while thin wisps of tattered, unbraided black hair clung to their sallow cheeks and bare breasts like cobwebs. I tried to choke my stomach back down. "Eternal Blade…"

"Lyn, get down!" I wasn't even sure what was happening when Jade shoved me roughly out of the way just as a crossbow bolt sprouted from the window frame above my head. The corpses dropped back into the darkness of the dining room as we dove away from the open window, terrified. In moments, the air was filled with bolts and arrows as Croeli fired at us from both inside the dining room and from the grounds below. The moon darkened under the onslaught. Frantically, we dashed for the safety of the towering chimney that rose above the rest of the peaked roofs.

Together, Jade and I vaulted over and slammed our backs against the other side of the chimney, followed only moments later by the pattering of arrows in our wake. There we crouched, trembling in fear and sudden cold as the open, unseeing eyes of our dead sisters bore their image into our memories. Around us, arrows rattled the roof like a dark and bloody rainfall. Jade whispered a quiet prayer to a blackened sky.

My first instinct was to dive down the chimney in order to escape the onslaught of projectiles. I thought we could use the secret door at its base to find sanctuary from the Croeli archers. But there was no way that Jade and I could disappear into the chimney without the Croeli searching it more thoroughly. They would find the urchins and kill us all.

With a frustrated cry, I finally shoved myself away from the safety of the brick, jerking Jade toward me as I moved. We tore across the roof together, trying to outrun the angry yells that rose behind us.

I practically flew across those rooftops. I felt Jade's terrified heartbeat in my own chest, but I could not stop to reassure her. Instead, I only sent what encouragement I could through the silver ties that circled us and pushed myself harder, knowing we would need all the momentum we could get in order to survive long enough to reach the urchins again.

The roof we were on ended in an overhanging eave that shadowed a section of the garden chapel beside the monastery. Though a ways off, with a strong enough leap, it was possible to make it from the main building to the pagoda roof. At least, it was in theory. Now we had only our terror and pumping hearts with which to carry out a maneuver that no one had ever truly tested.

Hearts in our throats, we dove for the chapel, barely reaching the green shingles of our destination with our outstretched hands. My shoulders shrieked in agony as I strained against the jarring force of impact, but I pushed away the pain. Without pausing, Jade and I swung through the huge, open windows and into the chapel proper.

Once inside the comfortingly familiar space, I finally allowed myself to fall to one knee and catch my breath. And Jade…Jade just knelt next to me, graceful as ever. Our racing heartbeats echoed in the empty hall for a moment before we forced ourselves to our feet.

The chapel was separated from the other buildings. Exposed. I knew we had to move on before the Croeli surrounded us. I opened my mouth to say as much, but Jade stopped me and gathered her voice. I shut up, excited for what Jade would bring forward. Even unascended, Jade was one of the most talented Cleroii I'd ever met, and I couldn't wait to see the spell that would unravel from her golden tongue. So I watched as Jade, in the silence of the starlight, whispered the softest of songs to the chapel. Its velvet threads twirled in the still air.

I was shocked as I listened to the familiar tune that had drifted through the chapel a million times before. It was not a war song, but one of worship and praise. A song of glory and gratitude. And, as ashamed as I was to admit it, it made me angry. We needed something that would hinder the Croeli rather than bolster the Goddess. After all, what could we possibly have to thank Illindria for at a time like this?

I almost growled at Jade, but I bit my tongue, ashamed. Was I not alive to offer gratitude? Had we not made it this far? Chastised, I prepared myself to accompany Jade in singing, but her song was already drawing to a close, and it draped itself around the chapel like a cloak.

In that moment, peace reigned. The calming presence of the Goddess enveloped us and warmed our hearts for the few moments that it took us to regain our composure and our wits. I ached with gratitude and regret. Never had I desired anything more than to simply lie at the Great One's feet and pray for everything to go back to the way it was. Surely the comfort I found there could not be found again in a world where the Croeli had defeated us.

The calmness of the room was shattered by a crash somewhere

nearby, and I was shaken from my reverie. The Croeli were coming. And no matter how hopeless it currently seemed, I wasn't ready to give up yet.

But where could we go from there? The entrances back into the monastery were sure to be guarded and trapped. It would be suicide to risk the Croeli magics without an ascended Cleroii there to help. It still didn't seem real that the Croeli had been able to take down Cleroii-Sung and Faoii-Ming. It just didn't seem possible. But it was, and we had to deal with it. With a stern gaze and steady hand, I crept up to the windows that faced the main building, searching for the best route back. There had to be a way for us to get back to the urchins and regroup. The Goddess would not let us die alone.

"Lyn. Do you hear that?" Jade's gentle hand fell on my arm.

I shook off the grip. "I don't hear anything. Which is perfect. They were all in the courtyard while we were on the roof. They'll have to come all the way around the building in order to get to us. If we—"

"Lyn. The Goddess is trying to get your attention." Jade's calm voice was insistent despite its sweetness, though I could hear the tiniest hint of impatience there too. I rolled my eyes and tugged my arm out from under Jade's hand again.

"We don't have time for this, Jade. Come on. We can—"

"Damn it, Lyn! *Listen!*" I froze, surprised. I'm not sure I'd ever heard Jade raise her voice before. With a final glance out the window, I pulled away and turned toward my shield sister.

Jade had always been more in touch with Illindria's subtle movements than I had been. She could have become a Preoii rather than Cleroii if she'd had more of a temperament for speaking out loud. And for the first time, I truly tried to focus on what Jade was hearing. But there was only silence. I opened my mouth to speak, but Jade stopped me with a gentle shake of the head. What could I do? I shut the hell up and *listened*.

There. I heard it. It was like listening to a breeze pass over a candlestick. So light, so airy, that it shouldn't have been able to exist at all. But it was there. A slight touch, like a piece of gossamer silk against my arm, caused me to turn, and my heart filled.

The Goddess's statue stood before us, proud and beautiful in the moonlight. The lovely, serene smile that I had seen a thousand times before was open and welcome. A beacon in the darkness.

The statue was apparently smaller than the ones that other Faoii monasteries boasted. I came up nearly to Illindria's shoulder, even though She stood on a pedestal while I had only my boots. The painstakingly carved details in the angelic face made the white embossment seem to be of human flesh and blood. Soft and real, like a woman lightly dusted with flour after baking.

Jade didn't say anything as she took small, graceful steps toward the pedestal. With a smooth bend of her knees, she knelt in a single, fluid motion and rested her clasped hands at the Goddess's feet. The intricate pattern of her Cleroii braid caught the moonlight as she bowed her head. I glanced toward the windows one more time, worried about the still-approaching threat, but I pulled away and followed Jade. With a resolute heart, I knelt too. *If we are to die tonight, then so be it. It is far worse to forget our prayers than to forget our fight.* I clasped my hands over an invisible hilt and rested my head on the statue's base.

A soft *click* sounded from the base of the statue as the stone slab beneath my fists shifted. I started as a tile near my knee popped up with a sprinkling of dust. Cautiously, I crept toward it and, with careful fingers, pried it loose. The gap revealed a set of steep stone stairs descending into darkness. I didn't have to look to know that Jade's eyes were twinkling in the moonlight as she peered over my shoulder.

"The Goddess provides, Lyn."

I almost whooped with joy as I pulled that maddening Cleroii from her kneeling position, kissing her forehead, cheeks, and lips again and again as she laughed. Finally, the urgency of the situation forced me to reassess this unknown catacomb, and together we descended into the blackness below, only stopping long enough to pull the tile slab back into place behind us.

The rat tunnels and mazes of the monastery above paled in comparison to the hidden labyrinth buried beneath the grounds. Jade's quiet contemplation of our pitch-black surroundings quickly produced a torch that had been set high in the wall next to the entrance. I wasn't even sure how she found it, but suddenly there was a quietly hummed tune and a spark of light. Jade smiled as the torch blazed, and her eyes glinted. I could only shake my head in shocked awe. "Blades, Jade, how do you *do* that?"

"You could do it too if you practiced more," she replied.

I rolled my eyes. "Not the time for a lecture, Jade." She smiled as I took a second torch off the wall and used hers to light it. "Let's see if we can get to the urchins from here." I passed the torch through the air in front of us, taking in the hand-carved walls. "Wherever *here* is. Goddess, what is this place?" Jade didn't respond. "Well, let's check it out. Come on." Together, we set off through the labyrinth.

Dozens of passages led to an assortment of long-forgotten bedrooms, training rooms, and even a primitive kitchen. All lay broken and entombed in the monastery's maze. Several times we came to a collapsed doorway or tunnel and had to backtrack through abandoned quarters and long-forgotten barracks.

"Look at this," I called to Jade as I pushed aside a broken bed frame with my foot. "Have you ever heard of any Faoii training underground?"

"The Order used to be larger." Jade shrugged as she ran one finger over a dust-covered carving. "Maybe they needed the space."

"Maybe." I carefully wedged my way past a fallen beam. "But there's a lot of destruction down here. Has there ever been an earthquake at the monastery?"

"Cleroii-Sung…" Jade fell silent for a moment, but then she found her voice again. "Cleroii-Sung said that the west wing was rebuilt when she was a girl. It had fallen before she was born."

"Maybe they stopped using this area when the supports began to give." I pushed a broken beam far enough aside to duck beneath it, then held it up as Jade followed. "It's got to lead back to the outside *somehow*, right?" Jade didn't reply.

After what seemed like hours of searching, backtracking, and searching again, we came to a spacious, circular room. The shattered remains of an Illindrian statue lay in its center, the arms broken and lying in pieces on the floor. Five exits led into the darkness beyond. I circled the space slowly, careful not to step on the remnants of the alabaster sculpture. "I can't tell which direction I'm facing down here. Which way is the monastery?"

Jade closed her eyes for a moment in order to center herself, then motioned down one of passages. I rolled my eyes.

"You could at least pretend it's slightly difficult to do these things, Jade." Jade only smiled as we started down the tunnel.

I don't know how long we walked before we found the dry riverbed. The smooth, cavernous floor and worked edges suggested that the monastery had housed a dock there once, but by the time we got to it there was only the dry sand of the shore surrounded by collapsed stone and rubble.

"I think we overshot the monastery." I hated admitting it, knowing that Jade probably knew exactly where we were. "Isn't there a dry riverbed near the old orangery, though?" She nodded, and when I saw the look in her eye, I knew that she'd probably known it for a while. "Damn. Well, let's circle back again." Jade nodded again and turned to go. I rolled my eyes and turned to follow, but something stopped me. Citrus. I paused for a moment and inspected the rubble of the timeworn docks. "Wait a second, Jade. Come look at this." Jade glided up behind me, peering into the small opening between stones. "It would be a tight fit, but I think the urchins could make it through here."

"And?" It was not a cruel question, just a simple one. Her large, dark eyes were curious.

"I can smell oranges through it, and the air here isn't stagnant like it is in the other rooms. There has to be an exit down that way."

"For the urchins, you mean." I nodded solemnly. I didn't like what I was saying any more than she did, but we both knew what was at stake.

"We're all that's left, Jade. We've got to make sure that, if nothing else, the little ones get out. It's better that than let them starve behind the dining room fireplace." She nodded slowly.

"We have to find them first."

One of the exits from the maze was serviceable, and it led to a dry storage cellar near the kitchen. It was almost empty, having been raided by first the Croeli and later by the few Faoii who had risked the completely exposed hallway outside its door. I hauled on a burlap sack filled with potatoes, pulling out what I could easily carry and motioning for Jade to do the same.

"I did not know there was a passage in this room." Jade whispered as she gathered a few of the vegetables that dotted the floor.

"Why would you? There aren't any hidden passages off this corridor. Or at least, no one thought there was."

"It will be difficult to get back to the urchins without a passage." Jade's voice showed no fear, but I knew it was there, lurking beneath that porcelain exterior. I gave my most reassuring smile and a wink.

"We're Faoii, Jade. We'll be fine."

Together we slunk through the deep shadows of the hallway, oozing like water through sand. Twice we had to freeze, holding our breath and willing the Croeli in the hall to look in a different direction. When they did, we sighed in relief and continued on. By the time we finally reached the rat tunnel that led to the fireplace, we were aching with the strain of fear and clenched muscles.

The urchins were huddled in the dingy closet, waiting anxiously for our return. They almost cried with joy when we pulled ourselves through the wall and into the small sanctuary. Kim-

Cleroii actually did begin to cry when Jade and I passed out those few meager potatoes that we were able to smuggle into the monastery's last haven.

"Where are Faoii-Ming and Cleroii-Sung?" Mei's quiet question broke the silence left after the children finished guzzling the slightly squished tubers. Jade stopped chewing at the question, and I swallowed with difficulty.

"They didn't make it." I hated the way the words tasted in my mouth, but I forced my eyes to meet Mei's. "We're all that's left." Her shocked gaze ripped into my heart.

"What do we do?" Mimiko and Keiko spoke in unison, trying not to let their voices quaver. I forced myself to smile and kept my voice even as I spoke, but I know those girls saw the heaviness in my heart.

"We're going to retreat."

16

We spent one more night behind the dining hall fireplace, and in the morning our stomachs rumbled incessantly as the rich smell of meat pies and porridge wafted into the hidden room. We tried to ignore the enticing scents as well as the Croeli's raucous laughter as we gathered what was left of our meager belongings. Jade and I went over the directions a dozen times before we sent the girls to the dry cellar, two at a time. They kept to the shadows and prayed all the way. We were lucky. The Croeli had evidently grown used to the ever-decreasing frequency of our attacks, and the corridors weren't heavily guarded anymore. Or maybe it wasn't luck. Maybe the Goddess was watching over her last little ragtag band, because we made it to the hidden maze without incident. Bless Her blade, somehow we made it.

Then…then we just waited. Day after day, I couldn't bring myself to lead those girls away from our monastery—our home. We hid like damned kittens in that maze for weeks, and all I could do was make up excuses for staying put. Every day I'd turn to the girls and say that we needed to recuperate from the mental torment of the monastery's fall or recover our strength from our involuntary fast. And they never argued; they just went through their daily rituals like we were still above ground. Jade stayed quiet too, but I saw the questions in her crystalline eyes. I knew how she looked at me from beneath her heavy lashes. But I had no answers, no words. So eventually I just stopped meeting her gaze.

We hid in the maze for two months, never attacking the Croeli or giving away our presence. But we never plotted our escape, either. Never tried to get away or start fresh. The younger girls continued their training in secret. We only risked the wrath of the Croeli by resupplying when we had no other choice. None of us, not even Jade, was willing to admit out loud that we needed to leave. I don't think any of us truly wanted to.

And all that time I just bit down on the doubt that wormed its way into my heart, unsure of why I was still so reluctant. I'd never been reluctant about anything before. I always had a plan, a comeback, a way of doing things. But now… now I was just lost. I prayed to the Goddess for strength to do what had to be done— to guide the girls away from that place of death and sorrow, and then at night I still gave the same stupid reasons to stay.

"We can't leave today. The twins said they smelled rain when they went to the orangery. We'll have to wait until after the storm passes." The girls agreed and went on with their daily routines, never questioning my judgment. Sometimes I wished they would.

I don't know how many nights I sat in the silence that surrounded the Goddess's broken statue, watching the urchins and Jade. The truth gnawed at my insides. We were all that was left. Six girls. Four of us at least had a sword ceremony under our belts, but that was it. Not a single one had even a fantoii to our still-unascended names. And yet we remained in enemy territory. Was it willingly? Or was it because I was afraid to go?

"What's wrong, Lyn?" Jade finally ventured one night, fading from out of the shadows behind me in order to lay a hand on my shoulder. I couldn't help but smile.

"You're getting better at sneaking, Jade."

"You taught me well." Jade folded her legs to kneel next to me. We sat in silence, watching the urchins sleep at Illindria's broken feet. Their faces were soft in the firelight.

I felt Jade's original question hang in the air between us, but she did not force the issue. She never did. The fire crackled quietly in the chilled air.

"Why are we still here, Jade?" I finally whispered with an angry sigh. Fury bubbled up inside of me, and I stabbed the ground in front of me repeatedly, frustrated. "I'm keeping us here, and I don't know why. We could have run by now. We could be in one of the cities, safe and making lives for ourselves. I could have ensured the urchins' safety, rather than keeping them here. But I keep coming up with excuses. I keep finding reasons to stay. Why?"

Jade's smooth answer came immediately, without anger or passion. Just a statement: "You are Faoii."

I brought my head up to snarl at the obvious, unhelpful reply, but Jade raised a hand, and I fell silent. Then, with a tune that I more felt than heard, her mind reached out, using that perfect, silver cord that had tied us together for as long as I could remember. And it *clicked*. All the things that I had felt and believed but had been afraid to say out loud filled the cold shadows of my heart and soul in a way that only Jade could understand.

You are Faoii. You do not run. You have never run before and Illindria would not have you run now.

As the thoughts came to me, unbidden, the air of those musty caverns suddenly smelled of freshly cut grass and jasmine flowers. It was like the cave was lit by a midsummer sun, though the firelight barely illuminated the worked stone and broken remnants of the Goddess's smiling face. Jade's unspoken words filled my heart. It was like feeling the Tapestry through my shield sister; a feeling that I'd gotten many times before from Jade but never with such clarity.

At the sound of that beautiful Cleroii's—no, not Cleroii; Preoii, as she should have always been—at her silent words, the Faoii Oath tumbled unrestrained from my beaming, unresisting lips. It was during those whispered phrases that I realized that I had not spoken the Oath since the Croeli occupation. And my new understanding of the Goddess and of Jade filled the unspoken gaps between the vows.

"I am Faoii. I am the harbinger of justice and truth."

You do not go to seek outside help because the Faoii fight alone. We have always worked alone. We shall finish this alone, as there are no others to wage this war.

"I am the strength of the weak and the voice of the silent."

We do not disappear into the night like dogs kicked by their masters. The Croeli have taken from us, and we shall fight back until we have nothing left to fight with.

"My blade is my arm, and as such is the arm of all people. Wherever I am, there will a weapon against injustice always be."

Running will not rid this plague from the world. You cannot allow it to spread behind you. You must act against it while you are near its source.

"And with this weapon, I will protect the weak and purge all evil in the land. I will be ready to perform my duty for the weak at all times."

We will not leave the sacred monastery and our fallen sisters' fantoii in the hands of our Croeli foe.

"And through this, I shall remember that all things are sacred and all souls worthwhile."

It is that strength that kept you here. It is that desire to strike back against the Croeli in any manner available to you that kept you from retreating. That fire in your heart.

"But my blade will be held above all, for it protects all, and shall be part of me."

You are the last to teach those that will follow. You are the voice that will educate the future, that will show these young ones what a Faoii is and what it means.

"For I am Faoii. My tongue will never forget the words of truth, for when I speak, then will the Goddess hear, and I am only Faoii in Her presence."

They need to hear the truth as it is meant to be told. They need to remember the voices that have been silenced.

"I am the Weaver of the Tapestry. I see the threads through all the world and guide them with the Goddess's eye. Above all, we are Faoii."

Yes, Lyn-Faoii. You understand. You have always understood. You cannot disappear into the night without one final strike. You cannot let these men tarnish the Tapestry without helping to guide its threads. You must release one final cry in the darkness to tell those that have tried to break us that we will not fall silently.

"Our blades will sing with the voice of every throat that has cried out against injustice and dance with the steps of every innocent child. And we will lead the choir, and the voices of our sword will deafen the ears of our enemies."

Why have you stayed all this time, Lyn-Faoii?

"For . . . I am Faoii."

Jade smiled in the dark and nodded. "Yes, Lyn. We are Faoii."

Two days later, I crawled back into the silence of the underground labyrinth with a smile that would have been frightening if anyone had been nearby to see. With a heart that was lighter than it had been in months, I hurried to the statue room. The other five stood at my approach.

"The dumb bastards have grown confident. They're not patrolling the halls or posting guards anymore. I even checked the rat tunnels and the alcoves. The traps have been removed. They're sure we're dead." Hastily, I drew a quick map of the monastery on the dirt floor. It was unnecessary. Everyone present had memorized it years before, but no one stopped me as the words continued to tumble out of my mouth in a rush.

"Everyone I saw was either wounded or drunk. There's talk of pushing north to meet with the rest of the force that's nearing the monasteries closer to the capital. But most of the men here aren't strong enough to make it yet. The Croeli are spread thin. If we can wipe out this group, the rest will be even weaker. We just have to strike before they mobilize."

Jade met my gaze with sparkling eyes. "All right, Faoii-Lyn. How do we end this?" The others nodded, waiting for my answer.

Faoii-Lyn. They called me Faoii-Lyn.

Smiling, I laid out my plans.

It was easier to sneak around the monastery when no one thought to look in the shadows, and the Croeli didn't seem to miss the oil that disappeared from the pantry or the grease that vanished from the smithy as we prepared for our final assault.

It took two nights to douse the monastery, and every terrifying and nerve-wracking minute dragged by with an impossible sluggishness. But we got it done.

The night after we had finished, Jade and I sent the young ones through the collapsed wall to the orangery.

"If we are not there by dawn, start running. Keep the fire and smoke at your back, and go until you can't go any farther. And remember always that you are Faoii." The girls clasped hands over invisible hilts in acknowledgment and turned toward the passage that led to the dry riverbed. Only Mei broke formation long enough to wrap her arms around my waist. I tried not to let her see the tears in my eyes as I hugged her back.

"I love you, Lyn."

"I love you too, Mei. You have always made me proud." Then Mei disappeared into the darkness of the maze.

"You will see her again, Lyn." Jade spoke quietly as we turned toward the chapel entrance. I smiled and blinked the tears from my eyes.

"We both will. When this is over, we're going to watch her dance."

That monastery lit like a candle. Jade and I had painstakingly blocked the exits leading outside. We set fire to the main corridors first. Then, scampering through the ceiling like rats on a sinking ship, we systematically boxed the Croeli in with traps and flame. The Croeli's surprised cries echoed through the smoke-filled corridors, and my heart *soared*.

When we had at last finished the grisly deed, Jade and I worked our way back toward the chapel. We'd left one door untouched, but we were smart enough to block the corridor leading up to it. We would have to crawl through the smoke-filled rafters to reach it, but I knew we could make it there, even in the dark. Our hidden passages would have to save our lives one more time.

I wish I'd foreseen more. I wish I'd known that one horrified and brutish Croeli had broken through the barricaded corridor and ran, burnt and screaming, toward the refuge of the outside world. Strips of charred, melted skin must have clung to his cheekbones as he drunkenly wove his way toward the unbarred door that would exit near the chapel.

I heard the screams before reaching the trapdoor that led down into the corridor, but the smoke had grown too thick, and it distorted the echoes that carried throughout the flaming structure. Between our strangled coughing and the distorted screams of men further inside the building, it didn't occur to me to try and peer through the inky blackness of night and smoke to see if one dying man might be below. Why would it? How could I know that someone would make it that far?

Everything would've been different if I had only looked.

When my boots struck the heated metal of the warrior's charred pauldrons as I dropped from the ceiling, I couldn't help but cry out in surprise. My yell was nothing compared to the pain-filled, terrorized scream of the man beneath me, though, and his fear must have been double mine. It gave me enough time roll away, but both of our training kicked in immediately.

You have to give the Croeli one thing—they're quick on their feet. I rolled away from that beast with an agile grace at the same moment that Jade leapt down to assist me. She must have heard my cry. She must have been afraid when she couldn't see me. She must not have thought—only acted. She wanted to save me. And the Croeli, despite his injuries, had been well trained. His criukli whipped forward almost instantly.

I still remember how Jade's blood sizzled as it sprayed onto his heated breastplate.

Two edged disks sprouted from the man's throat, and only one was mine. Eternal Blade, Jade made a hell of a Faoii, even when she was hurt. The Croeli's death cry came out only as a wet gurgle when he collapsed onto the heated flagstones of the corridor.

I didn't stop to gather our weapons. I just took Jade in my arms and shouldered my way through the door.

The cool night air was like the breath of a Goddess song against my face when we got out of the burning monastery. I hugged Jade close to my chest and turned toward the chapel, casting a glance at the stars as I moved. It took me way too long to realize that they were dimmed by tears rather than smoke. But I kept my eyes focused upward as I staggered toward the chapel, afraid and unwilling to look down at the heavy burden in my arms. Jade's leg was a fleshy mound of blood and flayed skin, and my knees were weak with even the muted pain that rode the silver cord between us.

"You can leave me, Faoii-Lyn." Jade whispered into the crook of my neck between pained gasps. I ignored her and kept going, refusing to hear. But she just kept whispering. "Get to the girls. Get somewhere safe. The Goddess will watch over you. And . . ." She paused, wheezing in my arms. "Know that I will always love you."

Get to the girls.

Get somewhere safe.

The Goddess will watch over you.

I will always love you.

Go . . .

I love you . . .

Those words repeated themselves over and over again in my ear. Weak, but persistent. Again and again, Jade whispered her swan song as I made my way to the chapel.

It was only when I arrived at Illindria's statue that I realized that Jade was gone and the voice I was hearing was my own quiet whispers into a night that never responded.

I left Jade there, at the Goddess's bare feet. Carefully, as one puts a baby in a crib, I offered Jade to the Eternal One's everlasting embrace. When I knelt for one final prayer, the pain from Jade's criukli wound had already faded, and the silver ribbon had left a gaping, savage wound in my heart that was so, so much worse.

The prayer was short but powerful. Not that it mattered. All the prayers and tears in the world could never ease that cavernous wound left in my soul. When I rose again, I lifted my eyes to the Goddess's face—angry, hurt, and scared. I wanted answers. I wanted some sort of hope. Jade would have known what to say, what to look for.

My gaze fell on the fantoii in the War Watcher's hand.

"I didn't even think about it. I just snapped the Goddess's hand off and took it with me. The fingers had crumbled away before I found the urchins in the orangery, and the look of pride in their eyes when they saw it belted at my waist . . ." Lyn paused, and Kaiya was surprised to hear her chuckle. "I've never even used the bloody thing. But it's a symbol. And with it in hand, I've made more out of these crumbling walls than I think anyone ever expected from me." She sighed, looking down at the fantoii for a long minute.

"It's a symbol I've carried all this time, all this way. Mimi and Kiki asked to kiss it before they stepped onto the ship that took them away from here, and I let them do it. I've held this symbol high for years now, proud of it and all it represents. And I'm not even supposed to have it." She looked down at her hands for a moment, quietly contemplating. Kaiya thought that the younger girl was going to remain silent, her story concluded, but Lyn finally whispered, "she was supposed to be Preoii. I know that now. I think I knew it all along. I thought about telling her to start training under Preoii-Chin, but I knew that if she was Preoii instead of Cleroii, I would be assigned a different shield sister and I . . . I didn't want to lose her." Lyn fell silent, staring at the glittering sword. "Not that it mattered."

Kaiya watched the tears fall from Lyn's lowered eyes before she finally laid a dark hand on one shaking shoulder. Then, without preamble or thought to custom, Kaiya drew the grieving Faoii into a warm and empathetic hug.

18

Kaiya watched Lyn subtly change as they returned to the chamber where the "urchins" danced. Her eyes dried and her back straightened. By the time they arrived, there was no hint of the heartbroken girl that Kaiya had embraced only a few minutes before.

It was an impressive show, but Kaiya knew what she had to do. After all that Lyn had been through, she deserved an ascension—a true ascension, and Kaiya was the only Faoii in a hundred leagues who could grant it to her.

This was not as simple a thing as it seemed. Kaiya had never had a true ascension ceremony, had never heard the words except for those spoken in her own dark memories. Reaching back, she remembered what Preoii-Aleena had said, the distant whisper snaking through the buried thoughts of her broken home. Slowly, a calm filled Kaiya, and the busy room seemed somehow hushed.

Kaiya stopped, grasping Lyn's elbow with a steady hand. Lyn turned toward her, annoyance streaking her face, but when the young woman's dark eyes met with Kaiya's pale ones, there was a recognition and serenity that Kaiya doubted the other had felt since her experience in the now-abandoned chapel. Kaiya smiled.

"I recognize what you have been through, Faoii. And while you stand strong and fearless before those that follow you, I know the dread in your heart. Do not fear, Faoii, for as long as your blade still sings, there will be justice. You must tell the world what has happened to our people and to be wary of the horned god that is trying to take hold of our lands. You must protect them as you have protected those you love, both here and in the ruins that have since fallen. You are strong, Faoii. I, and the Goddess, have faith in you." Kaiya placed Lyn's hand on her fantoii's hilt. "Take your sword, Lyn-Faoii. And with it, take your place as Faoii-Lyn."

Faoii-Lyn drew her sword, and for the first time, the blade *sang*. Its cry was that of angels, crystalline and perfect. All movement in the room stopped, and the song expanded outward like water spilling over the rim of a pitcher. The walls reverberated with its melody. Kaiya's heart rose and clenched with the sound. She wanted to weep. *This is what ascension is.*

Moments passed before the note finally faded. Released of its spell, Kaiya and Lyn found themselves able to move and turned to discover an entire room of eyes set on them. The reverence they saw there was almost overwhelming. "Thank you," Lyn whispered. "Thank you." She took a moment to compose herself before speaking again, louder this time. "Come on. Let's get something to eat."

The shocked awe of the surrounding women dissipated quickly, and ladies rushed to set up several long tables. The benches on either side filled almost immediately, and Kaiya was surprised to find how many people were actually here. Several hundred women filled the hall and, if Lyn was to be believed, this was only a third of the full force that had come for training over the last two years. The women sat quickly, brushing shoulders with one another, but the head of the table remained unoccupied, and Lyn took her place with an air of pride and authority. A space was quickly made for Kaiya as well, and she sat, her shield resting at her feet.

Here, however, the hospitality of Lyn's band ended. Emery stood awkwardly behind Kaiya's chair, and Tendaji flashed an amused smile from where he leaned against the back wall. Kaiya glanced to Lyn. The vulnerable girl that had told her the sorrowful story was gone. Lyn, in front of the women gathered at the table, kept up the appearance of an unbroken leader.

"I could order them to make a place for your…guests, Faoii-Kaiya. But that wouldn't really make you look like a reckonable force, would it?" The whisper was soft but stern. "I assume that's why you're here. To band us together?"

"It is." Kaiya frowned at the younger girl. Her face was completely expressionless. Was this some sort of test?

Lyn smiled. "Thought so. If you've got a plan, I'll listen. But if you want to *lead*, you'd better start now. No use in us having a power struggle later if you can't even get these girls to clear a place setting." There was the faintest hint of pleasure in Lyn's voice as she spoke. Kaiya set her jaw.

Damn if she wasn't right, though. At the moment, Kaiya was an outsider. Despite offering ascension and proving to be at least equal to Lyn in the Faoii Order, the hierarchy of their faith meant nothing to the women gathered here. For all that Lyn had done, these women were not Faoii. The strongest person they'd ever seen was a teenage girl who secretly doubted her own ability. They needed to see the true power of a Faoii warrior—the true strength of will and blade. Only then would they willingly unite with the growing army that was training under Faoii-Eili in the north.

Clenching her jaw, Faoii-Kaiya spoke in an iron voice, putting all the power of the Faoii into her words. "Clear a space for my companions." The command rang across the hall, and all conversation stopped. A sea of eyes moved between her and Lyn, seeking guidance. The silky-haired Faoii only stared back, her face deliberately expressionless. Slowly, the eyes turned back to Kai. As the silence lengthened, Kaiya hardened her glare. "I will not issue a command twice."

She did not even need to raise her voice this time. The room was so quiet and the words so laced with power a deaf person could have heard them. Another moment passed before a woman about halfway down the table rose to her feet.

"Faoii, we will not." Kaiya was surprised at the strength of the woman's voice, and more than a little perturbed at having her orders blatantly challenged. So much for an easy power shift.

Kaiya rose, planting both hands on the table as she locked eyes with the offender. The glare she shot across the table was filled with enough war magic to make a hunting dog falter. The other woman's eyes shook in fear for a moment, but she steeled them quickly, again taking Kaiya by surprise. Other women began to rise as well, turning toward Kaiya with steely gazes. Their voices rose sharply against the silence.

"No man has ever sat at this table. And no man will unless Faoii-Lyn demands it."

"You're lucky we let you sit among us at all, being untested."

"You don't look so big yourself. I bet we could teach you your place."

"You say you're Faoii. Let's see you prove it."

That broke the dam. Suddenly a dozen women rushed at Kaiya, filled with pride and the untested belief that they were warriors. Kaiya could almost hear Tendaji's chuckle behind her, his previous words coming back to her. *Don't say I didn't warn you.* Emery jerked behind Kaiya, but she had just enough time to throw him a warning glance. If she were to prove herself, she had to handle this alone. Emery backed up to stand next to Tendaji just as the first attacker reached Kai.

Kaiya spun, catching the nearest young woman with a double-fisted blow to the stomach. She doubled over, and Kaiya caught her around the waist, lifting and throwing her bodily across the table. The terrified girl collided heavily with one of the women that was trying to climb over the wood. They both crashed to the ground.

Another woman, wearing a sturdy leather jerkin, lunged toward Kaiya's stomach with a short dagger in each hand. Kaiya crouched low, grasping her shield. She yanked it upward with a single clean jerk, brushing the daggers out of the woman's grasp. They clattered to the floor. With another swift movement, Kaiya shoved the shield into the now-weaponless attacker, and she fell into the arms of those behind her.

Kaiya ducked as a platter was launched at her head. Crouching, she braced her shield against the floor. Then, leaping upward, she kicked a girl behind her in the chin as she somersaulted over the bronze dome, catching another woman in the shoulder with a booted foot. Using the momentum of her now-bowed back,

Kaiya pulled the shield up after her and brought it crashing down across two other women's outstretched arms.

Kaiya spun again and again, lashing out with arms, elbows, knees, feet, and shield, but never once did she raise her fantoii. Her battle cries filled the hall, and the women around her fell, bloodied and broken, but alive.

At last only Kaiya stood among the trembling bodies of defeated girls. She studied them with a knowing eye.

"You are all very brave. But being Faoii is not simply showing courage or even knowing how to hold a knife. A Faoii is more than a girl in armor, more than a warrior with a battle cry. Faoii-Lyn has taught you well to believe in yourselves, and that's a good first step. But you can be better than what you are. You can be true Faoii." She circled around, looking at each woman in turn, her eyes sharp and her hands steady. They stared back at her in awe—even those that were on the flat of their backs beneath her. At last she met Faoii-Lyn's eyes, and the dark orbs were strong with pride and defiance. Kaiya's voice rose in pitch.

"We are better than any regular fighter. We are more than just women hiding behind the strength of husbands and brothers. We are Faoii. We are the harbingers of justice and truth. We are the strength of the weak and the voice of the silent."

Lyn's eyes shone as she stood, and her voice matched Kaiya's. "My blade is my arm, and as such is the arm of all people. Wherever I am, there will a weapon against injustice always be. And with this weapon, I will protect the weak and purge all evil in the land."

Kim and Mae stood as well, and their voices joined the chorus.

"I will be ready to perform my duty for the weak at all times. And through this, I shall remember that all things are sacred and all souls worthwhile." Others joined, and the women on the floor began to rise. "But my blade will be held above all, for it protects all, and shall be a part of me. For I am Faoii. My tongue will never forget the words of truth, for when I speak, then will the Goddess hear, and I am only Faoii in Her presence."

Those that were not fisting their hands one above the other were making the inverted triangle sign of Illindria, their eyes shining and their voices rising. "We are the Weavers of the Tapestry. We see the threads through all the world and guide them with the Goddess's eye. Above all, we are Faoii. Our blades will sing with the voice of every throat that has cried out against injustice and dance with the steps of every innocent child. We will lead the choir, and the voices of our swords will deafen the ears of our enemies." The final statement was a battle cry all its own: "For we are Faoii!"

The energy of the room exploded outward, shaking the table and the wooden plates. Tears flowed readily, and those that had fought against Kaiya kneeled at her feet, begging for forgiveness. Kaiya rested her hands on their shoulders and cheeks as she forgave her would-be attackers, using what she'd learned from Faoii-Eili to will the power of the Cleroii through her palms. The bruises she had caused began to heal.

When Kaiya finally approached the table again, Faoii-Lyn had stepped down from her place at its head. She winked as Kaiya passed her. "I thought you were just going to challenge me. That was way more fun." Tendaji and Emery took their places at the table, unmolested. Then, with the dignity and grace that became a Faoii leader, Kaiya took her place in the high-backed seat. The entire room stared at her with a sense of unity that they had not realized they were missing. Kaiya smiled, nodding to herself.

We are Faoii, indeed.

19

The Faoii enclave was bursting with activity. Every day, Kaiya, Lyn, Tendaji, and Emery pushed the newest Faoii Order to a higher standard. Those that were not in sparring practice or dedicating themselves to prayer were forging their own blades and crafting their own leather armor. It was hard work, and months passed with frustrated tears and disappointment as blades failed inspection and women's arms faltered in fatigue, but there was never any sense of despair. The women, under Kaiya's steady and relentless gaze, did not accept failure. For they were Faoii now, and failure was no longer an option.

The women who worked the streets continued to seek empty eyes and hearts, but now with a different purpose. They had something real with which to fill that void: hope. Salvation. The ranks in the enclave grew. Soon the two warehouses were filled beyond capacity, and an adjacent warehouse (previously owned by a trader who was only too eager to sell it to a group of terrifying women with glistening blades) was turned into a barracks. This new warehouse had the added bonus of a cellar that, after some renovations, gave access to the sewers, and thus access to most of the town without the women ever having to use a door. Even with the added space and bunks, however, sleep could only be achieved in shifts. Night and day, there were continual battle dances, constant prayers, and the steady, never-ceasing clang of hammers on anvils.

Even men came to join the army, seeking a world and a strength that had been stripped away by the Croeli. The Goddess was never mentioned outside the enclave's walls, but Her presence was still hidden there, under the fog. And the people felt it, longed for it, and followed its pull. All found themselves at the enclave.

Through the months of torturous preparation for a war that everyone felt was coming but few talked about, Kaiya was always there. There was never a new batch of recruits that did not watch her steady fantoii dance through the air as she showed them the basic steps of sword fighting. There was never an Oath that did not carry her voice in it, or a lost and uncertain girl that could not look up and see her glinting breastplate as a source of inspiration. The final laces of a leather jerkin were never tied without her scanning the detail work, nor was a newly finished sword ever sheathed without her arm first testing its edge.

Kaiya was like Illindria Herself—everywhere at once and never faltering. She would disappear for possibly a half hour at a time to collapse onto the solitary cot that the soldiers had set aside for her, but she was always back among the others almost immediately.

Weeks passed in this manner, and while everyone looked to Kaiya for guidance and strength (there was no longer any doubt that she was the leader here), there was no denying that she could not have done it on her own. The silky-haired Lyn was always nearby, pairing soldiers (men and women alike now) to others that complemented them. Her eye was keen, and the ranks grew stronger as soldiers fought back-to-back, dancing their graceful circles of deadly beauty, their songs rising through the air like silver motes.

Tendaji taught those that were not suited for sword fighting how to ease through shadows like water through sand, training their innocent eyes to aim for the liver or kidneys with precise, deadly strikes. On the few occasions that Kaiya slipped away from the crowded warehouse in order to travel the streets (they seemed so calm despite the growing energy that engulfed the cobblestones), she could almost feel Tendaji's pupils following her on the rooftops, oozing their way between beams of moonlight. While she could not prove it, she wondered if these tests were not Tendaji's way of protecting her—*as though she needed protection!*—as well as a way of testing the pupils' newfound abilities. They moved like true Croeli infiltrators in the darkness. She never saw them, and never knew whether they noticed her quiet smile at his success.

As it turned out, Emery was a master bowman. Fletching and bow making were quickly added to the already overflowing roster of daily tasks. Kaiya, who had never learned the skill personally, worked tirelessly to perfect her techniques. If there was ever a spare minute that did not require her presence with another soldier, she could be found practicing her skills in their makeshift archery range.

Meanwhile, Lyn's scouts scurried across the landscape, seeking word of opposing soldiers. The Croeli's ethereal army was terrifying. Reports of enemy soldiers would come from the south, near the Danhaid Tribes, then from the remains of the Monastery of the Ivy Helm far to the west a week later. Tendaji said the Croeli had called the phenomenon "Blinking," and though Lyn made fun of "Croeli lack of originality" on several occasions, the term stuck. Reports continued to pile in as the Croeli army Blinked across the landscape in a dizzying, terrifying frenzy. No one could accurately report their numbers or locations, much to Lyn's constant ire.

"The information is coming from everywhere, but we can't even tell whether my girls are reporting the same battalion over and over again or if there really are three dozen armies all told." Lyn sawed at the slab of meat that could possibly pass for a steak, stabbing at the individual pieces irritably. "The reports are all similar, but there's no way to determine whether they're the same soldiers. If only the bastards would stop jumping around the country like some sort of deranged bullfrog." Exasperated, Lyn threw down her eating utensils and leaned back in her chair. "And now the girls have been stumbling across tonicloran, too."

Tendaji tensed. "Tonicloran? Where?"

"That's the thing! Everywhere. In towns, in fields, in village carts. When the girls asked, people seemed genuinely unaware that the most dangerous toxin known to man was so close at hand. Most of them weren't even aware that they were transporting it. They had just been paid to move goods, and they did." She shook her head. "I guess some people will take any job they can if money's scarce enough."

Kaiya looked around at the half-dressed women of the enclave, but didn't mention the irony of Lyn's statement. "If they're transporting it," she said instead, "they must know who it's going to."

"They don't, though. They drop the seeds off with other farmers, in random fields, in dirt patches near the road. They just . . . scatter tonicloran and they're not even aware of what they're doing." She cracked her knuckles impulsively. "It's in the fields, too. Growing wild. Look." She threw a sprig onto the table. Emery and Tendaji drew away from it almost on reflex, but Kaiya leaned forward, studying it through narrowed eyes.

"It looks like the chinol sprig on the Goddess statue back home." She reached out to pick up the innocent-looking plant, but Tendaji stopped her with a quick jerk of her arm. Kaiya put her hand back in her lap and refocused on Lyn.

The other Faoii snarled at the broad, flat leaves resting on the table. "We're damned lucky no one cut their finger on a thorn or something and died before making it home. Most of the girls didn't even know what it was. But it's growing in the places that the Croeli armies go repeatedly. Or at least, I think they go there repeatedly. It might be a dozen different groups jumping there one after the other." She slammed her fist on the table, frustrated. "Blades, I wish we knew how they did that!"

She cast an annoyed glance at Tendaji, who spread his hands. "I wish I had that information. I'm sorry." Lyn released a frustrated sigh.

Tendaji turned his attention to the plant, his eyes calculating. "For what it's worth, I doubt that Thinir's army is using tonicloran. There are no reports of melting skin or blisters or cauterized wounds from his soldiers' criukli. It is troublesome that it is growing wild, though. That is not safe for anyone."

"Didn't the Preoii forbid tonicloran ages ago?" Lyn asked heatedly. "I thought they destroyed all of that rubbish after too many people died trying to use it for 'enlightenment' or some such nonsense. Why is it showing up now?"

Tendaji frowned. "I don't know. But whoever is spreading it cannot have good intentions." As he spoke, Kaiya's mind worked to drudge up a conversation from long ago, nearly forgotten amongst things she'd once considered more important than her studies. She jolted out of her reverie when Tendaji nudged her shoulder. "Are you okay, Kai?"

"Yeah. Sorry. Just thinking. Cleroii-Belle once said that tonicloran was not made for this world, but for the one we reach after death. Part of the Goddess's world. If . . ." She paused, trying to put her thoughts into words. "If the Croeli are jumping from place to place, they have to be traveling through *somewhere*. Maybe that's where they go. Illindria can see everything. Her world connects to every part of ours. If they are finding a way to Her side, they could reappear anywhere they wanted to. Maybe they're bringing the tonicloran back with them and don't realize it."

Lyn's almond-shaped eyes narrowed. "Well, that's crazy." She turned to Emery. "Why are the pretty ones always crazy?"

Tendaji shot her a warning glance before turning back to his sister. "Kai, even if what you're saying was possible, there is no way that Thinir and his men are accessing the Tapestry. No deity would allow such a transgression."

Kaiya refrained from biting her lip. "I know, I know. I was just rambling. But if it were possible . . . you said that those who Blink come back . . . different. Without light behind their eyes. Would you be able to look at the Eternal Tapestry and come back completely whole?"

The table fell quiet for a moment before Lyn at last stood up with unnecessary force. "You're all imbeciles. Burn that thing and let's get moving. We've got shield instruction in five." She stalked away from them, still muttering under her breath. Kaiya watched as Tendaji set a candle to the tonicloran stalk. Its broad leaves wilted as Kaiya stood to leave as well.

20

The months of training hardened Kaiya. Her already feline legs and arms were like carved ebony now. So dedicated was she to each of those that swore themselves to the Goddess and her fantoii that she felt neither weariness nor hunger. Instead, there was only the burning desire to give these people the world they deserved—one where they could make decisions for themselves without fear of Croeli slithering through the shadows.

It was Tendaji that finally posed a question one night, crouching next to Kaiya as she pounded dutifully on a newly tempered sword. "When was the last time you slept? Or ate?" Kaiya's blows faltered for a moment as she realized that she did not know. Her brother released the slightest chuckle.

"Pretty little Kai. What good will you be to us if you do not take care of your most basic needs?" Kaiya did not respond, and

Tendaji offered his hand to her, pulling her to her feet. As though her realization had made it true, Kaiya's head swam, and the world tilted. With a graceful step to one side, Tendaji positioned himself between his sister and the ever-working soldiers, giving her the time she needed to steady herself.

Kaiya forced her limbs to still as she made her way to the only private chamber in the enclave. She had originally been against the idea of wasting space on her own bedroom, but Tendaji had dissuaded her from bunking with the other soldiers.

"If you want to keep up your appearance as a leader, you must always remind the soldiers that you are above them in rank. Letting your men—or women—see you sleep is giving them an opportunity to see your weakness. No one must see you as merely human." He paused, considering. "Also, you drool in your sleep. It's hardly flattering."

Kaiya had understood his words at the time and had accepted them, though the drool comment had elicited an annoyed glare from her and a far-too-innocent look from him. Now she was grateful for solitude as she leaned her head against the wall of her sparsely decorated quarters. Tendaji helped her unlace the leather straps of her breastplate. "When is the third quadrant due for their disarm examination?" she asked without lifting her head.

"Nine hours. I will make sure you're awake before then." Kaiya smiled at the wall.

"I know I don't say this often enough, but thank you, Tendaji."

Tendaji smiled as he removed her breastplate and pointed her to the bed. "I was never there for you when you were growing up. You did not need me then and you don't need me now. But I'm glad you let me stay, anyway."

Kaiya started to reply, but he shook his head and turned toward the door. Then he was gone, and the room was quiet.

Kaiya tried to convince herself to stand so that she could remove her leather armor, but the night had already enveloped her. A soft breeze blew in from the tiny slit of a window that the sparse room offered, and as Kaiya's eyes fluttered closed, she could just barely see the moon peeking out from behind the building across the street. She was tired enough that her eyes were evidently playing tricks on her, because it seemed like the shadows on the roof were actually moving to hide behind the looming chimney. The silliness of this thought carried Kaiya into a peaceful slumber.

Kaiya jerked awake at a crashing sound. It reverberated off the walls of the enclave like a great bronze bell. Kaiya shook her head until it faded. Disoriented by half-faded dreams and the passage of unknown hours, she scrambled up, belting her fantoii to her side even as she bolted into the enclave proper. Already a mob had formed next to one of the warehouse's massive doors. Kaiya pushed her way through the crowd until she came upon Lyn, who was crouched next to a small, terrified girl. The child was speaking rapidly to the older Faoii, and Kaiya waited until the narration had dissolved into quiet sobs before turning her attention to her lieutenant. "Faoii-Lyn, report." Lyn rose quickly and fisted her hands.

"She is from the next town over, Silentbell. Our activities have gained notice. The brothel there has been attacked. Nine women had their throats slit and their eyes cut out. The intruders made it into the brothel without alerting the women who were making their rounds on the street." There was a sudden clamor in the room as hundreds of voices fought to drown out the others.

"No one else was injured?" Kaiya's voice cut through the uproar.

"No. Just our sleeping girls."

"How did this one make it out?"

Lyn leaned down again to receive the girl's answer. Several minutes later, she rose again.

"She's trained as an infiltrator. She was hiding in the rafters. The poor girl watched what happened to her mother and the other women but was not able to stop the attack. When the Croeli left, she snuck through the sewers and then swam through the sewage canal until she could cut across the alleyways to get here." Kaiya raised an eyebrow, impressed at the girl's resourcefulness.

"Did she see any other Faoii on the way here? Alive or dead?"

"No. But there would have been none along the route she took. She did listen, however. No alarm was sounded. If there were any other attacks, they haven't been reported yet."

Kaiya nodded, then turned at the sound of Tendaji's slight growl. "This is the work of Croeli scouts. It is not a full battalion, but we've obviously drawn attention. They have sent people to investigate."

Kaiya clenched her teeth. "How long until their superiors know our location?"

"Probably not for several days. Infiltrators will make kills of opportunity—like the slaughter of several sleeping Faoii—but they don't report until their task is complete. Chances are they won't send word until they've not only found our main head-quarters but can also give an accurate report of our numbers. However . . ." Tendaji furrowed his brow, thinking. Even through his false-facing, one could see his troubled features.

"What's wrong?" Lyn's whisper was only a ghost of sound, but the question was reflected on most of the surrounding soldiers' faces.

"If they're killing the girls in Silentbell, they've probably already determined that the center of operations is not there. The women there have outgrown their usefulness and are no longer worth watching."

"So they'll keep looking. If we're careful about how we leave the enclave, they won't be able to find us and will move on," Lyn said, shrugging one shoulder.

"That's possible." Tendaji lowered his voice and locked eyes with Kaiya. "Unless they left one Faoii alive so she could lead them here." Upon hearing this, the girl at his feet broke down into more sobs. Lyn tried to comfort her.

"It's not your fault, little one. You warned us. Now we can protect ourselves." She looked up to Kaiya, and the unasked question danced behind her eyes: *Right?*

Kaiya took a deep breath and squared her shoulders. When she spoke, she spoke with the full power of a Faoii leader.

"Take her to my room. Let her rest. Bring my breastplate back out with you." Lyn's face hardened into a battle-ready mask immediately, and she rose to obey. Kaiya turned to Tendaji. "Gather your best infiltrators. Take them through the cellar and out through the sewers. Let's see if we can't find out where these Croeli bastards are hiding before they can gather the information they want." He turned to leave, but Kaiya's voice caused him to turn back. "Tendaji. We will *not* let a single one escape to report their findings." Tendaji nodded once, his eyes shining in a frightening bloodlust. In moments he had picked a handful of recruits and ghosted out.

Next, Kaiya searched the crowd for Emery. He had, like her, evidently been sleeping and was just fastening the final strap of his leather bracers. He slung a quiver of arrows over one shoulder just as she caught his eye. "Harkins, take your archers through the cellar next. Wait at least a minute between sets and exit the sewers from as many different outlets as possible, but I want as many groups on as many rooftops as you can get within the hour." Emery saluted and clicked his heels together, then disappeared after Tendaji. A throng of bow-wielding warriors followed in his wake.

"The rest of you—if the Croeli are truly aware of our presence, and if they are aware that we're looking for them, it may not take them long to strike. Our scouts and archers will be able to give us some warning, but we must be ready in any case. This is not a full army we will face. They are only scouts; we both outnumber and outclass them. But whatever comes, we *will not* let them report back to their superiors." She cast her steely eyes over the crowd. "Prepare yourselves." Suddenly the mob of soldiers was in motion, militant and orderly as they armed themselves and formed ranks next to their shield mates. There was no sound except for the scrape of leather and metal.

Lyn returned with Kaiya's breastplate and began to strap it on with steady grace. "The girl is resting, though her fear keeps her from sleeping. Mei and Kim are with her."

"Thank you. Did you barricade the window?" Kaiya felt Lyn's hands stop their task.

"The win—?" Lyn turned on her heel just as a shrill scream erupted from the bedroom. It was cut silent almost immediately.

In that moment, the enclave exploded into chaos. The high windows of the warehouse shattered. Wood splinters rained down, and grappling hooks caught on the window frames. Kaiya's breastplate clattered to the floor as Lyn sprinted across the room toward the scream's ghostly echo. Men and women braced themselves and faced the various exits in the chamber just as the main door leading to the barracks crashed open.

"They're not scouts! They're everywhere! They were just trying to draw us ou—" The woman's frantic cries dissolved into gurgles as an arrow sprouted from her throat, its iron tip protruding just below her chin. Kaiya spun to the window behind her, catching a glimpse of a solitary bowman on the roof across the street.

"Get your shields up! Watch for arrows from the windows!" Kaiya's barked orders pierced the hall. She snatched a longbow from the wall nearby and drew a bead on their attacker. An arrow from the east caught him first and he toppled off the roof. Kaiya grinned. At least some of her archers had made it to their positions.

"How long have they been watching us?" someone growled.

"Probably weeks." The whisper that drifted back shook a little. "There must have been a miscommunication. I bet those girls in Silentbell weren't supposed to die so soon. We weren't supposed to get a warning. That little girl saved our lives." Kaiya grimaced as she let loose an arrow through another window.

I saw them. Those shadows on the roof across the street. I saw them. And I didn't do a damned thing. She suspected that the Croeli posted next to her bedroom had been sent to kill her specifically. *If their attack had started even a little earlier, they would have killed m in my sleep. And that little girl would still be alive.* Kaiya shook the hurtful thought away, trying to expel a raw pain that was beginning to draw between her eyebrows. A great bell sounded in her ears. It took longer to fade this time. With a scowl, Kaiya released another arrow just as the windows darkened.

A dozen forms blocked the moonlight, crouching in the now-splintered frames. Their ghostly silhouettes were greeted with the chilling battle cry of a Faoii army. The shadows showed no fear and offered no response except for releasing a dozen small, steel balls that tumbled from their hands. The room exploded into blue smoke as the canisters hit the ground.

The makeshift bombs were meant to cause confusion as the ghostly Croeli leapt silently into the room. But the Faoii army held their ranks, blinking the inky smoke from their eyes. As the Croeli broke through the mist and reached the formations, they were cut down quickly. They never even released a scream.

Kaiya was proud that her army held their lines despite the disconcerting smog that broke up shapes and sounds. She urged them on and yelled in their shared triumph with every darting shape she cut down. Her blade was slick with oozing gore, and bodies littered the floor at her feet. The battle cries of her army filled the air. But the dark shapes from the windows continued to block out the moonlight in a constant stream, and the Faoii formations began to break under the enemy's swift, relentless attacks. Obviously trained for the smoky conditions, the Croeli darted from the fog to strike before ducking back into obscurity. While their blades mostly connected with the interlocking shields of the Faoii forces, the close quarters of the warehouse made traditional shield mates ineffective. The line began to falter.

Kaiya spun as a shape darted to her right. She spun again as it came from the left. Trying to keep her back away from the increasingly frightful foes, Kaiya turned again and again, making her way to the nearest wall. Finally, she saw a clear silhouette and struck out with her fantoii. Its blade caught him cleanly through the middle and came away coated in crimson. But too late did she see the second black shape dart from the side. A burning agony sprouted from her ribcage. She twisted toward this new assailant, but a third shadow sprang from the smoke again. Her leg buckled as he drove his criukli into her calf.

Kaiya landed heavily on one knee, still lashing out into the darkness with her flashing blade. They were easier to see now.

"Keep your formation! The smoke is clearing!" Her stout command came out with more strength than she felt she had. But there was the sudden sound of wooden and bronze shields locking into place. She grinned through her pain. These were Faoii.

A Croeli darted past her to the right, sprinting toward the battle lines. Kaiya lunged from her kneeling position and caught him in the small of the back. He fell heavily, and his blood pooled around his still-twitching limbs. Her victory was short-lived, however, as the punctured muscles beneath her ribs shifted and her vision became black splotches on a red background. The room wheeled, and the blood-splattered floor rose up to meet her.

Her fantoii clattered away, ringing like a bell in her head. The sound was louder now, more persistent. Kaiya tried to catch herself, but the pain blocked out everything. She could only tumble forward, one arm clenched to her side.

Kaiya never hit the slick, bloody beams. With a disorienting jerk, she was stopped in her tumble as a strong, protective arm wrapped around her chest and pulled her forcefully backward to the wall.

"Kai? Kaiya!" Tendaji's voice rose to a frantic pitch somewhere behind her. She felt his heartbeat in her ear, and it slowly drowned out the bell that was knocking around inside her skull.

"Tendaji?" Her tongue was thick and inconvenient. "Tendaji . . .

you're supposed to be out—"

"They were already waiting for us. We couldn't sneak up on them, so we retreated. Emery's men are picking them off one by one…" Kaiya's head swam, and her brother's voice faded. "Damn it, Kaiya! Stay awake!" Her entire body was jostled. "Come on, Kai!"

"The bells, Tendaji. I can't hear . . ."

"Fight them, Kai! Please!" Kaiya could hear the fear in the pitch of his voice, could feel his heartbeat quicken in alarm. She fought to obey.

After what felt like an eternity, Kaiya forced her heavy eyelids open. At first all she saw was flashing silver, and it sang with the heavenly voice of an angel. Then, as the pain regained control, everything became visible with shocking clarity. The world shifted in her vision, changing constantly as images superimposed themselves on top of one another.

The smoke had mostly cleared. Behind her, Tendaji was crouched, one arm still wrapped protectively around her torso, cradling her to his chest. His broken wings were lifted in shattered glory, and his amber eyes shone with a frightening intensity as he growled at those that tried to come against her. In his hand, her fantoii danced like a firefly, singing like an angel in twilight. *Singing? It's singing for him. It was supposed to be his blade all along.* Despite everything, Kaiya was suddenly amazed by the intricacies of the world. That she would find the correct blade for a brother she'd never known in a monastery that did not think the Croeli still existed… She drifted away with the thought, but Tendaji shook her awake again. "Keep your eyes open, Kai!" She fought to refocus.

The battle scene that spread out over the open floor of the

warehouse was frightening. Eyeless, chained warriors with broken, detached movements threw themselves against the flowing swords of golden angels. Even with their bound and bloodied limbs, however, their blades tore the angels down with a brutal efficiency.

But her soldiers were still in formation.

As the soldiers clashed against their Croeli foe, a brutal cry cut through the room as though it had been silent. Kai tried to stand but could only swing her head toward the roar. Lyn was suddenly there, bursting with a fiery glory from the locked shields of her Faoii sisters. Her blood-soaked, burning fantoii released the battle cry of a thousand demons as she slashed downward at a Croeli, severing his arm with a single stroke. The fantoii's cry rose an octave as she spun and skewered another man's throat, her flaming wings blurring as she moved. Then, Lyn's shieldless left arm shot outward, and three of the bladed disks imbedded themselves in a Croeli skull across the room. The Faoii's eyes were feline and ferocious when they scanned the area, piercing and beautiful despite their fury.

Next to Kaiya, Tendaji raised Kaiya's sword, and its song rose in pitch. The chorus of the two blades was the most beautiful and terrifying thing Kaiya had ever heard. And with it, her own throat swelled in a song of its own.

Kaiya had never heard of a Preoii song like the one she released that bloody night. It twisted and flowed with the fantoii's chorus, beautiful and haunting at the same time. It stretched and pulled at the determination, pride, faith, and unity that bound the Faoii army—and magnified it a thousandfold. The hearts of her soldiers nearly burst as they released their battle cries and pressed forward. Somewhere far away, a single note cracked out from the rooftops.

As the sound of splitting bronze faded, everything seemed to break at once. For the first time, the Croeli showed fear, and they turned to make their escape through the high windows. Some dropped suddenly from wounds that had hitherto not affected their stride, and they crawled toward the sanctuary of the outside world. But they never made it to their ropes before the Faoii were upon them.

The night was composed of screams.

When the last of the Croeli had died and the battle fervor had faded, Kaiya's song continued, shifting from the battle hymn to a softer, healing melody. All around her, wounds began to stitch themselves shut, and bruised or bloodied Faoii began to stand with the help of their shield mates and friends. People tried not to look at the dead women that remained broken at their feet, and instead chose to rejoice in the adrenaline-filled minutes that followed their first victory.

Eventually, as the wounds of her army dwindled into little more than scrapes and bruises, Kaiya turned the song to her own injures. Her broken flesh mended and the bleeding slowed, but as it did, Kaiya's voice finally faltered. She released a trembling breath as bone-weary, leaden fatigue crept into her limbs. With difficulty, she fought her way to her feet. Tendaji, no longer appearing as a broken angel to her eyes, had the sense not to help her up in front of the unascended, but he stood close by, nonetheless. Once she was standing, Kaiya forced her body to remain erect and steady despite her pounding head and blurred vision. When she spoke, the words were forceful and concise.

"Faoii, spread into the streets. If a single Croeli bastard escaped, I want him found. Someone find Harkins and send him here for his full report. Go." The soldiers vacated quickly, their steps in perfect unison. There were no sounds of pain or anguish, and Kaiya was surprised despite herself. Was it possible for a non-Preoii to issue a healing song of that magnitude?

She must have imagined the almost familiar voice and its response. *Ah, but you are Preoii now, aren't you?*

When the final Faoii had made her way into the street, the warehouse was deathly silent. Only Kaiya, Tendaji, and Lyn remained. Kaiya swiveled her head around to assess the damage, but her vision swam. Finally, her eyes roamed over a solitary figure standing to one side, hunched and shaking in the gloom. Kaiya moved toward it, but stumbled. Tendaji caught her and helped her to rebalance.

"Faoii-Lyn." The dark shape just barely moved its head in response. "Report."

"There are thirty-six Faoii dead in this room. Two more are in the bedroom. And . . ." The shape looked down, unable to finish. Kaiya shook her head once, twice, and willed her vision to clear. When it did, her heart wrenched in her chest.

Faoii-Lyn knelt there. No longer a howling warrior with fiery wings, but instead a broken human girl with a disheveled braid and teary eyes. Long strands of silky hair fell across her face and lay over the ashen corpse of Mei-Faoii. The shaft had been removed, but Kaiya could still see the entry wound of a single arrow in the young girl's forehead. Dark purple spider webs spread over her pale skin where the poison had left its mark, causing the area around the eyes to swell. Faoii-Lyn had not been able to completely shut them, and two dark orbs stared, unseeing, at the ceiling.

"Faoii-Lyn . . ." Kaiya took another step toward the grieving girl, but she could not will her legs to support her. They buckled again, and Tendaji caught her. With a worried glance, he finally gave up on custom and draped one of Kaiya's arms across his shoulders. Kaiya could only stare at Lyn, willing all the emotions she felt to color her face.

After a long time, Faoii-Lyn buried Mei's face in her chest and raised her eyes to Kaiya, seeking comfort. Instead, she saw Kaiya's trembling stance and bloody armor, and Lyn's face broke with shame.

"I did this to you. I didn't finish belting on your breastplate. I was supposed to be your shield sister . . ." Her voice cracked, and she sank wearily to the floor, still hugging her sister's corpse to her chest. "I have failed at all of the things that I was meant to do as Faoii. I am sorry."

Kaiya broke away from Tendaji and made her way to her lieutenant so she could lay a hand on the girl's shoulder.

"There is no shame in what you've done this day, Faoii-Lyn." Lyn only hung her head in response. The silence that followed spread into eternity.

Finally, Lyn's broken, almond-eyed gaze rose until it bored into Kaiya's skull. The rage and fire in those shadowed orbs crackled in the blood-soaked evening, and Kaiya realized that the fury and power in them was real, not borne of the visions she did not understand. Lyn's voice was hard and cold.

"You will stop these Croeli bastards?"

Kaiya nodded. "I give you my word."

Lyn looked down at her sweet sister's swollen, purple face one more time before lifting her eyes and brushing away tears with angry determination. She rose steadily to face Kaiya.

"From here on, wherever you go, I'm coming with you."

The next few hours swirled around Kaiya in a confused jumble. Emery's report. *The archers were hit the hardest. Eighty-seven dead.*

One hundred twenty-seven Faoii to bury.

Soldiers carried in the bodies of those that had fallen. The Faoii lined the walls; the Croeli were heaped upon each other.

Two hundred ninety-two Croeli. They'd been sent to destroy us completely.

But they failed. It was at a great cost, but we have earned this victory.

The others broke after the one on top of the watchtower fell. He was creepy. Too still. Ghostlike.

Faoii-Kaiya, will you offer a prayer?

A room full of dead. Tears and lamentation. Oaths and sworn vengeance. Pride. Strength. Determination.

The soldiers must sleep. Burials will begin tomorrow.

Faoii-Kaiya, are you well?

Thank you, Faoii-Kaiya. Your song saved those of us that were at death's door. Goddess bless you.

You have led us to this victory. We will follow you anywhere.

Prayers and Oaths. An order to rest. Cots set up when the barracks filled. Exhausted soldiers lying prone on the floor.

Bless you. Bless you.

Bless you.

Then silence.

Kai, can you hear me? A shake. *Kaiya?*

The people around her continued their sickening dance in Kaiya's vision. The firelight hurt her eyes. She tried to respond,

but her tongue was heavy in her throat. She tried to stand up—
When did I sit down? —but the room tilted. She felt nauseated. Hot.
She shivered as she tried to get her bearings. *Where is the fire coming
from?* She was on fire. She had to be. But she couldn't even muster
the strength to scream.

Emery, bring that torch here.

She clenched her teeth and bit back nausea as her leathers were
peeled away from her sticky, sweat-slick skin. Why weren't they
putting the fire out?

Goddess—she's been poisoned!

Emery, get a clean blanket on her cot. Bring water.

Suddenly, Kaiya was floating. The heartbeat again. Was that a
bell in the distance? At least it was far away now. Quiet.

Tendaji! The Cailivale watch has been alerted. They're coming now.

*Deal with them, Lyn. Tell them what has happened here. Let the word
spread. Others will come to the call.*

What about Kai?

We'll take care of her. Go.

Kaiya floated. The bells receded and a song took their place.
Quiet. Soothing. Kai had heard that song before. When?

Preoii-Aleena was there, singing a gentle melody. Her hand on
Kaiya's forehead was cool and soft. The song drifted to Kaiya
from across time and space. It was something she remembered from
long ago.

Pretty little Kaiya, Kaiya . . . Pretty little sweetling.

Pretty little Kaiya, Kaiya . . . May your pain always be fleeting.

Pretty little Kaiya, Kaiya . . .

Pretty little Kaiya, Kaiya . . .

21

When Kaiya woke up, her return to consciousness felt like swimming through deep water. Even when she surfaced, her skin was still clammy with salty residue and her limbs felt weighted. The chilled air coming through the open window made her shiver.

Tendaji was there, his back turned toward her simple cot as he hummed a familiar tune under his breath. But there was an agitated edge to the sound. Worry.

Kaiya finally found the strength to speak. "Tendaji." Her thready whisper sounded almost alien. "How long...?" Tendaji spun toward her, his pale blue eyes flooding with relief even as he set his lips into a grim line.

"Four days. The funerals have concluded, and Cailivale has recognized the Faoii army as a sanctioned militia. Our numbers have already grown since the Croeli defeat." He smiled as he moved black ringlets out of her eyes. "The world seeks justice. You have offered it to them with your army, Kai."

Kaiya shut her eyes as she digested what he'd said. Minutes passed before she heard her brother whisper her name, worry creeping into his voice again. She forced her eyes back open.

"I missed the burials. Those poor women . . ." Tears wet her cheeks as Kaiya turned her head to the wall in shame and anguish. Tendaji stood by silently, letting her grieve.

"The numbers could have been much worse, Kaiya," he finally whispered reassuringly. "You saved many of the soldiers with your song that night. Even those that had only slight injuries would have fallen to the criukli poison without your aid. But..." He fell quiet. The silence stretched for so long that Kaiya at last had to turn her head back to face him, afraid that he had disappeared into the disconcerting calm. He stared at her with a piercing gaze.

"Kaiya, this is very important. Do you still hear the bells you mentioned?" Kaiya closed her eyes and listened.

"No. They've faded."

"Thank the Goddess." Tendaji wiped a hand over his face. "Croeli-Thinir has grown stronger. He doesn't need to be physically present anymore to get into your mind. Had I known..." He fell silent for a moment before rubbing a hand over his eyes. "When you refused to heal yourself with your song, I thought you'd lost the fight against him. I thought..."

"Oh, Tendaji." Kaiya let her head sink back into the pillow, eyes closed against the bright light of the candle. Her head ached. "You think I'd turn on you now, after all we've been through?" She felt his eyes on her, but she couldn't find the strength to meet them. She tried again to reassure him. "I did try to heal myself. After I finished with the others. I just... I couldn't keep it up for long enough. I'm no Preoii." She could feel Tendaji studying her. He stood in contemplative silence for a moment, mulling over her words.

Then he chuckled. "You saved the infantry first?"

Kaiya opened her eyes again, looking for whatever it was he found humorous. He shook his head, still smiling. "Pretty little Kaiya. What good will you be to us if you do not take care of your most basic needs?" Kaiya rolled her eyes, groaning when even that hurt.

Still smiling, Tendaji turned away, busying himself near the tub of water that had been set next to the bed. Kaiya tried not to notice that the tub's rim had been dyed a rusty crimson—an indication that bloody cloths had been rinsed in its tin frame. A moment later, Tendaji turned back, his hands hidden in a web of cloth bandages.

"Are you able to sit up?"

Kaiya tried, but at first her shaking arms would not support her weight. She dissuaded Tendaji's supporting hand and tried again, forcing her trembling, resistant limbs to shove her up despite their protests. The pain in her side exploded, and sparks shattered her vision as she gasped for breath. The world spun, and this time she could not keep Tendaji from steadying her with a sturdy hand. "Easy, Kai. Easy. Lie back, or you'll pull out your stitches." Kaiya hadn't realized that she'd tried to curl into a ball against the agony. She let Tendaji ease her back onto the pillows he had propped up. When he was sure she wasn't going to faint, he diligently began redressing her side and leg.

As he worked, he hummed.

"That melody," Kai finally ventured. "I've heard it before."

"Have you?" His smile was soft and understated.

"I keep remembering . . . Preoii-Aleena. She must have sung it to me when I was younger."

Tendaji stopped his bandaging and held Kaiya's gaze. "Your Preoii? Are you sure?" That quiet smile again.

"It must be. But she's different than I remember. She seems so kind. So... happy."

Tendaji clucked his tongue at her. "Pretty little Kaiya. Think harder. *Focus*. Is the woman in your memories really the woman in your monastery?"

Kaiya thought, humming the tune as she did. "The eyes are different than Preoii-Aleena's were. Not as sad. Brighter. Her cheeks are fuller. Her hair has more red in it. Her smile . . ." Kaiya jerked upward, hissing as she pulled at her ribs again. Tendaji wrapped an arm around her and started to lower her back to the pillows, but she clung to his sleeve and stared at him. "Can it be?"

Tendaji smiled. "Siblings in our family do tend to look alike."

"Our mother. I didn't remember what she looked like. So beautiful . . ." Unable to lie back down, Kaiya maneuvered her legs over the edge of the cot and sat staring at the span of memories that stretched out before her. Tendaji made no objection and went to work at redressing her throbbing calf. As he stripped off the soiled bandages, Kaiya noticed that the reopened gash was packed with chinol. An image of the Goddess statue flashed in her mind for a moment, but she realized that this plant was different from the one depicted in the statue. Similar, yes, but the leaves were not quite as broad. Not as flat.

"Then Preoii-Aleena was . . ."

"Our mother's sister. Mother always did want you to call her 'Auntie.' But you weren't able to speak yet when we left you at the monastery."

Left me. "I . . . I don't understand. Why abandon us? Why. . .?" Kaiya broke off as a sudden, violent shiver racked her body. Tendaji placed a comforting hand on her shoulder. Her arms trembled and sweat broke out on her forehead. His concerned eyes were soft and gentle.

"Abandoned us, Kai? Look at you. You have become a stronger woman than most mothers can ever dream for their daughters. You are Faoii. What more could Mother offer you than that chance?"

"But she separated us. She left you with the Croeli. We hate each other."

"Do we? I thought we were getting along decently well." He smiled at her as he gathered up the dirty bandages. "I can elbow you more often if you'd like. Address you as witch, maybe?"

Kaiya gave him a hard look. "You know what I mean."

"I do. But I think Mother knew that the dividing line between Croeli and Faoii was to be erased one way or another. She loved our father, after all. And he was a Croeli clan leader. Aunt Aleena never did like that."

"Clan leader? Like Thinir?" Tendaji's eyes iced over.

"No. Thinir killed his brother and usurped his position while I was scouting far from home." His hands clenched into fists. "I didn't even know that our uncle had taken over until I returned to the ranks months later. I'd have been there sooner, but . . . I'd taken a detour to watch your monastery. I thought Father would want to know how you'd grown . . ." He stared into the distance for a moment before shaking his head violently.

"When I returned, they offered me my title—Croeli-Tendaji-Thinir, a lieutenant in his army. I knew I could never carry that title. I hadn't hated Uncle before, but I could not follow him. It took me three hours to plot my escape from the clan. It started with me offering allegiance to my mother's Goddess— and ended with my criukli in Croeli-Vilikir-Thinir's chest."

Now it was Kaiya's turn to offer comfort. She rested a shaky hand on Tendaji's arm. The steel in his eyes faded, and he continued, "That was almost two years ago. Right after the attack on Lyn's monastery. It's possible that is why your own battle was so delayed. After my betrayal, the Croeli would have had to start over and verify that my previous reports were true." He smiled.

"I'm glad of it now. The extra years gave you a chance to grow. You were more capable of defending yourself by the time they moved against your people. Though . . . I wish I had been able to warn you of what was to come." He fell into a contemplative silence.

"What did you do after you left?" Kaiya asked, stretching her stiff leg.

"After that I traveled in search of the other Croeli tribes. I found a few of them, but none seemed willing to break free of Thinir's influence. I was forced to retreat from the lands of my own people many times after they learned that I was willing to betray their god-empowered leader. A few individuals listened, though, and broke away from the others. We did what we could to counteract the mind-dominating magic that Thinir was only just beginning to dabble in. One group seemed close to a breakthrough before I left, and I did everything I could to support their efforts. If nothing else, we wanted those who joined his cause to join of their own accord.

"Eventually, though, our uncle got too powerful. He swore that he would slay your people and claim your lands, whatever it took. So I came back. I didn't want him to do to your people what he did to mine."

"That's when you went to Lucius." Tendaji nodded, absently rubbing at his side.

"Maybe I should have gone to the capital earlier, though I doubt it would have made a difference. Lucius was Thinir's puppet by the time I arrived, and he was only too happy to remind me of my treachery." Kaiya winced as she remembered the bulging rib and whip marks Tendaji had sported when they'd first met. Tendaji saw the grimace, and his eyes shot to her injured leg and side. When he saw no new injuries, he leaned back again. "The rest you know, I think."

"I am sure that Mother never wanted any of that, Tendaji. You would have made her proud."

Tendaji chuckled in response. "You speak only in past tense when you talk about her. Did you notice that?"

Kaiya's eyes widened and she moved to stand, astonished. "She's alive? Where?"

Tendaji shook his head and gently pushed her back down to the cot.

"I do not know. Preoii-Aleena was the last one to speak with her. It's possible that she left for reasons that we aren't supposed to understand." He sighed. "You have to realize, Kaiya: Mother knew more about the way the world—the true world, Illindria's world—worked than we do. She could...see things that we couldn't. She spoke of it like a ghost world, here but not here. Overlapping with the world we saw. She said it was what the Goddess sees all the time." Kaiya's heart faltered. She was suddenly very glad to be sitting. All of the superimposed images she had seen before danced in front of her like a ghostly ballet.

Tendaji was immediately kneeling in front of her, her suddenly pale features reflecting in his worried eyes. "Perhaps I should have waited to tell you all of this until you were stronger. Lie down, Kaiya. We'll continue this conversation after you've rested." Kaiya only shook her head, resisting the gentle pressure he placed on her shoulder.

The Great Illindria had been showing her the way since Resting Oak. For the first time, Kaiya was certain that there was a set path to victory, and she had been following it instead of just blindly swimming with a current she could neither battle nor cross. Those were visions sent by the Great Illindria, not Kaiya's own mind breaking under the weight of everything that had happened. How could she rest now when there was still so much to do? When Illindria needed her to keep going? She looked back up, her mind racing. "What is the status of the Croeli army?"

"Kaiya, now is not the time—"

"Tendaji, report." Her words were filled with power, even as the extra effort made her head spin. Tendaji frowned at her defiantly before slowly crossing his arms.

"There are no new reports yet, but Lyn has spoken of dwindling forces. It's only a hunch on her part, but I think she's right. The Croeli seem to be less threatening now than they were when I left the ranks. The Faoii at your monastery cut down more of them than any of the others did. Whatever magic Thinir is using to get into his enemies' heads, he has evidently not perfected it."

"And our army?"

"Last reports indicated that we are nearly four thousand strong. More join the ranks every day, and our most experienced Faoii are becoming combat trainers."

Kaiya frowned. "That's not enough. The Croeli may be weaker

now, but they still outnumber us. We need more soldiers." Kaiya tried to stand, feeling the need to pace, but Tendaji pushed her back down sternly. His eyes darkened dangerously, and Kaiya pursed her lips, but remained seated. "If we want to defeat them, we have to strike before they can replenish their forces. But we can't stay here. We need to move our army before the Croeli send others to investigate their missing fighters." She pondered for a moment. "We can move to another location; hide our numbers until we are ready to strike in the spring. Then we would have an entire season to train . . ." Her mind turned, faster and faster, the coming months spreading out before her as she followed potential paths with dizzying fervor.

"Kaiya, stop." Kaiya had not realized that her sudden and forceful oration had left her winded but battle-ready. However, when she looked at Tendaji, he seemed less than amused. She sighed before obediently lying back onto the cot. Tendaji stared her down until she had settled back into the pillow with closed eyes. Once he was certain that she was not planning to jump up again, Kaiya could hear him take out her leather armor and begin mending its pierced plates.

Eventually, Kaiya couldn't stand the silence and reopened her eyes. "Tendaji."

A sigh. "Yes?"

"See if you can find somewhere for us to station the army over the winter."

"If I promise you that Lyn and I will seek a suitable destination, will you go back to sleep?"

"Just do it. They'll have to move soon, or the snow will trap them on the trail."

Tendaji looked up from his work. "They? Are you not planning to join this crusade?"

Kaiya shook her head as she battled to keep her eyes open. "You and I can't. We have other Faoii to find."

Three days later, Tendaji fastened Kaiya's breastplate before turning to pick up her sheathed fantoii. He squared his shoulders and offered her the hilt. The Faoii shook her head.

"It's not my blade anymore."

Tendaji raised one eyebrow and presented it to her again. "Of all those here, you are the only one who is truly worthy to carry a fantoii blade." Kaiya smiled sadly and looked at the sword that she had carried since the monastery's fall. Then she lifted her eyes to Tendaji and pushed it back.

"The blade sang for you, Tendaji. It is meant to be in your hands, not mine."

Tendaji pondered for a moment, then unsheathed the fantoii and studied it with a knowledgeable eye. Kaiya waited. When he slid it back into its sheath with a dutiful click, she released a sigh of relief.

In a single, liquid motion, Tendaji belted the scabbard around his waist, where it hung from his hips as though it had been made to sit there. *It was. It was.* Kaiya nodded approvingly. A piece of the huge, wonderful puzzle that made up the Goddess's world had fallen into its proper place.

"We will have to find you another blade, Kaiya."

"We will." She smiled at him and turned toward the door. "The Goddess provides, Tendaji."

Croeli-Thinir yelled in rage as he overturned a nearby table with a flick of his criukli. The table flew across the room and collided heavily with the wall. *Imbeciles! All of them!* Some of the strongest refurbished soldiers he had left, and they were not able to take out a single outpost of cowardly prostitutes? It would have been better to send the masses of untrained fodder—they at least would have been guaranteed to attack at the same moment. A stupid mistake! If they had been able to strike at once, both factions would have fallen without difficulty.

Instead, three hundred of his best spies had fallen beneath the blades of whores and housewives. And because of his niece's ever-increasing power, he had only been able to refurbish a few of the Silentbell wenches for his own purposes. Such failure was not acceptable!

His pacing quickened. Now the untrained bitches had tasted battle. That first tendrils of uncertainty and terror could not be used against them later. They knew victory, and that assurance would strengthen their blades when their hearts faltered.

Worst of all, he had been unable to take control of the pretty little Faoii's stubborn little mind. She had gained too much power. Too many followers. It was no longer safe to allow her to continue her journey free of shackles. But he had already used most of the blood from the dagger tip to follow her movements, and now he was not sure there would be enough to gain control when it really mattered.

Out of frustration, he struck one of his refurbished slaves across the face. It, of course, offered no response.

And then they'd stabbed her! Stabbed her! Had he not given specific instructions to keep her alive? Why hadn't that half-breed Tendaji played his part yet?

He threw a chair in a different direction. It splintered against the door frame.

And let's not forget this new criukli poison. That vile pollutant. He'd already begun to suspect that it was the reason for his decreasing number of refurbished soldiers. Somehow it resisted the magic that the war god had granted him, and yet he could not be rid of it. How many times now had he tried to wipe it from his officers' minds? A dozen? Yet somehow, the majority still fought his influence and continued to coat their criukli before each battle. Threats of death or torture no longer worked; he had conditioned them past the point of knowing fear. But try as he might, he had not conditioned them past their use of that vile substance.

He needed to strengthen his hold on them, needed to increase the pressure he could put on other minds. He would start moving them more, forcing the soldiers to Blink from place to place. They would dull with every leap, making them easier to control. Some would eventually become too senseless to be truly useful, but even morons could swing a sword. They would become fodder, maintained only so that their blades could draw the blood of those who would take their place in the ranks.

Though Thinir could not stop seething over the failure to acquire his newest and greatest warrior, he could still see the benefits that might come from what he'd learned. In a way, it was better like this. Though he would lose many warriors over time, there could be a brighter side to having a smaller army at the end of it all.

The refurbishing was a difficult process, and only the strong survived it with their minds intact. No one had come away from its influence completely whole, but some were almost as they had been before. And all were content now that they no longer had a mind to question orders. When the wars were done, only the strongest would remain, and they would be happy with whatever Thinir rewarded them. If some men fell, it was only so that his portion of the spoils could be divided among those who were left.

Thinir chuckled darkly as he began devising ways to better control those he sought to dominate. For now, he needed more warriors, trained or not. Numbers could bring down the Faoii when skill was not available. It did not even matter whether the refurbished soldiers fell, as long as he had more to replace them with. All that mattered was that more Croeli than Faoii stood in the end.

So you're building an army, my niece? You can't even comprehend what a true army looks like.

Thinir's dark laughter filled the night.

22

"This is it, Kai. This is the last group of people I know that might even think about joining us. If they don't help, we'll have to go after Thinir with what we've got." Kaiya nodded to Lyn as she urged her gelding up yet another snow-covered hill. She'd lost track of how many people they'd spoken to in the last weeks—all had been too afraid or too weak to join the coming war. Maybe this time it would be different. *Goddess, please let this time be different.*

As they crested this final rise, a valley opened beneath them. Campfires dotted the acres between their knoll and the long line of trees on the horizon.

The Danhaid had bronze skin and dark eyes. The multicolored shells and stones threaded into their brightly dyed outfits and long, copper-colored hair caught the few rays of sunlight that struggled through the overcast skies.

"We should be wary, Kaiya. These people have had almost no

contact with outsiders since Lucius's war five years ago," Tendaji said quietly as they dismounted.

Kaiya nodded in response but did not reach for the short blade at her hip. Instead, her gaze roamed over the sun-darkened expressions of the people that were cautiously approaching.

"Not Lucius. Thinir." Kaiya could see her uncle on the plains, could feel his piercing gaze from across the past. She watched the nomads of five years before scatter at the sight of his lightning spell. There was a raw gleam in his eyes born from newfound power.

Kaiya watched the ghostly Danhaid warriors come with their bows and spears, but the demonic-helmed Croeli fell upon them without mercy. The summer grass ran red, and screams of pain and fear filled the air.

But there was hope. Amidst the turmoil a single, ferocious woman fought viciously. Foe after foe fell before her beaded spear, and her trilling cry pierced the battlefield. Others gathered behind her, and slowly the tide began to turn.

When the Croeli finally left, followed by the Danhaid that chose to worship Thinir and his brutal god, Kaiya watched the spear maiden gather those left behind. Broken warriors and frightened women gathered beneath her beaded spear. And when she prayed for them, Illindria heard.

Kaiya's breath caught as the vision faded, and she shivered as one of the nomads broke from the group and charged toward a tent at the back of the camp. Kaiya pulled her wool cloak around herself, bracing against the chill.

Tendaji glanced over. "Are you all right, Kai?"

"There is a Faoii here," Kaiya whispered.

Lyn gave Kaiya an incredulous look. "Here? There isn't a

monastery for months in any direction. The Order despised barbarian magics."

"I don't think she was trained in a monastery. Or anywhere. But she is Faoii."

"How do you know?" Tendaji whispered without shifting his gaze away from the people that were forming a semicircle around them. Kaiya opened her mouth to answer but was cut off when a wide-eyed woman started chattering shrilly in an unknown tongue.

"Well, I guess we all expected this," Lyn said as a dozen other nomads joined in. She reached for her fantoii, but Kaiya stopped her.

"They're not attacking." Kaiya motioned to the gathering crowd where the surrounding nomads continued chittering incomprehensibly while lifting their hands to their eyes in a repetitive motion, but they made no move toward the small group or toward their own weapons. Lyn tensed, anyway, eyes narrowed. "See? We're okay. Calm down," Kaiya whispered softly.

"You calm down," Lyn retorted, her back rigid. "What are they even doing?" Her hand didn't move from her fantoii hilt.

Suddenly the crowd parted, and a tall, lithe woman stepped out from the sea of bronze skin. Her long legs, uncovered despite the snow, reminded Kaiya of a tiger's, and her dark eyes were as clear and black as a stream at midnight. Bright, multicolored shells laced through her mane of coppery hair, catching the sunlight as readily as the glinting tip of her beaded spear. The nomadic woman's rolling stride was unmistakable, though. Kaiya breathed a sigh of relief at the sight of another Faoii.

"Hail, sister." Kaiya's whisper rolled across the ground that separated them. Next to her, Lyn deferred to Kaiya's greeting and immediately fisted her hands over an invisible hilt and bowed her head. On Kaiya's left, Tendaji mirrored the gesture after a moment's hesitation. The dark-eyed nomad's steady gaze passed over each of them in turn.

"I am no kin of yours." The words were soft around the edges, rounded by the woman's heavy accent. "Who sends you?"

"No one. We come of our own accord," Kaiya replied, slowly lowering her arms to her sides. The unnamed warrior shook her head.

"No. You are here by someone's will." She brandished her spear with an angry shake and pointed it at Kaiya. "Others have come and said they were not sent. But we all follow the paths that were chosen by those that came before, or by those that loom beyond the reflections of the life pond. Name your sender, outsider. Which deity is carved into the bark of your life tree?" Kaiya smiled and lifted her eyes, enchanted by the other woman's description of the Goddess. *Mollie, you would have loved her.*

After a moment's contemplation, Kaiya used her hands to make the inverted triangle of Illindria. The gesture seemed unnatural to her. The commoner's symbol was unfitting for Faoii, but the Danhaid leader obviously recognized it and visibly softened.

"She Who Speaks in Dreams has brought you here. I have told the others to prepare for those who claim to be Her messengers. Come. We will hear you."

Lyn gaped at the sudden change. "Really? That's it? Blades, Kai, I wish I'd had you as my negotiator years ago. Imagine what we could have done by now."

Kaiya rolled her eyes, but she smiled and took a few steps down the hill toward the gathered nomads. A hundred pairs of hands immediately rose to a hundred chests in an inverted triangle. Then, the bronze men and women lifted their hands to their eyes in the same repetitive motion as before. Kaiya stopped in front of the shell-laden Faoii.

"I am Faoii-Kaiya of the Monastery of the Eternal Blade. The woman at the top of the hill is Faoii-Lyn of the Unbroken Weave, and . . ." she stopped, not sure of how to address her brother. He was not Croeli anymore. But Tendaji's blade had sung for him. He deserved the title of an ascended. With a deep breath and a set heart, Kaiya applied the masculine conjugation to a word that had never been anything but feminine. "And this is Faoli-Tendaji." The word seemed almost natural as it rolled off her tongue. Tendaji, who had followed her down the slope, tensed beside her at the given title. Kaiya wondered whether it was a good reaction or a bad one. "May the Goddess guide your battles."

The spear woman set her weapon in the snow at their feet and laid both hands over her heart. Her unkempt hair fell over her face as she bowed her head. "I am Asanali of the Danhaid-anati. Though now there are only anati left. So I am only Asanali." She raised her head and looked over the group. "You are cold. Come. I will feed you, and you will tell me about She Who Speaks in Dreams. You will prove to me that you are Her messengers."

As they walked through the nomad camp, most of the people that they passed continued to bring their hands up to cover their eyes. Kaiya watched the display several times before asking what it was about. Asanali smiled.

"It is a sign of respect. They think that you are messengers of the gods."

"Why?" Lyn's voice was incredulous as she cast an apprehensive glance at one of the women they passed.

"Because of the man that came before, five summers ago. He was of dark skin and light eyes. He was a messenger of a god. A dark one. Your bodies and his were carved from the same branch. These people know you to be special, but they aren't yet sure which god you speak for. You will have to prove that you are for She Who Speaks in Dreams before they will follow you." They reached a large, brightly painted tent, and Asanali pulled back the flap that permitted entrance. Warm, coarse rugs covered the ground surrounding a fire pit in its center.

Kaiya frowned. "How do we do that?"

Asanali motioned for her guests to sit and began skinning one of the rabbits that hung to the left of the entryway. She spoke as though she hadn't heard Kaiya's question. "She Who Speaks in Dreams told me that others like him would come. That his life tree spreads far, over many lives. His branch may be the widest and easiest to see, but it is broken. But She said that whole branches would come, too. That they would be sturdy. So I have waited for you." She looked up as she set the now-meatless hide to one side. "Your Goddess, too, is powerful. Is She as powerful as the horned god?"

"Yes." Kaiya spoke without hesitation. "Illindria is perfect." Asanali smiled a knowing smile as she set a pot over the central fire. The rabbit meat and a surprising amount of summer vegetables went into it. Kaiya raised an eyebrow at the carrots and corn, glancing back to the tent's entrance. A flurry of snow lifted its corner just as Asanali began to speak again.

"The horned god has gifted his worshippers with power. They can dive through the life pond, then reappear at a different shore. He has offered weapons of steel and ash and cold. Horrific beasts of blood and fire and ice that aid in battles against children and ancients. Then, when the weak have fallen, the strong are taken as horned soldiers, and they follow willingly, without pain. Without fear." She met Kaiya's gaze. "What can the carver of your life tree offer to those who have heard Her starry whispers?"

Kaiya closed her eyes, unable to repress her smile. *What indeed?*

With a contented sigh, Kaiya recalled all the words Preoii-Aleena had declared at chapel—or, at least, the ones she had paid attention to. She regretted that now. She wished she'd been the unascended that Illindria deserved. But there were other things she'd paid attention to. Things she would never forget.

She thought of the cries of the ascended Faoii's fantoii as they swung through the air against a foe, and of the Cleroii songs that wove like breezes through wind chimes. She thought of the Oath, which swelled against the walls of chapels and hearts alike each morning. She thought of the camaraderie in the mess hall, of the jokes and laughter and songs. She thought of Mollie, and the silver bond that had been stronger than any of Thinir's iron shackles. She thought of Jade, the quiet Preoii she had never met but who had affected the world as greatly as any Faoii Kaiya had ever known. She thought of Lyn, who, despite her cynicism, made Kaiya's world brighter and her heart race when she came into view, and Tendaji, who made everything seem tranquil even in the most chaotic times. She thought of the sunrises that lit up the Goddess's pale statue, lighting the soft smile that looked down upon the Faoii with an intelligence that rock alone could never convey. Finally, she thought of the sunset that brought so much beauty to life.

How can one describe something that is everything?

As Kaiya contemplated, the tent flap blew open, and thick flakes of snow fell onto the woven rugs. No one moved, stunned at what followed.

Panpipes. Soft and feathery, barely louder than the wind, accompanied by the scent of sunflowers. It only lasted for a moment, but it was unmistakable. Outside, she heard exclamations of surprise and joy. Asanali, who had begun to slice a potato into the pot, paused in her task. After a moment, she resumed, evidently satisfied.

"Ah," she whispered, seemingly to herself. "It is enough. Those that were uncertain about following you will understand. The Danhaid will come and fight for you with hearts unburdened by fear. Your pack is growing, Faoii-Kaiya."

23

The trek back through the snow and ever-dropping temperatures of the heartland would have been nearly impossible had the Danhaid not accompanied Kaiya and the others. Kaiya knew little of wild magic—the Faoii were taught to distrust any spells that were not their own—but she could not help but admire the Danhaid abilities.

While the magics taught in the monasteries were refined and powerful in their simplicity, wild magic was unbridled in comparison. There was a fierce, barbaric beauty in the dances and elaborate outfits that the Danhaid used in their rituals. Kaiya's heart sped up to match the beat of the bodhrán as Asanali and her bronze warriors moved their bare feet in elaborate steps over the snow-coated plain each morning.

The days of endless marching were not comfortable, but they were easier than Kaiya expected a winter expedition to be. More than once, she and her companions would look off into the distance and see dark, angry clouds clamoring toward them on the horizon, threatening frostbite or worse. But these terrible storms never quite reached them.

While not able to say for certain—and Asanali was stubbornly silent on the matter, saying adamantly that the Goddess was the only controller of tempests—Kaiya couldn't help but wonder whether these miraculous bouts of luck were not to be attributed to the copper-haired members of their troop. The farther they traveled, the more admiration she held for the Danhaid, and for the Goddess that offered gifts to all who worshipped Her, no matter the manner in which they prayed.

"How did those behind your stone walls feed themselves, if not by accepting the land's bountiful gifts?" Asanali spoke softly as she crouched on the ground, streaming a magic that Kaiya did not understand into the snow.

"The people nearby offered us food and other goods. Most of our essentials came from Resting Oak." Kaiya gasped as a snow-white rabbit crept toward a barely noticeable sprig that sprouted from the slush. Kaiya drew her bow and aimed at the little creature. Then, releasing her breath in a slow exhale, she let the arrow fly. Caught in the side, the rabbit fell limply with only the slightest squeak. Asanali nodded and went to gather their dinner, whispering a prayer as she approached. "Our garden had some edibles, but it was mostly for medicinal herbs."

"The other tribes offered you their well-earned food?" Asanali's lips pressed together as she pulled the arrow from the carcass and cleaned it in the snow. She handed the unbroken shaft back to Kaiya with a slight frown. "The winds sing sad songs when they drift here from the north. It is whispered that those not part of the tribes starve under the demands of wolves that take what they did not hunt, and the deer have no ability to fight them. You are not these wolves?"

"What? No! Of course not! The Faoii are fair and just." But Kaiya felt troubled as she again remembered the too-thin cow. She had always been adequately fed. Was that not true for those outside the monastery?

Tendaji spoke carefully from a few paces away. "You say Resting Oak and your other wards gave you food out of gratitude?" Kaiya turned toward him as she slung the rabbit over her saddle. His features were guarded, unreadable.

"Yes. Most of them didn't have anything stronger than a picket fence. We offered patrols, soldiers. Of course they'd repay us for that security."

"Would you have protected them even if they had not offered these . . . gifts?"

"Of course! We are Faoii!"

Tendaji's lip pulled up in his quiet, ever-infuriating smile. "I see. Did they know that?"

Kaiya opened her mouth to give a heated reply but stopped herself. She didn't know whether the peasants knew of her Oath. Was it possible that the Faoii had remained fed and clothed while others starved and shivered because of . . . extortion, however unintentional?

"I'm sure that the Preoii would never let the people live in undue fear," she finally whispered. "We are not Croeli." Tendaji froze, his shoulders stiff.

"The Croeli never hid their intentions, Kaiya. People either paid their taxes or they joined the army. Everyone knew this." He studied his reflection in his fantoii before sheathing it and mounting his horse. "The peasants might have been starving, but we all starved equally. That was never in doubt."

"Wait. So this army we're going to face... they're just untrained, *starving* peasants?" Lyn's voice was almost mocking. Kaiya shot her a glance, aware that Tendaji was already on edge. Her brother, however, didn't even bristle.

"No more so than yours, Faoii-Lyn. Is not the majority of our army now composed of working women from the streets of various settlements?" He turned back to Kaiya before Lyn could reply. "Anyone that was capable of fighting was trained. The others were put to work creating armor and weapons, or put into the fields under the army's control. Most of those that joined before I left were volunteers—possibly because they knew that they would not have enough food to provide in tax season. Volunteers were treated better than indentured servants, though no one was abused. It was . . . not a bad system before Thinir took control."

"It must have been pretty bad. Seems like there was a lot of hatred taught in your homeland," Lyn muttered under her breath.

Tendaji cast her a cold glance. "Starve enough people for enough time, and eventually they will rise against those that have food. There was only one group that we knew of that never lacked for sustenance, and Thinir uses that to his advantage. It would not have been difficult to shift that hunger from people's bellies and into their hearts."

Kaiya stared at passing snow-covered fields for a long time. When at last she spoke, it was little more than a whisper. "They hate us, don't they?"

Tendaji shifted uneasily. "The ones that were fighting before I left did. Though now I don't know. The Croeli we have faced recently seem different. There is no hatred in their eyes, no hunger or fear. Just... obedience. Thinir was known for using magic to give his words more influence, but this is something else entirely. He's grown more powerful since I knew him."

"Someone doesn't gain that much power that quickly by natural means. We need to know how he's doing it," Kaiya said, eager to redirect the conversation toward a common enemy. "The men we faced in Cailivale were only shells in Thinir's control. No matter what laws you once had, I doubt anyone willingly signed up for that."

"And if he could do it to them, he can do it to any of us. Blades, he almost got Kai with it last time." Lyn brought her horse closer to Kaiya's, her eyes steely. "That's not happening again. Ever. We need more information before we face him next. Before Kai even gets close to anywhere he might be."

Tendaji nodded. "I agree. And..." He paused, his eyes suddenly brightening in realization. "I think I know who might have those answers."

Kaiya and Lyn both perked up their ears. "Who?"

"There was a resistance before I left," Tendaji said. "A small band willing to fight against Thinir. They might have continued making plans after I was imprisoned." He turned to Kaiya. "Do you remember how I told you that one group was close to finding a way to throw off Thinir's influence?" Kaiya nodded, thinking back to the hazy conversation they'd had in the enclave. He waved one hand as if her nod had proven an unspoken point. "I don't know whether they found anything definite, but there is hope."

"Let's go talk to them, then. I can send a rider to Eili so she knows about the delay." Kaiya was about to call a Danhaid Warrior to her, but Tendaji shook his head.

"If they saw a group like this coming, they'd attack or disappear before we could get close. They're not fools. But I had good friends there. And more than a few debtors. It might be enough to get you in and out alive."

"Kaiya's not going anywhere without me." Lyn declared. She turned to Kaiya. "Wherever you go, I'm going with you. I swore."

Kai shook her head. "Not this time, Lyn. Tendaji's right. Any Faoii presence is going to look like an attack. We must tread carefully."

"But—"

"Besides, I need you to regroup with Eili. Train the new troops. Keep an ear to the ground and be prepared to report anything you find out about Thinir or potential allies." Lyn looked like she was about to protest, so Kaiya raised her voice. "Is that clear, Faoii?"

"Yes, Faoii-Kaiya," Lyn at last conceded.

"Good." Kaiya turned back and let some of the power drain away from her voice. "We're growing too large. It will be harder to hide our numbers. Thinir may choose to strike again if he discovers us."

"We will be prepared for his coming." Kaiya had almost forgotten that Asanali was still with them, she'd been so quiet. Now she spoke with an assurance that was both comforting and sound. "The horned god has strong, far-spreading roots, but they have not yet dug so far into the soil that it does not yield true magic. Your dancers will know their steps before the sun brushes his warm fingers against the frosty crone. We will meet with your Eili and prepare the dance." She smiled broadly at the gathered forces.

Lyn frowned. "Uh . . . what?"

She says she'll have the troops ready before spring," Tendaji supplied.

Kaiya smiled. "Good. Emery and the enclave girls are almost directly west of here. Faoii-Eili should have met up with them by now. If you two continue on this route, you should meet up with them inside a week. Tendaji and I will be heading...?" She paused, looking to her brother for guidance.

"North," he responded simply.

"North. We will rejoin you with information as soon as possible. Look for us within the month. Keep your eyes and ears open. We still don't have all we need to win this war."

Lyn stacked her fists, her dejection melting away. Her voice was free of discontent when she spoke. "Goddess guide your battles, Faoii. And . . . come back, okay? I lo—I don't want to lose you."

Kaiya smiled warmly at her and reached out to grip her hand. "The same to you, Lyn. Don't worry. We'll meet on one field or another again soon."

Asanali also gave her well-wishes and prayers before moving with Lyn to the front of the nomadic flock that continued to push its way westward. Meanwhile, Kaiya and Tendaji turned their horses to the north and spurred them forward.

24

Kaiya and Tendaji traveled for weeks in the biting cold. Without the Danhaid nomads with them, however, the weather suddenly became vengeful and cruel. Many overcast evenings found them huddled in their cloaks around a windswept campfire, and the few inns they visited were only marginally more welcoming than the storms.

In each new town, Kaiya and Tendaji weathered dark glares and thinly-veiled hatred from angry, desperate residents. Kaiya remembered how she'd bristled at their wariness when she'd first traveled this way. She'd wanted to scream and fight their stares—make them understand that she was the hand of justice and that the Faoii deserved recognition. But even the word "justice" had taken on a different meaning since then. And she was no longer sure that "Faoii" was synonymous with it.

So they trekked on. Kaiya's heart dropped with each new landmark she recognized. The slope of that mountain on the horizon… the smell on the wind that reminded her of red hair and an easy smile… it all weighed heavily. Even without asking, Tendaji sensed her unease.

"Don't worry, Kai. We won't be going that far."

She frowned. "I didn't realize that there were Croeli this close. I spent my entire life thinking that you were just stories."

Tendaji shrugged easily. "We were taught well. We knew how to keep ourselves hidden. When Father was still our leader, we scouted the area primarily for knowledge of custom and rituals, things necessary for acclimation. The main force of our tribe always remained in the Blackfeather Wilds, but there were usually at least a few of us here."

Kaiya wasn't sure how she felt about that.

Days passed as Tendaji led Kaiya further north. They had just reached the edge of a vast, sprawling forest that would eventually lead back to the rocky bluffs of her childhood when he unexpectedly dismounted.

"We'll have to walk from here," he said, motioning to a deer path barely distinguishable between the trees. "We'll lead the horses."

"How far away are we?"

"A few days. If the Croeli don't already know we're here, they will soon. Be ready, just in case."

Kaiya nodded. After a moment of focusing on details she couldn't distinguish, Tendaji motioned her forward and began picking his way through the underbrush.

"What about traps?" Kaiya asked, glancing around.

"I know what to look for. We'll be all right."

They traveled in near silence for almost a day, navigating paths that were practically invisible to Kaiya, but Tendaji glided over them with a practiced ease. All the while, both warriors kept a wary eye out for their Croeli hosts.

It took much less time for them to be discovered than Kaiya had anticipated.

Dusk was barely falling, casting its long shadows through the woods, when one shadow separated itself from an overhanging branch, peering down intensely at the duo. Its booted feet made only the faintest crunch in the snow. Kaiya, despite her attentiveness, was slower to respond than her brother. He was on his feet even before Kaiya was truly aware that they weren't alone.

"Torin." Tendaji's voice was steady, but Kaiya still caught the faintest hint of surprise there. She glanced between her brother and the shadow, agitated and wary.

"Croeli-Tendaji. You've returned." It was a statement rather than a question.

"I have." The shadow swung down into the light of Tendaji's campfire. A lean man with light hair and wary eyes crouched in front of them. His dark leathers were muted, even in the firelight. He did not quite smile when he looked up.

"Most of the others will be pleased. Many will be surprised. A few will not be happy." The man rose steadily until he reached full height. He was not quite as tall as Tendaji and was narrower in the shoulders, but his body was lean and muscular, and when he moved, it was with a smooth grace. He put a hand out to the darker man. "I, for one, am pleased to see you. Leadership under Croeli-Amaenel-Tendaji has not been easy." Tendaji reached out to clasp Torin's arm. Kaiya raised an eyebrow at the given title but remained silent. Tendaji had told Eili that Croeli attached their superior officer's name to the end of their name and title. But that couldn't be right, could it?

She tensed when she realized that Torin was looking her over appraisingly. "Is this the help you promised to supply?" he asked.

"In a manner of speaking, yes." Tendaji moved to put out the fire he had only recently built. "Will you be escorting us back?"

"Not exactly. We've had to move."

"Move? Why? What's happened?" Tendaji was suddenly apprehensive as he turned his head too sharply to look at the other man. Torin glanced at Kaiya before spreading his hands.

"It is not my place to say. Amaenel will speak to you when we arrive. Just be aware that he will not be pleased that your supplied help is armed and unbridled. That was not your promise, Croeli-Tendaji."

Tendaji bristled. "I told everyone that any help I brought would be willing and unshackled. The Faoii need to be our allies, not our slaves."

Torin's face was not quite a smile and not quite a grimace. "Amaenel remembers your words differently. And has made sure that most of the others remember them differently, too. We only know that we need their help—it does not matter how we get it. He won't be pleased."

Tendaji sighed, and his shoulders relaxed by a few degrees. He rolled his neck carefully. "Amaenel's never pleased, anyway, but I thank you for the warning. You've always been a good friend, Torin."

"I hope you can still say that when this is all over with."

The light-skinned Croeli motioned the duo forward and began leading them through the forest in a different direction.

The encampment they eventually came to was haphazard and incomplete. Only a few temporary huts had been constructed, and those were built more out of hides and skins than of hardier wood and stone. The men who drifted around the camp did not try to hide their stares at the trio's approach, and Kaiya in particular caught their gaze. Like dogs eyeing a bone, the Croeli were not aggressive so much as desirous, but to Kaiya that seemed even more unsettling. The Faoii followed her brother quickly, trying to ignore the ravenous stares that trailed her every step.

At the far side of the encampment, a hard, solitary figure stood, his face hidden by one of the brutal horned helms that the Croeli were known for. He seemed to bristle at Tendaji's approach, but he saluted dutifully when addressed.

"Croeli-Amaenel-Tendaji, report," Tendaji ordered.

The man's piercing, vengeful eyes scrutinized Kaiya's lithe frame from beneath his grotesque mask before he turned away from her and spoke rapidly into Tendaji's ear. Tendaji's face darkened considerably as he listened, and the masked man gesticulated violently as he spoke.

Minutes passed with a continuous stream of heated words from the horned Croeli. He was interrupted only by Tendaji's infrequent and impassioned questions. Kaiya waited silently, not daring to disrespect her brother's stature here by stepping closer.

Finally, she caught some of Tendaji's words. "Has there been any information on the original? The one that refused us?" The masked man, Amaenel, shook his head.

"No. Stupid Faoii probably got herself killed. And now her mate's been looking for an ill-spent vengeance. We'll have to kill her."

Kaiya perked her ears. *Faoii? A Faoii had been here?* Tendaji spoke before she could voice her uncertainty.

"That's not necessary. Faoii-Kaiya is of the same Order. She'll succeed where we have not. This is salvageable."

The masked man let out a low growl. "Unlikely, but I guess you can try. You're probably just going to get your Faoii pet killed too." He gestured toward the forest with a drawn criukli. "There's something wrong with that witch. She's not going to let your kin live long enough to draw a blade, much less talk her down. My advice is to strike before she can do any more damage."

"No!" Kaiya hadn't realized that the cry was her own until it had already escaped. By then she was striding toward the masked Croeli, the air around her filling with an unbridled protectiveness and power. "I will not let you kill a Faoii!"

Amaenel turned on her, his eyes flashing from beneath his snarling mask. She held his gaze for an increasingly intense moment before he finally turned back to Tendaji, dismissing her as easily as one dismisses a stray dog.

"You let her speak for you too? You have fallen far, Tendaji. At least your uncle actually knows who the enemy is."

Tendaji's hand shot forward with devastating speed. His long, lithe fingers wrapped around the other man's thick throat, nails buried deep into the skin. His right hand had already produced the fantoii, its tip less than a handspan away from his opponent's abdomen. The fantoii song was quiet and terrifying in the sudden silence.

"You watch the words you say with me, Croeli-Amaenel-Tendaji. I am not above setting an example for those that will rise to take your place." Amaenel only chuckled lightly under his breath.

"Maybe you're still Croeli after all. But you'd best drop your name from my title. I'm only Croeli-Amaenel now." He sneered as he looked back toward Kaiya, ignoring Tendaji's hand and blade. "Go speak to your Faoii pet. There must be a reason you brought her here, and I know it's not the reason that everyone thinks it is. Or any reason that a true Croeli would endanger the tribe. You want something." He brought his eyes back to bore into Tendaji's skull. "Get her to get rid of her bitch sister. Then we'll talk."

"You do not give orders to me, Amaenel."

"Suit yourself, *Croeli-Tendaji.*" Amaenel spat the title, stressing each syllable. "But you know that Thinir is getting stronger with every minute we waste. If you want to know how much stronger, you're going to have to work with me."

It took Tendaji an uncharacteristically long time to release his foe, but when he did, the other only laughed. "The chief's hut is still technically yours. You may use it until someone more deserving settles in."

Blue eyes blazing, Tendaji spun from the horned warrior and stalked away. Amaenel called after him. "While you're there, you may want to teach her how to make the criukli poison. I am sure she'd love to learn it straight from the source!" Tendaji tensed but kept walking, his pace brisk. Kaiya followed, seething silently, trying to process everything she'd heard. *Tendaji had made the criukli poison? Could that be right? If he'd known about other Faoii, why hadn't he said anything? What else did he know? Who else had been here? What else could he be hiding? And why?* She wanted to believe that there was some reasonable explanation behind all of this, but her anger only increased as other people began calling out as they passed. These were not men that would follow the Tendaji she knew. Or thought she knew.

"God's axe, boy! We didn't think it was possible! A witch willing to help us? I thought the seas'd dry up before that happened!"

"When you're on a mission, you never fail to provide, Tendaji. I bet the stupid witches never saw you coming."

"Ignore Amaenel, Tendaji. He was never able to provide us a replacement like that!" Kaiya frowned. *A replacement? For what?*

"She might be a witch, but if she can take down that other one, maybe she'd be worth keeping around in chains." She could feel their hatred for her rolling off them in waves. *They expect me to kill my own sister. What kind of promises has Tendaji made to these men who have such bloodlust in their hearts?*

"Would you look at that! She certainly *looks* better than that first one. Can she fight, too?"

"Always a step ahead of the enemy, my boy. Always a step ahead."

Kaiya seethed but bit her tongue while the surrounding men talked about her like a battle trophy. Finally, Tendaji led her to one of the huts set up near the edge of the clearing. It was larger than the others and sturdily built. A tapestry of an amber-eyed wolf hung over the door, staring impassively at the approaching siblings. Tendaji lifted the rug and motioned her through.

They had barely made it past the tapestry when Kaiya's control broke and she gave voice to her uncertainty. "What the blades is going on, Tendaji? Are these really the type of men you would willingly associate with? The hatred out there—I've never felt anything like it." Before he could respond, she gave voice to a deeper hurt and stalked towards him, jamming a finger into his chest.

"And you've been lying to me! You knew there were Faoii left in this area, and you never said a blade-blessed thing! And the criukli poison? That was you?" She swept her arm, indicating the room and the surrounding camp. "No one that truly cared about the Faoii would be part of this rabble." She angrily blinked back tears. "'Find a replacement. Find a replacement,' everyone keeps saying. What replacement, Tendaji? How many other Faoii have come here? What have these people been doing to them?" Her voice rose in pitch. "And you let them believe I'd kill another Faoii? One of my sisters? You'd ask me to do *anything* for these bastards, after the criukli poison? After they…you…" She choked on the words, her eyes stinging as she pressed her finger harder against his chest. "You kept things from me. Why?"

Slowly, deliberately, Tendaji grasped her wrist with one hand. She tried to pull away but couldn't and at last forced herself to meet his gaze.

"Kai, I know you're angry. I know that this is a lot to process, but I need you to hear me. I did not do any of this to cause you harm. I would never betray you. I did the only thing I knew how to do in order to protect you and myself and my people. Blades, even your people!" His eyes sparked, then softened. Kaiya let go of some of the tension in her shoulders, and Tendaji relinquished his hold on her wrist. "I know what you think of the criukli poison. You've seen the agony it causes—the fevers and the slow, painful deaths. It is vile, Kaiya, but I need you to know that it was supposed to be something better." He sighed, rolling his neck wearily.

"When Thinir first started his rise to power, his ability to control the minds of his followers was imperfect. He had to cut them with his own blade to start the process. We thought it was some sort of poison. We thought we could create an antidote. We succeeded, in the end, but not in the way we'd hoped. The criukli poison is imperfect, but it's effective. And more importantly, it's all we have. If we want to fight Thinir, we have to do whatever we can or fall under his control. It's the only way to drown him out. The only way to keep those wounded in battle from rising again and joining his side. As horrible as it is, it is *necessary*. You must understand this."

Kaiya frowned. "It's such a high price to pay, Tendaji. The suffering those girls endured as they struggled to make it back to Eili. The ones in Lyn's monastery . . . You might have been trying to help, but you've traded slavery for torture. So much blood is on your hands."

"Damn it, Kai! Don't you think I know that? But they heard the bells! Without the poison, those girls would be in Thinir's army now. He would have made it into their minds, and they would have sworn themselves to his banner. Worse yet, he would have had *you* by now if our criukli hadn't burned him away! As horrible as it is, the criukli poison is the only answer we have!"

Tendaji again forced himself to calm down. With a deep breath, he continued in lower tones. "Our father believed there was a way for us to live in peace, and I'll be damned if I'm not going to do everything in my power to achieve that goal in his memory. If that meant keeping a secret from you for a time, knowing that I could tell you eventually, then so be it. I knew you wouldn't listen to me if I tried to explain first. You had to understand."

He gestured to the door. "These are the last of those that were loyal to our father. Loyal to me. They have escaped our uncle's influence and despise him for what he's done to the Croeli people. As much as they hate your kind, the hate him more, so they *will* work with us if we can show them that you and your army are worthy of their respect. Right now they're preparing to face Thinir in battle, but don't be misled. If the end comes and all that is left is to die by their own poisoned blades so that they won't be his unwilling slaves for a lifetime, then that's what they'll do. There isn't any other choice." He held her gaze for a moment longer, his eyes intense. "You have to understand."

After a moment, Kaiya met his gaze with soft eyes.

"You could have told me, Tendaji. I would have listened."

He chuckled. "Would you? Would you have trusted me if I told you that I was still a Croeli clan leader? If I had told you that my men, under my guidance, created the criukli poison? If I had acted anything like my men outside, with hatred in my heart and blood on my mind, would you have ever given me a chance?"

"I . . . I don't know."

Tendaji's voice softened as he cupped her chin in one hand. "Yes you do, Kaiya. You barely trusted me when we first met, and you would have killed me immediately if you hadn't thought that you were the last Faoii in existence. Now, after all we've been through, I need you to trust me for a little longer."

Kai took a deep breath and nodded. "I *do* trust you, Tendaji. And I'll follow your lead here. But those men outside—they're different. I don't know if our two armies could ever actually trust each other. I don't know if we can ever be true allies."

"And someday we will remedy that, but for now we need to remember that even if our methods are different, our immediate goal is the same."

"To stop Thinir. I think I could maybe work with them long enough to see that through."

Tendaji smiled brightly at her. "Thank you, Kaiya."

They stood in contemplative silence before Kaiya spoke again. "I still have questions, though, Tendaji."

"I know. Where would you like to start?"

"With the part that makes this trip worthwhile. What do I have to do before these people will give us the information they have? Before they might choose to fight alongside Faoii?" Her eyes narrowed again. "And Tendaji, know now that your answer had better not include me killing one of my sisters."

Tendaji nodded and motioned her to sit on one of the simple camp chairs that sat to one side of the hut. He pulled up a second so that it sat across from her.

"Amaenel says there's a Faoii somewhere nearby, screaming about her shield sister being stolen. She is more powerful than she should be, and she's able to move like Thinir's forces do. That makes us nervous. It's possible that this Faoii has allied herself with Thinir but blames us for her sister's disappearance."

Kaiya was surprised at how quickly Tendaji switched back into using "we" when describing the Croeli. It was almost like he'd never left the camp.

"Why does she think that your men kidnapped her shield sister?"

"I don't know. Another Faoii did come through here shortly before I went to Clearwall. We'd sent her a tentative offer beforehand, and we thought there might be a chance of forming an alliance. She had been unwilling to help us, though, and we sent her on her way. We were not allies, but we didn't part as enemies either." He paused, thinking back. "I never met this new woman. The girl we met—Faoii-Vonda, I think her name was—said at the time that her shield sister did not trust us enough to negotiate, and she had come alone. Apparently her shield mate's opinion has not changed."

"Negotiations? You tried to get help from another Faoii? Is that what those men meant when they asked if I was the replacement?"

"Yes. But you're not," he said adamantly. "That plan wouldn't have worked anyway."

Kaiya frowned but didn't push. "So I need to talk down an enraged shield sister. You expect me to do what your entire tribe couldn't?"

"Amaenel doesn't think you'll be useful at all, but he's nothing if not an opportunist. There's a chance that you can talk her down, and he's willing to let you try."

Kaiya didn't point out that pitting one Faoii against another meant that at least one of Amaenel's enemies would fall without him having to sacrifice any of his own people. Tendaji must have recognized it too, but didn't say anything as he continued. "She's gained an almost ghostly reputation, even among our kind. That's why they want you to kill her so badly. They're afraid of her. But if you can talk her down instead, convert her to our cause, the men will respect you." He lowered his voice. "Maybe even more than they do Amaenel."

Kaiya nodded. "That's our best chance. I'm sure she'll listen to Illindria's reason." She met Tendaji's gaze, content with what he'd had to say so far. "How do we meet with her?" Tendaji stood and began to pace, an action that Kaiya had never seen before. She wondered whether it was something that he normally did when he was alone.

"Apparently, she's been following this temporary encampment at odd intervals, and they've had to move more than once. But she always makes her way back to our original settlement. The buildings there are more permanent; they would make good landmarks for someone unfamiliar with the forest." He chuckled at Kaiya's surprised glance. "Yes, Kai, we had a home here, this close to your monastery. It wasn't grand, but it was stable. And it was the only thing outside the Blackfeather Wilds that was ours."

"Until this Faoii came." Kaiya frowned, thinking. "The original Faoii—the one you met with before—did she meet with you at the original encampment?"

"Yes. It makes sense that her shield mate would continue to look for her there. As far as I know, it was the last place anyone saw her." He looked down at his hands for a moment. "I am not happy about this, but her shield sister will be quite distraught when she learns that her search has been in vain."

Kaiya nodded grimly. "Hopefully it will be easier for her to take when she has another sister there to comfort her."

"I hope you're right, Kai. I didn't mean for any of this to make your life more difficult."

Kaiya let that hang in the air for a moment before broaching another question. "What were you and Faoii-Vonda negotiating before her disappearance?"

Tendaji did not look at Kaiya, but his pacing increased. "We wanted to convince her to help spread the criukli poison through your ranks. That way, even if your people were conquered by Thinir, we could at least be certain that no one would join him. His army was already composed of Danhaid and Croeli. We did not want to face Faoii too."

"You were trying to sell her on suicide? You thought that *that* would make the Faoii trust you after generations of suspicion?" She paused at Tendaji's sharp look and raised her hands. "Right, right. The poison is still better than the alternative." She tried to force a smile. "How'd she react to that little tidbit?"

"We honestly didn't explain that part very well at the time. We cared more about keeping Thinir's numbers low than anything else. We knew we weren't going to march next to the Faoii into battle—we just wanted to decrease the chances of facing you there, instead." He shook his head. "It didn't end up mattering. She refused, and we didn't push her. This was before your monastery had fallen, and we didn't want her bringing the entire Order down on us. So we cut our losses and let her go."

"And everyone thinks that I'm her replacement? That I'm going to spread the criukli poison across the rest of the nation?"

"The men might think that that's what you're here for, but Amaenel knows better. He's willing to give us the information we need if you talk to the Faoii that's at our old encampment. That's enough."

Kaiya sighed. "It's worth a shot. I'll leave tonight. Tell me how to get to there."

25

There was the faintest hint of a trail leading to the old Croeli settlement. Kaiya walked along it with all the surety of a Faoii, but she never moved her hand for her short sword. Above her, the trees rustled with a constant breeze that did not quite make its way down to the forest floor. At least Tendaji would be able to traverse the branches without worrying about noise.

Just after dawn, Kaiya sensed more than saw someone slide from the brush to step in front of her path. There was no denying that the newcomer was Faoii. Her stance was guarded and angry, her eyes fierce. While unkempt and ragged, her fiery red hair was tied into something resembling a braid adorned with dull iron rings. Even her blood-encrusted fantoii had lost its shine. The two women stood motionless, eyeing each other with cool indifference.

It was the unnamed Faoii that broke the silence first, her voice ragged and shrill. Kaiya shuddered at the sound.

"You? A Faoii? Here? No fantoii, but a sister. A sister here. Dark skin. Dark soul? Pale eyes. Like he that betrayed me. He that helped me. Kidnapper? Kidnapper in disguise? Or friend? Friend like shield sister. Sister. Sister. Sister here?" The girl looked around with eyes that were not quite focused, but Kaiya took a step closer anyway. *Goddess, what's happened to her?*

"Hail, Sister. I am Faoii-Kaiya of the Eternal Blade." Kaiya tried to make her voice sound as unthreatening as possible. "And I *am* your friend. In the light of the Great Tapestry, I promise that I am not here to betray you." Kaiya fisted her hands and bowed her head. The other girl flashed a smile of hope for a moment before her face twisted into a scowl.

"They stole her! Stole her! Asked her to help, and when she refused, they came for her in the night. Stole her! We fought them. Fought back. Fought. They cut me down, picked her up, and left. Stole her! Stole her!" She gesticulated wildly with her fantoii. "The poison! It burned! Burned like fire! I should have died, and Illindria never heard my cries. But men did. Men! They heard me. I thought they were the kidnappers. But they healed. Healed! Drowned the poison out! Brought bells. Bronze bells. Quiet bells. Quiet whispers in my skull. Behind my face. A man with dark skin and pale eyes—horned and powerful god! Not kidnappers. Not betrayers. Taught me to jump. Jump jump. Jumping. Back and forth. Other side. This side. Other side. Always jumping."

Suddenly the fiery-haired Faoii sidestepped and was gone. Kaiya stiffened. The woman appeared again some strides to the left. "Always jumping. Healed me. Helped. Told me to return. Find her. Strike down the kidnappers. Kidnappers! Kill. Kill!

Kill!"

The wild woman's voice faded for a moment, and she stared off at something that only she could see. When she spoke again, it was quiet.

"He still whispers sometimes. Behind my eyes. Tells me what to do. But I don't listen. Never listen." She suddenly grinned, and her smile was wide and terrifying. "Have to fight my own battles. My own way. He fights wrong. Goddess wouldn't like it. Makes him mad. Mad, mad, mad! And angry! Angry voices. Angry whispers. Helper. Helper, yes. But wrong! Have to fight him. Fight him. Fight him back. But when I do, he tears out the parts of my eyes. The parts of my ears. Takes them with him. Not much left. But it's just me. Just me." Her grin was happier now.

"Faoii." Kaiya spoke slowly, carefully. The other woman's tirade had unsettled her deeply, but she pressed on. "Faoii, what is your name?" The woman's fiery braid whipped back and forth when she shook her head.

"No name. No name. Faoii-Thinir? Croeli-Julianne? Faoii. Croeli. It's all the same now. All the same. Until I get her back. Only half without her. No name. No." Suddenly the woman was crying, her eyes streaming as she clawed at them with dirty nails. "I feel her. Feel the chains, the darkness. I feel her, but I can't find her. The silver cord is wrapped up. Twisted. Twisted! Lost! Stolen!" The woman's screeches rose into the trees, and even the wind stilled at the sound.

Kaiya tried again to calm the distraught Faoii, sifting through the anguished babbling as best she could. "*Shh*, Faoii-Julianne. It was Faoii-Julianne, once, before all of this, right?"

The woman nodded, releasing a frantic sob. Kaiya tried again. "*Shhh* . . . It's all right. We'll look together. If she's still here, we'll find her. And then you both can come back with me. We'll get you some help."

"Help? Help? What help? Where? Monastery's gone! Gone! Burnt! Ashes! Who would cut the chains, mend the cracks? No. No no no no. Only Vonda can help me now. Only Vonda. Have to find her." The woman looked like she would turn to run back into the trees, but Kaiya stopped her with a soothing motion.

"We will, we will, I promise you. But Thinir has taken a lot from you. We must seek Illindria. She can heal you. She can stop the voices and put all of the parts back together."

"Illindria?" Faoii-Julianne lifted her eyes to Kaiya's. "The Goddess! She speaks. Used to speak. Songs. Prayers. Pipes. Bells? No. Not bells. But music. Words. Speak, speak. Always speaking. Her voice was drowned out by the strong god. He hasn't found Vonda for me. Hasn't helped. Not helping. But the Goddess can find Vonda! The Goddess would know!" Suddenly Julianne flung herself to the side, Blinking out of existence. She landed at Kaiya's feet, grasping fervently. "You! You are the one that I have seen each time I have jumped. You are in Her world, in Her mind. She speaks of you. Would listen to you. Ask Her! Ask for Her to find Vonda! Ask! Ask! Please!" Kaiya smiled sadly and brought her hand up to lay it on the other woman's shoulder.

"Have faith, Faoii. The Goddess provides." Julianne's eyes flooded anew, and Kaiya truly saw the broken Faoii for the first time. The world shifted, and images superimposed themselves on top of what Kaiya had already seen.

A tattered, grimy blindfold hung limply from across Julianne's eyes and dingy shackles hung from her bloody wrists. Julianne had evidently clawed her way free of whatever bindings Croeli-Thinir had placed upon her, but the damage was done. The sweet, youthful face was now cracked and blemished, jagged like the shards of a shattered mirror.

As Kaiya watched, the broken mirror shifted, and there was the faintest hint of Thinir's pale eyes peeking up from beneath the glass of the Faoii's face. With a grimace, Julianne shoved him back. He faded, but another crack danced its way across Julianne's cheekbone.

Kaiya stared at the fallen Faoii with a heavy heart. She didn't know whether even the Great Illindria could heal all the broken pieces of this woman's soul. But even a broken mirror could still serve its purpose, and the Goddess was not known for throwing things away.

As though reading Kaiya's mind, Julianne looked up, and her eyes lit with a fire and devotion that burned its way through the broken glass of her marred face. Kaiya had to shut her eyes against the brightness she found there.

A short time passed, but the light behind Kaiya's closed eyelids never faded. Cautiously, Kaiya opened them again, but the fire had not diminished. She blinked a few times, trying to clear her vision. Julianne mimicked her with a confused expression that was decidedly not lit with the ethereal glow. Kai frowned. Whatever she was seeing, it was not coming from Julianne.

There. A glow from the ground behind Julianne's shackled visage. Bright, eerie, and red—a stark contrast to the whites and greens of the forest that lay in all directions. Kaiya moved toward the trees, toward a light that was there but not there. And as she stared, it moved, speeding away from her and into the foliage that surrounded the path. Without thinking, Kaiya followed it, only vaguely aware that the other woman trailed. Overhead, the leaves began to rustle with even more fervor as she crashed through them, following the beacon.

Goddess, let this be Your sign and not a trap!

Eventually they came to what could have been an outpost. The single-room building had not yet completely fallen to disuse, though someone had torn down the wooden door, scattering it across the clearing. Some sort of burrowing animal had dug long, deep furrows at its base. Kaiya cast a glance at Julianne's cracked and muddy fingernails but said nothing. Instead, she circled the building, staring past it, through it.

There. The beacon issued from the ground a dozen paces from the outpost. She walked toward it, and the earth seemed to open in a great chasm below her. At its base were a flame and a figure that Kaiya could not quite make out, flickering in the darkness of her mind's eye.

As she reached the beacon's source, the superimposed images faded, and Kaiya was left staring at only the forest floor. Somewhere far away, the sounds of panpipes rose, then cut off abruptly. This sound, more than anything, shook Kaiya from her daze.

"Here! Somewhere here!" Kaiya dropped to her knees, scrabbling at the ground with her bare hands. Julianne stared at her for a long moment before releasing a strangled yell and driving into the ground with her fantoii, using the blade like a shovel. Together, the two women clawed at the forest floor.

Increasingly desperate minutes passed, and Kaiya's heartbeat quickened. Something was wrong. She didn't know exactly what had happened here, but something in her gut made her more terrified with every passing moment. Somewhere in the distance, the panpipes struggled to rise against the rushing in her ears.

Kaiya's fingers struck something hard beneath the earth. A

wooden beam, thin enough for her to wrap her fingers around the edge. It spread out in front of her, beneath the dirt. She followed it, brushing the earth off with her fingers as she moved. The board ended after a few strides and gave way to a circular crevice that widened out on either side. Kaiya scraped dirt out from here too, moving faster and faster until she had completed the circuit. She rose slowly, her eyebrows drawn together.

In front of her was a round slab of earth nearly nine handspans across, with a board crossing it lengthwise. A trapdoor.

Kaiya wrapped her long fingers around the beam. "Help me pull it up!" she hissed at the other woman. Julianne bent over, her eyes wide and wild. "Pull!"

They pulled. Earth heaved upward from the path of the circle as the women yanked. Dirt and pine needles rained into the gaping hole that opened beneath their feet.

Throwing the round plank aside, Kaiya peered into the blackness, but she could see nothing. Her previous vision had faded, and she was left with only the dark reality before her. She straightened quickly, spinning around to scan the trees.

"Tendaji!" Even before the echo had finished its reverberations, her brother had detached himself from the surrounding shadows and glided forward. Faoii-Julianne released a piercing battle cry at his approach and charged, but Kaiya batted her blade away and grabbed her by the shoulders without moving her eyes. "Tendaji, what is this?"

The wrath in Tendaji's face seemed genuine. "I don't know." His voice deepened into a sinister growl. "But I intend to find out." He turned toward the hole just as another shadow broke free from the trees.

This shadow approached slowly, its hands raised in a placating gesture. Tendaji's eyes were fiercer than Kaiya had ever seen them when he recognized Torin. A deep growl rumbled in his chest.

"Croeli-Tendaji," Torin whispered. "Tendaji, we *need* her."

"What is down there?" Tendaji's voice was unforgiving. Torin licked his lips and took another tentative step forward.

"We couldn't wait for you to find a willing Faoii. He's grown too powerful. We weren't sure you'd ever come back with another."

"*What is down there?*" The growl was closer to a roar now, and Kaiya could hear Tendaji's fantoii scream even from within its sheath, but Torin continued as though he hadn't heard anything at all.

"She's too weak now. She can't do it on her own. And the other one wouldn't drop her guard long enough for us to get to her. She can just Blink out again anyway. We need your replacement. They'll all be his if we don't. You know that."

"Torin, so help me…" Tendaji let the threat drop, and his hand snaked closer to his wailing blade. Torin's eyes narrowed, but he did not move for his own weapon.

"She's willing now. It took some time, but she eventually realized that it was the only way. Slowing Thinir is our main priority. We all know this. And if you could look past your own blade-blasted pride for a minute, you'd realize it too." Tendaji's eyes narrowed, and he took a step forward. Torin moved to circle him. "Come on, Tendaji. Your family started this! You have the power to end it! She'll understand too, with time. The pain fades when you realize that the greater good outweighs all else." His voice softened a little. "Tendaji, you know this is the only way."

"No! This wasn't an option. It was *never* an option!" Tendaji's voice shattered the air around them, and his fantoii appeared in his hand, its tip pointed at Torin's chest.

Suddenly, a dozen more shapes dropped from the trees.

"We need a replacement, Tendaji. One or both, we'll make it work." Torin's face was forlorn as he slowly drew his criukli. "I'm sorry we couldn't make you see." Then there was only the soft rustle of leather as the shadows attacked.

26

"**K**aiya! Run!" Tendaji's voice rang through the forest just as he swung his blade against the first Croeli foe that reached him. Kaiya spun, drawing her short sword as she did.

Two Croeli dropped in front of her, and she drove her blade deep into one's shoulder before he'd even risen to his full height. The other snarled and lunged. Kaiya spun with an outstretched arm, trying to clip his helmetless head with her sword, but he ducked away, rolling to one side.

Meanwhile, Faoii-Julianne jumped around the forest with disorienting speed. Again and again she appeared, then disappeared, then appeared once more, each time striking out against a different opponent. In the glimpses that Kaiya caught between her own battles, she realized with dismay that Julianne's eyes grew wilder with each movement, until they seemed barely human. The effect of Thinir's Blinking was taking a rapid toll.

"Julianne! Be care—" Kaiya tried to warn the other girl, but a criukli clipped Kaiya's shoulder, and she was drawn back to the fight. But Julianne still Blinked in and out of her peripheral vision.

As the haggard, frantic minutes passed, the wild Faoii's movements became more and more sporadic, less controlled. She jumped, seemingly at random, again and again, constantly landing closer and closer to her enemies. Her blood frenzy drove her wild as she screamed. The cry pierced the forest, and the surrounding Croeli paused, uncertain.

Croeli-Amaenel's voice cut through the silence. "Stay on her! Chain her if you must! We need her in that pit!"

Shaken from their shock, Amaenel's subordinates circled Faoii-Julianne cautiously. The broken Faoii stalked back and forth like a caged panther before throwing herself to one side again.

When she Blinked next, she was on them.

One Croeli screamed as she appeared, but the cry faded into a low gurgle as her blade sprouted from his throat. The others pounced on her even before their comrade's body hit the ground, but she Blinked to the side, appearing behind them. Two more fell away from her outstretched fantoii, their heads rolling away from her booted feet as their bodies slumped to the ground. She Blinked again, this time forward, then immediately back.

Right into the arms of Croeli-Amaenel.

Faoii-Julianne struggled in his grip, cursing and biting, but he held her still. Enveloping her in a bone-crushing squeeze, the Croeli raised his boot and slammed it against Julianne's leg with a resounding *crack*. Her scream hadn't even begun to pass her lips when he swung the boot back to collide with her opposite knee. Its *pop* was somehow more disconcerting than the first strike had been.

Faoii-Julianne could not repress her cry as she fell to the ground, writhing in agony as she tried to drag herself toward her dropped fantoii. Croeli-Amaenel only looked down at her from beneath his scowling mask. "Blink now, Faoii witch," he growled.

Julianne weakly reached for the dingy fantoii that lay just out of her reach, then crumpled limply as her adversary brought his booted heel down on her outstretched hand. Kaiya stared in horror as he kicked the motionless body into the pit.

Almost lazily, Amaenel turned back from the hole and nodded silently. It was then that Kaiya realized she had been still for far too long as she'd watched events unfold. Far too long, indeed.

A man seemingly materialized behind her, his breath hot and sudden against her neck. It reeked of hatred and fear. Instantly alert, Kaiya sidestepped to the left, hearing the cold scratching of metal against metal as his criukli scraped against the right side of her breastplate. Her eyes narrowed and she spun to the right, twisting around the blade. Then she snapped her arm toward the Croeli's back, aiming for his lungs. Her short sword sliced through the dark leathers with a practiced ease.

But the blade caught.

So unlike her regular fantoii, this weapon was not weighted correctly. It did not release itself from her slain enemy's ribcage with the smooth elegance she was accustomed to. Instead, it stuck between the man's ribs with an infuriating tug. Kaiya wrenched it free with a violent jerk of her arm, but even those precious seconds were too much. She had not noticed the other Croeli lurking beneath her adversary's arm. She had not noticed the criukli posed to strike at her now.

She did, however, notice as the criukli rammed upward, sliding underneath the edge of her breastplate. She noticed as it lodged itself into the soft flesh of her belly, its blade breaking from the hilt with a twist of the Croeli's wrist. She noticed a high-pitched scream but did not recognize it as her own.

There were shouts from everywhere. Someone caught her as her knees buckled, cradling her against a sudden chill. Someone was screaming at her to sing. She opened her mouth to try, but her tongue didn't cooperate. Couldn't move. Then, just as suddenly, the arms were gone and there was more yelling. A fight somewhere. *I should be helping.* She reached for her sword but couldn't find it. There was only pain and fire. The world spun, and her flesh boiled. She felt the blisters explode from her belly even without seeing them.

Then the yelling increased and the ground was gone. The trees overhead were suddenly closer, fading in and out of her fiery existence. They spun and distorted, seeming to lengthen and spread apart as she struggled to breathe. Then she was falling. Pain exploded and the trees disappeared. There was only fire and darkness, tears and blood.

Then nothing.

Thinir could not repress his glee as he watched the minutes following his niece's downfall. His traitorous nephew's scream was unearthly as his former comrade plunged a criukli into Kaiya's stomach. Thinir watched as Tendaji frantically cut down two more Croeli in a rush to get to Kaiya, trying in vain to stop the bleeding from her abdomen. His body shook as he yelled at her, trying to raise his voice above her pained cries.

"Kaiya! Start singing! You've gotten through this before! You can do it again! Sing, Kai! Sing!" Kaiya tried to open her mouth, but her tongue, red and slick with blood, only moved faintly. He tried again but two men yanked him to his feet and Kaiya fell limply to the ground, blood pooling beneath her prone form.

Tendaji fought against these newest adversaries, screaming brutally in rage and fear, but they held him. It did not take long for him to exhaust himself within their grasp, bruising his arms already in the effort. Defeated, he could only stare in cold rage as Amaenel exploded on the aggressor that had cut his sister down.

"You moron! We needed her alive!" With angry movements, Amaenel crouched down and freed Kaiya from her breastplate and leathers, using his hands to staunch the blood that seeped from her stomach. Even from this vantage point, Thinir could see horrendous blisters puckering Kaiya's dark skin—boils that pulsed and oozed sickeningly with red and yellow puss. She screamed under Amaenel's touch, and several of the blisters burst like overripe cherries.

Stripping off his horned helm, Amaenel twisted his face into a mask of vehemence as he yanked out the blade that had broken off beneath Kaiya's skin. Blood sprayed, and she gasped, paling. Tendaji's enraged shudder matched Amaenel's as they watched the blood spread slowly over the forest floor. "You even poisoned the blade! Imbecile!"

The other man visibly paled, and Thinir smiled as he watched new rifts form in his enemies' ranks. "Croeli-Amaenel, forgive me. She would have killed us all before stepping into that pit." Amaenel leapt to his feet and backhanded the man with a resounding *crack*.

"Look at her! Who does she look like to you?" The

subordinate looked toward Kaiya, but Amaenel continued before the other man could respond. "We had other uses for her! Two left in the world, and you kill one! What good is she to us now?" The man licked his lips before speaking.

"At least Thinir can't use her now, right? And she can test the new formula. The Faoii in the pit might be able to use her poisoned blood to strengthen the Hag's bond. Maybe—" Amaenel cut him off with an outraged scream and buried the broken blade in his subordinate's chest.

"You want to test it? Fine." He spat on the man as agonized screams filled the air. "Die knowing that you have been our downfall." He turned away and barked at two more of his men nearby. "Throw her in. He's right about one thing. The other one might find a use for her."

Amaenel spit toward the pit with an angry growl. "Damn it all anyway. Hide this place. We won't be coming back."

Two of the men picked Kaiya up by her arms and legs. She didn't struggle at their touch this time. Tendaji renewed his fight, screaming her name, but Kaiya didn't move as the two men threw her into the gaping pit. He tried to lunge for her, but Amaenel blocked his path, smiling down at him as he settled his helm again.

"Well, that didn't go as I had hoped, but we've survived worse. Now that you are free of distractions, I am sure you can be convinced to focus on more important matters, Tendaji." He nodded to the two Croeli that were still restraining their newest captive. "Bring him with us. We only have one chance now. Let's make sure it isn't wasted."

Kaiya's discarded breastplate lay abandoned in the clearing as the men lifted Tendaji by his arms, bound him, and led him away.

The vision faded, and Thinir cackled gleefully as he ordered a nearby slave to remove the chalice. Kaiya was no threat to him now. Without her leadership, her army would fracture and crumble. Tendaji would become useless to the Faoii whores, maddened by grief. And, more importantly, he knew where all his woes were stemming from. Everything was falling into place.

Still grinning, he idly tossed the now blood-free dagger onto the table.

Nothing could stop him now.

endaji glared at Amaenel from his position on the ground. He had long since given up trying to struggle out of his bonds, though other than this indecency, he had not been mistreated. While he could not see what Amaenel was doing from this angle, he was acutely aware that his former subordinate was making preparations. Tendaji growled.

"That poison is not what I created, Amaenel. What did you do?" Amaenel shrugged but did not turn away from the table he was working at.

"The old stuff took too long. As Thinir grew more powerful, he could refurbish his victims more quickly, and from farther away. So we had to make it louder. Make it faster."

"What did you add to it?"

"Tonicloran."

Tendaji jumped, his muscles tensing painfully against the ropes. "What?!"

Amaenel sighed, and his shoulders slackened a little. He turned back to the table resignedly. "All the gods have abandoned us, Tendaji. We can't anger Them any more than we have already. So why not use any tool we can to bring down this tyrant? What else could he do to us in retaliation?"

"Illindria would not like it, Amaenel."

Amaenel released a barking laugh. "You still worship the Hag? Poor Tendaji. Look at your Faoii pet. At her armies. How could that witch possibly be worth the breath it takes to even whisper a prayer?"

Tendaji scowled but did not reply. The silence lengthened, and Amaenel glanced over his shoulder again. He snorted at Tendaji's belligerent stare. "What? Nothing to say to that?" The sound of metal instruments clicking together filled the void left in his laughter's wake.

"Where did you get it?" Tendaji finally asked. "The tonicloran, I mean."

"Why, we brought it with us, of course. Thinir had one of the original sprigs from the temple back home. He started growing it at the encampment even before he slew Croeli-Tendir." Tendaji's eyebrows lifted in surprise despite the sudden pain at the mention of his father. Amaenel caught the look. "God's axe, Tendaji, you really were *never* around to see any of this, were you? Bells, it's surprising you found your way back at all." Tendaji curled one thin lip, but Amaenel continued, "You should have seen the garden he created. Dark and brutal, but filled with such power. His horned god would be proud."

"My father knew of it?"

"Of course."

"How?" The sound was angrier than Tendaji had intended,

and after a moment, he tried again. "How did Thinir convince Father that tonicloran could be useful? Was he planning to use it to kill the Faoii if they refused us?"

"What? No, of course not. Broken blade, Tendaji, think about it. If Thinir was planning on doing that, don't you think he would have used it when he tore down their temples?" Amaenel took a few measured steps toward Tendaji and squatted on his haunches in front of him, resting his forearms on his knees. "I think he convinced your father that he was looking for an antidote, something that could be used as a peace offering for when we contacted the Faoii. The truth is much more believable, of course. I'm surprised your father fell for that story, knowing how much Thinir despised the witches.

"Thinir was sure there was a way to use tonicloran to reach the home of the witch goddess. Crazy bastard wanted to strike Her in the heart and enslave Her followers. Show them what it's like to go without." He chuckled. "Your entire family gets these weird ideas in their heads, don't they?" He laughed out loud at Tendaji's seething glare. "Never did quite master it, though—lucky for us. He had to expend all his forces on bringing down the Faoii temples, and it gave us time to twist the plant to our own use. Blessed tonicloran might end up being his downfall despite how much hope he put into it."

Tendaji spat at Amaenel's feet. "There is nothing blessed about tonicloran. You've seen what it does to people. And you're spreading it around the world for anyone to stumble over."

Amaenel shrugged. "Better for them to die that way than to become Thinir's unwilling slave." Amaenel straightened again and loomed over Tendaji. "You're right about one thing, though: there's nothing blessed about this plant. Thinir did find a way to use some part of it for that weird Blinking of his. Almost a dozen men died while he was experimenting with it, but eventually he must have done something right. I don't know how he made it work, but between that and his mind control, he's nearly destroyed us." Deep lines creased Amaenel's face as he frowned.

"You came back right around that time, didn't you? That last time. You must remember. There was always something wrong about those boys that came back afterward. Something gone from their eyes. And they always spoke of a world that wasn't ours." He sighed deeply, shivering from a nonexistent chill. "When you killed Croeli-Vilikir-Thinir, we all realized how bad it'd gotten. Most of us who deserted left then. We scattered. Until you found us." He looked down at Tendaji and inhaled deeply, as though considering what to say.

"Despite all of this, Tendaji, I'm glad that you freed us from that before we were all lost to whatever's on the other side of the void."

Tendaji scowled. "If you're so grateful, why keep me here? We both want to stop Thinir. One of our tactics might work. Why not have a contingency plan?" His voice was icy. "Why imprison me?"

Amaenel turned back again, this time holding a copper vial in one hand. He cocked his head at Tendaji, eyeing him with wry amusement.

"Come now, Tendaji. You're not stupid. Isn't it obvious?" He smiled as he stuck a cork into the vial's top. "You're the key to finding Thinir."

Tendaji's eyes narrowed as he tried to follow Amaenel's logic and failed. "Explain."

Amaenel chuckled. "Haven't you realized? Thinir uses the

blood of his victims to control them. Thaumaturgy. He keeps the blood of his lieutenants with him and uses it to control their actions, and in turn, they control others. A thousand dead and dying all connected by the same bloody web." His eyes shone. "Blood has power. Control the blood and you control the man."

Amaenel looked to the copper vial again before turning and placing it carefully back on the table. "Your father's blood would have been better, of course, but it's lost to us now. Thinir was smart. He destroyed his bloodline immediately so that we couldn't use it. But he spared you."

Tendaji frowned. "If what you say is true, he must have known that you could use me to find him. He wouldn't have kept me alive."

Amaenel shrugged. "I guess he thought you'd remain loyal. Thought he could still use you. He must have had dreams of you taking his place eventually because he kept your mind intact. Untarnished. You were the only of Thinir's ascended he did not refurbish after your father's fall."

"And what about Kai?"

"I don't pretend to know why he spared your sister. Maybe he had plans to use her too. Not that he has a chance now." Turning his attention to someone that Tendaji couldn't see, Amaenel headed for the door. "Prepare him. The full moon is rising. We only have one chance at this."

Meanwhile, far to the west, Lyn paced back and forth, gouging a deep rut in the snow. Asanali, sitting on one of the lower branches of a nearby tree, watched her movements silently. Eili, on the other hand, scowled through her ice-blue eye and webs of scarring.

"Stop that, girl. You ain't helpin' nothin'."

"They should be back by now!" Lyn snarled in reply. "The troops are getting restless, and we're sitting ducks here." She swept one arm to encompass the valley and surrounding woodland. Tents and campfires dotted the area. Women and not a few men spoke in hushed tones, their voices carrying on a wind that was not as biting as it should have been. Asanali's feet stopped twirling and changed direction.

"The pale-eyed messengers said they would not return until the night sun has shown all of her faces. It has not been so long yet."

"And you! Goddess's girdle, Asanali, I wish you would speak like a normal person!" Lyn kicked a clump of snow at the tree that the Danhaid leader was sitting in. The bronze woman moved one foot out of its line of fire.

"If I did, you would still only hear the words you ask for, not the one I speak." There was most assuredly no hint of contempt in Asanali's voice, but her soft smile was maddening, regardless.

"Blades! You are so infuriating!"

"Faoii! Enough!" Faoii-Eili's voice was filled with power, and Lyn tensed at its sound. Still belligerent, however, she spun and redirected her attack.

"Don't use that tone with me! I've earned my title, Eili. There are no superiors here." Eili exhaled through her nose in a dark *huff.* Slowly, the fire in her ice-blue eye faded. When she spoke, it was still stern, but without the sharp edge of battle.

"No, Faoii-Lyn, there are not. Which is why we should be workin' together rather than squabblin' like the unascended. We knew that Kaiya and the Croeli might not return. We knew that we might have to act on our own orders rather than theirs. We are full Faoii. Even Asanali there. We are more than capable of doin' what needs to be done."

"Which is what, exactly? We don't know what's making Croeli-Thinir more powerful. We don't know where to go to strike against him. We don't even know where to go to strike at his army. Even if we march to where they were last, they can just move again."

"Then we patrol. We keep 'im from taking any more of the people from the outlyin' villages. We scout and gather as we've been doin'. And we strike when we have the information we need."

"That's not good enough! He's growing more powerful every day! If we wait until we find more information, it'll be too late. We need to strike now, while his army is still weak from the battle at the last monastery and their defeat at Cailivale."

"What would you suggest then, Faoii? I'm listenin'."

Lyn flashed a dark smile. "We know where he holds at least some power. I say we strike at the only stationary hold we can. Overtake it, if possible, and force him to come to us. If we strike hard and fast, we can take control. We can defend rather than attack."

"Clearwall? The capital?" Eili's remaining blonde eyebrow shot up. "That's treason, girl."

Lyn's eyes were filled with bloodlust and spite. "Everything we do is treason. We might as well own up to it."

Eili chewed this over for a minute before lowering her eyes. "I suppose yer right. And it does make a certain kind of sense."

"The eyes on the wind will see us travel. The dark god's pack will rise to meet us before we reach his walls of stone and sorrow."

"Then we meet them before we reach the capital gates. Either way, we draw them out. It's got to be better than wasting energy and rations wandering the world and searching for them."

"We might not even need to do that much." Eili rose to her feet and pointed toward the field. A single dark figure, a woman of lithe build and clad in Cailivale leathers, dashed across the snow-covered plain. As she got closer, Lyn finally heard the frightened cry of a bugle pressed against white lips. Eili frowned and donned her ivy helm. "Maybe you were right. We have been here too long."

Thinir's army had found them.

28

Tendaji steeled himself as Amaenel approached with a wicked-looking criukli and the copper vial. Night had fallen, and a full moon lit up the harsh, deep furrows that had been carved at Tendaji's feet. If viewed from above, they formed a crude, simplistic star surrounded by a series of angular symbols. Amaenel's men had placed a wooden altar at its topmost point before shoving Tendaji into the center.

"How much blood do you need?" Tendaji asked without fear or even anger. Amaenel faltered in his step for a moment, surprised.

"You have finally realized that this is necessary, Tendaji?"

"I realize that there is nothing I can do about it. And you're right; we need to find out where Thinir is. I understand that."

Amaenel nodded and stepped close to his old superior. "I am glad to hear you say that, Tendaji. Truly. I do not need much."

More quickly than even Tendaji's eye could follow, he slashed down with the virgin blade.

A moment passed, and Tendaji almost remarked on Amaenel's poor aim for missing a stationary target at close range. Then there was suddenly a warmth on his chest, and when he looked down he saw crimson blood oozing in a steady stream along the center of his ribcage. The stream had barely begun its slow trickle before the copper vial was there, chilly against the warm flesh of his torso. Amaenel pressed it under the wound firmly, and the precious life force filled it.

When he'd finished, Amaenel made his way to the altar and began to chant. His whisper rose out of the silence of the forest, and at first Tendaji wasn't even sure he'd heard it. But as it rose, its cadence changed.

Soon Amaenel's voice became hollow, booming through the ground like a far-off earthquake. It reverberated its way through the clearing and the trees, growing louder until it surged through the night. Tendaji didn't understand the words, but he shivered as they rattled across his skin, his bones, his soul. When Amaenel turned around to face the gathered Croeli, the whispers swirled around his cloak and the earth gasped as he poured the contents of the copper vial into an ornate chalice that had been placed at the altar's head.

Tendaji lost track of the chant as it continued to spin and twist in the air. Then, abruptly, it was over, and in the sudden silence, Amaenel discarded the copper vial and criukli blade. He grasped the brim of the gleaming cup with both hands, his face glowing red with the reflection of the firelight as he peered into it. His eyes were wide and eager.

The wind *screamed*. The night erupted into chaos as the chalice exploded with an unseen force that shook the earth and the men standing around the ritual site. Tendaji set his feet and remained erect, but he could only watch as Amaenel's head was thrown back with the force of the chalice's power. The wind around him caught at his hair, his clothes, his scowling eyes. Then, with a screeching howl that roared from the earth like a geyser in the night, the wind and Amaenel were *gone*.

In Amaenel's absence, the chalice's glow intensified in hue, and light sprayed forth from its brim toward the night sky. It swayed there like a desert mirage, flickering unsteadily. Tendaji peered at the shifting image, drawn by the glimmering red trees and firelight that appeared within.

He had only a moment to admire the ghostly tapestry, however, before the projected trees suddenly zoomed past with sickening speed. Twisting through the trunks like a bird in flight, the image covered miles of forest and valley, carrying Tendaji forward without grace or comfort, over rivers and fields, past landmarks that he could just barely glimpse. Zooming. Twisting. Ever forward.

Finally, the apparition sped up the side of a mountain that Tendaji did not recognize by sight and rested at the base of an old, dilapidated keep. Vines snaked their way up the broken turrets, and crows released their mournful cries in the shade of the broken stone. And yet, despite the desolate and worn exterior, there was a darkness within that turned Tendaji's insides to water.

He tried to peer into one of the black windows of the keep, sure that whatever was beyond it would enlighten him to something he could not currently comprehend. But as he peered, a flash of light burst forth, blinding him. Above it, a feminine war cry rang out, equally similar and strange—like something he knew from long ago. He tried to place the cry, but it was immediately drowned out by the sound of metal scraping against metal, and a great bronze bell. Then there was only the sound of the dying wind through the forest as the image blinked out of existence and Amaenel reappeared.

Amaenel grasped at the altar, knocking over the chalice with his shaking, groping hands. Tendaji watched his own blood pool on the ground at his former subordinate's booted feet. He felt shaky and nauseated. The entire experience had lasted no more than a handful of seconds, and yet he felt sure he had seen a lifetime's worth of events between the images he understood. And he had only experienced a fraction of what Amaenel had seen.

"A map. Get me a map," Amaenel gasped out as he struggled to stand. Torin produced one, and with a violent movement, Amaenel drove his blade into its surface. Tendaji strained his neck to see and was not surprised that the criukli point pierced a hole in the forest where the abandoned keep would be. Amaenel took a few unsteady steps to the chair that had been set out for him and sank into it, his breathing ragged.

"My lord?" Torin finally ventured. He set a steadying hand on Amaenel's shoulder, but the older Croeli shrugged it off.

"I saw the keep that he calls home. I know where to go." He clutched his head and growled under his breath, his voice filling with a rage that Tendaji did not understand. There was something different about Amaenel's eyes when he brought them up to stare at the full moon that hung above them. "But there was more, too! Something else that I couldn't quite wrap my head around. There was a war cry. High-pitched. Faoii." He spit the last word. "The other soldiers were right. Wherever you go when you Blink, it's not of this world. There's information there that we aren't supposed to grasp. But I think we need it. Whatever Faoii released her cry—we need her for some blasted reason. And I don't even know who she is!" Torin narrowed his eyes while Amaenel fumed.

"Do you want to use one of the other soldiers, my lord? We still have one more virgin blade, and Croeli-Tendaji's blood has already proven to be effective. There are a few men in the camp that have Blinked before. They might be more capable of getting the information you need, if it is a matter of navigation."

"No. No more Blinking. We need everyone at their full capacity when we do this. We're already spread too thin."

"What do you wish to do then, Croeli-Amaenel?"

Slowly, Amaenel raised his eyes to look at Tendaji, and a slow smile crept over his face.

"We need the Faoii. Of that I am certain." His eyes darkened, but his smile never faltered. "Tendaji knows. He knows every Faoii left. Get the information from him."

Daytime. It was daytime again, Tendaji was sure of it. He'd survived another night. Or had the blackness only been caused by pain? He didn't know; he didn't . . .

The broken warrior could not hold back a cry as one of his former brothers pressed the red-hot sword tip against his thigh. He struggled against the bonds tied to the branch high above him but found no more success than before. Torin leaned against a tree a few paces away, his arms crossed over his chest. His expression was more of disgust and discomfort than rage.

Tendaji tried not to look toward him, but his old friend's presence was somehow comforting. Constant. The scout had never been far away during the last few days while Amaenel's men had tried to extract the location of the Faoii army from their newest prisoner. But he had also never helped with the administrations of hot irons or barbed wire. Torin had not torn Tendaji's fingernails off with blacksmith tools or carved deep gashes in his chest. Instead, every time Tendaji had been pushed past even his tolerance for pain— each time he had finally fallen into the bottomless well of unconsciousness—Torin had been there when he woke again, administrating bandages or salves.

Tendaji wasn't sure whether Torin was still a friend or whether he was only trying to convince him of such. That uncertainty was a torture all its own.

The searing blade was pulled away, and Tendaji sagged against the bonds that held him upright. His cut, bloodied legs had long since refused to support him, and his arms had gone numb days before. He hadn't broken. He wouldn't break. And part of him wanted to take comfort in how infuriating that must have been to Amaenel.

He'd seen the other Croeli a few times in the last few days, but only in passing. The new Croeli leader seemed more than content to allow Torin to administer to Tendaji in whatever way he saw fit. But Tendaji still saw the impatience in Amaenel's eyes, the hard edge to his jaw.

As though reading Tendaji's mind, Amaenel stepped out from behind the trees that surrounded camp. He wore one of the horned war helmets, and the snarling mask glinted in the firelight as Tendaji's tormentor reached to pull another blade from the fire.

"Enough. He's never going to break. None of us would under the same circumstances." Amaenel spat into the blood at Tendaji's feet. "You can't expect a Croeli, even a treacherous one, to give up information he doesn't want to."

Torin rose and gave a slight bow. "What would you have us do, Croeli? Kill him?" There was no hint of remorse or disgust in the question, only duty. Tendaji's heart sank, but he squared his jaw and remained silent. If he was to die here, at the hands of his brothers without remorse, he could at least do so with dignity.

The scowling helmet seemed even more sinister when Amaenel replied. "No. Traitor or not, he's still Croeli, and one of the few people in the world not under Thinir's thumb. We can find Thinir with what we've already learned, and we can sure as the broken blade kill him without a Faoii witch's help. No matter what the Hag says." Amaenel stepped close and lifted Tendaji's bruised, bleeding face until their eyes met. "You were right, Tendaji. I need a contingency plan. You think that you can succeed against Thinir where my men can't? Fine. Give it your all. Just don't get in my way." The last words hung in the air between them, filled with steel and ice. He took a few slow steps backward before turning on his heel and storming back toward camp. "Release him. Then prepare the horses. We ride against Thinir at dawn."

Surprised and a little wary, Tendaji stared after the war-hungry general. The snow flurried in the wake of his blood-red cloak, masking him from view among the grey trees. In that haze of white dusting, Torin stepped forward, his criukli drawn.

Torin was fast. Faster than Tendaji remembered. When he was within reach of Tendaji's bonds, he flicked his wrist upward, severing them with viperlike speed. Tendaji had just long enough to realize how easily Torin could have killed him when his legs gave out under his weight. He crumpled sideways, his eyes rolling back as his agonized legs began screaming anew, the numbness giving way to a torrent of injuries he had, thus far, not been forced to face en masse. The world tilted dizzyingly, and he fought against his darkening vision. Then Torin was there, supporting Tendaji with a strength that was not obvious in his lithe form. While Tendaji fought in vain to regain his balance, Torin lowered him carefully to the ground and went about bandaging his most recent injuries. Tendaji focused on staying conscious.

"For what it is worth, Tendaji, I hope you succeed." Torin barely whispered the words as he sewed up one of the gashes that littered Tendaji's dark skin. Tendaji blinked, surprised. It was the first time Torin had spoken to him since the fight next to the pit. He turned his bloodied face to meet his old friend's dark eyes. They seemed sincere.

"Even after all of this, you'd say that to my face?"

"Of course. I've always been your friend, Tendaji." Torin seemed hurt by the question, and after some thought, Tendaji reached out to lay a hand on his shoulder.

"Come with me then, Torin. Fight beside me as you once did." Torin shook his head.

"I cannot. We are Croeli, Tendaji. 'We are the harbingers of justice and truth. We are the strength of the weak and the voice of the silent.' And that strength comes from unity. You know this." Disappointed, Tendaji removed his hand and nodded once, leaning his head back against the tree. Torin finished the last stitch and pulled it tight. When he spoke again, his voice was firm. "The Croeli are divided. We are all weaker because of it. You cannot ask me to fragment that strength further."

"No. I can't." With difficulty, Tendaji rose on shaky legs, then squared his shoulders and steeled himself. He put a hand out to Torin, who grasped his forearm in a friendship that still, even after all this time, seemed unbreakable. Tendaji wondered how he could have doubted that. "I wish you luck, Croeli-Torin-Amaenel. When Thinir is dead, maybe we will be able to meet again under more pleasant circumstances." Torin nodded, and Tendaji released his arm, then turned away and limped out of camp. He wondered how he would tell the others what had happened here. It had been his idea to bring Kaiya alone. They had expected him to keep her safe. And now…no matter what their reaction, he doubted they could blame him any more than he blamed himself.

Yet another person's blood on my hands. He cast a glance toward the sky. "Kai, I'm so sorry," he whispered to the clouds.

If his little sister was able to hear him in the afterlife, she did not answer.

29

These were not men. They were silent, their eyes dull and listless, their attacks precise and deadly. Their kills were quick and fierce, but they attacked continuously, mechanically. No defense. No strategy. No fear.

And when they fell, they made no sound.

But the battlefield was far from silent. For two days now, piercing, terror-filled screams had spread across the blood-soaked plain. Women fell in droves against swords that dripped green with poison. Lyn watched in horror as skin boiled beneath the poisoned blades that her opponents cleaved the air with. The fast-acting toxin was different than what they'd seen before. It cauterized the wounds immediately, leaving the victims to die in a slow agony as their flesh boiled away in huge, open sores. The Faoii screams twisted Lyn's stomach. And yet she pushed on.

Pain didn't seem to affect the Croeli or hinder their continuous onslaught. The enemy continued forward as long as their limbs were still attached and as long as blood pumped through their veins. Those that fell, fell only because they lacked legs to move or enough blood to keep their hearts beating. But the Faoii still dropped like mortals. Beyond this, the Croeli were inexhaustible, and fought on despite fatigue or the plummeting temperature after nightfall. It seemed hopeless. And yet, the Faoii fought on.

The women fought in shifts now, and while one half rested, the others held the line through darkness, snow, and pain against an enemy that was affected by none of these things. The battle was no war—it was a slaughter.

And it had gone on too long.

Asanali's warriors had taken the night battles because they were less affected by the freezing air, and their still forms lay huddled in the trees behind Lyn. Eili had tried to bring a squadron around to attack Thinir's flanks, and Emery had taken the archers to try to gain the higher ground. Lyn had not heard from either team in several hours, and though she had waited as long as she could, she needed to end this.

Setting her jaw, Lyn readied her voice for a phrase she'd never expected to utter again.

"Retreat." Her whisper seemed alien, even to her, and she tried again. "Retreat! Fall back!" She willed her voice to carry over the din of battle as she turned her horse back toward the tree line. "Retreat!"

Terrified girls turned to run at her call, only to fall beneath the ever-advancing criukli blades. Lyn growled from her saddle, hacking at a Croeli helm before her. It split and fell beneath her fantoii, splattering brains and blood onto her horse's barding. She grimaced and turned to another foe. The enemy came at her in a tidal wave.

The Faoii weren't going to get out of this. They would die here. Still hacking with her blade, Lyn could only pray that somehow Kaiya could succeed where they had failed. She could only pray that somehow, somewhere, this could all end.

Screaming rang in her ears, and the stench of blood and melted flesh burnt her nose. But there was something else, too—sunflowers. Dew. A flute.

Somehow, above the din of battle, Illindria's presence still prevailed. And that, above all, sickened Lyn. Did She still believe even when Her followers had all given up all hope? Illindria had always taught the Faoii not to retreat, not to give up. And yet, what else could they do?

Lyn clenched her blade and hacked at another foe. He kept coming, and she hacked again, giving the woman in front of him a chance to run. "I'm sorry, Great Goddess Illindria. But I cannot do what You ask of me." She was about to turn and follow the fleeing maiden to the tree line when something caught her eye.

There, on a hilltop, wrapped in a black cloak, a single Croeli stood, watching the battle from behind his masked helm. He was motionless, a stone monolith surveying the progression of the slaughter below.

Rage filled Lyn in a red cyclone that beat against her breast and filled her gut with raw tension. Was this Croeli bastard so sure of their victory that he did not even feel the need to raise his sword? Was he so sure of their utter destruction that he felt he could simply sit atop his hill and watch as though it were a play performed for his benefit? She screamed and spurred her horse.

If they were to lose here, then so be it. But she would forsake the Goddess's love before she let an enemy *mock* their last moments with his inactivity. By the Eternal Blade, the Faoii deserved a true enemy in this final confrontation. Every Croeli would fight tooth and nail for that final victory.

Every. Single. One.

Lyn rode up almost to within blade length of the Croeli on the hill before he even seemed aware of her. Her fantoii was slick with the gore of those that had stood between her and her target, but she did not even notice as she raised it for its final strike. The Croeli's dull eyes flicked toward her. Too late. With a smirk, Lyn realized that there was fear in those eyes—a sudden understanding that the other warriors did not share. For a moment, the dark eyes flashed blue, pale as ice, then filled with a rage that rivaled even her own. *It's not enough, you bastard.* Lyn lobbed the horned head off at the neck. The body slumped as she turned away.

Finally, the screaming began. Screams of pain and terror filled the air as Croeli dropped their poisoned blades and grasped at the oozing wounds that littered their skin. Many tumbled to the ground, exhausted and broken from a fight that had not affected them until now.

It seemed to Lyn that hours passed before she truly understood what was happening. By then, most of the remaining Faoii had already retreated to the protection of the forest, but those that remained gained the advantage. The enemy moved differently now—guarded. Aware. They were poorly organized without their unspoken orders, and Lyn realized that most of them were thin, barely able to lift their weapons. Like cattle, they fell beneath the Faoii force.

The tides changed quickly then. While the Croeli continued to swing their criukli, it became painfully obvious that these were not trained warriors. Less than an hour passed before the Faoii had felled those that left them no choice and captured the rest, encircling their prisoners in a bloody wreath of short swords and longbows. The field was littered with bodies, and the metallic smell of blood washed over everything.

There were not many Cleroii in Lyn's army, but the few healers they had worked with Asanali's tribe to help those left alive on the field. There were not many. The Croeli's new poison was terrifying, and most women had already ceased their screaming, staring blankly at a sky that seemed too dark for midday. Those who had not yet succumbed could only cry and moan, vomiting in pain and terror as their skin boiled off in ribbons. These women were offered quick, merciful deaths by their sisters.

Lyn gave orders without faltering, cleaning up the last tattered remains of battle as she waited for news. Eili, Asanali, and Emery were all found, and they gathered around one of the wagons left standing. Emery looked down momentarily at the steady stream of blood that oozed from one bicep, his face ashen, but said nothing and took his place on a fallen log at the edge of their improvised circle. It wasn't until he moved his arm into the campfire light that Lyn saw the fletching protruding from his leather armor. The arrowhead poking out from the other side dripped steadily with blood.

"We were so close to capturing that hill," he said, catching her gaze. His grin was weak but triumphant. "I couldn't very well stop firing, could I?" He winced as he tried to rotate his arm slowly. "I . . . uh . . . I might have aggravated it a bit, ma'am."

Eili barked out a laugh. "Ya got an arrow through yer arm and ya kept firin'. 'Aggravated' indeed. We'll make a Faoii out of ya yet, boy." The older woman's voice was rough and mirthful, but Lyn caught the tremor of rage in her gaze as she eyed the arrow's shaft. Her eye glared darkly in the direction of the Croeli prisoners.

Lyn was not sure when the band of Faoii had accepted Emery as one of their own, but there was no denying that they all cared about him. He might have been quiet and withdrawn, but he was also sturdy and loyal. Of course he would worry more about capturing a hill than about his own pain. *Faoli.* That's what Kaiya had called Tendaji. A masculine conjugation to what had always been feminine. There was no doubt that Emery was Faoli too.

The sudden reminder of Faoii-Kaiya's absence pulled Lyn back to the present. She drew her mouth into a thin line.

"Faoii-Asanali, see to him." Lyn only gave Asanali a passing glance as the bronze woman moved to cut off the archer's leathers and tunic. Eili, however, stared steadily for a little longer until she was satisfied with Asanali's administrations. Lyn fisted her hands and bowed her head to the older Faoii when their eyes met.

"Faoii-Eili, I know you must be angry. I ordered the retreat without receiving orders. But if you'll hear me out..." Eili drew her pale eyebrows together in irritation.

"Quiet, girl. Now's not the time for self-pity. Ya did fine and ya know it." Lyn brought her head up sharply, surprised and pleased. She refrained from smiling, however. No reason to make it obvious.

"The War Watcher should be pleased as well," Asanali said. "It was the silky-haired Lyn that cut off the snake's head and allowed the body to shed the wicked skin that had it enshrouded. The War Watcher offered this victory through her screaming shining blade."

"War Watcher?" Lyn glanced at Asanali. "I thought you called the Goddess 'She Who Speaks in Dreams.'"

"Today She is not speaking in dreams," Asanali responded matter-of-factly.

Lyn chuckled and was about to reply but stopped short. Her smile disappeared at a sudden choking groan and quick, harsh breathing. She turned back in time to see Asanali drop a bloody arrowhead into the snow.

"Hush now. The life pond is not ready to reclaim you yet." Taking Emery's shuddering shoulder in one hand, Asanali wrapped her long, bronze fingers around the drenched fletching of the shaft. Slowly, methodically, she pulled the remains of the arrow from his arm, the skin tugging against the wood and blood oozing down her bronze hand. Then it exited with an inaudible *shuck*, and Asanali moved quickly to bind the gaping hole that remained. Emery's breath came in quick gasps, but she only smiled. "Hush, hush, Light Arrow. You will live to draw your bow again. Breathe easy."

"Light Arrow?" Emery chuckled through clenched teeth. "I kind of like that. Thank you, ma'am." He gasped again as Asanali set her palm against his shoulder, squeezing his eyes shut.

"It is a fine name," Asanali replied. "I *was* going to call you 'ma'am-caller.'"

Eili barked out a laugh, and Emery offered a pained grin.

"I'm just glad that they don't coat their arrows like they do their swords, or I'd be gone already," he managed through clenched teeth. Asanali's smiled faded and she nodded.

"It is a dark brew indeed. Not of this world. It smells of blood magic and despair—the work of a vengeful god left to his own dreams for too long."

Eili raised her remaining eyebrow as Asanali spoke. "Actually, that's a fine thing to muse about." The blonde Faoii turned to Asanali and Lyn, her scarred face pulled into a scowl. "This poison is different than what we've seen before. Do we have any idea as ta why?"

Asanali's response was quiet but sure. "It is tonicloran."

"*Tonicloran?*" Lyn screeched. "They used tonicloran against us?" She clenched her fists.

Asanali nodded. "The horned wolves have crossed a river that even the vilest serpent would not breach."

"Tonicloran." Eili shook her head. "Were we such a threat that they would stoop to *that*?" She looked toward the dead scattered on the field. "Eternal Blade. They were only girls. What did they do to deserve tonicloran?"

"I don't know." Lyn shook her head. "But someone has to." She called two young Faoii to her. "Find a prisoner that knows about the poison they coated their blades with. Bring him to me. Let's make all this death mean something."

Almost an hour passed. Lyn and Eili helped Asanali administer to Emery as best they could before guiding him to the wagon to let him rest. Twice Eili tried a Cleroii song, but to no avail. The women did not know whether the tonicloran-tainted blood had sucked the magic from the field or whether it was only Eili's heavy heart that dampened the song's power. Dissatisfied, the aging Faoii had offered her cloak to the archer and prayed for his health. He was asleep now, his face grey, but peaceful. Asanali had assured Lyn that there would be no fever and that he would recover completely in time.

Lyn was about to go looking for the women she had sent out into the field when they finally came into view, dragging a struggling Croeli between him.

"We are sorry for taking so long, Faoii," one of them said, bowing her head. "The Croeli don't seem to want to talk about the poison. But this one might know something."

Lyn and Eili both turned to the Croeli. The man at their feet was thicker and sturdier than the other prisoners, but he raved madly, his voice hoarse and his eyes wild.

"Kill me! Kill me!" His plea was sharp and angry, though there was terror hidden there as well. Lyn peered down her nose at him and crossed her arms over her chest.

"Why are you so desperate to die, Croeli scum?"

"It's not over. It will never be over." He pulled against the women that still held him by the arms, thrashing wildly. They restrained him with a surprisingly collected agility. "They'll assign a new lieutenant and it won't matter anymore. All of us that you refused to kill? That *mercy* you hold in such high regard? That will be the death of you—and us! Thinir will call us back to the other side and bind us again. The cycle will continue, and you will fall. We'll all fall!" He fought to bring his hands up in a pleading gesture, though it was somewhat less effective while the Faoii restrained his arms. When he realized his helplessness, he sagged, and the rage in his voice ebbed slightly.

"Please . . . Please, Faoii. Kill me with your fantoii. Or give me my own poisoned blade. I'd rather die that terrible death than be controlled again. Please."

Lyn narrowed her eyes, and her words were biting. "Maybe I should. You're willing to suffer through the tonicloran death? So be it." She motioned to the corpses on the field. "You showed no mercy to them. Why should I?"

A sad, sobbing laugh escaped his lips as he dropped his head. "No mercy? No mercy?" The edges of hysteria crept back into his features. "You don't understand, Faoii. Not at all. The poison was our way of saving you from our fate. It *was* merciful."

Lyn barely registered the words. All she heard were her sisters' terrified, agonized screams. All she saw were the boils and ribbons of flesh. Her eyes filled with fire, and she grabbed the Croeli by an ear and dragged him a few strides toward the field. Asanali and Eili trailed behind.

Lyn stopped in front of one of the dead Faoii, her red, blistered body left uncovered beneath the noonday sun. The young woman's lifeless eyes stared imploringly at the Croeli as Lyn shoved him forward. He stumbled toward his former enemy, staring at the ruined flesh that had been flayed like a fish's scales. Lyn's voice practically dripped acid when she spoke.

"Merciful? Look carefully, Croeli. This is what your mercy has done. The criukli poison was one thing. But this... You turned to the most hated of all poisons. You deserve far worse than death." The Croeli stared, his face ashen. He licked his lips once before replying.

"The old poison was not potent enough. It used to be able to burn out the sound of the bells, but he grew stronger. He overcame it. You couldn't die free. You got up, picked up your blade, and followed his will. But the tonicloran... it burns out the bells' cry." He suddenly grasped at his head and yanked at his hair.

"Curse those damned bells! They drive your mind to the other side, and when you come back, your thoughts aren't yours! You just...follow. They bring you to your new lieutenant. They bind their blood to your blade so you can cut down new recruits. Then the salve we weren't given before, the tonicloran... it becomes our bane. It's adulterated, tarnished. Made into a drink. And it *doesn't* kill you like it should. It just opens up a door you're not supposed to go through; makes you Blink. And you're his."

The Croeli's voice rose to a screech as he spoke faster, seemingly afraid that he wouldn't have a chance to finish. His wild eyes rolled in their sockets. "The tonicloran is supposed to kill you. It was supposed to be our salvation. It was supposed to kill us all. It's not supposed to be made into doors that he can control. It's not supposed to make you into his slave. But he's tarnished it. Now Thinir only has to control a dozen people, and each of those can control a hundred more. It spreads across the land like a spider's web, like a plague. Like the wind.

"We don't feel pain or fear. We see our target and we destroy it. But we can still feel the bars, hear his bells. We know we're trapped. And it's the part of us that knows the truth that wants to escape. It's that part of us that turns our eyes and hearts to something else. Something quiet. Panpipes. Flutes. Sunflowers. We focus on those things. Whatever it is that lets us hear those songs, smell those scents . . . that's what lets us gather the poisoned leaves scattered across the fields and roads. That's what lets us resist Thinir's will long enough to brew our poison and dip our blades. That's what lets us pray that it gets to you before he does. We use those songs to turn his instrument of enslavement—his tonicloran—into the key to your release." He cackled wildly, sobbing through his teeth. Faoii-Eili came up behind him, her face pulled together in a scowl.

"Ya keep saying yer able to resist Thinir despite his power. That the Goddess finds ya anyway. What else do ya know?" The Croeli sobbed harder.

"There are rumors... and cut me with the broken blade if I don't believe it...All of this—the bells and the sunflowers, the willpower that keeps us out of his reach—it's all because of a Faoii!" He laughed, and the sound was wild. "I grew up hating your kind, and yet I am more grateful to her than anyone alive. A Faoii saved all those out there on that field. She saved everyone! And if you give me back my blade, she'll save me, too!"

His laughter became more maniacal, and it grated against Lyn's eardrums. She turned away from the mad Croeli, her skin crawling. "Take him back to the others. Do not harm him." The two Faoii picked him up by his arms and carried him away. His laughter echoed in his absence.

"Do you think any of it's true?" Lyn asked Eili after a few minutes.

"Who can tell? He seems ta have a few cogs loose. Maybe he ain't even sure of what he's sayin'."

"Maybe the others know more." Lyn glanced up at the sky. "We've got some time to question them. The soldiers need to rest, anyway. And we need to determine the true extent of our casualties. It will be a few days before we leave here. Let's bury our dead and see what there is to do for the living."

The Croeli's sobbing laughter echoed in the distance.

This victory was not like the one in Cailivale. While dozens of women had fallen there, the majority had risen again, virtually unscathed. Faoii-Kaiya's song had saved all but a few. If only that were true now.

There were no smiles or high spirits at the end of this battle, no feelings of accomplishment or pride. Only grim determination depression, and regret as the survivors gathered the bodies of those less fortunate. Broken, limping women with haunted eyes were led away from those whose eyes still stared, unseeing, at the greyness overhead. Others were carried, unable to rise above their sorrow. Still others remained silent and drawn as they stared down at the lifeless corpses of their sisters before bending over and moving the bodies to where the mass pyre was being constructed. Crows cawed their delight as they landed and feasted, and the weary Faoii were not always able to keep them away. Many of the fallen that were added to the pyre were eyeless in their parting.

It was nearly noon on the second day when the last of the Faoii bodies had been laid to rest. The air was clogged with sickening, flesh-scented smoke and the wails of Faoii that had finally broken against the tide of angst and woe. Lyn pulled her lips together grimly, blinking smoke-induced tears from her eyes as she took stock of what provisions had been salvaged from the wrecked wagons. Though there was less than she had hoped, the death toll was disproportionately larger. There would be more than enough to survive on until they could decide what to do. She didn't know how to feel about that.

Asanali stepped from the trees, her bare feet soundless as she glided to Lyn's side. The bronze-skinned Faoii's eyes were downcast and shadowed with dark smudges, her copper hair listless and limp. When she spoke, her voice was barely more than a whisper.

"Many boughs have been broken here. Will you cut all of them so cleanly as to let new roots take hold?"

Lyn sneered and rolled her eyes, hoping that her tears were not obvious. "Goddess's girdle," she hissed under her breath. "What are you trying to say now?"

Asanali drew herself to her full height and spoke slowly, as though to a child still learning to how to use full sentences.

"There are many left on the field. New life cannot grow if they are left there—the ground will sense your hatred and shy from it." She grasped Lyn's arm with a gentle hand. "I know that they wear the faces of snarling beasts and hatred, but they lie there, nonetheless. Their eyes hold no joy, no sorrow. What are they waiting to see?"

"They'll see whatever Illindria is willing to offer them now that they've betrayed Her. Isn't that obvious?"

Asanali released an exasperated sigh. "No, not with those eyes—the mortal ones. The ones made of blood and heart."

"What? They're dead. They don't see anything."

"The world sees them. And it sees you. Will you offer the gaze that it seeks? Will you look past the snarling beast eyes and see the eyes of men instead? Men who could not hear the World Watcher, because the bronze screams rose in pitch?"

"Blasted heart, woman! I have no idea what you're trying to say!" Lyn spun to face Asanali, glaring at the moonlit eyes that stared back so earnestly.

"She means, are you goin' to bury 'em, burn 'em, or leave 'em?" Eili hollered from the campfire a little ways away. "Are we going to show our hatred for 'em by leavin' 'em where they lie, or are we going to offer them a true funeral?"

Lyn balked. "They killed most of us. They almost killed all of us. Why should we do them any favors?"

"Well, if that crazy Croeli was tellin' the truth, then they didn't have much of a choice, now, did they? They might be victims as much as us."

"And She Who Speaks in Dreams still whispers to them. Cuts

through the cloud of sleep and death. The broken wolf said as much. She still loves them. Cannot we love them as well?"

Lyn tensed her shoulders and narrowed her eyes. She was about to release a torrent of colorful language at the idea, but then she bit her tongue. She could smell sunflowers.

Lyn finally sighed. "Yes, Asanali. We can honor them, too. Tell the women to construct another pyre."

31

The remains of the last Croeli were little more than grey and black ashes dancing in the smog-choked air when a solitary figure crested one of the hills on the other side of the valley. The hunched silhouette stood out against the dreary backdrop of soot and sorrow, though it flowed through the scene like water through a too-fast current—liquid, but jerky in unexpected places.

Asanali was the first person to spot the approaching form as it stumbled toward them from over a distant hill. At first, she thought he was only another of Thinir's wolves, a pack member late to the fight, but she recognized the man soon after. She pointed him out to Lyn.

"Tendaji returns. He looks wounded."

Lyn and Asanali rode to him together, and Asanali caught him as he stumbled and fell. Even Lyn could not hide her apprehension as he struggled to stand, his legs and torso slick with blood and angry bruises.

"Tendaji, what happened? Where's Kai?"

Tendaji's shoulders shook as he spoke through clenched teeth. "They... killed her," he whispered, the words sounding strangled in his throat.

Lyn gaped, unbelieving. Tendaji slowly dragged his head up to meet her gaze. His fury, anguish, and regret were palpable as he shuddered out the next sentences, his words dripping venom and grief. "They killed her. A criukli through the stomach. I tried to stop them, but the tonicloran . . ." He choked and staggered. He leaned heavily on Asanali's horse until he'd regained his breath enough to continue. "They used my blood to find Thinir. I know where they're going but"—another gasping breath—"he's immune to their blades. It will be a slaughter."

Lyn's jaw tightened. She felt a brutal cry rise from her chest as she thought of Faoii-Kaiya, their leader, their savior, their friend, the only person since Jade that made her feel like... like...

Dead.

The angry gasp broke from her lips in clipped, strangled syllables. "Let it be a slaughter, then." She felt no pity, no remorse. "We need to watch out for our own first. Starting with you. Let's get back to camp."

Asanali wasted no time in treating Tendaji once they were back in their encampment. The others waited anxiously for her to finish her administrations, pacing or sitting near the campfire with agitated eyes and wringing hands. A universal sigh of relief escaped them when the bronze-skinned nomad took her place at the edge of the campfire once more. Asanali spoke quietly as she used snow to clean the blood from her fingers. "His wounds are sealed. They had already been sewn together once, then pulled apart again in his passage here."

"What caused them?" Lyn tried not to sound overly anxious, but she could not stop pacing. Eili and Emery sat quietly, the latter having woken up in better spirits several hours before. His good humor had been stripped away, however, at the sight of Tendaji's blood-soaked body and Kaiya's complete absence.

"Unnatural claws. Blades. Harsher tools. This was not done by the creatures of the forests between here and his old tribe's den."

"By man, then." Eili spit into the fire. "Is there any sign of poison? Criukli? Tonicloran?"

"No. His wounds were meant to hurt, not kill."

Lyn narrowed her eyes and continued her agitated pacing. "Torture. What seditious bastard would resort to that?" She snarled. "His own damned people. He went there trusting their blasted loyalty, and they tortured him for it. *Tortured* him." She cast worried, angry glances toward the wagon that Tendaji currently resided in, having fallen to exhaustion even before he had reached the camp. "Why? What were they looking for? Entertainment? Revenge?" She kicked at a tree in frustration, her boot striking its trunk with a resounding *crack*. "Blades! Why did he *trust* them?"

Asanali spread her hands. "They did leave him alive. They healed his wounds with care and sent him to once again join our course. Had they wished to, they could have cut his branch rather than only carving into it."

"Like they did to Faoii-Kaiya?" Lyn bit back. The others fell silent.

"They're goin' after Thinir," Faoii-Eili finally said. "I ain't willin' to call 'em friends, but they *are* the enemy of our enemy."

"It doesn't sound like it will do any good, though. If what

Kai—" Emery stopped, closing his eyes. He tried again. "If the stories are true, Thinir can't be hurt by normal blades. Tendaji's old tribe will barely slow him down."

"They might be able ta cut a hole through his army. Get us right up next to 'im."

Lyn shook her head. "No good. Without knowing Thinir's weakness, we'd just fall like those in Kai's monastery, our blades ringing off his skin."

Asanali sat quietly, contemplating. "She Who Speaks in Dreams knows the way to cut him down," she said finally. "The dark god's servant learned his sorcery from those beyond the life pond's veil, where the Carrier of Eternal Blade and all those who love or rise against Her sleep. The answer waits there.

Eili sneered, "Don't be stupid, girl. That ain't no answer. No one learns secrets like that without dyin' first."

Asanali only shrugged. "The wolf did."

That made everyone fall silent. She was right. Thinir had found a way to communicate directly with the gods in order to gain his invincibility and the secret of his Blinking. It *was* possible.

"He has taught the secret to his pack, too," Asanali continued. "They pass between the life waters—through the veil in giant leaps. Though it is quick, like a swallow through the branches of a tree. Too fast to see what we need to see. And it dulls their eyes and minds each time. But he holds the secret to the Tapestry nonetheless." She sighed down at the ground, watching the moonlight shimmer against a patch of snow. "If the horned god knows this imperfect passage into the Tapestry, the Carrier of the Eternal Blade, the War Watcher, She Who Speaks in Dreams . . . surely She knows the correct path."

Eili frowned at her fantoii. "Ah, the Tapestry. The Oath always made it sound like we were destined for great things. Like we couldn't fail. 'We are the Weavers of the Tapestry.'"

"'We see the threads through all the world and guide them with the Goddess's eye,'" Lyn responded immediately. Eili nodded, her frown growing deeper as she thought. After a moment, Lyn ventured, "What is it?"

"I dunno. Some story that my Preoii used to tell." Eili's one blue eye stared into the distance as she pondered. "The Weavers weren't always a metaphor. They were an actual group of Faoii— well, Preoii—handpicked by the Goddess..." She scrunched her eyebrows together. "They watched the Eternal Tapestry... and used what they found there to govern our Order." She shook her head and shrugged. "It was a long time ago. Before her time, and certainly before mine. I always thought it was just a legend, but... I don't know. She always seemed so disappointed when she talked about the Weavers. Always wanted to be one herself, I guess, but the initiation was banned. Somethin' about bein' too dangerous."

Lyn rolled her eyes. "There are no initiations in the Order."

"I know that, girl! I was just musin' about what Asanali said."

"Wait a moment, ma'am." Emery sat a little straighter, and he treaded onto unfamiliar Faoii territory carefully. "Faoii-Lyn, when we were in the enclave still, you mentioned that tonicloran was banned because too many people were getting hurt while trying to achieve 'enlightenment.'"

"Yeah. Stupid people used to think that they could see the Goddess's world if they survived tonicloran poisoning. Most of them were right—but it was a one-way street."

"The Croeli you interrogated said that Thinir used tonicloran to make his soldiers Blink. If it's not true, then how would rumors like that start?"

"Who knows? Same way any other rumor starts. Someone hears something and it spreads. Doesn't make any of it true."

"Don't be daft, girl," Eili broke in. "You know that all rumors that last more than a fortnight have at least a grain of truth to 'em. The Faoli's onta somethin'." Her blue eye glittered in the firelight. "What if that's how Preoii used ta became Weavers? By survivin' tonicloran?"

Asanali tried to speak, but Lyn cut her off. "That's insane! No one would willingly subject herself to that torture. Did you see what happened to those girls on that field?"

"Kai . . ." Emery swallowed and tried again. "Kaiya said that the Goddess's world is everywhere at once. It's next to everything. If you had the chance to gain that kind of power, to see everything. . . do you think you'd be willing to suffer a few hours of pain?"

"Not like that. That's . . ." Lyn shook her head. "Even if the Croeli are using the tonicloran to do their weird Blinking thing, why would they also be using it to kill those that they want to save from Thinir's influence? It can't be Thinir's main weapon and his bane."

Again Asanali opened her mouth to speak, and again she was cut off, this time by Eili. "Why not? The crazy Croeli said that it's mostly a blood ritual that gives Thinir power. The tonicloran might just be part of it. A catalyst. And like most catalysts, if the balance ain't exactly right . . ." Eili trailed off, looking once more to the dark silhouette of the pyre on the horizon.

"Hear me!" Asanali's voice was barely louder than its regular soft contralto, but it carried with it the full strength of the Faoii, making the others jerk back in surprise. When she spoke again, her voice was once again at its original pitch. "The Carrier of the

Eternal Blade is of two parts. She is light and dark, sword and shield, War Watcher and Dream Speaker. She is the sun and the moon, the drowning flood and the life-giving rain. Her tools are also two flowers of the same root. The tonicloran is both a weapon and a gift."

Eili and Lyn stared at her. No one had ever heard Asanali speak so much at one time.

"She's right," a voice said from behind them, and the group whipped around to see Tendaji approach. He walked stiffly, carefully. "My old tribe is using it as both a poison against Thinir's control and a window to the Goddess's world. It can be both."

"You should not be awake yet." Asanali's voice was disapproving. Tendaji held a hand up and continued toward the circle.

"I heard your conversation. This is important." The wounded fighter sat on one of the available logs and rested his arms on his knees. His eyes were intense as he looked at each of his companions in turn. "The tonicloran isn't just a poison. Thinir experimented with it until he could reach the other side of whatever veil separates us from death. He learned the secrets of his immortality there, and he uses it to make doorways for his soldiers. Amaenel, one of my old allies, used it in a dark ritual to see through Illindria's eye and find Thinir. Thinir's soldiers use it to drown out his influence when they are struck down. It is a poison, but if it's used in small amounts and under the right conditions, it is also . . . a gateway. A key." He paused, his pale eyes smoldering in the firelight. "And that makes it the most dangerous substance I have ever heard of."

"It has always been such," Asanali said knowingly. "It is a venomous panacea, filled with glory and death. My people knew of its secrets long ago. We pulled it out by the roots when we discovered it. Destroyed it when we could. Too few can use it as it is meant to be used, and we thought it was better to remove it entirely than let young pups with ideas of glory try and die. But we watched those beyond their stone walls meddle with what they could not control. Too many died trying to fight their way to the sides of gods." She shook her head. "It is wrong that somehow the horned wolves have gained even a sprig of the power available there. They didn't even have to see the door with their mortal eyes first. It is an affront to the War Watcher."

"Wait. Are you saying that normally you'd have to see the Goddess's world with your own eyes before you can use the tonicloran and become a Weaver?" Lyn's voice was incredulous. "That's even crazier than the last thing you said."

"It is as the story goes, though I do not know how the night wolf swam across the world pool without seeing the path first. Maybe these 'experiments' that Tendaji mentioned—"

"We ain't experimentin' with no tonicloran!" Eili exclaimed. Asanali shrugged and fell silent.

Lyn nodded fiercely. "She's right. And there's definitely never been someone who could just see the Goddess's world without some sort of magic. Not even children's stories have those kinds of crazy dreams."

"No...No. They're not crazy dreams at all." Tendaji rubbed his palms against his weary eyes. "Our mother was able to do it. I think our aunt, too. Maybe, if she'd been given the chance, Kai could have..." He fell silent for a moment, staring at the stars on the horizon. The snow around his feet swirled a little in the night breeze. "Kai might have learned how to do it, too, if she'd been given enough time."

The silence lengthened until there was only the sound of the wind through the branches overhead.

"She died free, Tendaji, sir," Emery finally whispered over the embers. "She died as Faoii-Kaiya and not as a servant of Thinir."

"Thank the Goddess and her unnamed servant for that," Eili growled out in reply. "As long as there's someone out there workin' in Illindria's name, Thinir's army doesn't need ta get any bigger." She sighed. "I just wish there was some other way. The tonicloran is a heavy price to pay, even for freedom."

Tendaji opened one pale eye to glance Eili's way. "What do you mean, 'the Goddess's unnamed servant?'"

Together, Eili, Lyn, and Asanali explained what they had learned from the Croeli prisoner. Tendaji listened carefully, his eyes narrowing. Eili watched him as he stood up to pace.

"What is it, boy?"

"I think I know where she is." Tendaji's voice was steady, his face unreadable. With decisive steps, he began striding toward the horses, his movements deceptively steady. The others moved to intercept him, but he shook them off despite his injuries. "Your Faoii—she's in that pit." Quickly, his eyes glinting in the darkness, Tendaji went over what had happened in the Croeli camp. The others listened, their expressions masked. Only Emery stared on with wide, uncertain eyes.

"She probably knows more 'bout tonicloran than anyone alive, if she's been able ta spread it like that," Eili said. "And she has ta be powerful if she can override Thinir's will. She might even know his weakness."

"We'll have to hurry. Who knows what kind of state she was in before Amaenel abandoned her? However, I think we can—" Tendaji stopped as something on the horizon caught his eye. He motioned the others to be still, immediately falling into a defensive position as his gaze roamed the distant hills. His eyes darkened in the night.

"No." It started out as a whisper, then got louder with each repetition. "No. No. No!" The others turned to follow his gaze, reaching for their weapons as a thin line of soldiers crested the horizon. Though there was only a dark silhouette of a horned helm against a grey sky, Tendaji glared in its direction.

"What is it, Tendaji?" Lyn asked, drawing her fantoii as she stared at the dark line against the far-off trees.

When Tendaji replied, his voice was low and tortured.

"I led them right to you."

"Come on, Kai. I'm not going to get stuck mucking stables again just because you can't get up like a regular Faoii for chapel."

Get up. Get up. Kaiya tried, but the world only spun in sickening, violent pain. She groaned miserably as her stomach voided its contents in a gruesome splatter. Agony exploded through her with each heave, and even after everything had been expelled, she could only lie there, gasping in the dark. She tried to speak, tried to beg Mollie to get Cleroii-Belle, but her mouth couldn't form the words. Finally, she managed a strangled gasp:

"Mollie, please . . ." The sound was a desperate mockery of her regular voice, and she could only curl in on herself as she waited for the spasms to pass.

Eventually the pain began to subside, and Kaiya was only too aware that no one came to her aid while she suffered. She tried to call out again but only choked on her own bile. Where was Mollie? Had she already left? It must be time for chapel by now. Weren't those the morning bells she heard?

Kaiya knew she had to sit up. She had to get to chapel. Illindria would be proud of her strength and discipline. The Cleroii would help her there. Preoii-Aleena would comfort her. If Kaiya could make it to the chapel, this pain would stop. She just had to make it. She had just had to . . .

But she was already there. With the sudden awareness that someone experiences when they first distinguish the difference between a dream and reality, Kaiya felt the chapel all around her. The air was clean and pure, as though a rain had just fallen and been dried by a pleasant sun. The Cleroii must have already sang one of their songs and purified the area. How could she have missed it? It smelled like lavender and apples. Crisp and pure. Perfect.

Finally, blessedly, Kaiya was able to open her eyes. She wasn't alone.

She saw the hand first. Pale like honeyed cream, the delicate fingers gave way to a graceful, curving arm that beckoned to Kaiya. Straining, Kaiya followed the curve upward, past the bare shoulder and slender neck, then over a thin frame and the long, gossamer folds of a floor-length gown.

The woman's soft, round face was framed by sinuous, strawberry-blonde hair and lit up with a beaming smile. Glittering sapphire-blue eyes sparkled at Kaiya's recognition.

Had Kaiya been standing, she would have fallen again. As it was, she was only able to roll awkwardly onto one knee, bowing her head and fisting her hands in front of her. Her eyes flooded with tears as she caught a glimpse of her soiled, blood-crusted leathers and vomit-covered leggings. Her heart plummeted with shame.

"Goddess, I . . ." Kaiya did not know what to say. She wanted to apologize for having failed. She wanted to say that she had tried, that she had done everything she could. But she could not lie to Illindria. Even if Kaiya's false-facing had been better. Even if she had practiced more, the lie would always be plain. The Goddess knew all. And Kaiya had failed. The Faoii hung her head and simply whispered, "I'm sorry."

Kaiya wasn't sure what she expected. A gentle scolding? Words of disappointment? A speech of failure and embarrassment? She didn't know. She knew only that she most certainly did *not* expect what came afterward. A tinkling sound. Like pieces of glass at the bottom of a stream.

Illindria was laughing.

At first, Kaiya felt wounded. Was she not already disgraced enough as it was? But the hurt faded as she listened again. There was no malice in that laughter. No anger. Timidly, she raised her eyes until she could see the Eternal One's face.

Her savior was beaming.

"Faoii-Kaiya." The voice was regal and rang with authority despite its softness. "Do not be ashamed. You have done everything I have asked of you. Your strength and dedication have brought you here—to where you are supposed to be." Illindria, still smiling, reached for Kaiya's hands and drew her to her feet. Kaiya frowned down at her cracked, bleeding nails, feeling unworthy. The Goddess, however, only smiled. "You were always meant to find your way here, Faoii."

"You knew that I would die?" Kaiya's heart wrenched, and she drew back a pace. She was aware that death would come for her eventually. She was even pleased that she had fallen in battle, rather than in her bed long after the battle cries and glory had faded. But she had thought the Goddess's guidance was a sign that she was supposed to succeed, not have it end… like this.

Kaiya felt betrayed. Why had she fought so long and hard, received so many signs of hope and guidance, only for it to end here? Why would the Eternal One offer so much encouragement if the outcome was to be the same?

Her face must have shown her doubt, because the Goddess smiled and reached out to lift Kaiya's chin until they met each other's gaze.

"Die? This is not death, child. Only a forgotten place." The woman's pale arm swept around them, encompassing the vast emptiness that spread into eternity. "Many have passed through this place before, and I hope that someday, many will again."

Smoothly, she turned back and reached out her hand once more. "Come with me, Faoii. There is something I would like to show you." Kaiya stared at the delicate hand for a moment before once again examining her own blood-encrusted fingers. Illindria clicked her tongue. "Come, now. I wielded a sword against demons long before you were born. Do you think I would shy from the blood of one of my heroes?"

Kaiya blushed and obediently placed her dark hand into the cream-colored palm of her liege.

"There are few in the world who could do what you have done," the Carrier of the Eternal Blade said softly as She led Kaiya forward into the whiteness that surrounded them. "The secret of my tonicloran is nearly lost, shrouded in fear. The deaths of the overzealous long ago frightened those who should not be afraid and enticed those who should have been cautious. Now dark, brutish men claw at the walls of this place, catching glimpses of what they cannot possibly understand on their way back to your world." She sighed, shaking Her head. "They will learn little, of course. But it hurts me that they would tear their minds apart for a few scraps of meat they cannot chew."

Kaiya looked around at the vast emptiness and frowned. "Goddess…I don't understand. There is nothing here."

That soft, tinkling laughter again. "You are still using your mortal eyes, Faoii-Kaiya. You look to the air and see only air. You see water in rivers and sand on beaches. But you've seen more than that. You have danced in these halls before. You've seen the fiery wings of my warriors, the amber eyes of my scouts. You've seen mountains blossom where only dirt appeared and chains where your enemies have shackled the souls of others." She looked down at Kaiya, Her eyes sparkling. "Did you think that those truths were any less real than that which you could touch?"

Kaiya shook her head. "I . . . I don't know."

"You have always been able to see this place, this world of mine where all paths, past and future, intertwine. My beautiful woven Tapestry. But it is the tonicloran that lets you pluck the strands." She smiled lovingly and reached out with the hand that was not grasping Kaiya's, brushing Her fingers through the air. And for a moment, Kaiya *did* see it—a ripple in the white clouds that surrounded them. A humming shroud that vibrated beneath the Goddess's fingers.

As Kaiya watched, images formed in the white haze, standing out against the spongy oblivion that encircled them. Landscapes and timelines formed in the nothingness, jumping out at Kaiya in stark realism. Then they shifted, and different forms emerged like bubbles from the bottom of a pool. These images, too, faded and shifted to other scenes. Endlessly. Tirelessly.

The pace increased. A myriad of colors and pictures danced their sickening swirl before Kaiya's eyes. The world and all within it spread out along the emptiness of the white room. Trees sprouted and spread across a landscape that grew, burned, flooded, and flourished. People spread like ants across hills, mountains, forests, and oceans. A thousand voices and a million heartbeats pounded in Kaiya's ears.

Kaiya's head spun nauseatingly, and she tottered back a step, squeezing her eyelids shut. But the images were still there, growing. Spreading. Changing. She pulled away from Illindria's gentle squeeze and pressed her palms against her eyelids, but the visions didn't fade. She thought she would go blind with all the sights and deaf with all the sounds. She couldn't move, couldn't breathe. There was too much . . . Too much . . .

There was a soft whisper from the Goddess, and her mind's eye closed. The ripple disappeared, and the world grew quiet.

Kaiya felt Illindria's hand slip back into hers as She waited for the Faoii to settle again. Long minutes passed before Kaiya could open her mortal eyes once more. The soft whiteness surrounded them, warm and inviting despite the secrets encased within its walls.

"It takes practice to master, of course," the Goddess said, squeezing Kaiya's hand. "And as there are no longer any Preoii to prepare you, no guides to teach you . . ." She sighed sadly. "Do not worry. You will learn."

"What . . . what was that?" Kaiya's voice shook. Her heart was racing, her head spinning. She swallowed. Once. Twice. She was glad she had already voided her stomach recently.

"Why, this is my Tapestry—the weave of the world and all

that are within it. The past, the future, the present—and every variation of each." The Eternal One gave the air a loving caress, smiling like a new mother. "It is the ward of the Preoii. They have always watched it. Followed its threads. They have always used its stories to guide my people, choosing the paths that offer the most favorable outcome." She moved her hand again, and an infinitely long cloth formed, spreading out on all sides. "Try again, Kaiya."

Unable to help herself, Kaiya looked. A million characters stared back, and she focused on a child sleeping against his mother's breast. He could only be a few hours old. So small. So innocent.

As Kaiya watched him, the Tapestry spiraled out before her, pulling her through all the possible outcomes of that boy's life. In the span of seconds, she watched him age a thousand times, each version slightly different from the last. A thousand outcomes danced outward with every action, every word, every deed. Those choices spread, each to a million other points, affecting a million other people.

If he steals a loaf of bread here, it will force that woman there to go to another store tomorrow. A button on her dress will snag on the counter. The seamstress that sells her a needle and thread will be able to buy food for another day. She will share a bit of wisdom with a pair of twins . . . But the already disheartened baker will begin to hold resentment for other people in his heart. He will pass it on to his son over the next decade . . .

Their reactions shaded other stories, leading to a million other choices. A million other outcomes. She watched as uncountable versions of the unnamed boy's life passed before her. Death at a hundred different hands. Laughter at a million jokes. Love in the arms of a dozen different women. And each choice led somewhere else. A dozen different families. A million different lives. The choices colored generations, all created or destroyed by a single man who remained completely unaware of his impact.

If he meets the tailor's daughter, she will bear him two strong sons. They will become politicians and help shape their country. But if he goes to the smithy first that day, she will be gone before he meets her, away to deliver her father's wares. Then he will marry one of the women in the next town over, and the tailor's daughter will marry a traveling merchant from . . .

Kaiya tore her eyes away from the lives she didn't know, the futures she didn't want to see. How could any one person decide which of those million futures were the best? How could anyone look so far into a limitless expanse and come back human? It was too big. There was too much.

She felt someone's hand petting her unkempt hair, and Kaiya realized that she was shuddering on the ground, sobbing into Illindria's gossamer skirts. The Goddess only whispered sweet words in reply.

"The future is the hardest, child, I know. But you will learn." She soothed Kaiya until the wracking sobs dissipated. "It has been a long time since Preoii were trained to enter this place. It was their choice to ban the tonicloran and stop training young Weavers to watch the Tapestry. That decision has forced me to stay in this form, among you, so that I may offer guidance when I can. But one person, even a Goddess, cannot control everything at once."

"It's too big. It's too big," Kaiya sobbed, still shuddering.

"Of course it is. It is too much for a single Preoii. In the old days, hundreds of Weavers would watch the Tapestry, working together. United. Now there is only you. Poor child. It must seem like too much. But you must rebalance. Then you will be able to train others to work beside you at the loom." She sat Kaiya up, grasping her shoulders. Her sapphire eyes bore into Kaiya's with a sincerity that hurt. "Faoii-Kaiya, you must restore my Order."

"How?" The word was barely a whisper, clutched by a gentle breeze and carried away.

The Goddess smiled. "By continuing as you have done. The tonicloran was in many of your futures, but it was not your only fate to discover this Tapestry now. For now, worry only about the mortal quarrels you and your sisters have suffered. Strike back at the heart of this evil that has unmade your world. You may worry about the Tapestry afterward. Deal with Thinir, then return to me."

Kaiya brushed the tears from her eyes and nodded. After the enormity of having seen the entire future, the task of dealing with one mortal Croeli seemed mundane. But as she thought of the huge, weaving Tapestry again, her stomach churned and her knees shook.

"I don't want to come back here. I don't want to have the world laid out before me. I don't... I can't..." Kaiya floundered.

"By the time you return, you may want it."

Kaiya released a harsh, sobbing giggle. It seemed desperate, even to her own ears. "So I will come back? I'll survive this?"

Illindria's laugh was high and pretty as She clapped Her hands. "I have no idea! I have seen your deaths and your victories. I have seen you laugh and cry, give up and endure, crumble and strengthen. Your choices are your own, and they are infinite. A single moment can destroy or create a hundred thousand different outcomes. It is what makes the Tapestry beautiful and terrifying. But if you return, I will be here."

Kaiya opened her mouth to say something, then closed it gain. The Goddess watched her face. "I recognize that look, child.

You want to know whether you should look at the threads and see all the ways that this could end. You wonder whether it can help prepare you."

Kaiya nodded. Illindria smiled, Her eyes knowing. "But you are afraid. You think that seeing it will change it and new futures will unravel. You're afraid that once you fall into that hole you might never be able to climb back out."

Kaiya nodded again, her face grey as the enormity hit her. This time, the Goddess put a gentle hand on her shoulder. "Now you understand. That is why you have been selected as one of my Weavers, Faoii-Kaiya. Because you, of all people, know that looking at it one moment at a time is the only way to keep your sanity. No being in existence could look upon that Tapestry alone for long without losing themselves in its many threads."

Kaiya opened her mouth to speak again, but the Goddess shook Her head. "Not now. You must return to your world. There is someone there who will help you reach this place again, should you so choose." She smiled thoughtfully. "I suppose you may not like where I put you back, Faoii-Kaiya, but it will be the easiest place for your first journey. My power is strongest there, and I will help you do what so few others have achieved."

Kaiya wanted to ask what She meant, but suddenly she was falling, hurtling away from the white room and the cloudlike softness that enveloped it.

Illindria's bright smile followed her into oblivion.

Kaiya woke up suddenly, her body screaming in pain. Her mind strained under the weight of infinity. Was scattered and pulled apart like taffy. At first a soft voice helped her pull the strained pieces of herself back from that looming void, but it grew distant as the seconds passed. Kaiya clung to it, and the dizzying effect lessened by degrees until only agony and silence remained. Kaiya reached out for the soft warmth of Goddess's embrace, but there was nothing—only grime and chill. The smell of vomit and death. She cried out in frustration and anguish for Illindria, for Mollie, for anyone.

"Mollie . . ." she finally sobbed. "Help . . ."

Her plea was answered, but in a voice that was decidedly not Mollie's.

"Oh. You're alive."

33

The remaining Faoii were already weary of this battlefield and its thousand cut-off screams. Broken by the Croeli and enslaved by desolation at the sight of their tortured, maimed sisters, much of the Faoii will had shattered with the previous dawn, carried with the pyre smoke into the marshy darkness of morning. Amaenel's soldiers fell upon them eagerly.

Lyn tried to rally those around her, her voice ringing high, mixing with Eili's in the dawn. Their songs danced across the field in ribbons, twisting around each other in an unbroken hymn of rage and glory. Upon hearing the sound, the faintest hint of hope sparked in the eyes of those girls that were still left, and they raised their short swords higher to meet the oncoming horde. Lyn smiled as she pushed forward, raising her fantoii at the front of the charge, Eili close behind. Together, they screamed into the face of their enemy and into the night that plagued them. Into the death that chittered at their pain.

Eili's battle song cut off suddenly. Death's mocking laughter echoed hollowly in its place. The air around Lyn grew chill in the sudden stillness.

When time started again, it was faster than before and heated with a battle rage that sprouted in Lyn's heart and shot forward from her outstretched arm, into the fantoii that still led the charge. Lyn spurred her horse, her eyes set on the dark, cruel helmet that glinted in the mist ahead. Somewhere behind her, she heard Emery scream in pain. She clenched her teeth and brought her head down, glaring at the leader as she urged her horse faster.

The horned helmet turned, ever so slowly, to face her, the eyes beneath it filled with madness. He watched her approach with a wild stare. Lyn's blade let loose a cry of a thousand demons.

The cry was cut short with violent efficiency.

The Croeli warriors appeared from everywhere at once, oozing from the mist to surround her in a semicircle, clawing at her arms and legs, pulling her from the horse with an unexpected force.

Lyn fought against her adversaries despite her surprise, cutting down two even as she slid from her saddle, her arms and legs lashing out in all directions as she fought to gain her feet. Then they were on her, pinning her arms and legs as she struggled against them, spittle and curses spraying from her mouth. The fantoii fell from her hand, dropping dully onto the bloody plain.

Lyn quieted by degrees, raising her chin defiantly and barring her teeth as the helmeted leader of the Croeli approached, leading his—*no, not his, that is Kaiya's gelding!*—horse by the reins. He stopped a few strides away, bending from the waist to retrieve the fallen fantoii. It looked deformed and tarnished in his calloused mitt of a hand.

"She has more fight than the rest, hasn't she?" Amaenel said with a laugh.

Lyn snarled and pulled against her captors, gnashing her teeth in unbridled fury. The Croeli leader looked over her fantoii with lazy apathy. "Put her with whatever other survivors there are. I think we have enough. Oh, and bring me any other witch blades you find. We'll show them to our children when they ask what the Faoii were."

Lyn was dragged back to the tree line, where a ramshackle circle had been constructed, ringed by a handful of Croeli warriors. She spat on one of the guards' feet. *There is no reason we should have been beaten by so few. It should have taken no less than an army to bring us down.* She was more disgusted, however, by the obvious lack of Faoii survivors. Of the thousands of warriors that had walked onto this field a week ago, only a few hundred remained, their faces downcast and their spirits broken. *We were not prepared for another battle. Not so soon.* Lyn was pushed roughly into the group, but she walked forward with a sure step, scanning those that were left alive. *Too few. Far too few.*

Emery was there, white as death. His bound hands pulled his injured shoulder at an uncomfortable angle, the stitches stretching against his torn, bloody skin. He struggled up to one knee when he saw her, but Lyn only laid a hand on his good shoulder and knelt in front of him. She searched him over for new injuries but saw none. "Faoli, report."

He said crisply, "I haven't gotten a full count, ma'am. There are at least a hundred of our warriors here, two hundred at most. I have not seen the other ascended." He dropped his gaze.

"I'm sorry, ma'am. They got me early. I didn't give them as much of a fight as I should have."

Lyn rolled her eyes. "You were already injured, Emery. There is no failure in what you've done."

He cracked a wicked smile at her. "I killed three of them as they came for me. I couldn't nock the next arrow in time, but I got three."

Lyn smiled and squeezed his shoulder. "You've done well, Faoii." Lyn glanced around. None of the surrounding women were bound. Emery seemed to be the only exception. With an angry growl, Lyn fished a dagger from her boot. The Croeli had done well in stripping her of the fantoii and her throwing disks, but they had missed the simple, almost useless boot knife. Not that it mattered. It would do little good against the Croeli now. But she could use it to assist her friend.

Carefully, she extricated Emery from his bonds. He sucked air in through his nose in pained gasps as he shifted his shoulder to bring his arms to the front again. After a moment, he nodded, and Lyn helped him to stand. Together, they moved through the huddled masses of the surviving Faoii, searching for familiar faces and hope in a crowd that spoke only of sorrow and defeat.

Eili was not well off. Her already-scarred face was bloodied with a deep wound on one side of her head, her blonde hair soaked crimson. Asanali was with her, using strands of long copper hair to stitch the skin back in place like a demented rag doll with a ripped seam.

Eili closed her eyes in relief when she saw the others approach, and Asanali even offered her dazzling smile to the pair. It seemed out of place next to the desolate faces of those that surrounded them.

"Eternal blade! Ya made it, girl!" Eili laughed as they approached. "I watched ya charge on ahead, crazy thing. But it did my heart good to see a Faoii hold tha line like that." Eili rose shakily, her disfigured face dripping with blood as she fisted her hands in front of her. "Goddess bless ya, girl. And you too, Faoli. Even with a hole in yer arm, ya fought like a true warrior."

Emery gave a smart salute, clicking his heels together. "Thank you, ma'am."

"Faoii-Eili, have you seen Tendaji?" Lyn asked.

The hints of a smile melted from Eili's face as she sat back down. Asanali went back to work on her torn cheek.

"He wasn't prepared for a fight. You saw 'im. Barely able to stand. They musta been lookin' for him specifically, 'cuz a group of the bastards flowed 'round our girls like water 'round a rock to get ta him. He fell pretty quick, and they moved on." Her single blue eye misted a tiny bit. "I'm sorry, girl."

Lyn was about to respond when Asanali cut her off. "Worry not for the carver of the shackled tree. He remains on this side of the life pool's many shores. His roots are deep, and they spread wide." She smiled softly. "A Croeli found him nearing the pool and pulled him back, whispering songs from the winds and skies. I saw the blood on that one's hands, the hatred in his heart. But those eyes held fear for the Goddess's light-eyed warrior. Even here, Tendaji is not alone."

Lyn frowned, not sure what to make of that. As she pondered, Emery settled next to her and glanced around.

"So what do we do now?" he whispered under his breath. "Regroup from here and try to take out the guards?" Asanali's shoulders tensed, and she stopped working just long enough to glance over her shoulder at Lyn. Even Eili regarded her warily through one bloodshot eye.

Lyn shook her head. "No. Look around. These girls couldn't

defeat them when they were armed. Now they're exhausted, and the will's been beat out of them. It would be a bloodbath." She popped her knuckles compulsively. "There must be a reason that these Croeli bastards are keeping us alive."

"They're goin' against Thinir. They might just be plannin' to use us as fleshy shields. Even unarmed, we could serve 'em that much."

Lyn narrowed her eyes. "We have to convince them we're worth more than that, then." She leaned in, her eyes glinting. "I'll be damned if we made it this far just so that we can die unarmed in the last battle. We need these Croeli scum to think of us as something more than battle trophies. Convince them that we make better allies than shields. Give us a sword, and we'll double his fighting force, no matter what the numbers are."

Eili frowned. "We're prisoners of war right now. There's no reason for this leader to trust us."

"War prisoners are only a drain on rations and resources. Any sane man would be willing to switch them out for something useful. We can be useful."

Emery glanced around at the broken girls nearby. Lyn caught his chin and pulled his eyes back to hers. "I know what it looks like. But we are Faoii. This isn't over yet."

Eili grinned. "If ya think ya can pull it off, girl, we'll follow yer lead."

"Good. Rest while you can. The girls are going to be busy soon.

34

Two days passed before the Croeli suddenly packed up camp and herded their prisoners back onto the road. With most of the Croeli on horseback, the pace was faster than Lyn would have preferred and grueling to the war-sick women that had been given only a tiny portion of the rations left. But she set her jaw and urged them on, watching her captors with a trained eye, listening to their conversations when she could.

It did not take long to learn that they were heading east, toward the mountains that bordered her own home and long-abandoned monastery. She knew of the forests on those mountains. She knew of their shadowy underbrush and chilled airs. And now she knew of its darkest and most dangerous inhabitant.

We are coming, Croeli-Thinir. You will pay for every death that was guided by your hand.

Weeks passed, and Lyn worked tirelessly. Kaiya had taught her how to be a leader, and Lyn still remembered her ever-present determination in the enclave. But this was different. *Kaiya, I love you, but even you couldn't have prepared our army for this particular battleplan. Watch how the Monastery of the Unbroken Weave works when behind enemy lines.*

The air began to change. Slowly—oh, so slowly—she guided her girls. First, they began to feel hope again. Then she led them farther, training them in subterfuge that she knew would come easier than even swordplay had. Like water grinding down stones in a stream, the women of Cailivale gradually began weakening the Croeli resolve with soft smiles and warm eyes. It did not surprise Lyn to see the guards disarmed by women who had spent a lifetime learning how to get close to men when it was profitable. In fact, she had depended on it.

Slowly, it worked. The Faoii began to regain their spirit when they saw what they were looking for in their captors' eyes—a need. A longing. They heard it in the guards' strained laughter. They felt it when they batted their long lashes and gave their soft smiles. The air in the camp began to change. When the men practiced their swordsmanship, it was fierce and jagged with unreleased tension. Fights broke out more often.

Soon the women knew the men almost as well as the men knew themselves, and Lyn smiled in the background. She wanted these warriors to at least see her girls' usefulness—on or off the battlefield. She wanted them to consider her girls an asset rather than a liability. Maybe they did not want them as allies in war. Maybe they didn't yet trust them. But there were many ways to gain trust. And there were always needs to be fulfilled.

Apparently, their new leader saw it too, and it displeased him.

His glower deepened as the women became more alluring and the men more lustful with each passing day. Lyn did what she could to use that to their advantage, training her girls to act willing and loving at first, only to pull away in "fear" if the Croeli got too close.

"The captain will punish us," they whispered, casting frightened glances at Amaenel's tent. "He's forbidden it. We can't."

Dejected, the Croeli would then cast dark glares in the direction of their leader and storm off to participate in their increasingly frequent sparring matches. Lyn laughed, still amazed at how little the Croeli were in control of, for all their postering. There was not a battle in which the Faoii didn't have the upper hand.

The Faoii drifted through the prisoners' circle like moths, plotting together as they chose their next targets. There was a fire in their eyes as they stalked their prey, but they buried it under sweet glances and soft lips when the Croeli looked their way. Over time, the wedge between the ascended and unascended Croeli grew.

Lyn could taste the coming revolt in the air before it happened. There was an unseen force between the captors and their alluring prisoners, an unspoken war cry that stemmed from the most bestial and primitive part of man.

It was a lithe, young Croeli that finally broke and reached up to stroke a fair Faoii's breasts beneath her dingy leathers. The girl responded immediately, letting out a shriek and pushing him off her with the full strength of a Faoii warrior. The others fanned out behind her immediately, encircling the Croeli like wolves around a wounded hind.

Lyn hung back and laughed to herself while she and Eili watched the women shriek like wildcats. The men wanted them. They *needed* them. But they could not have them. Croeli-Amaenel himself stormed up to the offending Croeli before dragging him away from the prisoners and publicly breaking his nose. The other Croeli watched from beneath furrowed brows, but Lyn still felt the need. The desire.

Everything was unfolding exactly as she had planned.

Lyn was not surprised when Croeli-Amaenel summoned her to his tent the next evening. Eili clapped her on the back as she rose gracefully to saunter after the guard that had brought the summons. "Good luck, girl. Let's see whether all this sickenin' work has paid off." Lyn only smiled and winked over her shoulder before following the guard to his superior's tent.

Amaenel was pacing when she entered, and he looked up angrily at her approach. She responded with a sweet smile and sultry eyes. Amaenel growled and gestured angrily toward one of the chairs positioned on either side of a low table.

"What do you want from me?" Lyn purred as she lowered herself into the seat. Amaenel tensed. His scowl was almost as dark as the one on his horned mask.

"I want you to get your little whores to do what they do best."

"Aw. Been away from home for that long, have you?" Lyn cocked a smile at him and leaned back in her chair, bouncing her crossed leg. Amaenel pursed his lips.

"My men are holding off now because I have demanded it. One of my soldiers has crossed the line and paid for it, but the others have not been as deterred as they should have been. Your women have been leading them on behind my back, and I know it."

"You can't blame your men for wanting a woman's touch, Croeli." Lyn leaned forward and plucked a date from the bowl on the table. "I've noticed that there are no women in your army. No concubines brought from home or taken from our monasteries. You could have had any number of women by now, but it was your decision to put forbidden fruit within reach of starving men."

"We do not rape those that we conquer. Not even Faoii whores."

"No, you only enslave them."

Amaenel's eyes darkened for a minute, and when he spoke it was with a forced calm. "There has been no work required of your hands since we conquered you. You have not had to take care of the horses, hunt, cook, or do any manual labor. We have treated you fairly as prisoners. I hope to keep what little peace there is, but my men are getting restless. You and I both know that if my men try to force themselves on anyone, there would be a lot of blood on both sides."

"Maybe that's what the women want." Lyn smirked and raised an eyebrow at the Croeli general. "We are Faoii. It is better for us to die in battle than live as slaves."

"Don't mock me, girl. I'm not stupid. You've got some vague hope of surviving this campaign. If you were to fight against my men without your weapons, it would be a bloodbath. I don't want that any more than you do."

"Don't you?"

"No. If I wanted you dead, you'd be dead already. Don't pretend you don't know it's true." Lyn shrugged casually. Amaenel continued, "So you're going to get them to do what the men want, and we're going to keep the peace."

Lyn waved a hand dismissively. "Fine. That's easy enough."

Amaenel looked down his nose at her, distrust in his eyes.

"I did not expect you to give in so easily."

Lyn stretched luxuriously and smiled at him. "All you have to do is pay them."

"What?" The growl was deep and angry. Lyn shrugged.

"Pay them. Gold. Clothes. A cot or bedroll to sleep on for a night. Trade it for food if that's what it takes. You want their services; you have to offer a trade." She looked him over, sizing him up like she would a cabbage at market. "You're not exactly a merchant, are you?"

"We're not going to pay any horn-blasted whores! They get their lives in exchange. That's enough payment for an hour with a real man."

"Please." Lyn rolled her eyes. "'Real men' or not, these girls are Faoii. Their honor is worth more than their lives, and we all know you're not going to kill them. If you were, it'd be done already." She laid her chin in her hands and batted long eyelashes at him. "Threats won't work, love. Make an honorable proposition, won't you?"

Amaenel stood up abruptly. "Honor? What honor do whores have?"

Lyn's eyes widened with fire. She rose to her feet and met his gaze with a steady stare. "They have the same honor as any of you, stupid Croeli. They have stood by their own codes, their own standards, for their entire lives." She stepped around the table until her chest was nearly touching his. Her nostrils flared. "And you're right—they are whores. But they were whores long before they were Faoii. Even then, they gave nothing that they did not choose, and they learned every way imaginable to keep their goods to themselves unless in fair trade that *they* agreed upon.

They were without sisters then, without help, and still they fought tooth and nail to keep what was theirs. If you ever try to take that away without consent, you will be walking against Thinir with far fewer men—and no Faoii at all."

Amaenel glared down at her for a long time before taking a rigid step backward and easing himself back down into his chair. After a moment, Lyn lounged lazily in her own again, her body loose and casual in the seat. "Don't pretend you don't know it's true," she added, smiling coolly. Amaenel glared in her direction for a long moment before finally offering a steely nod.

"The men have some goods they can offer in trade," he finally conceded.

"Good. The girls have traded in scarce times before. It shouldn't be hard for both sides to come to agreement." She straightened in her chair, her eyes stern. "My girls have the right to refuse an offer if they see fit."

"You're pushing my patience, Faoii."

"If my girls think they're being robbed, or if your men think that we demand too much, either side may come to us to resolve the matter. We're both fair people. We can ensure that they are, too."

Amaenel crossed his arms over his chest but nodded. Lyn smiled. "Good. It's settled, then." She rose from her chair and turned toward the tent flap. Just before reaching it, she turned back and willed all the power she could muster into her voice as she spoke. "Oh, and Amaenel," she purred, smiling softly over her shoulder, "if any of your men break this agreement, I will kill you personally."

She was gone before he could reply.

35

"**W**ho are you?" Kaiya whispered into the darkness, seeking the voice that she'd heard upon waking. The answer came from much nearer than she expected.

"I am Faoii-Vonda. Or I was. I have earned my Preoii title by now, I think." Kaiya turned towards the voice and waited for her eyes to adjust to the oubliette, where only a few strands of grey light trickled down to the grimy floor. When at last they did, she gasped in horror at the image that greeted her.

A frail, emaciated woman stared at her with haunted eyes, her wide lips too big for the gauntness of her cheekbones. Her eyes were grey, as was her skin and what was left of her thin hair. Her wrists were only bones chained into shackles that must have been far too tight when originally fastened. At her feet was a pool of greenish liquid as thick and dark as blood. Tonicloran grew from it, thriving despite the darkness.

Preoii-Vonda watched Kaiya with a soulless gaze. "You survived the tonicloran. You must be the one I watched enter Illindria's hall. Kaiya."

Kaiya nodded. "Have you been there? To the Tapestry?" Vonda shook her head.

"No. Not at all. Only people that have survived the tonicloran in all its potency have succeeded at that. I am no Weaver. But you know that Thinir and his men have gotten to its doors because of blood and tonicloran together. I did too." Vonda leaned her head back to rest on the rocky wall, a crooked little smile lifting the left side of her mouth. "Now I stand there, watching the flow of the weave's magic. It dances across the world into all of the Goddess's playthings. And as long as I am part of the tonicloran, I go with it."

Kaiya froze. A cold dread crept into her bones. "You're the one that convinces the Croeli to coat their blades with tonicloran. To poison my sisters."

"Yes." Vonda caught Kaiya's disgusted glare. "It was easier to believe the Croeli capable of such a thing, wasn't it? I know. I wasn't fond of it either, in the beginning. But the tonicloran has power in it. It keeps me alive and nurtures me even as I nurture it. I am wise enough to know that if I cannot offer my sisters a life of freedom, then I can at least offer them a death without chains. So I spread the tonicloran, hoping that I can get there before Thinir can. Sometimes it works."

"You're . . . you're forcing it to *grow*? Is that even possible?"

Vonda shrugged. "It has a life force as much as anything else in the Weave. A bloodline, you might say. I could control you if I had the blood of your mother and the right words, and I could control you, your mother ,your aunts, and your cousins if I had your grandmother's blood. All of this tonicloran was grown from the same sprig. A relic of the Croeli, brought from the Blackfeather Wilds." The clarity faded from Vonda's eyes as she pulled a long weed from the bowl that sat between her chained legs. The shackles on her arms jangled as she moved. "Such a simple weed. Easily passed over. Ugly. But oh, the power in it." She grinned and set the sprig back in the bowl. Kaiya shuddered at the sudden madness in her eyes.

"How long have you been down here, Faoii?"

The insanity ebbed away as Vonda focused her gaze on Kaiya again. "Not long. Well, my body has been here for longer than I even know, now. But I don't spend much time here. I stand outside the Goddess's halls, watching the tonicloran grow."

"You watch it grow, and you . . . what? Use the air around it to spread a song? Force the Croeli to coat their blades?" Kaiya tried to think of a magic that would work like that. None of her battle songs were similar, and even Asanali's savage wild magic was incapable of performing such feats.

"Don't be silly. You've already seen that tonicloran can be used to dominate the wills of others. Thinir uses it to control his soldiers through their blood. It binds them to him. But he isn't using it as he could. He focuses on *their* blood, *their* minds. He focuses on the dominated. I focus on the *dominator*." Vonda cackled, her chains rocking in the darkness. "This pool? That's me in there. Thinir controls his men through the tonicloran, but I *am* the tonicloran. I am part of it as much as it is now part of you. You have the panacea *inside* you. It will always be there. But me? I'm *inside it.* My blood has nourished it. I am its mother, its rain and sun. And where it is, so am I.

"I use its dominating effects to spread my will: coat your blades, spread my seed, and cut off the power of the man who would use me for evil rather than good."

"But your tonicloran is the only reason Thinir can even get to the Goddess's halls in the first place!" Kaiya nearly yelled.

Vonda spat into the blistering pool. "You think I want to help him? He rapes me every time he shackles a new prisoner to his blade. The tonicloran was made to be the Weavers' final ascension. It was supposed to be something of beauty for those who were worthy. But Thinir pollutes it. He's tarnished the purest element this world had to offer, and he doesn't even realize it. So I fight him. I scream and drown out his bells. I let my poison—my strength—shred the tendrils he tries to snake into my sisters' and brothers' minds. He uses me, tears at my skin and eyes trying to get to the Eternal One's door, not realizing that I am aware of him. But I see him, and I fight him back. He thinks he can control me, but I am destroying his army and his control, one un-refurbished Faoii at a time!"

Kaiya bit her lip, confused by the other woman's smile. "You…you're happy, then? With this situation?"

Vonda's mad eyes cleared. "I was not at first. I thought I was enslaved by the Croeli, imprisoned by these walls. I refused to do as they asked. I spit on them when they explained how to drown the horned god out, how to use the dominating power of the tonicloran to convince the remaining armies to coat their blades. I refused to hear them, sure that Illindria could not have any use for a torture as foul as the tonicloran end.

"But eventually I saw the good I could do. I knew I would be trapped here whether I refused to serve or not. So I decided to help. Once I realized that even a harsh death was better than a chained life, She released me, and She let me see all the world through Her most humble creation." The madness returned slowly as Vonda reached once more into the bowl, picking the sprig up by its long stem. "Such a simple plant. A weed, really. But like the Faoii, it will once again spread all across the world, digging its roots deep into an earth that has forgotten it. It will spread across the entire world, and I will travel with it."

"But don't you want to be free of this place?" Kaiya frowned. Had all of this happened so that she could rescue someone who did not want to be saved?

"Free? Freer than I am now? Oh, Faoii, I have access to every place that my tonicloran grows. I ride on the blades of every Croeli soldier. I dance as the wind carries my seed. And in all of this, I scream against the stars and drown out Thinir's bells of hatred and fear. I am the freest of any of you. You who are enslaved to the war, to the blood and the death, to the morals of your finite decisions. You are slaves to fear and choices. You are even enslaved to me." She cackled and spread her hands as far as they would go against the chains. "You are a prisoner here, shackled to the earth as truly as though you had fetters. You, the last Weaver, with the power to see any time and be anywhere . . . you are only a prisoner. And until you use the keys that the Goddess has given you, your shackles are of your own making."

"What do you mean?"

Vonda laughed again. "You're trapped in a world that was not made for you. You're trapped in circumstances that you wish to control but cannot. I know. I know everything about you. I am inside you now. I'm mixed with your blood. I am the one that opens the gate for those who survive my poison. I am the one that unlocks the door to the Goddess's hall. You have been there with your mind—an impossible feat. But you need to dig deeper than that. You need to go with your entire being—your mind as well as your physical body—and you need to do so while keeping both intact."

"Like the Croeli do? Like Julianne?" Kaiya shuddered as she thought about the maddened, barely human shells she'd faced before.

"The Croeli? The Croeli try, but they only have slivers of me and are only able to keep ahold of slivers of themselves. Their minds claw at walls they're not welcome in and slip away as their bodies Blink across the plains. Their souls ooze from wounds they can't see, dripping into the blades that Thinir controls. And Julianne… poor Julianne… her soul cracked like broken glass without the tonicloran's power."

With grieving eyes, Vonda looked to something at Kaiya's side. Kaiya followed her gaze and saw Julianne's body for the first time, her frame twisted and shattered from the fall. Kaiya bowed her head. *Goddess grant you better battles, Faoii.*

Vonda's gaze lingered for a moment longer. "There is nothing we can do for her now except take action to ensure that she is one of the last. Thinir uses parts of me to get the results he wants, but his jumps are not perfect, and he loses a piece of his men each time he tries. But you—you are perfect. You can do what the wolves cannot. You can go to the Goddess's hall with all of you intact—and once there, you will see how to destroy Thinir." Her grin widened. "The Tapestry can show you everything."

Tendaji stood at the edge of the encampment, staring at the stars on the horizon. He had seen Lyn and Emery in the prisoner camp. He had watched the Faoii manipulate Amaenel with graceful ease. He thought that he should be proud of her and of the Monastery of the Unbroken Weave's tactics, but he felt nothing—only a coldness that had crept into his bones and wrapped itself around his heart.

Some part of him knew that he should be on the other side of the guards' circle. He should be there, next to them, one of the prisoners that whispered in the firelight on the other side of camp. He belonged there, among the group that had called him Faoli.

But he did not want to face them. He did not want to sit in that circle, staring at the empty seat that would never again be filled. He did not want to have to look into Emery's eyes and explain Kaiya's death, or have to face Asanali's forgiving smile.

No. There were only two things that he wanted now. He wanted to make sure that Kaiya's was the last empty seat to haunt that ring. And he wanted to make his uncle suffer.

He wasn't sure which one he wanted more.

Kaiya wasn't sure how many times she'd tried to obey Vonda's orders. *Open your mind's eye. See the Goddess's world. Open it. Open it!* She had seen Illindria's world unbidden so many times before, its ethereal images dancing across her vision in a superimposed ballet. But she had never forced it to happen. It wasn't something she knew how to control.

Kaiya sagged, sweat dripping from her forehead as she gasped on hands and knees. She tried again, prying at the door she could just barely sense in the center of her forehead. It cracked ajar, threatening to slam shut again even as she pried. Straining, she pushed harder . . .

There. It snapped open with an almost physical blow as, for the first time, Kaiya purposely coerced her mind's eye to obey her will. The images shook in her vision for a moment before breaking apart. The door slammed shut again, and Kaiya's head reeled as she gasped for breath. Vonda scowled from her chained dais.

"No, no! You're using your innate abilities. You must use *me*."

"I...I can't," Kaiya gasped out, her arms shaking.

"No? And why not? Come on, Faoii! You've already accomplished the impossible just by seeing those fading images! Your mind is there. The next part is easy. Even the brain-dead Croeli can do it."

Kaiya hung her head.

"You can do this, Faoii! So why don't you?"

Kaiya knew the answer, but she didn't want to admit it. Fear clawed at her like inky tentacles, wrapping around her face in a suffocating scarf. She couldn't. It was too overwhelming. She was too helpless in that world of endless possibilities—endless mistakes.

"I..." She let her voice taper off, hanging her head. Bile rose in the back of her throat, and her stomach rolled. "I..."

"Faoii, look around you!" Preoii-Vonda spoke with the full power of the Order, making Kaiya's head snap to attention. "Your world and everything in it is *dying*! Your friends are walking to their deaths, and they will fall painfully by my hand. I cannot save them, but you . . . you have the power to keep them alive, and you let your own fear control you?"

Kaiya heard the unspoken question: *How dare you?*

Tears of shame and anger leaked from her eyes, and in their glistening pools she saw those that had stood next to her through everything.

Eili with her firm gaze and gravely laugh. Lyn's quick, saucy wit and lingering glances. Asanali's open smile. Emery's loyal salute. Tendaji's quick chuckle and concerned eyes.

Her friends swam before her vision, their paths spreading out into a rocky, uncertain future. She watched them die at the hands of Thinir's unthinking minions. Impaled, hacked apart, burned by tonicloran, their lifeless bodies strewn across a blood-soaked battlefield. And their eyes—lifeless, listless, and yet so accusing—stared at her across dozens of realities and unrealized—*but avoidable, changeable!*—destinations. The accusations in their gazes barely brushed aside the fear in her heart. And that's what it was—fear. She was afraid of the choices she'd have to make. Afraid of the failure.

Kaiya tried to expel the accusatory glares of the friends she had abandoned, but they only swam closer. She shut her teary eyes against them, but they did not dissipate. Tendaji, Eili, even Mollie stared at her with tortured, broken gazes, agonized and raw.

Kaiya watched them all. She watched their fights and their falls. She watched as they died and burned, again and again, spinning through her visions at a dizzying speed. Their anguished screams deafened her with an incessant, mind numbing tirade. The monastery, her Faoii sisters, Mollie, Lyn, Emery, Asanali, Eili, Tendaji . . .

NO!

Kaiya wasn't sure whether the cry was of her earthly voice or her internal one, but it was real either way, and it shattered the broken faces of her companions, silenced their plaintive cries. The shriek filled the gloomy pit for only a moment before being cut off.

Preoii-Vonda smiled as fading echoes filled the place where Kaiya had been.

"Well done, Faoii. Well done, indeed."

36

The Goddess's white halls were darker than Kaiya remembered. A chilly wind blew through the open windows and toyed with the frayed edges of the Tapestry as she fought her way to her feet. Preoii-Vonda's laughter echoed from far away, fading into a haunting mist. Then there was only the sound of the wind and the rustle of the Tapestry. With a deep breath, Kaiya turned toward it and stared at the infinite cloth with unfocused eyes. There was so much information there. So many things that she could do to save those that she loved. So many questions she could ask and answers she could seek.

An infinite number of ways she could become lost in the Tapestry and never break her way free.

Kaiya dragged her eyes up to focus on the images before her. She searched the Tapestry for Croeli-Thinir. That, above all, was her goal. She could return here and lose herself in the Tapestry or stay clear of this place for all eternity if she wished—but only after Croeli-Thinir was gone. Doing her best to not focus on anything other than her objective, she explored the Tapestry for her loathsome uncle and his ever-present horned god.

When she found him, the weight of his influence was staggering. A thousand images, a thousand possible futures that were at the mercy of his will rushed forth. Kaiya's head spun under the weight of the horrific map that Thinir wove, its threads coloring a world of displaced citizens and lives filled with fear under his growing fascism. Their hatred and terror rolled off them in waves, paralyzing her.

She did her best to subdue the hurricane of emotions, and eventually she freed herself from its grip. Her heart filled with rage for the innocent people caught in his bloody web, and she pushed forward with her search. There had to be a way to defeat him. There *had* to be.

Time passed, and still the storm rolled on. The images continued, over and over, swarming around Kaiya in their steady stream. Eventually, certain patterns became clear. In the endless possibilities that flooded the hall, some things were consistent no matter what decisions were made before. Taking a deep breath, Kaiya forced herself to focus on these repeating themes, searching them with steady eyes.

Thinir's brooding keep was always nestled between the tangled trees of the eastern forest. She saw his cruel eyes and soulless, unblinking army. She watched a thousand different battles on the same vast plain. She watched dozens of soldiers make their way to him, fighting through the horde of mindless fighters. Each fell, however, as their sparking, screaming blades cracked against his impenetrable skull. His laughter filled the night.

Still Kaiya watched. The possibilities piled up, and the Faoii stared hard as warrior after warrior made their way to Thinir only to be cut down. Hundreds of possible outcomes, and all ending the same—in failure. A thousand soldiers that came within reach of ultimate victory, and a thousand broken blades that rang like bells against his tattooed head and body. A thousand deaths beneath Thinir's crackling criukli or lightning spell.

It was easier to focus on the Tapestry when you looked at only a specific point. Kaiya did not dare to wander off and find out what became of those fallen warriors' families. She did not watch for the tears shed or the oaths uttered after each fall. She only stared at each of Thinir's attackers, quickly moving on after each one failed. The millions of other images beckoned to her, called to her, but she held steadfast. *There must be a way to defeat him. There must be.*

There. A shadowy figure. Feminine. Faoii. Wielding a blade unlike any that Kaiya had ever seen. Her cry was brutal and beautiful, and in its lingering echo…Thinir lay dead at the woman's feet.

Kaiya focused on the woman, but the past webbed out before her, leading to a hundred different people, a hundred different warriors that could possibly wield the blade that would be Thinir's downfall. She frowned.

It's the blade's *fate to destroy Thinir—not the person's.*

Could an inanimate object even have a fate? Kaiya didn't know, but she kept her eyes on the Tapestry, searching over and over for Thinir's death in the midst of his thousand victories.

There. And there.

Each time the flicker of Thinir's demise graced the Tapestry, it was because of the same sword.

That settled it, then. The sword was the key. She had only to find it.

Kaiya took a shaky step back and let the images fade. She sighed and waited for her mind to clear and for the ache in her head to subside. She knew the future. Now she had only to look to the past. Surely that would be less distressing—the past was finite. Decided. Her task should be easy: find the sword, retrieve it, and kill Thinir with it.

Taking a deep breath to steady herself, Kaiya stepped up to the Tapestry again.

The past bombarded her with a force nearly as devastating as the future. She had known that the past was set. She was not, however, aware of *how much* there was of it. All her sisters, her friends, the innumerable refurbished forces, the millions of common citizens barely aware of the war—all of these combined were little more than a raindrop in a hurricane of the billions and billions of lives that the world had seen. They swarmed over her, drowning her.

Kaiya was thrown back from the Tapestry, her mind pressed flat under the weight of all that had transpired. Trillions of people had come and gone. Billions of wars had been waged and lost— an infinite number of victories and defeats. Each had seemed as important in its time as her current battle seemed now. But this war, and all of the people who would survive its aftermath—the dozens of generations that would thrive after its conclusion— were no more than a single grain of sand on the life pond's many shores. How important could her work truly be when her entire world and everyone in it . . . was only a single fiber in the Eternal Weave? Surely there was nothing etched onto that grain of rice that was worth the pain of digging through so many memories in order to find it.

Kaiya wanted to give up as she stared at the millions of lives and dreams that had already passed by and been forgotten. In the wake of all of those people, how could any single Faoii—or even the entirety of the remaining Order—be worth anything? Could any of it matter? Could anything...?

And through this, I shall remember that all things are sacred and all souls worthwhile . . .

The Oath floated to Kaiya from the voices of a thousand silenced Faoii, their pride and determination—their loyalty and faith—dyeing the tapestry a hundred beautiful colors. Kaiya heard it and set her jaw, batting the tears from her eyes. Resolutely, she fisted her hands and bowed her head.

"My blade will be held above all, for it protects all, and shall be a part of me. For I am Faoii." Determination in her stance, she forced herself to see the Tapestry again, darting her eyes across the cloth until she found the blade she was looking for. The one the Tapestry demanded. Waves of uncertainty and fear crashed against her from both the future and the present, but she ignored it all and focused solely on what she needed to see.

Thinir fell before her eyes, cut down again and again by the glistening sword, though its wielder shifted beneath her ghostly gaze. Kaiya ignored the numerous warriors that met him with their steely eyes and hearts filled with grim determination. Instead, she focused only on the blade that sang out with the voices of a thousand angels as it clipped through his surety and skull.

Focused on the sword, she followed its glittering thread backwards. Back through the battles against Thinir. Back through the bloody war that had not yet, and may never be, waged. Back through mountains and plains. A hundred paths it took to get to Thinir, but always from the same roots. The same beginnings. Like a bloodline, Kaiya tracked the fantoii's path back to its origins.

And gasped at where the road ended.

A grave with an iron Goddess symbol at its head. A rainy night and bloody hands tearing the symbol from the muddy ground. A broken edge. A tortured cry. A blacksmith's pale blue eyes filled with pain and tears. A single Faoii's final dirge. A lump of iron left, forgotten, in a forge that would never again echo with a hammer's fall.

Kaiya remembered Leonard the blacksmith, whom she had passed during her final trip through Resting Oak. She had seen his shop and the pain in his heart, but she had not stopped to truly *see* him. The story in the Tapestry unraveled before her.

Leonard had made hundreds of blades in his lifetime. He had prepared for war even when no one else had seen it coming on the horizon. Both criukli and fantoii had been crafted by his steady hand. Kaiya saw the blades he crafted, watching each take shape beneath his bulging arms. Dozens passed through the Tapestry, sold off and used to kill men or save families. She did not watch their passing but kept her eyes trained on the smithy in Resting Oak, waiting for the blade that would save them all.

It was never forged.

Sure she had missed something, Kaiya watched Leonard again and again. The blades swept by her, and she recognized them by his technique even before the blade was finished.

That one is forged, pounded again and again to make its edge. It will become fantoii. That one is crafted by cutting the blade from steel. Stock removal.

Criukli. Fantoii. Criukli. Criukli. Fantoii.

The blades swept by, and as she stared, Kaiya began to recognize the flaws in each, the minute differences that could ultimately mean victory or defeat in stories that she didn't want to read. Meanwhile, Thinir's tattoos made their impressions on her mind.

After watching the swordsmith go through his life—and death—a dozen times, wondering how many times she must hear his screams before they stopped haunting her, Kaiya was sure that the blade she had seen in her vision of Thinir's demise had not been crafted by Leonard. But its thread traced back to his shop.

Kaiya slammed a fist into the marble wall of the Goddess's hall and prepared to watch it all unravel again. It had to be there! It had to be!

Finally, something caught the Faoii's eye. After Leonard had been cut down and dragged away, the rain washing his blood into the gutters, the image of his workshop remained. And there, on the dusty floor of the abandoned space, barely visible in the darkness of the eaves, was the broken remnants of a Goddess's marker, coated now with dried blood and dust.

Kaiya saw the potential in that twisted metal. It had been broken and tossed away, forgotten by everyone, and yet she still saw it for what it was—a tool of Illindria. An instrument of glory. The markings of a tomb.

It would be hard—nearly impossible—to refashion a decoration into a blade. But it would not become just any blade. Thinir's swirling tattoos protected him from fantoii and criukli alike, but she had seen the inherent weakness in those already. She would craft something that none before her had created. For the first time in millennia, she would reunite the Croeli and Faoii and combine their blades as one.

After all, my child, how else can you expect to conquer Thinir?

With a resolute nod, Kaiya refocused on the Tapestry, preparing to watch Leonard again. This time she gave into the emotions that rolled off him as he worked, pushing past the fear of being overwhelmed. It was necessary. She could withstand it. She *had* to know what made him feel victorious when he forged a blade, what movements felt like mistakes. She had to know exactly what he did to create his weapons and how to prevent any imperfections.

Again and again she watched his life pass before her eyes.

Time in the Goddess's hall seemed unmoving, and Kaiya never felt like she needed food or drink as she watched the Tapestry day after day. But when she finally felt like she'd learned everything there was to know about Leonard's skills, a glance at the Tapestry told her nearly a month had passed, and her friends were quickly making their way to Thinir's keep. There wasn't much time left, but at last she knew what to do.

With a surety born of determination and will, Kaiya focused on her goal, letting the Tapestry fade away as she fell willingly into the oblivion that would take her where she needed to be.

ow that Kaiya had forced her body through
the Goddess's gate once, it was not so difficult to
force it back, though her head spun when she found
herself on hands and knees in front of Leonard's
long-abandoned forge.

It was a disjointing experience, and she had to fight for several
moments to piece the scattered parts of her mind back together.
The insanity of the Croeli made more sense now. Had Illindria not
assisted her in that very first attempt, Kaiya, too, would have lost
her mind to the Blinking spell.

An ear-piercing scream broke behind her, and Kaiya rolled to
her feet, immediately on edge. A frail woman stood in the street,
clutching a parcel to her breast.

"Witch!" Her shriek rose above the dingy shops and dust-
covered shingles, shattering the night. Kaiya frowned. Her time
in Resting Oak was already limited.

The woman backed away before turning to run down the street in the opposite direction, screaming her accusations as she went. Already Kaiya was aware of the sounds of booted feet striking the cobblestones in a dead run, heading in her direction. She looked down at her cracked leathers. She had no sword, no breastplate. She was not prepared to take on the Croeli alone.

Grimacing, Kaiya sprinted into the dusty remains of Leonard's shop. His anvil stood, a silent monolith over the mass grave that Resting Oak had become. At its base lay Kaiya's prize.

The Faoii scooped the disfigured Goddess symbol to her chest and spun to face the oncoming Croeli soldiers. Their criukli dripped venom, and their scowling masks burned in the moonlight.

Kaiya willed herself back into the Goddess's hall, leaving the Croeli in a frustrated huddle as they swung at empty air.

Once she gathered herself again, she turned the disfigured metal over in her hands, its jagged edges glinting in a nonexistent light. There would be nothing left over, especially after she cut down the sides after the forging. But there would be enough.

There had to be enough.

Kaiya felt the power in this hunk of metal. There was love there. Not just for Illindria or for the Order, but for things even more binding than that. Kaiya had not known of anything more powerful than those Oaths and songs while in the monastery, but her time outside it had shown her the things that Leonard had cherished: the love of a wife, a family. The love of living and being allowed to live without fear. The love of joy and the freedom of choice. The love of children's laughter. Leonard had poured his love of all the things that he held dear—all the things that tied him to this world and gave him a reason to continue existing in it—into that one beautifully crafted symbol.

If there was anything in the world more powerful than the Goddess's love, it was the love that people had for one another—father for son, wife for husband, sister for sister. The roots of the life tree might spread wide, but the branches that humans chose to nurture supported the most weight. Kaiya saw that now.

Unbidden, without even looking at the Tapestry, Kaiya saw the devotion that had brought them here: Lyn's loyalty to Mae and Jade, and eventually to Kaiya. Eili's faithfulness to her troops and her lost lover. Tendaji's devotion to his sister. Their parents' love for each other. Those were the things that had led them this far. Their victory was not based on prayers or Oaths, but on the faith they had in those around them and the desire to get through this ordeal together.

Kaiya looked at that broken scrap of metal and knew all of this. She knew that she could make it whole and beautiful, not because she desired to create this blade for the War Watcher and Her immortal will—but because she desired to save her friends. That had been the final lock that had separated her from the Tapestry. Her love for them tugged at her more than any Oath or battle spell.

"The Goddess doesn't ask for our worship through words or songs. She cares about our love of justice and strength. Our faith in honor and virtue. She cares about the strength that comes from being us. We don't have to worry about pleasing Her."

Oh, Mollie. Did you understand even then? I never went to chapel because the Goddess asked me to. I went because I knew it would make you happy. I knew that going would make me a better Faoii for you and all the others. It made me part of something more than just myself. And I loved it.

Kaiya knew where to go. Throughout her life, she had always

depended on her sisters more than any deity, alive or dead. There was a strength there that no war song could ever dominate, a compassion that grew far deeper than Thinir's hatred could scratch. That was where her sisters had always been and where they yet remained. Now she would have to depend on them again.

My blade will sing with the voice of every throat that has ever cried out against injustice and dance with the steps of every innocent child.

Focusing on the Tapestry, the metal shard still gripped in her hands, Kaiya willed herself through to a place she'd never thought she would return to.

Now that Lyn's warriors and Amaenel's soldiers were cooperating, life was easier in the camp. Many of the Faoii maidens had begun trading their services for blades and bows, and they were given their own training times in the evenings. Most of the hand-forged blades crafted in the enclave had been stripped from the Faoii maidens and left to rust on the plains, but those that had been salvaged were slowly doled back out as Faoii's physical prowess and skill became evident. Lyn even earned the right to wield her fantoii and throwing disks again, and her followers' hopes grew.

Once or twice Lyn saw Tendaji drifting among the Croeli warriors, his gaze lifeless and his movements ghostlike. She'd called out to him, but he only looked through her with soulless eyes and continued on his way. The other Croeli gave him a wide berth, but none showed the animosity that had laid him low on the bloody plains. Even Amaenel tolerated his presence, displaying the broken warrior like a demented battle trophy.

Tendaji's deep scars were easier to look at than his soulless eyes, but all of it made Lyn's blood run cold. She hoped that killing Thinir would help Tendaji heal. She hoped that Thinir's blood would cover the wounds carved across the land by his mindless slaves. But as she looked at the still-empty spot in the circle that she and the others still sometimes formed, she knew that some wounds might never truly close.

Kaiya, we still need you. I still need you. Please watch over us. Help us end this.

Her whisper drifted, unanswered, over the dark forest.

38

The broken, skeletal remains of the Monastery of the Eternal Blade loomed above Kaiya. Shards of rock and fallen towers jutted toward the sky, grasping at dark clouds. Again Kaiya tried to pull the scattered pieces of her mind back toward her. They finally fell into place with a snap, and with it, all of the emotions associated with this place came tumbling forward. Shivering at her unchecked memories, Kaiya took a tentative step in the direction of the monastery's looming gates, now asymmetrical and partially fallen. The broken walls shimmered for a moment, fading into an overlaid image of their original splendor.

Kaiya gasped out a startled breath. Dozens of leather-clad girls in the superimposed vision materialized before her, filing through the open entrance, laughing and joking on their way to training. The sun was painfully bright, and the first buds of spring were peeking their way through the grass. The faintest hint of Cleroii songs danced on a nonexistent breeze.

Kaiya had never wanted anything more than she wanted to join those girls. She wanted to walk with them again, to go to chapel and to sing her songs—she wanted to go back to a time when the worst thing she had to worry about was Cleroii-Belle's stupid staff. She wanted to walk through those gates and *go home*.

As Kaiya took her first step, however, the image disappeared. It did not fade away slowly like the visions she had had before, but vanished with the force of a window falling closed and shattering on impact. The girls and their bright smiles winked out of existence, and Kaiya was left staring at her booted feet on the muddy path. She turned the Goddess's symbol over in her hands before taking another step forward. More images appeared: playing tag with other unascended when she was barely big enough to walk. Practicing swordsmanship with sticks and wooden shields. Dancing in the summer with other girls that were just old enough to start discovering their true selves. With each step, the best parts of growing up in the monastery swirled around her, only to be swiftly and violently shattered as she stepped forward again.

Just when Kai was sure she wouldn't be able to take any more, the visions changed. Darkness surrounded her and the chilling rain continued to fall, but the ghostly maidens did not dissipate as they had. Kaiya stared. A hundred Faoii stepped toward her through the broken gates, greenish and translucent against the inky blackness of the monastery's remains. They came to Kaiya, their bodies bloodied and broken, reaching out to her with transparent hands. Terrified, she backed away.

The girls stopped at the sight of Kaiya's retreat, their eyes filled with hurt. Shame filled Kaiya. These were her sisters. They had been with her for her entire life—even after their own lives had been extinguished. And now she feared them?

Mollie drifted forward from the crowd, her bright red hair subdued to an ashen hue. Her smile was no less beautiful, however, and Kaiya's eyes flooded upon seeing it.

Mollie. Beautiful, sweet, loving Mollie . . .

Kaiya wasn't even aware that she'd knelt until Mollie was crouched in front of her, concern etched at the edges of her ghostly eyes. Kaiya knew she could banish these spirits if she tried—knew she could force her senses back into the living world rather than this place that sat somewhere between her world and the next. But she didn't. Instead, Kaiya reached forward to grasp Mollie's hand, wishing to feel the warmth of living flesh and a heartbeat beneath the skin.

This time, however, it was Mollie's turn to step away, and she only smiled, just out of Kaiya's reach, gesturing toward the monastery's awaiting gates. The other Faoii fanned out behind her, lining the muddy path, beckoning Kaiya forward.

Kaiya obeyed. She followed her sisters' spirits and entered the charred ruins of her old home. She walked by the scattered pillars that had once been the grand hall, then through the training quarters and past the demolished armor stands, careful to step over the melted remains of bronze breastplates and ivy helms. Eventually she came to the forge behind the armory.

The forge was unadorned in construction. It did not have the high, vaulted ceilings that the rest of the monastery sported but was squat and square with a flat stone roof. Kaiya realized that this is what had kept the forge standing despite the effort to demolish the entire sanctuary. *Goddess, bless whoever designed this place.*

In the middle of the room was the huge circular forge, its chimney rising up through the stone slab. Kaiya circled it slowly, checking for damage. Though the mortar was broken in a few places, it was otherwise solid. Surprised and pleased, she set to work gathering untouched coal from the stone cutouts in the walls.

Kaiya had never been in the forge before. As one of the unascended, she had been forbidden to enter this place. But her work in the enclave had taught her the basics, and watching Leonard's life over and over had honed her skills. She could do this.

She could do this.

Kaiya worked for six days, the rain outside pelting down on the ceiling with an almost continuous thundering beat. She forged the blade from the Goddess's symbol as she would a fantoii, beating the red-hot metal into shape before resting while it cooled, then starting again. Again and again she repeated the cycle, sleeping as the blade cooled and awaking again to reheat and reforge the metal. Slowly, it began to take the shape she'd seen in the Tapestry, but it wasn't yet perfect.

During the last forging cycle, Kaiya purposely left the metal nearly three times thicker than her ultimate goal. Then, using a red-hot chisel and mallet, she cut a third of the thickness from each side, shaping the fantoii and honing its edge. This is what made the blade different from any of its predecessors, a mixture of criukli and fantoii—light and dark. Perfect.

She was ready now. Kaiya smiled at Mollie's ethereal face as she lifted the newly forged blade. It glowed in the warmth of the fire.

"I'm going to end this, Mollie. I promise." She wanted to hug her shield sister in a final farewell, but she only fisted her hands in front of her, gripping the new blade's hilt with both hands.

"*I know, Kai,*" Mollie seemed to say. "*May Illindria offer you a thousand glorious battles in Her hall when this is through.*" Mollie's ethereal green eyes glittered as Kaiya Blinked back out of existence.

Thinir screamed into the wind, cursing the Faoii goddess and all her false glory. Still the Hag and her followers sang of equality and fairness. Still she said that she loved all her children, and that all were worthy in her eyes. But he knew—HE KNEW— that his niece had somehow reached the halls that he had been fighting his way toward for as long as he could remember. All were supposedly equal, and yet only a few were allowed access there? Only some were offered power while the others starved, fighting over scraps of meat? What made his niece worthy while he was not? What made her able to see the whole world without sacrifice, while he had had to give up so much—*too much*—for only a fragment of what she had received? And she would *squander* it. She would not use the knowledge to reshape the world into something beautiful and great. She would declare it dangerous and keep it under lock and key. He knew it.

It was not fair that she should continue to hold power despite all his work to tear it from her. She had been handed everything since the day she'd been born, and he and his men had slaved to come as far as they had. They would not stop here. If pretty little Kaiya was the only one capable of using the Hag's power, he would have to access it through her. He could reach that power and this tonicloran demon at the same time.

He pulled himself together as a scout approached. He had long since searched for the source of the poison that had drowned out his calls. His own nephew—his own brothers—it had not occurred to him to look so close to home.

Oh, how they would suffer for having plotted against him. They would grovel at his feet even as he cut out their eyes and tongues for their disobedience. This—all of this—had been for their benefit, and this was how he was repaid? The knowledge that they were willingly coming to him barely eased his heart. They thought that his niece was dead. How, oh how, would they react to discovering the truth? Would they be willing to fight her once he enslaved her mind? It would be a priceless image—and the last thing they ever saw.

He chuckled and turned to the approaching soldier. "Take a group to the old outpost. There is a pit there, and inside it is the last barrier between us and our final reward." The warrior nodded and turned to leave. Thinir's eyes glinted as he called the soldier back.

"Oh. And bring two virgin blades. Faoii-Kaiya will come to save the tonicloran witch. Be prepared for her and use the blades to destroy the chained one and make Faoii-Kaiya mine. It won't be long now before you may choose the site on which to build your wife's new home."

The wind in the Goddess's world screamed, beating against the white walls and howling through deserted gardens and corridors. The last Weaver had to brace herself as she stared at the Tapestry for what she hoped would be the last time. Its images crackled before her.

Kaiya saw everything. She saw the last band of free Croeli herd their prisoners toward Thinir. She saw the traps that he left for them and watched his captains plot their ambushes. She watched Lyn saunter forward without fear in her eyes—sure of a victory that she could not hope to grasp. She watched her brother limp on, his eyes wet with unshed tears, his heart fallen. A year ago, she had not known of his existence, but now she saw him watching her through all her years of childhood, always there, just behind the scenes. He had grown up next to her, protecting her, loving her. And her death had broken him. He was not walking to a final victory. He was walking toward an unattainable revenge, and he knew it. Tendaji was walking toward suicide.

Eili and Emery were less sure than the others. They tottered on the edge of hope and despair. They steeled their hearts and minds while they clenched fists that would not be graced with bow or sword, prepared to give it their all, anyway. Asanali walked beside them. She was unafraid, but did not harbor the hopes of vengeance that pushed Lyn. She simply followed the course of the river with her friends, prepared to help them cross however she may.

Thinir's ambushers were not the only dangers. Another group was coming, Blinking sporadically across the weave. Kaiya saw them through the Tapestry and the Goddess's high, glassless windows. They leapt through Her fields and gardens, making their way to the pit below the Croeli stronghold. Making their way home.

They will destroy Vonda. They will kill her and stop her song—stop the only voice that can drown out Thinir's bells. They will make his reign complete.

Kaiya could wait for them there. Wait and break their spirits and spines with this new blade with its beautiful, terrifying cry. But Kaiya was not sure she could hold them all off, and if Vonda fell, her remaining soldiers would only join Thinir's dead and dying army.

She could meet up with her Faoii—use her blade to lead the charge. But even that held the chance for defeat. She knew she could fight her way to Thinir's dark, brooding walls, but how many would she leave bloodied and broken behind her?

No. Kaiya scowled and gripped her blade, her eyes locked on a specific spot in the Tapestry's eternal weave. Enough people had died already. She would end this alone or not at all.

I am coming for you, Uncle.

The Goddess's halls stood empty and silent.

"This is it, then. We always knew we'd end up here eventually." Eili stared at the mossy trees that covered the dark mountain. "They've probably already seen us. If they don't strike tonight, they might wait until we reach the tree line. Easier for foot soldiers to maneuver, even with the incline."

"If even one of us is able to make it to him," Lyn said sharply, "it'll be worth it. No matter what, this ends tomorrow." Despite her tone, everyone heard the significant *if* at its beginning. It hung in the air among them, and no one dared mention the overwhelming numbers of the opposing force, the lack of sufficient weapons on their side, or Thinir's seeming invincibility. The wind cackled mockingly at their unspoken fears.

Emery rose to his feet. "No matter what happens at dawn, I want you all to know that it's been an honor serving with you, Faoii." He snapped a salute and clicked his heels.

"May the ever-flowing waters bring you to your desired shore. If your flame is extinguished in the coming day, I hope we meet again on the far bank." Asanali smiled as she rose to embrace him. Neither Eili nor Lyn pulled away when she turned to offer them both the same affection.

"Aye. It's been good knowin' you all, and it'll be good to fight beside you in the end." Eili tried to smile, but it was forced.

Emery and Asanali returned it anyway.

Three sets of eyes fell on Lyn expectantly. The silky-haired Faoii only shrugged and pulled out her fantoii. She didn't look up as she began sharpening the glittering blade.

"I don't know why you're all looking at me. I'm planning on walking out of that keep tomorrow. You're all welcome to join me if you think you can keep up."

40

Kaiya appeared in the heart of the dark forest that encased Thinir's keep and stumbled into a tree. She gasped for breath, trying again to pull her mind back into place. It didn't fit back quite the way it had before—like a puzzle with worn-down pieces. With an effort of sheer will, she snapped it into place and pushed herself vertical.

The forest's shadowy trees whispered ominously all around her. Kaiya focused on the black towers that sprouted just above the tree line a few miles from where she stood. Kneeling, she pulled her sagging boot to a more comfortable position and tightened the straps before straightening again. With a set jaw and steely eyes, she began her journey up the mountain.

The trek was more arduous than Kaiya expected, her muscles unaccustomed to hiking after the tonicloran poisoning and their disuse in the Goddess's hall. However, she continued to move with unbroken strides, drawing on her Faoii training and the wild magic Asanali had begun to teach her in order to keep the tremor out of her legs and the sound out of her step. She glided through the forest with a grace it did not deserve, and the patrolling Croeli seldom became aware of her presence. Those that saw her had only enough time to recognize danger through a fog-addled brain before she cut them down. Their blood slaked the dying forest's thirst.

Kaiya knew that Thinir or one of his lieutenants would eventually see her through the subordinates' eyes, but she pressed on, anyway. She did not fear their coming.

She'd only gone a few miles when the trees that pressed in on all sides suddenly gave way to the lofty keep with its dark walls. The wind and snow howled around the cracked stone, tugging at Kaiya's braid as she walked into the chilled shadow that fell below the castle's crumbling ramparts. Torches from the windows blazed in the blackness, silhouetting a handful of Croeli lurking in the shadows.

Kaiya ignored these lighted beacons and the scowling masks in the crossbow slits. She looked past the poor cockroaches under Thinir's thumb and forced her eyes upward until they landed on the central balcony of the foreboding keep's top floor. Only a few torches lit the black stone there—a few bleak fires warming the dying bones of her wicked uncle. He did not need to see those halls that encased him—not while he looked through the glassy eyes of a dozen other warriors, who in turn saw through the lives of a thousand more. She knew that he waited there in the dark, commanding his forces across the worlds and valleys, controlling events miles from here—and yet completely unaware of how close his greatest enemy truly was.

Twice now have I died, Uncle. Do you think you can kill me a third time?

Stepping from the safety of the trees, Kaiya made her way to the foreboding keep. To her uncle.

To the end.

Lyn had just barely fallen into a troubled sleep when surprised, agonized screams filled the night without warning. The crash of metal upon metal and the cries of battle rang out over the camp. She was on her feet and reaching for her fantoii immediately. Eili was next to her in an instant, her one blue eye scanning the fray.

"This ain't good, Lyn." The sounds of battle were coming from the far side of their encampment—the area farthest from the blackened stronghold. While more trusting of the Faoii and their prowess, the small band of Croeli rebels had still chosen to use their prisoners as a buffer—a meaty shield against the possibility of approaching foes. But Thinir's men had circled around and flanked the Croeli with ghostly ease.

"They must have Blinked," Lyn snarled. She had expected this, but Amaenel had ignored her council. Now they'd all end up paying for his arrogance.

As if on cue, rustling from all sides suddenly surrounded the Faoii who were already in battle formation. Asanali and Emery joined Lyn and Eili, watching all around them as more of Thinir's soulless-eyed warriors emerged from the darkness. Emery and Eili had no weapons, and Asanali carried only a rough-hewn branch she had picked up on their journey here. Briefly, Lyn wished she'd been able to bargain for more.

"May the War Watcher guide you." Asanali's voice was as soft as it had ever been, but her eyes were fierce.

Lyn tightened her grip on the fantoii as one lip curled. "She always has before."

The collective war cry of the Faoii filled the sky as the Croeli broke from the trees, shattering the night with their howls. Lyn plunged her fantoii into one of the Croeli's necks as he rushed her. Her foe didn't even hit the ground before she pulled the blade out with a spray of blood and spun to cleave an arm off another opponent. He continued toward her, undeterred, swinging his criukli overhead. Lyn ducked beneath the blow and Asanali was there, swinging her staff with a trilling cry. It collided with the scowling mask, bending it in at the temple. Jellied eye and blood dripped from a socket as the Croeli crumpled.

Eili scooped up the two dropped criukli and tossed one to Emery, who caught it with his uninjured arm. They circled together, parrying the Croeli advance even as more poured in from the trees.

"We're too open here!" Emery's strained cry rose over the din. "We have to get to cover!"

"Watch yourself!" Eili spun to cleave open the face of a Croeli that had flanked him.

"Try to get to the trees!" Lyn's voice held the full power of a Faoii, and the others fought to obey her command. Back to back, the quad desperately tried to make their way to the safety of the forest, and their kinship aided every stride.

The assembly had been trained to work together, to watch out for each other. The Croeli attackers had no sense of empathy, no altruism. They thought only about their own ends, their own swings—no care, no strategy, no help. Slowly, desperately, the Faoii gained higher ground.

A criukli shot out suddenly, snaking past Lyn's deflecting fantoii with a grace she did not expect. It slid across her shoulder, near the neck, but did not quite cut deep enough to clip the collarbone. Lyn danced back a step as she scanned this newest foe.

A myriad of scars and healed wounds shone on what exposed skin she could see, and it surprised her. *A true warrior, then—not a simple farmer masquerading as something more.* Lyn smiled. *If I am to die here, then at least the Eternal One saw fit to offer me a worthy battle.* She centered her weight and rounded on the Croeli again, blood seeping across her chest. The masked warrior stumbled back beneath her blows, parrying her thrusts with the ease that comes from muscle memory.

Lyn pushed forward and brought her blade up under the horned helm, flicking the visor off with a twitch of her wrist. It tumbled through the air, end over end, and as it fell, Lyn paled. A long, ratted braid snaked down from where the casing had been, its metal rings clicking on the armored breastplate.

Lyn's arm faltered. This was a Faoii in front of her. A sister. Her armor was different and her fantoii gone, but surely, somewhere in that shell, the Faoii remained? Surely Thinir had not been able to reach that part of her that made her Faoii?

Without reason, without logic, Lyn suddenly wanted to find that girl, that warrior who had been forced to face more than she could handle and who had received a punishment worse than death. It didn't make any sense, but in that moment, Lyn wanted to bring her back.

The refurbished Faoii lunged at Lyn again, and this time the blade pierced the shoulder all the way through. Lyn released a tortured howl, snapped from her reverie. The pity was gone. The hope for this girl's future was suddenly and brutally absent. Instead, there was only rage—rage at Thinir, rage at Kaiya's death, rage at everything that had transpired since the Croeli had taken their first filthy steps onto her land. She rounded on her adversary again. This was no Faoii. This was an abomination. And whatever remained of her sister deserved better than this.

Lyn didn't think about her training as she threw herself back into the fight. She didn't think about Faoii-Ming's voice in her head, shouting from across time and space, *Faoii! Never attack from the shoulder unless you have no other options. You are Faoii, but your opponents will be no small child. An overhead strike will leave you open for a counterattack. Even with a shield, you will be unprotected. Block, Faoii! Always block!* Lyn didn't hear the voice that tried to snake its way to her from through the trees. She could only hear the sound of her fantoii striking against the criukli in front of her. She could only think about how each of her blows drove her opponent back another step—how each one of her attacks was stronger and more orderly than her opponent's had been. She could only think about how the trees were so close, and *by the Goddess, this abomination was going to die at her feet like a Faoii rather than live like a slave.*

Liberation was near at hand. For all of them.

Her group had made it clear to the tree line, and Lyn had the upper hand. A single strike could clear the way and give her friends—her valiant friends, who were still fighting on all sides of her, tiring at the incessant onslaught—at least some reprieve in the trunks' cover. She could do it. She could end this.

With a scream, Lyn lifted her blade over her head and brought it down toward the emotionless face with all her might.

Goddess grant you a better eternity, sister. I will see you on another battlefield.

But her fantoii never made contact. Instead, the fallen Faoii brought forth her mighty shield and, with a swing of her arm that was unhindered by agony or strain, forcefully slammed it into Lyn's side. Lyn flew through the air before crashing into one of the very trunks that she had sought as a refuge. The sudden impact made her head spin as she tried to focus. Her eyes cleared just enough for her to see Asanali spin around to where Lyn had been only a moment before.

Just in time for the broken Faoii's criukli to slide down across her chest.

Lyn's scream shook the forest. She tried to rise. Red anger fueled her. She lurched forward, rushing at Thinir's shackled monster and the wide-eyed, ever-gentle Asanali, who was slowly— oh, so slowly—sinking to the ground.

A shadow appeared in front of Lyn before she could reach her target—a shadow that oozed from the trees above her, clad in dark, cracked leathers, with black skin… and pale blue eyes. Tendaji's fantoii cut through the night with its terrifying scream, hewing Asanali's assassin from collarbone to navel like a reed through water. The dead woman toppled without a sound.

"Get into the trees!" Tendaji bellowed as he scooped Asanali up into his arms and backed into the forest. Eili and Emery followed, still hacking at the surrounding Croeli, their movements fueled by adrenaline and pain. There were no angelic or demonic cries from their blades, only the sounds of bloody flesh and crunching bones as they followed Tendaji's retreating footsteps. Lyn made her way to her feet and dashed after them.

They ran like gazelle, in zigzag patterns, Tendaji gripping Asanali's body to his chest. Even with his uneven gait and rasping breath, he sped across the forest in a liquid dance. Eventually, the slower, brain-dead Croeli were left behind.

"Tendaji! Sir! We have to stop! We're getting too close to the keep!" Emery's cry broke over the sound of their footfalls. Tendaji skidded to a halt, Asanali choking wetly in his arms.

"Here, let me see her." Eili pulled Asanali from him with shaky fingers. Emery was already stripping down to the waist and laying his cloth tunic on the forest floor, his eyes wet and terrified. Eili immediately started barking orders to the young man, only glancing up from Asanali's bleeding torso long enough to catch Lyn's gaze. "Take watch, girl. They won't be far behind."

Obediently, Lyn spun on her heel to watch the trees. She was dizzy from pain and adrenaline, but even that was drowned out by the rage in her heart. She didn't look at Tendaji as he stepped up next to her, his body tense.

"I thought you'd abandoned us."

"My sister loved you. She would have died to keep you well." He drew his lips into a thin line. "I could do no less." There was a racking sob behind him. Tendaji's eyes stayed unnaturally steady at the sound. Lyn didn't bother using the Sight to try and determine what he was feeling.

"We're not going to be able to move her again," she said through gritted teeth.

"No. And Thinir's men are coming."

"I won't let them get to her again."

"No. We will not." Tendaji redrew his blade and circled until he was at Lyn's back. They tensed as the Croeli emerged from the trees.

41

The men in the hallways and stairwells offered little resistance as Kaiya rushed past them on her way to the center balcony. They dropped limply, barely having time to raise their swords as she flew by. The stairs fell away before the Faoii as her pumping legs carried her higher. Nearer.

A solitary soldier stood at the top of the stairs that led to Kaiya's final destination. Small and hunched, he was not much of a warrior, but he swung his sword and moved his legs like a good puppet, and Kaiya faced him as an adversary. His wooden, predictable movements did not offer much of a challenge, and when she swung her blade, his head rolled away without resistance, the helmet clanking down the steps into the darkness.

Kaiya was about to leap past the body and continue to her final goal when something caught her eye. She slowed, staring at the decapitated head that looked up at her with a mournful gaze. She recognized the face.

"Oh, Ray. I'm so sorry." For the briefest of moments, Thinir was forgotten, and Kaiya's heart was heavy as she knelt to close the open eyes, remembering the couple that had helped her in Resting Oak a lifetime ago. Astrid had told her that Thinir had taken their blood, but Kaiya had forgotten. She'd thought they would be safe. She'd thought Illindria would keep them out of this war.

She'd thought wrong. No one was untouched. Every person had been called to fight—to take a side whether they wanted to or not. Thinir's horned god had promised unity, and that unity had been provided at a high cost. She said a prayer over Ray as she swore yet again that Thinir would not be allowed to "unify" another innocent soul.

The whispered oath did not take long. Even in her guilt, Kaiya could not afford to linger. She rose, stepping over the corpse of the fallen civilian with a silent stride. Calmly, soundlessly, she glided into the room at the top of the stairs.

Thinir's chambers were empty except for a few stone columns and bits of broken furniture. Rain pelted in through the high balcony's open doors. Tattered curtains blew in the wind. A few weak torches cast their dying lights across the stones, filling the room with twisted shadows.

From behind the ruined curtains, Kaiya saw him. Thinir's tattooed scalp glowed eerily in the torchlight, his robes fanning out behind him in the wind and rain as he stared down across the battlefield. An icy chill filled Kaiya as she stared at the uncle that looked like her in so many ways. She'd never hated anything as much as she hated Thinir in that instant.

The chill spread into Kaiya's chest as she took a step forward. Her heart thundered beneath it as she took in the room and its lone inhabitant. The lack of traps and guards infuriated her. Was her uncle really so sure of his invincibility?

Of course he was. This was a man who had looked through the eyes of others for so long that he no longer remembered what reality felt like—a man who had grown used to sacrificing the helpless so that he could linger on. This was a man who had no concept of humanity—or of fear.

The ice melted away, and in its place raged a fire so primordial that Kaiya could not contain it. It broke through her, pushing her forward with an anguished howl. She charged from the stairwell, her battle cry ringing against the columns, her heart and legs fueled with the deaths of every person that had fallen at this demon's hands. Thinir turned toward the sound, his pale eyes shining in the darkness, infinitely large with the things they saw.

Was there a smile on those lips? A glint of fear in those pale eyes? Kaiya saw a million emotions under the clean slate of her uncle's features and ignored them all. Those weren't his emotions that she saw, only his puppets' shadowy echoes. A thousand terrible, unholy deaths played within the cracked mosaic in his eyes.

The criukli in Thinir's hand jerked, and Kaiya felt the power burst from it, rushing toward her as she sprinted forward. She Blinked past the lightning spell, and it hurtled into the iron stands that supported the room's few torches. She ignored their clatter and drew up to Thinir with her sword raised high. *One death too few, Uncle. Yours will be the last.* The cold rain drenched her cheeks even as her inner fire burnt them from the inside out.

There was a hint of fear in Thinir's eyes for a moment as she appeared before him, but it quickly gave way to amusement, and this time the look was his. He smiled in the darkness, so sure that her sword would be as harmless to him as all the others had been. So sure of the invincibility his god had granted.

Kaiya wondered whether Thinir had time to realize his mistake as her blade bit into his skull, slicing through the tattoos, the certainty, and the invisible chains with ease. Blood sprayed across the balcony in a warm, coppery fountain, drenching the stones at Kaiya's feet.

Thinir dropped limply, his blood red and so very human. There was no clash of thunder, no screaming of demons.

His death was overwhelming in its simplicity.

Kaiya rested her hands on her knees, breathing heavily, trying to massage the cracked pieces of her mind back into place. Behind her, soldiers ran in from the stairway, evidently summoned by their now-dead lord. They took only a handful of steps before stopping, their teeth chattering in sudden fear and adrenaline that their undominated minds were not prepared to face.

Kaiya sighed and straightened, rounding on these newest foes. Several turned and ran while others simply slumped to the ground, sobbing into bloodied hands. Horrid, frightening laughter bubbled up from Kaiya's chest. Thinir had been so certain that no one would make it to him, he had not even bothered surrounding himself with real warriors. Only farmers. Merchants. *Ray.* At least they were free now.

The weary Faoii breathed deeply, trying to calm her shaking limbs. The air was thick with blood and gore. Her eyes stung with smoke. The fallen torches had lit the old, broken furniture strewn across the room, and the flames were spreading quickly. Kaiya turned to escape into the outside world, which promised fresh air and a fresh start. A fresh existence.

But something stopped her. There was someone there—a figure just behind the haze. Someone who shouldn't be. Kaiya exhaled slowly and lifted her blade yet again, forcing her arms to steady despite their exhausted protests. Glassy laughter issued from the darkness.

"Fear not, my child. You have done well. You've done all that I could ask of you." The Goddess's white dress swept across the grimy floor as She approached Kaiya from the shadows. Her smile was bright and beautiful. Clean. Lovely. Perfect.

Slowly, Kaiya lowered her sword to the ground. Her eyes flooded as she gasped out a sobbing laugh at Illindria's approach.

"It's over, then?" She could hardly believe her own words. "It's finished?" The Eternal One nodded.

"For now. But the Weave is eternal. Others will rise and fall. The balance must always be maintained."

Kaiya nodded, taking a shaky step forward. A nagging feeling dragged at her feet, however, slowing her advance. She frowned, coming to an uneasy halt. Something didn't seem right. There was something in the smoke, something hidden in the blood-splattered walls. Something . . . wrong.

The spreading fire cast dancing shadows on the surfaces of the keep as it greedily made its way across the room. The hair on the back of Kaiya's neck rose, and a chill came over her despite the blaze, warning her of something different—something she couldn't quite see...

Drawing on what Preoii-Vonda had taught her, Kaiya focused her mind's eye and forced the Goddess's world to superimpose itself on the scene before her. The castle stood, soaked in blood and death, but it almost melted away into trees and forests. Thinir still lay broken at her feet, truly and blessedly dead. But it was not him that was strange. Kaiya brought her eyes up to scan Illindria's smiling face.

It was hidden by the horned god's scowling helm.

Both images swayed there, unsteady, until Kaiya wasn't sure which was real and which was not. *They both are. Do you think one truth is any less real than the reality that you know?* Her blade fell shakily from her hand, and she gaped around trembling lips. She saw, but she couldn't comprehend.

"It was you? The entire time?" Kaiya's voice was cracked, broken.

"Of course." Illindria's smile seemed frightening now, a scowl beneath eyes that had lost their kindness. "They are my people. They are all my people. A mother does not like to see her children fighting."

"But... the tonicloran. All of that suffering. All of the death."

No. No, no, no.

"There was no other way to ensure its spreading. I had to make sure that you would eventually be exposed to it. I need a Weaver, Faoii. Someone must guide my children after I am gone. They can't be let loose to ruin things."

"But . . . a war? Why?" The Goddess took a dainty step toward Kaiya, but the Faoii drew back. The Eternal One stopped and folded Her arms.

"You and the Croeli would have been separated forever otherwise, slowly harboring grudges against myths and letting them fester. I saw it coming when I chose this form, when I chose to walk among you instead of returning to the eternal waters. The other gods said I would lose myself in this body, but I saw that you needed me." Her eyes glittered as She spoke.

"I tried to unite the clans through peaceful methods first, through your mother and father. But your mother refused to be my Weaver and ran away from my Tapestry. She deserted her children in hopes that they would never learn of it. Her death was painless, but it forced me to look to others who could fulfill my needs." She took another step forward. Kaiya scooped up her sword and backed up again, eyeing her Goddess with uncertainty and fear.

"You cannot comprehend how long it has taken for things to finally fall into place, Faoii-Kaiya. Convincing that young Faoii to become one with the tonicloran took patience. Without her, your uncle would have become too powerful. I wanted him to lead his men to this place so that you may at last all meet as equals, but he used my gifts without care or boundaries. There had to be balance. The tonicloran offered that.

"But more importantly, without her spreading my most prized plant, you would have never encountered it. You, the last Faoii to see through my eyes. The last one who could watch over the Tapestry once I am gone. Those that were lost to the tonicloran had tragic ends, but it was all for you. My Weaver." She smiled and reached out Her hand toward Kai's cheek. "My pretty little Weaver."

Kaiya pulled her cheek away and did not lower her sword. "You keep saying that you'll be leaving. Why?"

"This body is not a proper vessel for a goddess. It takes so much power to maintain it. In the past, the Weavers did what I am doing. They watched the Tapestry and guided my followers. But the Order failed me. They neglected their duties. They feared the role they were meant to fill. I had to remain in this form until

I could find another Weaver to start the tradition again. And I have."

"You had to have known the other plans would fail. You had to have seen my mother, the oncoming war. Mollie, Lyn's sister . . . you sent them all to their deaths."

"Yes. But I knew that, if they came to pass, then those failures would set the groundwork for your success. Your father's death gave your brother the resolve to begin this war against Thinir. Your mother's death gave your aunt a reason to train you harder. Even your guilt for your shield sister kept you moving when you would have otherwise given up. Do you see how perfectly it all fits together?" Illindria smiled and clapped her hands.

Kaiya saw it. And a cold rage filled her heart. "You're a monster." The Goddess nodded.

"Yes, of course. A creature of duality, you remember."

The cold rage deepened, and Kaiya's heart burned. Red haze colored her vision, and blood pumped in her ears. She leveled her blade on Illindria, her eyes steely and her growl icy. When she spoke, the sound erupted from her chest.

"No! It's not enough! The tonicloran, the Tapestry—you used us as your playthings, and those were your tools! The Faoii of old didn't cut off that world because they were afraid of it—they rose above it! They were trying to save us from your tyranny! They tried to live for themselves, instead of living as your... your bloody puppets!"

She swung her blade, and it screamed its terrible scream. Illindria's fantoii appeared from nowhere, rising to counter Kaiya's blow. Kai's voice rose to a shriek, carrying over the blades' terrifying cries.

"Maybe the women in the days of yore weren't yet mature

enough to prosper without guidance! Maybe they *did* need you to hold their hands—but we're past that now. We are more than children who must be guided away from flame for fear of burns." A howl of rage from Illindria's fantoii flooded the room, causing the steadily-growing fire to flicker and rise. The Eternal One's eyes were cold as stone.

Kaiya did not shrink away from that glare, only continued to voice her rage, fueled by horror and hurt. "We have mastered your fire! We have earned the right to govern our own fates!"

The shriek of the Goddess's blade rose in pitch, like demons in a maelstrom. The fair woman's face purpled with rage.

"You ungrateful *worm*! I have given you everything! I have stayed in this form all this time for *you*—for all of you!"

"Look around you! You have provided only death and suffering!"

"Without my influence, you—all of you—would have known nothing but war and pain!"

"That's all we've known anyway!" Kaiya slashed down with her beautiful blade, forcing her opponent to retreat a few steps. "If we're going to suffer, then we deserve to make the decisions that lead to that ending ourselves! You *think* your children would end up slaughtering each other without your influence? Look around! Could it be any worse than this?" She shoved her liege into the wall and drew up to her full height.

"Even you cannot be positive of what we would do without you pulling the strings. I've seen the Tapestry. I've seen its infinite possibilities. Nothing is set in stone. Not even you."

Her blade fell in a sudden and uncanny silence.

A moment later, Illindria's unearthly scream shook the keep.

The air vibrated with a force more crippling than any of the spells Kaiya had ever seen summoned, blasting outward from the Goddess's mortal vessel. Kaiya crashed to her knees, grasping at her head as Illindria's power broke free from the body that had encased it, howling through the castle like a torrent of demons in the night.

The enormity of the Tapestry seemed miniscule next to the immensity of the Goddess's power. Once released, it spread through the crumbling keep, shaking the broken chandeliers and cracking stones with its force. Outside, it broke across the trees, ripping its way back through a world that had struggled without it for too long. It soaked into the alcoves and crannies of a realm that had forgotten the meaning of magic—of Faoii.

Resting Oak, Clearwall, Cailivale, and a million other black holes that had been devoid of meaning while the little bit of power that had trickled through the Goddess's sieve had made its way into monasteries, sucked from the too-small vessel by women who felt entitled to the world's most precious and scarce resource.

Kaiya watched Illindria's body die, and suddenly the world felt... *right*, somehow. Filled and cleaned, like a dry riverbed after a rain. It was never meant to be a place where all the power of creation and life rested in the hands of a few. People were not meant to be controlled like puppets, led down a predetermined path to meet the demands of some ethereal tapestry. She knew this now, and, as crazy as it sounded, she thanked the Goddess for helping her see it. Because even if the Goddess was not a single being anymore, She was still there—everywhere. In everything. As she should have been all along. In the trees and air and stone.

Stone. Kaiya jerked from her reverie, unaware that she was

kneeling in a puddle of blood that had once belonged to the most powerful creature in existence. She had not realized that the stones around her were falling rapidly as the earth beneath them shook and shifted. She straightened just in time to dodge a beam that dislodged itself from the ceiling above. Another fell after it. And another. Kaiya sheathed the still-dripping blade and rolled away with one quick movement as the ceiling collapsed entirely.

Illindria's lifeless body was buried in stone and dust, and Kaiya did her best to avoid a similar fate. But the keep around her was crumbling too quickly, and the ground beneath her feet was unsteady. Twice she stumbled as she made her way to the tower's door. Twice the keep shook apart at its foundation, breaking the frame before she could reach it. Kaiya tottered to a stop. She spun, her eyes darting warily, looking for an exit. There were none.

The Goddess is dead. She is part of our world and everything in it. Does the world she made for that vessel still exist?

There was only one way to find out. With an unsure step, Kaiya Blinked.

The Goddess's hall still stood, but was disintegrating quickly. The Tapestry spun out of control through the room, its future changing in a million ways. Kaiya focused on it only long enough to see the ever-changing present, now so full of fear and uncertainty. *Has it ever been any different, though?*

She found her destination and willed herself through just as a chunk of the marble ceiling fell. The Tapestry tore under its weight, and for a moment Kaiya found herself in a limbo she did not understand. Illindria's angry shriek echoed in her mind, mixed with an eternal cry of blessing and gratitude. The sounds swirled around Kaiya, suffocating her. Strangling her. Was that a bronze bell in the distance? Was that Mollie who was singing?

Kaiya gasped for breath, looking for the end of the tunnel she was now trapped in. For a moment, she thought she could see a light, but it faded quickly, drawn into the vortex that also swallowed the screams and pain.

The end was here. She'd tried to make it a good one for everybody. Goddess, how she'd tried.

Kaiya let it take her.

42

Tendaji recognized the change in his opponent's expression just in time. The glazed, undead eyes focused for a heartbeat, glistening with terror and confusion.

His mouth moved a second too late, and his blade fell from his hand just a little too early to be caused by the fantoii swinging toward his neck. Tendaji stopped his blade just as his opponent brought his hands up in surrender.

Next to him, Lyn's fantoii sliced through her adversary's neck, and the helmeted head rolled to her feet. The face beneath the scowling mask retained its grimace of terror. Tendaji gripped Lyn's arm as she raised her blade to swing again. In front of them, the other Croeli had stopped too, their eyes clear and their bodies trembling. A few even tore the scowling helms from their heads in shock and dismay.

"What the blades is happening?" Lyn refused to sheath her fantoii as she circled warily, watching the Croeli with suspicious eyes. Tendaji cast an eye in the direction of the keep.

"Thinir has fallen."

"How can we be sure? How do we know this isn't a trap?" Tendaji opened his mouth to respond when a powerful wind suddenly rushed past, making their very bones tingle with an unseen energy. He shuddered in surprise and looked to Lyn for confirmation that she had felt it too. She paled a shade and nodded.

"Tendaji! Come here!" Eili's voice was frightening in the sudden silence, and Tendaji glanced at Lyn only long enough to see her nod before sprinting to the scarred woman's side.

Asanali lay gasping on the ground, her liquid eyes roaming the silvery stars that had broken out overhead. Her normally-white smile was stained red. For a moment, Tendaji almost let himself believe that she'd simply been eating strawberries.

"She wants ta talk to ya. I tried ta sing for her, but the wound's deep. Even without the tonicloran . . ." Eili shook her head. "I ain't a very good Preoii, Tendaji." Tendaji set a gentle hand on Eili's shoulder before kneeling closer to Asanali's blood-soaked lips. Heat radiated from her skin as he drew near. She seemed to be laughing as she spoke.

"Their shackles have fallen away like ripe figs. Their wings unclipped. He's fallen." Tendaji took one of Asanali's hands even as she choked. Blood bubbled up from between her teeth, but her smile didn't fade. Eili pet her tangled hair.

"Easy, girl. Easy. Goddess willin', yer gonna make it outta here."

"Goddess. Dream Speaker. War Watcher. The wind through the leaves and the water through the ice. She was of flesh and blood, but now She's a part of the pool again." The dark eyes fluttered for a moment. "Better this way. I can see Her. She's free now, too. No longer trapped in a mortal body—a bird in a cage too small. Thought it was better. Thought She could hold it all together with mortal rope. But she's released. Free. Perfect." Asanali's words faded and her eyes drifted closed.

"Girl? Girl, can ya hear me?" Eili shook Asanali, who only smiled weakly in response.

"She wants to thank you. I see your eyes in the pool..." The bronze nomad frowned. "No. Not your eyes. Green. Pained. In the keep." The Danhaid spear maiden's eyes flew open again, flooded with a concern so deep that Tendaji knew it wasn't for herself. Asanali would never be afraid of something as natural as her own death.

He squeezed her hand, but Asanali only shook her head, speaking in quick, clipped phrases that were only briefly punctuated by gasping breaths. The weak tremor to her words was gone, replaced with an urgency that was frightening.

"The world is crumbling. The flood waters will change it. You'll need Kaiya to guide the flow. She waits behind the bloody stones. You'll need... You'll need..." Her strength exhausted, Asanali gasped into silence. The light in her eyes faded, and her body fell limp. Eili released a tortured sigh, but she did not try to revive the fallen warrior. Instead, she only offered a prayer and closed the lifeless eyes. After a moment, she gazed up at Tendaji with wet cheeks.

"What do ya think she meant by all that? Maybe—" She was cut off by a sudden rumble and earsplitting boom. Tendaji and Eili whipped their heads to the north just in time to watch the keep's highest tower crumble to the ground. Eili sighed.

"Whoever made it to 'im ain't goin' to have an easy time makin' it back out. At least they got the bastard."

Tendaji stiffened as something clicked into place. His heart pounded in his chest as he made sense of Asanali's final words. *Green eyes. In the keep.* Then he was dashing through the trees before Eili even had a chance to stop him.

"**Kaiya! Kai!**" The trees around the keep were rocking back in forth with the force of the falling walls. Tendaji ignored them, sprinting between the trunks with a determination that blocked out everything. He pushed himself past the limitations of his broken gait, past the pain in his body and the sickening worry in his heart. Everything that Asanali had said might have been the final ravings of a dying woman, but if it wasn't...

Something glinted out of the corner of his eye. Spinning to a stop, Tendaji focused on the line of trees that separated the forest from the falling stronghold. It glinted again, hidden beneath a layer of dirt and broken branches. Heart quickening, Tendaji had barely hit his knees before he was shoving aside the rubble with shaking hands, nearly cutting himself on the glittering object beneath the grime.

A sword. The most magnificent sword he'd ever seen. But it meant nothing to him because he could see the hilt. A dark hand, battered and covered in blood, encased it.

Tendaji kicked the piece of metal aside and went to work on freeing that bloody hand. The shaken, fallen leaves and broken trees gave way to an arm, a battered leathern jerkin, a tangled braid, and finally…

"Kai." Tendaji's whisper barely broke the sound of rustling leaves as he exhumed his sister from the earthy tomb she'd been incased in. Chunks of marble and bark fell away as he pulled her gently to his chest, just cogent enough to briefly wonder why there had been marble in a military keep and how it had made its way this far from the crumbling ruins. Then that thought was gone, and he was concerned only about the blood on his sister's face, her arms, her armor. He lowered his ear to her chest, terrified of what he might not hear. His own heartbeat quickened to a thundering beat, so loud that for a moment he couldn't hear. Couldn't tell …

There. The steady, quiet thumping of Kaiya's heart was the most beautiful thing he had ever heard, and he wanted to cry for joy. Instead, he only drew Kaiya closer to him and hugged her close. After everything, she'd somehow made it through alive.

"Tendaji?" Tendaji twisted to face Lyn as she approached from behind. She put her hands on her hips at the sight of the former Croeli. "Why'd you run off? There are still things to—" She gasped, wide-eyed, when she saw the woman in his arms. "Oh, blades—Kaiya…" Before Tendaji could reply, Lyn had already crossed the space that separated them, pushing him to one side as she grasped Kaiya's shoulders in both hands.

"Kai? Kaiya! Answer me, Faoii!" A light slap to the face. "Come on, wake up!" Lyn was rougher than Tendaji would have been, but there was an urgency, a fear in her movements he'd never seen in in her before. He stood slowly, watching as Lyn's voice rose by degrees. "Damn it, Kaiya! Come on! Answer me!"

Finally, blessedly, Kaiya's jade eyes fluttered open, and the weight that lifted from Tendaji's heart was nearly staggering. Lyn's entire body sagged in relief, and she roughly brushed the hair out of Kaiya's face while cursing under her breath in clipped syllables. The cursing only stopped when Kaiya tried to pull away.

"Lyn? What are you doing here?"

The silky-haired Faoii narrowed her eyes. "What am *I* doing here? What are *you* doing here?" She shook Kaiya once before pulling the Faoii into a tight embrace, kissing her forehead, her cheeks, her mouth tenderly, her tears washing away some of the grime. It was a long time before she released Kaiya enough to meet her gaze.

"Damn it, Kaiya, I told you I'd follow you anywhere. How dare you try to leave me after that?!" Kaiya hesitated for a moment before finally giving and resting her head on Lyn's shoulder.

"I'm sorry. It won't happen again."

"Never?"

"Never. Wherever you go, I'm going too. Forever."

A sudden crash rocked the ground around them, and Kaiya was immediately on her feet, spinning toward the falling keep as it groaned in its decay. Seconds passed in rigid agitation before Kaiya finally relaxed a little and turned to survey her surroundings. Her gaze fell on her brother.

"Tendaji." Her voice cracked as she took a few hesitant steps toward him. He nodded once before enveloping her in a relieved hug.

"It is good to see you, Kai." And then, quieter: "Goddess, how good it is to see you." Something about what he said caught Kaiya and she stumbled away, quaking violently. His heart clenched with concern. "Kai?" There was no response. "Kaiya?"

Lyn strode forward with quick, deliberate steps. She scowled at Tendaji before spinning Kaiya around to search her face. "What is it, Kai?" She snapped her fingers. "Come on, Faoii. Talk to me."

"I… I killed…" The shaky whisper was cut off by Kaiya's suddenly chattering teeth, her eyes trained once again on the keep as it fell away into the forest. Lyn relaxed.

"Thinir. We know. Don't worry, Kai. You did well. Illindria is proud of you."

"No!" Kaiya shoved herself away from Lyn and took a step backward, out of reach, still staring at the towering ruins. "No. Not Her. Not the Goddess. She couldn't… I can't…" She released a sobbing laugh and stilled. "She's dead. I killed Her."

"You . . . *what?*"

Kaiya turned back toward the other two, her eyes streaming in the starlight. "I killed Her." She shook her head. "I wish I could tell you all that I learned. All that I saw. I need to tell you. And the Faoii. And the Croeli. Not only the ones here, the ones in the Blackfeather Wilds—everyone. We need to . . . I have to . . ." Her voice cracked, and she tottered.

Lyn caught her, and Tendaji knelt in front of her quaking form, contemplating what she'd said and what it could mean. He kept his voice soft and gentle when he spoke. "You killed the Goddess? Alone?" He shook his head slowly, laying a gentle hand on her arm. "I'm sorry, Kaiya. We should have been with you."

Kaiya opened her mouth to speak, but Lyn shushed her immediately. "That doesn't matter now." She threw a withering glance toward Tendaji, then returned her attention to Kai. "It doesn't matter. What matters is that you're back now, and you're alive. We can… we can worry about the Goddess later." She glanced at Tendaji again, softer this time. So much had changed. For good or bad, things would be different now. He smiled reassuringly and clicked his tongue at his little sister in a quiet way.

"She's right. There's time to figure out everything. We'll begin gathering the people that are left. We'll meet up with the remaining warriors and send a diplomat to the north. We'll decide what to do."

"We'll decide." Kaiya smiled up at the sky, her eyes closed. Tears leaked out of the corners and trailed down her cheeks. "Yes. For the first time, we'll decide for ourselves." She released a shaky sigh. "I don't know what's going to happen, but at least we'll all be uncertain together. We've earned uncertainty."

Lyn helped Kaiya stand, and they turned back toward the field that now held more than Croeli and Faoii—it held the warriors that would usher in a new age.

The scent of sunflowers and dew carried on the wind as Thinir's keep finally settled.

A Letter from Andarian
(Glossary)

Art, if you're dead set on visiting Clearwall, then I figure I'd better tell you what I know of it. Not just the town, but that entire country is . . . different. And you'd better know a few things before you go getting yourself killed. Read through this. Carefully. And don't ask how I know any of it.

-Andarian

Faoii (Fah-yee): Leave it to women to make their most important word the most complex one. The word Faoii is a title. And an adjective. And probably some sort of curse word. Mostly, it's used to describe an entire order of women that serve the Goddess Illindria. They're Her soldiers, healers, speakers, whatever. If you see a woman with a sword, she's a Faoii of some sort. If you see a woman using magic, she's a Faoii of some sort. If you see a woman that looks like she could kill you without much thought, just assume she's Faoii of some sort and act accordingly. It doesn't matter if she's in full armor or not. They can look like a baker, a prostitute, or even some mad woman talking to herself—those witches can be *anywhere* and *everywhere*.

-And for the love of the eternal blade, never call them witches!-

Oh yeah. There are different types of Faoii, too. I'll tell you about the others in a minute, but if you can't tell at a glance what type of Faoii she is, just call her Faoii. Out of the three branches, the Faoii (which translates into "warrior") are the most common, and the entire organization answers to it without offense.

If one gives you her name and she says Faoii at the beginning of it, it means she's *ascended*—like a graduate of the order. She's proven herself and has earned more respect than the girls with Faoii at the end of their names. Even if a girl is unascended though—like someone named Dawn-Faoii—she still might cut your eyes out if you offend her or the Goddess. So please, *please* don't be your regular self around any of them. If they figure out what a philanderer you are, they might kill you on principal.

Preoii (Preh-yee): Translates into "speaker." There aren't many of these women, but they're still part of the Faoii Order. Supposedly, they used to be the ones that could see the Goddess's Tapestry—and could use it to see the past, present, and future. I guess there hasn't been a true Preoii in generations—the ones that are around now are more of a political head of the society rather than true oracles. Still, they're as good at fighting as a regular Faoii, so don't say anything stupid, and you'll be fine. Knowing you, though, you'd still get your head chopped off, so thank the Blade that they pretty much only stay in their monasteries. If you ever have the chance to meet one, then it means something is *very, very* wrong. Keep your head down and get the hell out of there.

Cleroii (Cler-yee): Translates into "healer." More common than Preoii. Less common than Faoii. These women are the best at using magic to heal others. They are also trained to be diplomats rather than warriors most of the time. Don't get me wrong, every branch of the Faoii can use a sword better than you or me, but these women are the ones most likely to be found in Clearwall. I've heard they're less likely to draw steel than the others in the order, but don't push it, okay?

Farᴛoii (Fonᴛ-yєє): This is the long, single-edged sword the Faoii carry. Each one is unique and tied to the woman that wields it. Some say the blades scream in battle. Others say they sing. I'm pretty sure that what you hear depends on what side of the fight you're on, so just do your best to never hear one at all, okay?

Thє Oaᴛh: I didn't tell you how to pronounce the Oath, because if you can't figure that out on your own then you're dumber than you look, and no amount of help on my part is going to save you from your own stupidity.

Anyway. The Oath is the promise that the Faoii make every time they wake up, go into battle, take a sword, help someone, or whatever else it is they do. Blades, they might say it before they go to the bathroom, I don't know. But they say it a lot. It's absolutely sacred to them and apparently gives them access to the magic they use. They know it forward, backward, and everything in between. If you ever make fun of it or try to get a Faoii to break it in *any* way, they will probably kill you. I've attached a copy of it for you so you're less likely to mess something up and sprout a fantoii from your stupid face.

Croєli (Crow-єl-єє): No one else knows about any of this, so keep your trap shut about it, okay? The Croeli used to be part of the Faoii order. Don't ask me how I know. And if you ask any of the Faoii today about it, they 1) won't believe you, and 2) will probably kill you for saying so. But it's true. Centuries ago the Croeli and Faoii were part of the same order, but they interpreted the Oath differently and it caused a divide. Then a war. Eventually, what we know as the Faoii today came out on top and banished the Croeli to the Blackfeather Wilds. No one has seen them since. But I'm telling you, they're out there, and they're going to want revenge. I don't know when, but it will happen. It's best to be prepared.

Criukli (Kree-oo-klee): The Croeli blade of choice. Shorter and broader than the fantoii, these single-edged swords are often slightly jagged. They tend to maim, rather than kill, so if you ever see one, RUN THE OTHER WAY.

Toricloran (Tah-ric-lore-ahn): A plant with flat, broad leaves. Legend says that it used to be used for some sort of Faoii ritual. I don't know how since it's literally the most poisonous substance on the planet. That stuff will make your flesh boil and your skin come off in ribbons. Stay away from it.

I know I've told you all the reasons that a Faoii might kill you, but truth be told, they actually seem like good people. Most everyone respects and reveres them. Most don't have any problems with them and are grateful that they're around. But, unlike most people, you're an idiot, so I had to get the point across somehow. Take care of yourself.

-Andarian

Excerpt from *Faoii Betrayer*
(Available Now!)

I lahna Harkins always associated Faoii with fire. The Proclamatic Order of Truth had a long list of characteristics that told them if a person was Faoii—weird symbols, breastplates, swords, braids, spells, lies… but not every Faoii had these things, and some had different incriminating items or behaviors altogether. Over the years Ilahna had learned that no single thing could tell you someone was a witch—except that they all ended up engulfed in flames.

That's how it had always been. That's how it was even now, as Ilahna watched one of the cloaked Proclaimers set his torch to the base of the pyre in the temple square. The two witches lashed to its towering stakes, a man and a woman, cried out at the sudden crackling tinder at their toes, and Ilahna focused on their faces for a moment. They were middle-aged and seemed normal enough from the outside. No armor. No shields. The woman didn't even have her hair in a braid. But the Proclaimers had found them guilty of some sort of crime against Clearwall (Ilahna didn't think that the exact accusations mattered anymore), and now the citizens of Clearwall had gathered to watch the cleansing purge of yet another threat. Ilahna crouched on the roof, watching the flames engulf the witches' feet. Around her, other children dotted the roofs that surrounded the temple courtyard, their small, round faces bright in the light of the pyre.

One of the urchins nudged her, pointing into the crowd. Ilahna followed his finger and locked on two children standing not far from the pyre. Madame Elise, the First Proclaimer, watched the two youth, as well, searching their faces for a reaction from her raised dais. Behind her, the witches screamed louder as they burned.

The two children stood motionless, hands clasped. There were no tears or sniffles. No pleas for mercy or screams for their parents. In fact, the darlings didn't show any emotion at all, their stoic faces reflecting the light of the fire. Ilahna shuddered despite herself. It was the unofficial trial of Clearwall. Someone that showed remorse or anger at a Faoii pyre was automatically declared guilty for crimes against the Kingdom of Imeriel and Her capital city. These were not the first children who had turned inside of themselves while they were forced to watch their parents burn.

Ilahna nodded to Kilah next to her. "Go get them. They're one of us now." The urchin nodded and bounded into the crowd. It wasn't much, but all of the mazers in Clearwall knew what it was like to be abandoned. They could at least make sure that no one was alone during those first terrible nights when everything changed. And being part of their little group of petty thieves or moss gatherers was safer than being sucked into one of the more violent aspects of Clearwall.

Ilahna didn't know anything about the witches on the pyre. She didn't care. But she wanted to make those children feel a little less destroyed when morning came.

Kilah was already talking to the siblings in the crowd, but his whispers were lost amongst the triumphant screams of the surrounding mob as the flames caught the witches' clothing. They weren't moving anymore, and Ilahna turned away.

Kilah and the other mazers would take care of these newest urchins. Ilahna wasn't even sure why they looked for her approval each time rumors spread of children being left to the Maze in the wake of a pyre. But so many of the younger mazers took comfort in her presence, and she had taught most of them how to survive in a world that didn't care whether they lived another night. She would help to teach these two, as well, now that Kilah had pointed them out to her. But not tonight. She'd already left Jacir alone for too long.

Trying to brush the smoke out of her eyes and the smell of burnt flesh out of her hair, Ilahna turned and leapt across the rooftops, leaving the temple and the triumphant screams of its people behind her.

Acknowledgements

Thank you to every Faoii that pre-ordered a copy of this book so that we could make it possible. While I am grateful to have moved away from the publisher that made those original pre-orders necessary, I will never forget that this could not have happened without your initial support. This is your victory as much as mine and it has been an honor to have you by my side through everything. Shields up.

Also, a special thank-you to my father for being there every step of the way. You have read every version of this story, seen every change and progress update from its conception, and have always had the most honest and helpful suggestions. Whether I needed an editor or someone to vent my fears to, I couldn't have made it this far without your help. Thank you for raising a Faoii rather than a damsel. I love you dearly.

For More Information
about Tahani Nelson and the Faoii
Please Visit

TahaniNelson.com

Printed in Great Britain
by Amazon

74945828R00227